Additional Praise for The Curse of Hester Gardens

"Ringing with lyricism and suspense, *The Curse of Hester Gardens* is a compelling vision of the horror of trying to raise sons in public housing haunted by violence. Despite ghosts and the uncanny, the true terror is the trap of poverty, which tests a mother's love to its limits. Tamika Thompson's sharp characterization and insightful storytelling make this a must-read."

—**Tananarive Due**, Los Angeles Book Prize– and Bram Stoker Award–winning author of *The Reformatory*

"The chilling journey of loss and madness is magnificently told through characters who became so real I was emotionally vested in their fight to protect their loved ones in the end."

—**Linda D. Addison**, award-winning author, HWA Lifetime Achievement Award recipient, and SFPA Grand Master

"*The Curse of Hester Gardens* is a chilling and vital debut that uses an underseen setting and distinct characters to give the genre a jolt."

—**Johnny Compton**, author of *Devils Kill Devils*

"Excelled in truly gifting the experience of living with a persistent haunting . . . The pinnacle of modern-day gothic."

—**Vincent Tirado**, Bram Stoker Award–nominated author of *We Came to Welcome You*

"Compelling and eye-opening."

—**Geneve Flynn**, Bram Stoker and Shirley Jackson Award winner

"A powerful debut that explores love, grief, and violence with aching emotion."

—**Sara Tantlinger**, Bram Stoker Award–winning author of *The Devil's Dreamland*

"Poignant, chilling, and immersive."

—**Christi Nogle**, Bram Stoker Award–winning author of *Beulah*

"Thompson doesn't pull any punches, startling us with tragedy and truth. A modern classic from one of horror's best new voices."

—**Lee Murray**, five-time Bram Stoker Award–winning author

"Horror at its best, rooted in the real-life terrors. An emotional rollercoaster that I'll remember for a long time."

—**Justin C. Key**, author of *The Hospital at the End of the World*

"A testimony to art imitating life. Poignant and deeply unsettling."

—**L. Marie Wood**, Bram Stoker Award–nominated author

"A necessary tale in our current times, written with heart and soul and stunning attention to detail."

—**Brandon Massey**, author of *Nana* and *The Landlord*

"A supernatural twist to a parent's worst fears, from structural racism to gun violence, ultimately asking the question: What if your children had to pay for the worst mistake you ever made?"

—**Lindsay King-Miller**, author of *This Is My Body*

"An almost Shakespearean tilt to the tragedy, in a place where secrets, lies, and ghosts tug and tear at people's lives."

—**Maria Haskins**, author of *Wolves & Girls* and *Six Dreams About the Train*

"A great and nuanced story that also changed my perspective—I'll never be the same."

—**Ivy Grimes**, author of *Glass Stories*

"Relentlessly real despite its supernatural premise."

—**Jonathan Louis Duckworth**, author of *Have You Seen the Moon Tonight? & Other Rumors*

"Raw and unflinching, emotional and spellbinding."

—**Zachary Rosenberg**, author of *Hungers as Old as This Land*

"Horror with a conscience, something that chills the soul as much as it challenges the heart."

—**Kenya Moss-Dyme**, author of *Seed*

"Any fan of Thompson's will find a new favorite with *The Curse of Hester Gardens* and any newcomer to her work will find a new top author."

—**Zaq Cass**, anthologist of *Error Code*

"Brilliant, crafted writing that bleeds with terror and humanity. She is the future of horror."

—Horror editor **Josh Darling**

The Curse of Hester Gardens

Tamika Thompson

an imprint of Kensington Publishing Corp.
erewhonbooks.com

For a full list of content warnings, please see p. 438.

EREWHON BOOKS are published by:

Kensington Publishing Corp.
900 Third Avenue
New York, NY 10022

erewhonbooks.com

All Kensington titles, imprints, and distributed lines are available at special quantity discounts for bulk purchases for sales promotions, premiums, fundraising, educational, or institutional use.

Special book excerpts or customized printings can also be created to fit specific needs. For details, write or phone the office of the Kensington sales manager: Kensington Publishing Corp., 900 Third Avenue, New York, NY 10022, attn: Sales Department; phone 1-800-221-2647.

ISBN 978-1-64566-319-5 (hardcover)

First Erewhon hardcover printing: April 2026

10 9 8 7 6 5 4 3 2 1

Printed in the United States of America

Library of Congress Control Number is available upon request.

Electronic edition: ISBN 978-1-64566-323-2

Edited by Diana Pho
Interior design by Leah Marsh
Excerpt from "The View from the Cloakroom" on p. ix courtesy ofTom Deady

The authorized representative in the EU for product safety and compliance
is eucomply OU, Parnu mnt 139b-14, Apt 123
Tallinn, Berlin 11317, hello@eucompliancepartner.com

For my uncle, Richard "Larry" Revels,
and for all of the people who have lost their
lives to gun violence in America

My feet hit another obstacle and I know it's not a desk. It's a body. Not a classmate, not a friend: a body. It's how I have to think of them if I'm going to survive.

—Tom Deady, "The View from the Cloakroom"

Prologue

May 28, 2002

Nona never enjoyed being apart from her boys. When they were asleep, she missed their giggles. When they bravely entered their classrooms on the first day of school, she was the one in tears as she exited the campus. So dropping them at their neighbor's for the afternoon was no simple task. She spent ten minutes just hugging and kissing her babies goodbye.

"Don't go, Mom. I can help you cook dinner." Her oldest, Kendall, had recently started calling her Mom instead of Mommy. She was still getting used to the new name. Now that he'd completed first grade, she had to call him "little guy" instead of "precious baby," and he allowed only a light peck on the forehead.

"I can help you clean the house too." He rested his tongue in the space left by his missing top tooth. He smelled of the waffles she'd made for breakfast.

"I know, Little Guy. You're always my big helper. But the time will go by so fast."

Morning sunlight poured into the front door as Kendall slumped his shoulders and shuffled into the home, several housing units across the courtyard from their own. Before too long, the day would be unbearably hot.

"Mommy, stay." Her middle son, Marcus, at four years old, squealed and squeezed her as she pulled him into a tight bear hug and plastered smooches all over his forehead, his cheeks, and the tip of his nose. A bandage covered his skinned knee. His sandals were on the wrong feet.

"I'm not going far. Just to the store and then back home to make a special dinner for Daddy. I won't be gone long."

Marcus poked out his bottom lip, but no whining this time. With Kendall as his guide, Marcus was maturing so quickly.

And even in his five-month-old baby sleep, her youngest, Lance, silently grinned when she gave him a soft kiss on the forehead, careful not to wake him.

"The store's gon' be closed by the time you finish loving on these boys," Mother Lincoln said. She knelt and gathered Kendall and Lance into her embrace as they filed into her living room. Moles and wrinkles crowded around the outer edges of the woman's eyes; her floral-patterned housedress seemed too warm for the weather.

Nona didn't know what she'd do without her neighbor, who watched her boys with little notice and sent them home filled with food and love.

"I have the Madden game," Peter, Mother Lincoln's grandson, said. The boy lived with the elder whenever his parents were in jail or on the streets, and his face lit up when he spoke to Kendall. Peter and Marcus were both four years old. She imagined Peter always wanted an older brother and was willing to borrow Marcus's.

"Will you play with me?" Peter whispered to Kendall. "It's new." His lisp wasn't as pronounced as the last time she'd heard him speak.

"Oh, yeah? Cool." Kendall giggled. The dimples he'd inherited from her made an appearance. She lived for those tiny dips in his cheeks.

"I'd kiss them a hundred times each if they'd let me, Mother." Nona removed Lance's diaper bag from her shoulder and placed it on Mother Lincoln's. Nona's milk-heavy breasts ached as she handed off her baby in his carrier. "I'll be back as soon as dinner is eaten."

"Baby, take your time. This is a big anniversary." Mother kissed Lance's tiny fist. He cooed but still didn't wake. "These boys can stay all night. Peter's got clothes and games enough for them all."

Nona couldn't leave her boys overnight. Not at Mother Lincoln's. Not at anyone's. But before she could speak, knobby-kneed Peter glanced up at her.

"Can they spend the night, Mrs. McKinley? Please. Pretty please. We won't give them berry pop. No chocolate neither."

Peter was laying it on thick. The "berry pop" actually wasn't soda at all. It was the iced tea from the bottling plant where Nona worked, and she didn't allow her boys to consume that much sugar. She also didn't like for them to spend long hours playing video games, but Peter lived by different rules.

"I'll check with their dad and see what he says." Nona knew Vance wouldn't care if the boys stayed the night, but it was easier to put the blame on him when she eventually said no.

Seeming satisfied with her answer, Peter nodded.

"Okay, my babies. One last kiss," she whispered as Lance stirred in his sleep.

Kendall and Marcus ran over, and she knelt again for a group hug. Peter remained in the doorway behind his grandmother, eyes wide and wistful as he fiddled with the game controller and watched them. Peter's forlorn eyes tugged at Nona's heart, and she extended her hand to him.

The boy crinkled his nose with glee. He rushed over to join the group, where he pressed in beside Kendall, who draped his arm around Peter as well. Mother Lincoln chuckled as Nona leaned over and kissed Peter's sweaty forehead like he was one of her own. As Peter giggled, she could smell the "berry pop" and chocolate on his breath.

Hours later, Nona cut through the alley, crept beside Hester Gardens' brick walls, and tucked into the shadows spreading across the concrete. Up ahead, two men argued, their shouts and curses drowning out the hum of a helicopter that circled in the distance. So far, the day had been perfect. She was determined not to let any turmoil cloud her wedding anniversary, but perhaps she shouldn't have taken this alternate route home, where she was isolated and hidden behind the crumbling façade that partially blocked the sun.

She'd pinned her curls into a French twist for the occasion. Vance liked the variety, the novelty of touching the new hair, the new her. She imagined the boys at Mother Lincoln's: Kendall playing video games with Peter, Marcus chatting up Mother while he helped her cook, and Lance practicing his new sitting skills on the pillows in the middle of the woman's floor. As much as she hated to part with them, she was grateful Mother took them, so they wouldn't drop paint on Nona's polished floors and grab at her skirt while she cooked steak, green beans with potatoes, and cornbread. Everything would be just so. Vance would be so surprised.

The argument continued in the distance, not far from a dumpster brimming with refuse that spilled onto the ground around it. Sweat gathered beneath her bra as she shifted her bulky seventy-percent-off purchase from her left hand to her right. For six months, she'd stuffed ones and fives into an old purse at the back of her closet to afford the fishing pole. She imagined Vance's face lighting up when she gave him the symbol of his bass fishing weekends with his late grandfather. Keeping the gift a surprise was the entire reason she'd chosen this roundabout way home. She slowed her stride, in case the disagreement intensified.

The memories of her life with Vance danced in her mind: their first night together in the back of his Camaro at Medford Lake, their slow dance to "Come Rain or Come Shine" by Ray Charles at their wedding reception, the morning their firstborn emerged from her body and cried.

She hummed a Mary J. Blige tune about real love as she ignored used needles, discarded cigarette butts, and empty liquor bottles littering the path. Ten years. Three boys. Tons of love. And although Vance hadn't gotten her the standalone home with a backyard, he was at least saving for the down payment. She wouldn't complain, though sometimes she wanted to.

The men's shouts escalated, interrupted her song, and echoed off the brick: "Motherfucker" this and "Shut the fuck up" that.

She scanned the windows. All the curtains were drawn. No one watching. Not a soul around to witness the incident, and with the chopper above coming and going, it seemed only she was aware this fight was occurring.

She searched for an exit. She needed to leave between the buildings. She girded herself as she stepped over two dead mice to do so. Vance would be home soon, and the surprise would just have to be spoiled before dinner.

"No. Please. I'm begging you."

She also avoided a splintered skateboard and a used condom as she moved toward the ray of sunlight peeking between the brick buildings. The silhouettes came into view. One figure lay on the ground, and the other towered over him. Luckily, they didn't notice her.

Seconds before she could slip out of the alley, the man on his feet spoke: "Should have thought about that before you messed with my money."

She stopped. Dropped the pole. Beads of sweat dampened her hairline. That voice was the one that woke her every morning with "Hey, my forever." The voice that teased her sons with "Where are Daddy's hugs and tickles?" The last voice she heard at night: "I love you, my forever. Pleasant dreams."

Sobbing and propped up on his elbows, the man on the ground dragged his lifeless legs behind him. "No, Vance. Please. Stop."

She opened her mouth, but her voice was locked in her throat. Silence enveloped her. The alley tilted. A wren swooped low and fluttered past. The wind from its wings brushed her skin. Her ears rang. Her mind screamed, *Run!* but paralysis took hold of her feet and planted them like the limp weeds growing between cracks in the ground.

As she closed in on the scene, raised her hand, and shielded her face from the warmth of the May sun, her husband and the father of her three boys, who told her he got his extra cash from his dad's body shop, beat another man with a pistol.

Thwack. Thwack. Thwack.

A surge of heat raced across her scalp. Each blow echoed against her chest, her stomach. She braced herself against the back of the nearest unit. The brick crumbled and left behind red flakes on her palm. Her husband was a bear—wild, panting, with sweat pasting his T-shirt to his chest. He held the very .38 she'd told him to get rid of. Blood had sprayed his khakis, the tan pants she'd ironed for him that morning.

As she revealed herself from the shadows, his name left her lips in a constrained shout. Their eyes met. He paused the beating. Pain crept into the set of his mouth.

"Vance" was all she could manage that time, and even that was a whisper.

Thick blood oozed from the crown of the man on the ground and slid like blessing oil over his eyes, nose, cheeks, and chin. Noticing her, the man dragged his limp body closer, his shoes inadvertently taking those littered cigarette butts and discarded needles with them.

He reached a swollen, bleeding hand toward her, his broken fingers trembling inches from her skirt. "Don't let him kill me."

Let. The man uttered that word as if she had the power to allow and disallow her husband's actions. She raised her gaze to Vance, who stared at her and mouthed, *Baby, please.* She wanted to help the injured man, to focus on the letting and not letting, but she had detached from her body, had lost her sense of smell, could no longer feel her hands or feet.

Between gasps, the man on the ground managed another plea: "I. Will. Pay. You. Back."

Beyond the housing units that concealed this bloody event, a truck rumbled along the road, a basketball bounced, children squealed, the sounds foreign, from another world.

Vance brought the pistol down on the man's head a final time, and Nona's exposed shins caught much of the spray of red liquid. She bent and reached for the man, but he fell silent and slumped forward, arms splayed like a downed bird.

Part One

One

May 28, 2016

Only a few Hester Gardens townhomes faced north, and in Medford lore, they were the reason the public housing complex was haunted. When the sun rose on the eastern-facing units that overlooked the Rodgers Freeway, light poured into the tiny windows, baking the occupants from May through September and reminding them of summer the rest of the year. For the homes that faced west, the setting sun bathed the walls in eerie pinks and purples reminiscent of late-afternoon funerals down south. The handful of southern-facing dwellings were dim most of the day except around noon, when the sun was high enough to peek through curtains like an intrusive neighbor. But the haunted quarters were the ones facing north, or so everyone said. For those homes, the sun never seemed to rise, the days were cast in a never-ending pall of gray, and the murdered just didn't know how to leave.

Nona McKinley's unit faced north. On the morning of her middle son's high school graduation, she showered, powdered herself, and primped in her bedroom mirror. It was a quarter past six, and she'd been up since four a.m. cleaning and fretting, filled with a range of emotions she couldn't quite place. She fastened her favorite bra—the best of the three she owned because it crafted the deepest cleavage—and hummed along to a gospel tune flowing from the television Pastor Davis had bought her. The song had also played at her eldest son's funeral.

Kendall.

That wound was still so raw.

Being home alone was a rare but welcome event. A full bed alongside a milk crate draped with a neighbor's discarded curtains completed her room, and the makeshift nightstand housed her blessing oil and Bible. The bars on the lone window and the narrowness of the room were her prison. Back when Vance still lived there, the space had seemed larger. His mere presence had stretched apart the walls and pushed up the ceiling.

She searched her closet for something that might dress up the outfit she would wear. At the back, she found the skirt she'd worn that day in the alley. It had taken her weeks to remove the bloodstains. Vance had made her promise not to throw it in the trash.

"I can burn it," she'd offered.

"Nothing out of the ordinary," he'd countered. "Just clean it and hang it again like you do with all of your clothes on a normal week."

The memory of NaDarius came to her, of his hand reaching for her skirt, but she wouldn't let him haunt her this day. Not at such a special moment. The occasion she'd been waiting for, when all of her hopes and dreams and backbreaking work were finally paying off.

She wasn't expecting the boys to return home before the ceremony. In fact, she was set to meet them there. So when her front door groaned open and slammed shut, she drew in a breath and stared at the image of her own wide eyes.

With her bra hooked but backward on her torso, she snapped off the Brooklyn Tabernacle Choir and waited for familiar footsteps—deliberate if they belonged to Marcus, the graduate; dawdling if they were Lance's, the middle schooler's.

These footfalls were neither; they rushed across her floor as if set aflame.

Was it a junkie? Or one of the boys from the local gang, the Hester Boys, rummaging through her kitchen drawers? How would they have gotten in? She had wrought iron on the front door, and there were but two ways a person could force entry, one of which involved a screwdriver.

Only she, Marcus, and Lance had keys, and her boys would never lose nor loan theirs. She prayed it was Marcus stomping across the living-room floor, drawing closer to her room. Perhaps he'd forgotten the printout for his speech?

"Marcus?"

She didn't like the way the movement stopped on the other side of the wall. The clock ticked louder than usual. Across the hall, the toilet bubbled. Sweat formed on her upper lip and about her temples, and she pressed her palm to her chest, hoping the gesture would calm her breathing.

No answer from the living room.

She rushed forward and pressed the dime-sized gold lock on her bedroom door. With trembling fingers almost too thick to work, she tugged her bra into place, slid on her blouse, and zipped her hips into her pencil skirt.

She tiptoed back to the dresser and quietly searched the top for her phone. Mable. She'd call Mable Cleveland. Mable lived several doors down in Hester Gardens and was always armed, even at funerals, even in line at the neighborhood food pantry. Where was Nona's cell?

Blush brushes, BB cream, and her bottle of blue-black mascara covered the dresser top, but no phone. She eased open the top drawer in case the device had fallen in. It wasn't there either.

Nerves stabbed her stomach and chest. She must have left it on the kitchen counter. Her only way to call for help was on the other side of her home, out where the steps gave way to a dragging sound, a heaviness being pulled across her floors.

"It's me," someone said. The voice moved to the hallway, outside her bedroom door. Closer. Louder. "It's me."

She snatched up the metal baseball bat she kept beside her bed, careful not to make a sound. She didn't know who was on the other side of the thin wood, but the voice—deadpan, bass-heavy, and evil—didn't belong to any of her sons.

How could such a flimsy lock keep her safe? She backed up, bumping her nightstand and knocking her Bible to the floor. She regretted making Vance get rid of the revolver he'd kept in the milk crate.

Floorboards creaked on the other side of the door.

"You better get out of my house if you know what's good for you." She drew closer to the wood again, hoping to sound like a large, menacing person who had a weapon and perhaps also knew how to throw a punch, but her voice came out shrill and weak.

The doorknob rotated slowly, the motion barely emitting a sound. The handle squeaked in protest as someone moved it left, right, left, right. The lock Pastor had installed worked after all. The metal held.

When she didn't open the door, the intruder violently shook it in its frame. A crack the size of a strand of hair appeared near the edge; it wouldn't take much more pressure to break through. She wished she hadn't told Pastor to install those irons on the bedroom windows and the front door. Now she had no way to get out.

She pressed her ear to the wood; the post of her stud earring dug into the flesh behind her lobe.

Everything came to a stop.

She brought the bat to her right shoulder anyway, gripping the handle and gearing up to swing. Her pulse throbbed against her temples. Tears burned the outer corners of her eyes. The clock beside the bedroom door ticked. As the red hand crept forward, the thin rod counted down the seconds until she came face to face with this prowler. She waited. Her pounding heart echoed in her ears.

Ten minutes passed. Outside the bedroom window, children laughed and a car's engine roared to life, but no noise from her home.

Was he gone?

She unlocked the bedroom door, and after the handle clicked and the hinges creaked open, her entire home seemed to sigh.

No sunlight graced the narrow walkway that led from her and the boys' bedrooms and past their shared bathroom. She gripped the bat with both hands and elbowed the light switch on.

The overhead bulb illuminated the only frame she'd ever hung on the wall: the family portrait in which she stood next to Vance, the two of them smiling, with their three boys seated in front of them, also grinning.

Expecting someone to leap from the open door of the boys' room, she peeked inside. Their closet sat open, their dirty shirts, shorts, and socks spilling out. Light from the window passed beneath their mattresses and illuminated the spots under their beds. She crouched and squinted. No one was under there. Same for the shower in the bathroom—curtain open, space empty. The final place to check was beyond the hall.

She inched along the wall, her palms moist on the bat as she braced for someone to reach out of the shadows and grab her. She kept her eyes trained on the archway where the hallway opened into the den.

The console table snagged her skirt as she passed, but she refused to take her eyes off the hall's threshold as she backed up and freed the fabric from the splinters in the wood.

The closer she got to rounding the corner, the stronger a sickening and familiar smell became. The air reeked of her mother and father in the moments before they passed, when they were in the liminal space between the living realm and the next, with the heat leaving them, sweat gathering under their arms, and feces leaking into the mattress beneath them.

The sharp odor of smoke reached her nostrils.

With her bat still poised to strike, she paused at the edge of the hall and squinted at the dim den, expecting open and ransacked kitchen drawers and cabinets, perhaps an overturned couch, a missing television, maybe. The sweat from her soles squeaked against the floor as she entered. She held her breath.

Vacuum lines from her four a.m. cleaning session coursed up her couch's fabric. The bowl of plastic apples sat undisturbed in the middle of the dining table. The refrigerator remained closed, the photos of her boys taped to its front untouched. The tiny coat, linen, and utility closets that spanned the entry wall were open, and the jackets and shoes were organized how she'd left them hours before. Nothing was out of place, but someone had broken in. Had made a ruckus doing so. Yet the physical evidence of the noises she'd heard did not exist. Had she imagined the entire thing?

Smoke billowed from the stove, but nothing was cooking on the eyes. The flames on the right rear burner grew as if she'd poured gasoline on them. Her breath escaped in a loud gasp as she dropped the bat and reached for the knobs. They were already off. The fire reached higher, above the back of the stove now, and might have continued if she hadn't smothered it quickly with a damp dish towel.

She wrestled with the window, opened it, and fanned the smoke that floated around her kitchen. With her index finger and thumb, careful not to burn herself, she snatched up the dish towel and flung it in the sink. All flames on the stove were gone.

Her phone sat on the counter. Coughing and sweating, she turned her back to the kitchen sink so her home and the hallway she'd just exited remained in view. She still felt under siege, even if no one was home but her and her fear.

She picked up the bat and rested it against the kitchen table, within arm's reach. She scanned the room's every nook as she unlocked her phone and opened her contacts. Marcus answered on the second ring, and she sobbed when she heard his voice. Choked up, she struggled to get through the entire story of what had just happened, but Marcus managed to get the gist of what she said: There had maybe, somehow, been an intruder.

"Someone broke in? I'm on my way back," Marcus shouted over the din of teens laughing in the background, some shrieking as they likely lined up and practiced for their ceremony. She hated she was worrying him on such an important day.

"No. Stay. I'm fine. I just . . . It wasn't real. I must have . . . I needed to know it wasn't real."

"But if somebody was trying to break in—"

"No. I had my gospel music on too. The sound might have been somebody over in the Taylors' unit or something."

She didn't fully believe that. The voice had seemed so real, but there was no proof now that it'd happened at all.

"'"But if it's an emergency—"

"There's no emergency." She regretted calling. Was kicking herself for making Marcus responsible for her emotions. "Just me losing my mind."

"Being scared doesn't mean you're losing your mind."

Scared. Yes. She was scared, but that's all she could really say with certainty. She had no idea what had just happened to her.

Maybe a burglar had tried the door, rattled it, and then realized her unit had bars and would be too difficult to break into.

What about the voice?

Again, Marcus insisted on coming home.

"Nope. By the time your bus arrives here, I'll already be there."

He paused, likely weighing this information and trying to come up with another way to take care of her.

As the morning sun rose higher, it punched through the windows, rested on seat cushions, filled the corners, spilled across her shelves and counters, and dissolved the shadows. Sunlight in her home was rare, so she was grateful for it. Even the smiles in those refrigerator photographs seemed brighter, with her boys' faces saying *What's the problem, Mom?*

"Okay." He still sounded unconvinced. "Text me as soon as you get on the bus."

"Soon as I get on." She didn't enjoy feeling like the child in this exchange. "I promise."

"Knew I shoulda told Lance to keep his butt at home this morning."

"It's fine. You know he uses any excuse to get out the house."

"All right, Mom. Sing it with me now."

She smiled, pretending she didn't want to belt out the tune they'd begun singing his first day of kindergarten, when he'd gripped her hand tight enough to leave creases from his toy watch on her wrist.

Back then he'd asked, "How long I gotta be 'way from you?" She'd knelt before him, took in his unlaced sneakers, the snot pooled above his lip, the thumb he'd begun sucking during the walk up the steps, and she'd told him, "When the little hand is on the three and the big hand on the twelve." She'd whispered the song to him. He'd joined in, and it was only then he'd been willing to bunny hop with the other students into the classroom.

"Better sing it now, or I'm coming home." His smile came through the phone, and it made her giggle.

They sang the chorus to "I'll Always Love My Mama" by the Intruders.

Marcus whispered the lyrics, likely pressing the button on the side of the phone, increasing the volume to hear her over the hubbub.

He chuckled, and her heart was bursting. She wished his day hadn't been clouded.

"Better now?"

"Better."

But as soon as she ended the call, the sun passed behind a cloud, and the light filling her home turned to gray. Shadows again rested on seat cushions, filled corners, spread across the counters and shelves, and darkness even passed over her boys' pictured faces—their smiles now those of aggrieved men.

She was not better. Her eyes ached as she faced the empty space in the hallway, the area so dark she could no longer make out the family portrait in that grim passageway. Behind her, the *tick, tick, tick* of the pilot light, and the stove lit itself again.

Two

By nine, she sat two bus stops away, in the Kitledge High auditorium be- side her youngest, Lance, noting with pain in her chest the absence of her husband and her firstborn. A flood of energy rushed through her hands and feet as she peered out the window at the gray clouds that had formed in the sky. She should have been happy Marcus's big day had finally arrived, but her thoughts remained on that voice she'd imagined in her home. *It's me.* That's how they all usually called out when they entered, and she'd recognize the voice immediately. Only this time, that hadn't happened.

Rain pelted the roof, slowly at first. Anxiety? No. She wasn't experiencing anxiety. Not exactly.

She received two text messages. One from Pastor: The big day is here! I'm putting the finishing touches on tonight's graduation party. Give Marcus a big high five for me. Btw, I can't wait to see you. I missed talking to you this morning.

A surge coursed through her body when she read his message. Her cheeks flushed. She turned her phone so Lance couldn't see.

The rain shower became a storm that grew louder than the din of the gathering crowd. Folks filed in fussing and sopping wet. The women with curls where straightened hair should have been complained that poor weather forecasting had cost them time and money on their blowouts.

The second message was from her nephew Harlan: Just got put on a breaking news story at work. Won't be able to make the graduation after all. Tell Marcus I'll see him tonight at the party.

Harlan's empty seat on the other side of Lance doubled in size. She was disappointed, so she knew Marcus would be as well. Another man absent from his life. She couldn't be mad at Harlan, though. He was such a fine example for Marcus to follow. Harlan had made it out of Hester Gardens, and now Marcus would too.

The graduates marched in to the beat of whistles, cheers, and hoots. A live band played "Lift Every Voice and Sing," and the crowd filled in the words of the Black national anthem. Nona's throat burned from yelling "Marcus!" Her cheeks flushed when he caught sight of her, waved, and blew her a kiss from the front of the line.

The sense of foreboding she'd woken with in the morning returned. Was it related to his graduation? Was she already missing him because he would head off to college in the fall? No. That wasn't quite right either. She wanted him to leave, to get as far away as he could from Hester Gardens.

Marcus waved to alums, parents, and underclassmen huddled in the audience. Two years before, her firstborn had done the same. Back then, Marcus and Lance had held up a homemade poster that said *Way to go, Kendall!*

Kendall, you'd be so proud of Marcus today. She pictured her oldest outside the windows, seated among the clouds, grinning back. Was this weight in the pit of her stomach related to her grief? No. That heaviness lived inside her every day, had become its own painful limb. This was something else.

In his speech, would Marcus mention he'd be attending an Ivy League school in the fall? She wanted to sing it from the third row: *My middle baby is going to an elite private school. Yes, honey, I raised him right!*

Once the rain-soaked audience took their seats, the ceremony dragged on for forty tortuous minutes. A few administrators gave speeches about "the future," and she nodded off twice, her head landing on Lance's shoulder. That all changed when the principal introduced Marcus.

Her middle son strode to the podium. His military gait and upright posture resembled his father Vance, who'd been eighteen when she'd met him.

With aching cheeks and a wet chin, dressed in the only suit she owned—a navy pencil skirt, a matching blazer, and a polyester blouse so shiny it looked like plastic—she sat up straight, cleared her throat, and snapped several photos of him on her phone.

Comments floated from the attendees around her. With praise like "You must be so proud" and "You raised such a fine young man," she was as much the star of this event as Marcus was. Her unsettled feeling from moments before could have been from a different day altogether.

"Family, friends, and teachers, those of you who have helped and guided us, you are witnessing a rite of passage for the future leaders of our nation. I hope not only that you take great pride in our commencement exercises today, but also that you consider the critical role you played in getting us here." Marcus's words thundered through the auditorium, the timbre of Vance's voice speaking through him. The crowd cheered and whistled. Lightning flickered across Marcus's face as he continued. Seconds later, thunder cracked. Before too long, rain pounded against the roof and windows.

The downpour echoed around them. Latecomers crowded into nearby rows, their pants and skirts soaked, with newspapers and plastic grocery bags covering their blowouts.

"They like to refer to us as the 'working poor,'" Marcus continued, "as if chastising us for making poor decisions, as if that phrase isn't an oxymoron, as if it isn't an indictment of their systems, which seek to keep us downtrodden, desperate, and disenfranchised."

"Amen, young brotha," a man in the back called out.

"But we know how to survive, don't we?" Marcus smirked. "We know how to take the pain, suffering, and mistreatment and turn it into joy, laughter, and miracles. We know how to stare down greed, hatred, and the violence of neglect and stand firm in our ability to give, to love, and to build community."

"Yes," a woman near the window shouted.

"And we're not without some responsibility in this, are we?" Marcus's expression grew stern, as if he were an elder; his eyes searched the faces of his fellow graduates. "We must accept responsibility for our actions because that's where our agency lies. We can build bridges in our community, but where are those bridges leading us? Are we voting? Are we pushing for ballot initiatives that address our concerns? Are we using our device screens to learn about electoral politics or to watch the latest reality show, scroll our social media, and take personality quizzes?"

The crowd chuckled.

"I'm not trying to cast aspersions on us or blame us for our condition, but our oppressors are not going to change our lives for us. My mother named me after Black nationalist Marcus Garvey, who said, 'If you want liberty, you yourselves must strike the blow.' And I believe this wholeheartedly. I might not be a separatist, but I think the brotha was on to something."

Laughter and thunderous applause erupted.

"Preach," a man in front of Nona said as he clapped. Whistles from behind her and an "all right, now" resounded above the ovation.

Nona couldn't contain her smile and nudged Lance in the ribs to get him to grin, but her youngest did not comply. He sat stiffly in a hand-me-down church suit that, until that morning, had been hanging untouched in the corner of the closet that belonged to Kendall.

Kendall.

From his first-row seat next to his grandmother, Peter nodded at Lance. Just the sight of Peter made her stomach pull in on itself. Even though she was a Christian and had had a hand in rearing Peter, she had grown over the years to despise that boy.

When Lance lifted his hand to wave, she slapped his bony flesh, sending his palm back down to his lap. Lance glanced at her, then at Peter, shaking his head. Peter grinned, shrugged, and returned his attention to the podium.

"I know a thing or two about having help," Marcus continued. "Everything my brothers and I have ever accomplished is because someone made a sacrifice for us. One day, I hope to be a U.S. senator to make a way in this country for the very people who paid for my sneakers, offered me and my brothers a ride to Kitledge High on a bitter winter morning, shoveled snow from our walkway so I could attend student council meetings before first bell, and handed me the last five from their wallets because they knew, as hard as my mother worked, on occasion, the fridge was empty."

That part.

Nona grew warm about the collar, and she worried sweat would frizz her hair. She wanted to cover her face, but it was Marcus's truth. As much as it stung, he was justified in saying it.

"That's all right," a young woman called out.

Lightning flickered through the windows. Nona jumped at the boom of thunder that followed. Wind pressed against the glass, and a sheet of moisture slid down the panes like slime. The storm reminded her of the darkness in her home and the voice from that morning.

"And I'm not just talking about our young people. The need to accept responsibility extends to our elders. Particularly when our school board year after year votes to spend thousands on gymnasium floors and turf for the football field while peeling paint mars classroom walls, while the air conditioning and heat are busted most of the time, while half the dollars spent on campus go to police resource officers who handcuff students more often than they high-five them."

"Tell it!" a young graduate shouted from the front row. She raised her cap and waved it in the air in Marcus's direction.

Marcus was telling the truth. The school had been built in 1952, when the city of Medford had been mostly working-class white folks and a smattering of middle-class Black people. Now, the administration still maintained the building's original wood cabinets and fixtures—and "maintained" was being generous. The three-story structure was the spitting image of Hester Gardens, with concrete, red brick, and rectangular windows like those lining a train car. The floors were scarred tile and laminate where better schools had polished oak or cedar.

Marcus and Principal Watkins were the same shade of brown, but the bald man seated behind Marcus's pimple-faced salutatorian Avery grew crimson about the forehead and scalp, and his mouth pulled into a sheepish grin the girl turned and captured on her phone.

"Money's tight and savings are light for everyone," Marcus continued.

She fully expected a standing ovation for this speech when he finished. She wished Kendall could see Marcus.

"You can tell a person's character by what he chooses to spend his little savings on."

Principal Watkins rubbed his brow and glanced at the school board president, who adjusted his necktie. In Medford, regular unleaded had risen to four dollars, but minimum wage hadn't gotten over double that, so Marcus's words drew claps, whistles, and more shouts of "Tell it, Marcus!"

Marcus paused, and the spotlight created a halo above his blue graduation cap. "And I would be remiss if I didn't mention my big brother, Kendall, killed in a drive-by shooting three blocks from where we're gathered right now." Marcus grimaced, choking down a sob.

Silence fell over the crowd. The storm quieted down. Light taps of rain on the roof filled the space as the audience grew stiff in their seats. Nona grabbed Lance's hand and squeezed.

Her lips quivered. Tears inched down the crevices beside her nose, puddled on her chin, and fell to her shirt, sticking the fabric to her chest. She was a mess, and about every head turned toward her, only adding to her self-consciousness about her ugly cry. If Kendall were looking down on them, he'd know she'd gotten no better since the day she'd lost him.

With the break in the rain, melodies from the sparrows perched in the trees outside rose and filled the space where the people's whispers had previously been. It was odd the birds were chanting in a storm. She'd been in a storm for years and hardly felt like singing.

Marcus cleared his throat and wiped a tear from the corner of his eye. A flood of panic rose from Nona's feet and rushed up her legs.

Principal Watkins, likely relieved Marcus had changed the subject, shouted, "It's all right, young brotha. Take your time."

Eyes glassy, Marcus nodded at his elder and returned his gaze to the third row, where Nona and Lance were, and where Vance and Kendall were not. Marcus's nose was red. He sniffled.

Nona used a tissue from her pocketbook to dab the tears on her blouse. From the corner of her eye, Kendall appeared in the first-row seat he'd occupied two years before. He'd been in this very space, wearing his own graduation cap. He'd winked at her; his high school graduation had been their mutual triumph.

Nona was no longer warm. She was hot. She was cold. She was frantic. She was calm. She didn't want Marcus to talk about Kendall. Actually, she wanted him to talk about Kendall.

Marcus cleared his throat again. "Most of you already know I adored my brother."

Rows ahead, Peter shifted in his seat. Mother Lincoln turned her church hat–adorned head and stared at the side of her grandson's face.

Lance, whose hand was limp even as Nona still squeezed it, lowered his gaze to the floor, seeming disappointed Marcus was not speaking of him.

A little louder, Marcus said, "But my love couldn't keep him alive. The last conversation we had, he actually reprimanded me, told me that no matter how difficult our life became, we had to remain honest men, said it was my responsibility to do better than he did, and then to make sure our younger brother does better than us both. Today, I honor my brother . . ."

Marcus's voice cracked on the final "brother," and the unbridled display of emotion was what Nona had been dreading.

Thunder pounded. The raindrops picked up again, striking the roof faster, harder.

She finally brought the tissue to her eyes, soaking the paper to the point that she had to fish out another. She held the new one to her nose, her shoulders trembling. Mother Lincoln blew her a kiss, but Peter did not move from his spot where he stared at the floor. Lance rubbed Nona's shoulder, rare affection from him, which signaled she must have looked a mess.

"Don't cry, Mom," Marcus whispered, his words amplified by the microphone as he sobbed.

Her mascara clumped beneath her lashes and ran thick down her cheeks along with her tears. She wanted to flee, to run back to the room where she'd identified Kendall's body and climb onto that metal table with him. She wanted to go back and take the bullet, let them cut her open for an autopsy and place her remains in a box underground. Anything she had to do to make Kendall alive again.

Marcus straightened his cap, bit his lip, and aimed his eyes at the back row. He gaped for so long at that spot near the double entry doors that Nona and the others checked the area as well. Who had entered? Or perhaps, who had waved to Marcus? There were no folding chairs near the entrance. No one stood there.

Marcus whispered again. "Not today."

Nona and Lance exchanged a confused expression, then searched again for the invisible person Marcus had spoken to. Principal Watkins cleared his throat, twirled his index finger to bring Marcus back to his speech.

Marcus nodded, seeming embarrassed, cleared his throat, and returned his eyes to the empty space near the door. He picked up his diploma from the podium and raised it toward the invisible person there. When he pointed to his name, lightning flashed through the auditorium windows, as if Marcus controlled the storm.

"This diploma, my future . . . it is all for . . . my big brother Kendall."

Nona didn't know what to make of what was happening, but she joined the crowd in clapping for the end of his speech. A couple of people behind her whistled and patted her shoulder.

As she rose to her feet, a cold emptiness passed over her, and this time, she got the sense she was forgetting something. No. "Forgetting" wasn't quite it either. The emotion was more specific than that.

Amid the thunderous standing ovation that seemed to drown out the storm, she swiveled her head to take note of Marcus, then followed his gaze over her shoulder to the double doors, where a lone beam of sunlight cut through the rain clouds and shot between the gap like a bullet. And then it hit her. She was experiencing dread. A deeply hidden but growing terror, a knowledge that something, perhaps everything, was about to go wrong again.

Three

Lance had no intentions of arriving at the graduation after-party with Marcus. Soon as the bus arrived at the Prescott stop, Marcus mounted, but Lance headed to the alley.

"Where you going?"

Lance didn't break his stride. Marcus was always pretending to be a Goody Two-shoes, but there were two sides to Marcus: Schoolboy Marcus, who wrote award-winning essays and aced tests he barely studied for because he "just knew the material," and Evil Marcus, who'd recently lit a bag of postal letters on fire because he was angry the mail carrier was misdelivering their mom's paychecks. Their mother was unaware, and the mailman never made that mistake again.

Neither version of Marcus had the standing with Lance that Kendall had. Kendall had been good-natured, honest, a protector, but Kendall was gone, and Marcus could go to hell.

"Be up there in just a sec."

"You got thirty minutes to arrive at that church or I'm sending Mom after you," Marcus shouted.

Lance threw up a peace sign without looking back. He was banking on Marcus getting to the party and forgetting about him. Apparently, forgetting about Lance was easy. Marcus and Mom never paid Lance much mind, long as he kept quiet and didn't inconvenience them.

Lance glanced back just before Marcus turned away, and he caught a glimpse of Evil Marcus, with the V that spread across his forehead whenever he frowned or scowled. That version of his brother had arrived right after Kendall had been killed. Lance thought the V resembled devil's horns, smack-dab in the middle of Marcus's head just above his eyebrows.

Tears stung Lance's eyes as Kendall's face flashed in his mind. Lance rounded the corner, and six of the Hester Boys were waiting in the alley between the complex's buildings—Peter, Solomon, Donnell, Cedrick, Rayvon, and Red—cigarettes hanging from each of their mouths.

Lance fanned the smoke. He never knew why his mother avoided the area, but whatever the reason, it made the color leave her cheeks, made her scramble forward, faster, faster, and she'd get the oddest expression on her face, like she was seeing something on the ground when nothing was there. He should have asked her about it, but he took it as a sign that he could get away with almost anything in this space because it was hidden, and because his mother was afraid of it.

When Donnell saw Lance, he raised his fist and said, "All right, now." Donnell had donned a "wife beater" to show off his sleeve of tattoos, the most recent a picture of his mom, Mable. Donnell rubbed his newly tatted skin and said, "Here comes Little Bit."

Lance hated the nickname. He was fourteen and thin, but he was inches taller than he'd been the previous summer and had sprouted hair on his face. He must look like a young man now, because the chicks who noticed him were easily seventeen. Those same girls would have patted him on the head the previous year.

"I ain't gon' be too many more of them Little Bits, man."

The HBs grinned, and Peter stepped forward to give Lance a dab. Peter, known on the streets as Pacman, wore his usual sunglasses and his cap low, which cast shadows on his face. "Drink up." Peter handed Lance a red cup with brown liquid. It smelled like battery acid and Coca-Cola. "This will help us get through that boring-ass party."

Lance had never had alcohol before. Had only smelled it on others. So when he brought the cup in the vicinity of his face, he wanted to sneeze. He took a sip, Peter eyeing him the entire time, and when Donnell spoke, Lance was relieved that they all stopped staring at him.

"You only think it's gon' be boring because your ass flunked out." Donnell's cup was probably filled with grape pop and codeine. They all called it "lean," and lean was definitely what it made Donnell do.

"I quit school." Peter rounded on Donnell, who took a step back, lowered his eyes, and threw his free hand up in surrender. "Lot of good your diploma done you. You out here just like the rest of us."

Lance took another sip. It burned less that time, so he downed the entire thing in four gulps.

"Fellas. Fellas." At six foot eight inches, Solomon towered over everyone and dribbled his basketball. He'd graduated in Kendall's class and hadn't worked a day since. "Why any of y'all going?"

"Well, Peter gotta go see his baby mama." Donnell was obviously drunk because he never got this bold with Peter. Lance moved a few inches to his left; any minute he expected Peter to sock Donnell in the nose.

To gauge reactions, Lance scanned the faces of the others gathered. Rayvon, shirtless, swayed like he was preparing to jump between Peter and Donnell or, better yet, jump out of the way.

Red fluffed his curly auburn hair with a pick and stared at the ground.

And Cedrick, shorter and thinner than Lance, even though he was a year older, stared into his smartphone, from which he was blasting "Bling Bling." The only reason they didn't call Cedrick "Little Bit" was because he'd been in the group longer. Cedrick lowered the volume. Silence pressed into the alley and surrounded them.

Peter didn't lash out this time. Just shot Donnell a nasty look followed by a grin. "My grandma say we gotta go support Gretchen. But, man, fuck Gretchen. I'm going because of my grandma. Y'all know how I am about my grandma."

Everyone chuckled nervously. Everybody in the city of Medford knew how much Peter loved Mother Lincoln. Until he'd had a baby, Peter only smiled when his grandmother was around. Now he smiled when he held his son too, but the kindness didn't extend to the child's mother.

Lance belched, and tears burned his eyes. He brought the empty cup to his face and pretended to be drinking still. He needed to cough, but he held it. Sniffled instead, hoping the urge would pass.

Donnell eyed Lance. "Proud of your brother, huh? Heard he gave a big speech this morning."

Lance shrugged and removed the cup from his face. "I mean, I guess." He wasn't sure how he felt about Marcus. And the speech had been type weird.

"I know Kendall would have been proud." Donnell paused. Solomon stopped dribbling his ball and shook his head no. A warning.

Peter glared at Donnell, the two of them having an exchange that Lance couldn't read. They each extinguished their cigarettes on the ground, Peter angrily, Donnell slowly, their gazes never faltering. The others followed suit. What had happened? Why did it look like they were all squaring up? Nervous, Lance tried to cut the tension.

"Yeah. My dad wasn't around to see the graduation either. Shit is fucked up." He'd slurred those last words. His face muscles went slack; his brain was suddenly filled with cotton.

The shift in Lance was enough to bring the group's mood back from wherever it'd been about to go.

"Little Bit is faded." Solomon chuckled and pointed, breaking the eye contact between Peter and Donnell.

"You good?" Peter asked like he was embarrassed. Lance had never seen that expression on Peter's face. Was he reacting to Lance's drinking or the mention of Kendall?

"Me? I'm straight, man. So straight. I'm good." He wasn't straight or good. He was definitely lopsided and bad. He needed to sit his ass all the way down. Everyone else he'd ever seen drinking had just gulped down their cups. Wasn't that what he was supposed to do? He was suddenly angry with his mom and Marcus for keeping him sheltered and in the church all the time. Keeping him from knowing basic things in life, like how to drink alcohol without looking a fool.

"Got a job for you, Lance, if you want." Donnell threw the contents of his entire cup into his mouth in one large gulp. If Lance could do that and maintain himself, they'd probably stop calling him Little Bit.

"What kind of job?" Lance's eyes darted toward Donnell's waistband, where he typically holstered his gun, a Glock 17 Donnell referred to as "Grave Digger," his "baby," and sometimes his "one and only girl." The bulge was there, but when Lance returned his gaze to Donnell's face, Donnell's expression was matter-of-fact. Lance couldn't read him and wished Donnell could give him a hint of whether this was a simple job or something more. Lance's answer depended on it.

"Let me ask you this." Peter walked over and put his arm around Lance's shoulder. Lance did not like the weight of Peter on him, but he didn't move. "Aren't you tired of asking Mommy for money?"

"I guess."

"It's time for you to stop guessing and start knowing." Peter gave Lance's shoulder a shake, like they were the best of friends.

"Donnell doesn't let everybody in on his jobs. So, when Donnell says he's got a job for you, instead of you asking 'What kind of job?' you need to ask, 'When can I start?'"

They all stood stock still, staring at Lance. Every muscle in his body loosened. The burden he'd been carrying for the past four years, from losing his father to prison to burying his older brother, lifted and floated up from his shoulders into the sky. He wasn't exactly happy, but everything in his life felt a little less heavy. And here Peter and Donnell were, solving a problem Lance hadn't realized he had before now.

"Got it," Lance said, with a tongue fat and slippery and lips increasingly thick. "When can I start?"

A blue ball rolled along the ground near the group, coming to rest near Peter's feet. Peter and Donnell jumped at the sight and checked behind them. The rest of the young men pressed their bodies against the red brick of the buildings, and, mouths agape, they all stared at the shadowy corner from which the ball had originated.

Lance coughed. It seemed this was the right time to release it, when no one was paying attention to him. "Uh. What the fuck is y'all looking at?"

"Man, shhhhh." Donnell squinted. He held his hand out to Lance like he was preparing for an attack.

Nothing happened. Cedrick picked up the ball and threw it back down the alley, where it bounced off the brick and came to rest in a corner. It was the kind of toy a kid might use for kickball.

"I don't think he's showing up this time," Cedrick said as the group continued to stare down the empty alley at the overflowing dumpsters, two brick walls, and cracked concrete ground overgrown with weeds.

Because the rows of townhomes continued all the way to Prescott Road, there were plenty of spots where the light started and stopped, and lots of empty corners with no sun. The place was pretty common looking, but it also gave Lance the heebie-jeebies.

"Y'all gon' tell me what the fuck is going on?" He knew he was drunk now, because he was feeling familiar, bold, agitated. "Who ain't showing up?"

"Little Lonnie," Donnell said.

"Who?"

All eyes were on him now.

"You never heard of Little Lonnie?" Cedrick seemed truly surprised. Not a hint of sarcasm in his voice.

Lance waited for someone to explain.

"The ghost?" Rayvon whispered, stepping closer like he was afraid of being overheard.

"You didn't know the Gardens is haunted?" Red, too, was whispering.

Lance was laughing inside that these supposed-to-be-tough guys were acting like shivering bitches. "Y'all know my mother acts all holy and whatnot. We don't talk about anything like that. She'd start shouting 'blasphemy' or some shit."

"Well, this whole place is haunted." Donnell wasn't whispering, but his voice quivered. "And in one unit, out front, folks move in but don't make it past one night. They run out screamin', cussin', scatterin' half their shit—clothes, cash, phones—across the grass as they leave. Say they woke up at night and found a bloody boy about seven sitting on the end of their bed giggling and holding his head, where his brains were spilling out.

"It's Lonnie Tompkins. We all call him Little Lonnie. When folks were fighting over crack turf back in the eighties, he was in second grade and a stray bullet killed him."

Lance didn't know if it was the alcohol or the story, but he had the urge to tell them to stop sharing. At home, he often sensed he wasn't alone when he was the only one there. It started just after he lost Kendall, when it sometimes felt like he was being watched. He'd check over his shoulder and find a shadow just out of sight.

Like there'd been a man standing there. And now, he imagined the boy, Little Lonnie, sitting at the foot of his bed, and gooseflesh spread over his arms and neck.

"Little Lonnie don't bother nobody, man." Peter checked over his shoulder, where the ball sat, like it was listening to them. "He does a lot of silly shit like taking heads off Barbie dolls. And he likes to kick his ball around the Gardens. You see the blue ball? Means Little Lonnie is nearby. Gretchen said he once showed up and pushed a girl out the way of a stray bullet. So he's, like, trying to save kids and shit."

"You believe all this?" Lance hadn't taken Peter for someone who believed in ghosts. Peter had once declared he was an atheist. How did this fit?

"Didn't at first, but I saw him. He was with a group of kids who walked past my window. I could tell it was him 'cause his clothes was all outdated and shit and covered in blood."

"Never noticed anything strange in *your* crib, Little Bit?" Solomon palmed the basketball.

"My place? Hell no." Wasn't no way he'd tell them about the feeling he got when he was home alone or about the man always standing just out of sight. Lance glanced at the blue ball. It was still far away, but it seemed to have moved a couple of feet to the right, into the sunlight. Lance wished Solomon would start bouncing his ball again. "Why?"

Solomon smirked and cut his eyes at Peter and Donnell. "I guess you'll find out eventually."

"Y'all. Get the fuck outta here with this bullshit." Lance was definitely drunk. Felt like he was talking to them from the other end of a tunnel.

"Ain't bullshit." Donnell seemed offended. He checked over his shoulder again but didn't seem to notice the shift in the ball's location.

"There's others too," Peter said. "Last year, one lady say she saw Junior running through this alley like he did just before he got shot and killed. Somebody saw Monica in her bathroom mirror applying makeup to bruises on her face and neck just like she did when she was alive. My own grandmother say she saw my parents right here in the alley, and they were both covered in blood, just like when they got killed. Somebody else saw Grace holding her doll like when she got shot."

Lance thought of Gretchen's twin sister, who was killed right next to Gretchen. It always made him think about how random death was. Like, why Grace and not Gretchen?

Peter went on. "And you know my grandma thinks all this ghost shit is an 'abomination of Christ,' so if *she* saw it? Must be true. Then there was Carlotta. Hooker who was choked to death. She sometimes mixes in with the other hos on Prescott, and when a john accidentally picks her up, she'll give him a blowjob, then take a bite."

Lance laughed. The others did not. "Can a spirit really bite a dude's dick?" he asked.

"Hell yeah, man." Donnell was shouting now. "If they can roll balls around the alley, they can sure as hell bite."

"Basically, folks who get offed never leave. They stay in this shithole, trapped, just like the rest of us," Peter said, checking the alley behind him.

Lance wondered whether anyone had seen Kendall after he was killed. If Kendall revealed himself to Lance, would that be a relief, or would he be scared out of his mind?

"Ah, shit." Peter raised his voice, and everyone jumped at the sound. Donnell reached for his waistband as Peter moved to the right of the alley and headed toward the sunlight. "I'm out."

Lance and the others followed Peter's gaze down the alley, beyond the bands of light and strips of shadow, where a boy stood in front of the dumpster, his back to all of them. He wore dark shorts, sneakers, and a T-shirt, but they were tattered. The boy's head was bowed as he stared down at the blue ball.

Solomon put his hand on Donnell's shoulder. Donnell nodded and removed his hand from his waistband. Grave Digger wouldn't make an appearance after all.

Gooseflesh spread up and down Lance's limbs, and the numbness from the alcohol left him. They all waited in silence as the boy turned and slowly kicked the ball back down the alley toward them. The boy's image was shrouded in darkness. Lance kept his eyes on the round object as it came to rest near their group. When he searched the other end of the alley again, the boy was gone.

A live trio of hatted men played jazz music. Balloons in blue and gold, Kitledge High's colors, floated above the ballroom tables. Medford Church of God in Christ's event hall was Nona's second home, where she and Vance had had their first dance after tying the knot, where they'd served a potluck dinner after Kendall's baptism, where she often passed plates of turkey and mashed potatoes smothered in gravy at church socials and Thanksgiving soup kitchens. Yet tonight, the space was foreign, worldly, as if it weren't inside a church at all.

Her cheeks burned when Mother Lincoln hugged her and whispered, "Looks like somebody went all out." Everyone called the gray-haired woman Mother Lincoln because she was a church elder, a mother in the church, but she was also a mother figure to Nona. In addition to each woman being the main babysitter for the other, they also loaned each other money here and there when things got tight. As Mother aged, Nona took on the role of dutiful daughter, tending to the woman's laundry, housekeeping, and errands, but as the boys grew, and Peter gravitated toward street life, a noticeable strain developed between Nona and Mother. Nona loved the woman, but Mother let a lot of things slide with Peter that Nona would never tolerate from her own boys.

With a smirk and a wink, Mother held Nona's hands. The woman's loose flesh and wrinkles melted into Nona's palms. "And I mean, aaaaaallll out." Mother threw back her head and cackled.

"You know I can't afford any of this." Nona tried to smile but sensed the expression appeared forced.

She took in the room: Framed baby photos of Marcus served as centerpieces, and she assumed Pastor Davis had resurrected those images from the church's archives; cake, steak, and shrimp topped gilded plates; lilacs finished the decor, and a banner across the back of the room where the windows let in the pink sunset read *Congrats, Marcus. Ivy League, here we come!*

She'd merely thrown Kendall a potluck gathering in the Hester Gardens' courtyard with a few balloons and a generic congrats banner. By comparison, this event was over-the-top.

"Well, looks like Pastor's got you covered, baby." Mother winked, released Nona's hands, and, with a barely perceptible limp, waddled to the line forming at the buffet table. Church congregants and Kitledge High parents whispered. They must have been talking about Nona. *Why, exactly, is Pastor spending so much money on Nona's son?*

"This is too much." She chastised Pastor as he sidled up to her and squeezed her shoulder. A bespectacled server passed by, and Pastor handed Nona a champagne flute from the waiter's tray. The glass was heavy in her hand.

"Most of the kids around here are only ever feted when they're freed from prison. So don't tell me this is too much," he playfully fussed back, giving her a whiff of the alcohol on his breath. "Your job is to stand here, enjoy Marcus's accomplishments, and look beautiful."

That last bit sent a flutter from her stomach to her thighs. She didn't sip the bubbly drink—she gave up drinking when the police carted Vance away for drug trafficking—but Pastor's words gave her a tingle in her middle. If Pastor delivered that sort of line to every sweet thing in the congregation, she wouldn't have grown damp all over.

Pastor had prayed with Nona after Vance had gone to prison, and again when she lost Kendall. Pastor became the person she called when she questioned whether she should continue living. Then he fixed her busted air conditioner and got the refrigerator up and running whenever it conked out. He talked to Lance when her youngest came home with an F on a school assignment. He gave Marcus work at the church as a way to indirectly give Nona money for the house. And four years later, here he was, throwing a lavish gathering for Marcus.

The church's first lady never attended any outing Pastor had with Nona and the boys, and Nona would be lying if she said she didn't carry guilt about the arrangement.

Marcus slinked by, giggling with Avery, and Nona used his proximity as an excuse to get space from Pastor. She handed the undrained glass to a bow-tied waiter and grabbed Marcus by the elbow, dragging him over to Lance. Shoving the two of them together, she called out, "Photos!" to their united groans.

The band played the instrumental version of Nina Simone's "Four Women," an interesting choice in a church. The music gave Nona the urge to dance, but she didn't. She'd given that up as well when Vance had gone to prison.

"Stand closer." She loved staring at her boys. Like Kendall, Marcus only smiled with one side of his face, the one with the dimple, as though he never wanted to give his all to anyone. While Marcus had Vance's voice, posture, and gait, Lance was the spitting image of Vance: narrow eyes, a broad smile, and charming to a fault. It's why she trusted Lance as much as she trusted Vance—not at all.

They seemed neither happy to pose together nor pleased she was taking the photos, but she snapped ten anyway. They didn't fuss too much at her demands.

"Put your arms around each other."

"Smile."

"Pretend you like each other."

They squirmed in most of the shots, like they did when they were in toddler sandals and Bermuda shorts with skinned knees and their cheeks smudged with finger paint.

"You must join in." Pastor grabbed her phone and insisted Nona get in several pictures. Then he handed it back, asking for one of him with Marcus and Lance, and another of him and the graduate.

Marcus seemed to enjoy Pastor tossing an arm around his shoulder, pulling him in close, and playing the part of the proud father Vance should have played. This was why Nona was conflicted about Pastor. He wasn't some player trying to sleep with her. He was trying to be a part of her family. She never knew what to make of that.

Tears stung her eyes as she pictured Vance whole, happy, living a legitimate life. Her boys never spoke of Vance, but they must have missed him.

Marcus and Pastor floated off to mingle with more guests, leaving Nona with Lance, who hadn't consumed anything since they'd arrived, but who also smelled like a bottle of liquor. His eyes were red. She wanted to bring it up, but this was the exact wrong time to do it.

"What are you planning to do this summer, Lance?"

"Chill, I guess."

Her stomach sank. That was his answer to most things these days, and it wasn't an answer at all. At six, when his front teeth were missing, he spent his summers playing soccer on the rec center league, rushing to hug her when she arrived for his games after work, waving to her whenever he scored, his eager face seeming to say *Look, Mom. Aren't you so proud of me?* She wanted to go upside his head for the idle thing he'd turned out to be.

"Then I'm signing you up for basketball camp at the rec center."

"Yeah. Okay."

He glanced around the room and then back at her. Was he waiting for her to say something? She was at a complete loss. Why was talking to her middle schooler so awkward?

"It's weird, right?" Lance chuckled, but his eyes were narrowed, his jaw tight. "That Pastor's doing all this? He even used the church shuttle to get folks here from the Gardens."

"Folks didn't want to get on the bus in their nice clothes." She motioned around the room at everyone in their Sunday best. Couldn't he see that fancy was good sometimes? "I think it's nice he did all this."

"You don't think it's strange he made this Marcus's party? I mean, Gretchen and Shelby graduated too." Lance's eyes never met hers when he spoke.

Why did Lance care? Was he sulking because Marcus was getting all the attention?

Lance rubbed his chapped lips, which showed off the grime beneath his fingernails. Had he smoked marijuana too?

She leaned in and whispered back, "Marcus is valedictorian, is going to an Ivy League school. Shelby's brother is out on bail, and Gretchen . . ." She couldn't finish that sentence without being an awful Christian.

"Gretchen, what?" Lance clenched his jaw, and his red eyes finally met hers. She longed for the days when she watched television on the couch with her sons' bony limbs pressed into her sides.

She avoided looking at the girl traipsing around with that baby on her hip. Gretchen was a teen mom, thanks to Peter. That's why Pastor hadn't made her a guest of honor. Nona wouldn't apologize for raising a good son.

"Why don't you go congratulate your brother? Have you even done that?"

Lance stormed off, to the exact opposite end of the ballroom from where Marcus was, and seemed at ease joining the conversation between Donnell and Peter, two boys she wished Pastor hadn't invited. The pair had arrived with the rest of the Hester Boys. They'd had the decency to at least put out the cigarettes they'd been smoking on the church's front steps before entering.

In a checkered shirt, unbuttoned save for the bottom two, Donnell rolled up the fabric on his right arm to show off his latest tattoo to Gretchen and Shelby. The movement put the bulge in his shirt on display. Just like his mother Mable, Donnell was always armed. According to neighborhood gossip, Donnell was the gang's deputy now. Secured most of the little money they had and kept tabs on their rivals over at Dempsey Woods. Donnell shouted, "You good, Little Bit?" as he patted Lance's shoulder.

Nona wanted to go over and remove Donnell's hand. It wasn't lost on her that these no-good young men hadn't befriended Lance until after Kendall was gone.

The HBs grinned. Peter stepped forward and grabbed Lance around the neck in a playful hug. In the span of a few years, Peter, who was younger than Donnell, had taken over as the leader of the gang. He sold drugs and pimped out young women. No one messed with him. Everyone feared him.

Then Solomon leaned down and hugged Lance. Why were they seemingly congratulating him? What had he done? Her hackles went up, but she told herself perhaps they were all showing Lance this affection because they hadn't seen him in a long time.

Solomon towered over everyone, and she was so used to him dribbling a basketball, it was odd for her to see him without one. He was born the same year as Kendall and, instead of being the gang's leader, was like its elder advisor. Solomon had actually boarded a plane and had seen other parts of the country while playing ball in high school. He'd almost made it out of Hester Gardens for his sport. Almost.

There was Rayvon, in a thin T-shirt with several gold chains draping down his torso. Rayvon lived next door to Nona with his sister Shelby and their parents, Brother and Sister Taylor, who were cutting up the dance floor with the bop.

Standing beside Rayvon was Red, who fluffed his hair with a pick. He might have felt overdressed in the church suit he was wearing with a tie, but she was grateful he'd dressed up. Rayvon and Red delivered the gang's drugs, which was why they were always in and out of police custody for possession.

And Cedrick stared into his smartphone. Kendall used to date Kiandra or "Kiki," Cedrick's older sister, and Cedrick used to look up to Kendall when he was alive. All of the Hester Boys did. Kendall had been the counterpoint to the gang. Where Peter had illegal jobs for them, Kendall had gigs for them working odd construction, gardening, or church jobs. Along with his cousin Harlan, Kendall would take these young men to the community garden and show them how to grow their own food. When Nona's oldest was killed, she wasn't the only one who lost a son; the entire neighborhood did. They'd lost hope. They'd lost vision, direction, and many of them had lost a future.

A wave of grief washed over her, but God threw her a lifeline. The ballroom's double doors opened, and her nephew Harlan entered. In dark denim, a collared casual shirt, and a black blazer, he waved to her and scanned the room for Marcus and Lance. He kept one hand behind his back, and with the other he brushed sweat from his forehead. He seemed rushed, between appointments. He hadn't made it to the graduation, and she sensed he wasn't staying for the party.

As a boy, Harlan always misplaced his sneakers and accidentally left his schoolbooks at her house. As he searched the room now, he had that same harried nature about him.

From opposite sides of the space, she and her boys made a beeline for her nephew. Her boys were busy hugging him and clapping his back before she even made it over. For a second, she imagined the three of them were Kendall, Marcus, and Lance, happy and together again. She blinked away the tears before she could get choked up.

Peter and the Hester Boys stared at Harlan. They probably wished they could hug him too. They likely missed Harlan as much as her sons did, but when Kendall died, Harlan cut ties with everyone at Hester Gardens except Nona, Marcus, and Lance. Harlan extended that severance to Pastor as well.

"You made it." She pushed between her boys to give her nephew a hug.

Harlan gave her a peck on the cheek. "Barely, Auntie. And I can't even stay."

"What?" Lance groaned, sounding five years old again.

"You have to," Marcus said, his smile fading.

"Y'all know whenever there's a shooting, I have to cover it."

"Another one?" Nona asked. She had been so busy with Marcus's graduation she hadn't kept up on the news.

"This morning. Yeah. Not around here, but close enough I needed to go. Now I'm on deadline to write it."

"Let me guess," Marcus said. "White folks."

Her nephew and her boys all exchanged a look. Kendall was the unspoken center of this conversation, as was the fact that shootings in their neighborhood were rarely assigned a reporter, and when they were, the victim was treated like a criminal in the write-up.

"You know it, Marcky. You know it." Harlan handed Marcus a gift bag. Marcus's face lit up as he opened it and pulled out a book.

"It was the gift your dad gave me when I won my first writing contest."

Marcus held up the cover for her to see, and it was *Soledad Brother: The Prison Letters of George Jackson*. Early in their marriage, Vance used to carry the book through their home and sit on the side of their bed, his head bent forward over the text. It would have been lost on her boys that their father was a reader and a thinker, since she never spoke of him. Harlan was Vance's blood nephew. Of course he would invoke Vance's name at a time like this.

"Got one for you too." Harlan handed Lance a bag, and Lance's face brightened. She liked this softer version of Lance. How different he was around Harlan than he'd been minutes ago hugging the Hester Boys. This Lance had a hopeful face. This Lance was her baby. "You know I can't forget about you, Lance."

"Good. Because everyone else does." Lance didn't look at her when he said it, but Nona sensed the statement was directed at her. A wave of guilt coursed through her. Was she neglecting Lance?

Harlan pulled Lance in for a one-armed hug. "This book changed my life. George Jackson was killed ten months after this was published. It's an indictment of the system that oppresses us and that oppresses people across the globe. Uncle Vance gave it to me because he wanted me to know how powerful the pen is. How ideas and words are such a threat to the ability to reign over a people that the powers that be would kill someone simply for sharing their thoughts. Why? Because thoughts, ideas, have the power to dismantle . . . everything."

"Whoa." Lance turned the book over and over again. "Dad said that?"

Harlan shot a look at Nona, and her cheeks burned. His unspoken statement was that in keeping the bad parts of Vance from his sons, she was also keeping away the good parts. The parts of Vance that she had connected with. The man who thought a wonderful date was the two of them sitting in the library discussing the books they read. Before the boys, she and Vance would spend entire Saturdays arguing the finer points of works by James Baldwin, Angela Davis, and several of the contributors to the Harlem Renaissance.

Marcus scanned the back of the book. Was his silence about the book or about the idea that his dad had read it? She could have added that Vance had sent a copy of the book to Kendall when her oldest had graduated, but she really didn't want to prolong this discussion.

"Yes," Harlan continued. "Your dad said that. He really wants us all to be thinkers and scholars. I mean, I even think he's disappointed that I'm just a journalist and not a college professor." Harlan chuckled, and in that moment, he looked like Kendall. The resemblance was uncanny.

At Kendall's funeral, Harlan had broken down and started wailing. His on-again, off-again girlfriend had tried to comfort him, but he was inconsolable. Shortly thereafter, Harlan had switched to covering the crime and youth violence beat at his newspaper. She'd never asked but had assumed he'd requested it.

"What do you say, boys?" She cleared her throat and beat back tears.

"Thanks, Harlan," they both said.

"Hey, fellas, walk me out." Harlan glanced at her, his eyes narrowed, his jaw tight. "We gotta have some man talk."

Harlan gave her another quick hug. Her boys followed Harlan the way they used to be glued to Kendall, and she looked away so the tears stinging her eyes wouldn't fall.

"Nona, baby. Was that Harlan?" Mother Lincoln was back, having made a plate for herself and Peter, when Peter should have made a plate for his grandmother instead. Nona nodded, sensing the woman's disappointment that Harlan hadn't greeted her. "You must be so proud of Marcus. I certainly am, but I must admit, I'm a little sad too."

"Sad? Why, Mother?" Nona sensed it was because of Peter, but she didn't want to presume.

"Our babies all came along in groups, didn't they? Kendall, Solomon, Kiandra, and Donnell all graduated together. And this was the year for Marcus, Peter, Shelby, and Gretchen. I'd always expected, had hoped at least, that Peter would be right up there beside those three." Mother handed a plate to Nona and found her balance by gripping a nearby chair as she adjusted her church hat. The woman's eyes were moist, and her voice trailed off.

"I always pray for Peter," Nona said. She mostly prayed that God would send Peter away from Hester Gardens, but she didn't want to hurt Mother Lincoln's feelings. "Every night. You know I do."

"Always been his own person. From birth. Even screamed instead of cried when he left the womb. My daughter used to ask, 'Why can't he just cry like other babies?'"

Nona followed Mother's gaze to Peter. He held Grayson, the baby he shared with Gretchen, and bounced the squealing boy up and down between kisses on his chubby cheeks. She'd hoped becoming a father would improve Peter's behavior, but so far, it only made him money-hungry. The sun had gone down, and he still wore gold-rimmed sunglasses. Hadn't even adhered to the "Sunday best" attire requested on Pastor's invitations. Mother maintained a closet full of church clothes for that boy, and yet he'd come out of the house in ripped jeans, sneakers, and an extra-long white T-shirt, with his matted beard and scraggly, uncombed hair.

Marcus and Lance entered the ballroom again and went their separate ways. Lance returned to the Hester Boys, showing off *Soledad Brother*. Marcus dropped off Harlan's book at the gift table and then arrived at Nona's side. He pecked Mother's cheek, making the elder woman giggle. Since they'd arrived at the event, he kept giving Nona and Pastor the most suspicious looks.

"I'll let you two talk," Mother said, seeming wistful at how affectionate Marcus was. "My Peter's gotta eat."

The woman shuffled off, carrying the plates to her grandson, who smiled at her as he handed off the baby to Gretchen, found a chair, and helped his grandmother into it. Peter then hunched over the plate and stuffed food in his mouth like a dog.

"Have I told you how proud I am of you?" Nona gave Marcus another hug, forced to tilt her chin up to reach his shoulder when, a few years prior, it'd been the other way around.

"So you knew about all this?" He kept his voice low, but his stiff smile told her he was unhappy about the fanfare.

"No. I knew the church wanted to throw you a party."

"The church? You mean Pastor?" Marcus's question held an accusation.

She missed Kendall.

"So what happened at the end of your speech?"

His forced smile dissolved, and his pursed lips looked an awful lot like Lance's. And therefore Vance's.

"What do you mean?"

He knew good and well what she meant, but she was willing to play along. More stares from the crowd, and she didn't like being watched.

"I don't know. You seemed like you were . . ." She didn't know how to say it without making him sound unhinged. "Did you see Kendall?"

"Did I see . . . ?" He grinned, shamefaced. Checked the crowd around him again, and then homed in on her. "You mean when I was choked up?"

"Not then. Later. It was like you saw him. Or somebody else. You know I don't sugarcoat things. I don't mean—"

"Thanks for calling me weird, Mom, but no. I didn't see him. You're the one imagining things."

His comment cut so deep she drew in a breath and held it, her mind racing. Marcus always comforted her and supported her, just as he had that morning on the phone. And it's not like she did that sort of thing all the time. Yes, she had been a mess when they lost Kendall, but who could blame her? She got herself together within months. Went back to working long hours at a dead-end job she hated, attending parent-teacher conferences, helping the boys with homework, registering them for sports. She'd been confused in the morning, obviously, and upset. Now Marcus was throwing it back in her face. And for what?

"Marcus." Pastor swooped in. "I've someone I want you to meet."

She wasn't sure whether Pastor sensed the tension, but she exhaled when he guided Marcus away to meet the musicians. Before heading off, Pastor touched Nona's forearm and winked.

She excused herself to the ladies' room, Marcus's comment repeating in her mind. *You're the one imagining things.* Was she?

Moments later, locked in a stall, she took a few calming breaths. Outside the bathroom, people laughed, dishes clinked, and the band had moved on to Coltrane.

Marcus was right. She had imagined the voice in the hall, but the odd ending to his speech? Was that all in her head too? Maybe he had just been choked up. She could only guess what it would be like to give a speech about a loss so heavy.

Ready for the party to end, she checked the time on her phone and the date on the screen leapt out at her: May 28. How could she have missed it? Had she been so caught up in preparing for Marcus's big day that she'd distracted herself from the anniversary?

Back in Hester Gardens' alley, her husband, teeth bared, back spread, resembled a bear as he brought that pistol down, down, down, *thwack, thwack, thwack*. The young man, NaDarius, pleaded, "Don't let him kill me."

Today was the day, wasn't it? May 28. The date, fourteen years ago, when she'd stood in that alley and discovered who her husband really was. The date, four years ago, when police raided her home and carted her husband off to jail, and not for his crimes in that alley. The date, two years ago, when her firstborn was killed. That's why she'd startled awake this morning. Why she'd been up cleaning at four a.m. It was May 28.

Pastor had told her several times "It's a mere coincidence, Nona." And it seemed now that Pastor was right. Because the day had arrived, and despite her overwhelming emotions, her scrutiny of Marcus's every word and action, and even the voices she was hearing, Marcus was fine. She was fine. Even Lance was fine. Mostly.

She left without checking her sweaty features in the mirror. When she emerged, silence had fallen on the room, and everyone faced the corner near the door. Pastor slowly set his champagne flute on a table, as if waiting to pounce on someone.

Marcus raised his voice. "You think I'm playing with you?"

The band stopped.

The space shrank. Marcus's back straightened and spread. He was half a foot taller. His posture, wide-legged. His fists, clenched.

His voice echoed and bounced off the walls. "You think this is a game?"

It wasn't like Marcus to shout at anyone, and it was definitely out of character for him to shove another person, but there he was, like a bear, like Vance in that alley, shoving Peter.

Nona rushed forward but stopped when Marcus threw a punch to Peter's chest. Peter was smug. Perhaps he'd gotten the reaction he wanted.

Her heartbeat echoed in her ears. She scanned the room. Her face flushed as everyone stared at her son, the one to throw a punch, the aggressor. This was not the boy she'd raised to turn the other cheek, the valedictorian, the one who was leaving for the Ivy League in the fall.

Time stopped. It was May 28, in the alley, NaDarius's body lifeless and crumpled on the ground. It was May 28, in her living room, her husband and boys spread-eagle with guns against their backs. It was May 28, in the morgue, Kendall's face stiff and surprised in death.

It.

Was.

May 28.

Peter collapsed onto the gift table, splitting the cloth-covered wooden legs and sending everything to the floor. Gift bags with tissue paper peeking out, wrapped boxes, sealed cards, and the framed photo of Marcus in his basketball uniform, his MVP plaque in hand, landed at Marcus's feet with a thud.

Panting, stalking back and forth before the symbols of his accomplishments, Marcus grew even taller. Nona's ears rang.

The Hester Boys did not intervene, which she found odd. Not one of them helped Peter. Not one of them stood between Peter and Marcus. Their backs were pressed against the wall as they watched alongside everyone else. Did they not know what was happening, or had they accomplished what they'd planned: to disrupt the party?

Pastor lifted the overturned table and placed his body in the midst of the crowd of boys. Peter slapped a hand against the wall, found his balance, and stood. Marcus snatched at Peter's wrist, but Peter twisted his hand away and hissed, "It's mine now."

Finally, Mable Cleveland's good-for-nothing son Donnell stood between Marcus and Peter to prevent Marcus from attacking Peter again, as Pastor, with help from Gretchen, restored the tablecloth, gifts, cards, and photos to their previous positions.

"I'll get back what's mine," Marcus growled. Or it at least sounded like a growl. Her wits having returned, Nona marched toward Marcus, and from the opposite end of the room, Mother Lincoln closed the other side of the circle.

Nona's heart sank as she remembered Peter and Marcus as four-year-olds, sitting on her living room rug, giggling as they watched *Sesame Street* together and played video games with Kendall, smelling of "berry pop" and chocolate candy.

"Chill, Marcus," Donnell said as Peter, fully standing now, recovered from the body blow.

"Peter!" Mother Lincoln whistled and clapped her hands twice, the way a person called a pet. The typically soft-spoken woman's voice projected and echoed in the silent space.

Peter towered over her, and Nona knew he took a deep breath, closed his mouth, and hung his head out of respect for his grandmother, not because the woman could put him over her knee.

By the time Nona touched Marcus's shoulder, Peter had stormed out, along with no-good Donnell and the rest of the Hester Boys. Mother was on Peter's heels, wagging her finger and fussing, "I raised you better than that" as she went.

Nona's hand was firm on her son's shoulder. Marcus rocked from side to side, taking deep breaths, clenching and opening his fists.

"What are you doing?" Nona whispered, aware of all eyes on her from around the room.

The waitstaff swept the broken glass. The murmurs began. One person whispered, "I don't know. Something about Kendall."

Marcus finally met her gaze, his eyes bloodshot, his cheeks flushed. Sweat had gathered about his temples. She was seeing Vance. She'd seen this wild face before, but never on Marcus. None of this tracked.

He shook his head repeatedly, the way one does when regaining consciousness after a fainting spell.

"Answer me." She was firmer, but it wouldn't matter. He wouldn't tell her. He'd long since reached the age where she was a nuisance, not a confidante. She'd been certain she'd failed as a mother, but Pastor had assured her that pulling away from his mother's counsel was a natural part of Marcus becoming a man.

"He said something about Kendall. And I . . ." His cheeks flushed red. Seeing his remorseful face actually made Nona feel better. At least this was the Marcus she knew.

"What did he say about Kendall?"

Marcus shot an angry look at Lance before turning and embracing her. "I'm sorry, Mom. It's nothing. Don't worry about it."

Receiving Marcus's hug, Nona eyed Lance, but her youngest stared at the door. Marcus's body trembled. Why would Marcus behave this way? He knew this was how she'd lost Kendall. A fistfight. Then shortly after, a fatal shooting. This was how every mother in her neighborhood lost her son.

Marcus released her and slowly made his way around the room, apologizing to everyone. Telling people, "Don't worry. Some folks will try to mess up any happy occasion."

"What was that?" she whispered to Lance, sensing judgmental eyes from around the room on her again. She wanted to hide, to shield her burning cheeks and ears, her confused face from view.

Lance usually kept Marcus's secrets, but this time, he whispered back, "Peter stole something."

"What? From Marcus?"

"Something like that."

"Something like that? Something like what?"

Lance wasn't listening to her anymore. He was focused on Marcus, who'd made his rounds and was now standing before the gossiping crowd.

"We're not going to let anything stand in the way of us eating this shrimp, are we?" Marcus was smiling again. He was the version of himself who'd grinned in all the photos with Pastor and had made Mother Lincoln blush with a kiss on the woman's cheek.

The crowd chuckled. Marcus twirled his finger, and the band played again, Charlie Parker this time. Marcus led his salutatorian and Mr. and Mrs. Taylor to the food and drink table, and the servers began piling shrimp and calamari onto everyone's plates. The bow-tied waitstaff circled again, refilling glasses.

Nona searched for Pastor and found him whispering with a young man wearing a gold chain and a suit that seemed tailored, someone who appeared more like security than a deacon or minister. A nephew? He looked too street to be a minister-in-training. Once the fellow had slinked off, she asked Pastor whether he knew what had gotten Marcus so angry. She didn't care who watched their whispered conversation this time. She needed information.

"Boys being boys."

"Please, don't."

Pastor's face grew serious, and his eyes bore into Nona's with real empathy, not pity.

"Forgive me. You have every right to fret over Marcus and Lance after losing Kendall."

Her throat tightened. Pastor always named her pain. They had similar upbringings. He'd grown up in the rough part of Medford less than a mile from the projects where Nona had lived. Even though the first lady was upper-middle class, "made" him, and never let him forget it, as Pastor put it, Nona sensed the man was still capable of acting like "the street," with menacing-looking characters always around him and an angry facial expression she'd only seen once, when a fight broke out at one of the church's youth events. The glare at his staff that day was so harsh it seemed it could cast out demons.

He'd told her he'd seen violence with his own eyes, so he always said Kendall's name, never alluding to "all you've been through" or how "strong" she was, and that was validating.

"Peter was being who he always is," Pastor said. "An instigator. Seems he made a snide remark about Kendall, and Marcus just wasn't having it. Don't think it will amount to much beyond this."

She wasn't so sure. Maybe Peter was just envious of Marcus's attention and wanted to ruin things, but she didn't trust him around her boys.

"Lance said Peter stole something from Marcus," Nona said. Her eyes followed Marcus as he grabbed Shelby's hand and began to dance, but in a silly way, as the two of them did the funky chicken. The band took the hint and switched to up-tempo Latin jazz. The Marcus from moments before didn't seem to exist at all. Another figment of her imagination.

"Remember, Nona, you've put Marcus on this wonderful path. You have to see him through this summer, and he'll be out of Medford and away from the workers of iniquity."

She was beginning to believe him, that this argument probably wouldn't amount to much, but she wouldn't be at ease until Marcus was away at college and she could worry about things like whether he was eating enough between classes or focusing on his studies and not partying too much. Three more months. Not a lot of time, but an eternity in Hester Gardens.

Marcus flapped his arms and wiggled his hips as Shelby's giggles gave way to hoots and cackles. Marcus noticed Nona eyeing him. His grin faltered briefly, and the darkness from moments before seemed ready to reemerge, but Marcus returned to flashing her a winning smile. Just as he spun his dance partner around, he fixed his gaze on Nona and winked.

Four

On Kiandra's bus ride home from her hospital job, she told her brother all about the young man who'd been shot. She overshared her patients' near-death stories because she wanted to scare Cedrick into straightening up his life. So far, her efforts seemed futile.

It was dark out, but as they drove by, she still pointed out the fancy homes in the suburbs. Cedrick put in his earbuds, but she continued to take in the manicured lawns, the shiny cars in the driveways, the knee-high planters out front with orange and fuchsia flowers, which the homeowners replaced seasonally so the petals were always fresh.

"Their gardeners maintain everything for them, you know," she chattered on even though Cedrick didn't seem to be listening. "They don't do it themselves."

Cedrick nodded at her, but she knew he wasn't listening. He'd taken on the job of riding home with her after she'd been groped on the bus late last winter. As she'd gotten on, a man had reached out and squeezed her breast as if merely grabbing an armrest. She happened to be holding a nursing text, and she took the hardcover book to his head until blood spurted out his nose. Afterward, she was afraid to take the bus alone. So she appreciated Cedrick riding the bus to the hospital, waiting for her, and then sitting next to her on the trip home. He'd never missed a pickup; he'd never been late.

After getting off the bus, Cedrick said he was going to stop by a friend's house.

"What friend?"

Cedrick removed one earbud. "You my mama now, Kiki? Damn." He put the device back in and moseyed away.

"You better not be visiting any girls."

His back still to her, he gave her the middle finger and disappeared around the corner.

Her guard went up as she trudged in the moonlight from Prescott Road toward her front door alone. She scanned the courtyard. No one was out, but she told herself she had nothing to worry about.

She knew everyone in her section of the Gardens and many in the outer ring of the projects too. Folks typically left her alone. The Hester Boys would harass other folks—snatch their purses, rummage through their pockets, pick fights with those who had jobs and places to go, like they wanted to punish their neighbors for the situation they were all in—but they protected her. They knew Kiandra worked at Medford "Deadford" Hospital and was saving so she could one day afford to take Cedrick and get the hell out of the Gardens. The other families seemed proud of her. They'd call her when their daughter had a fever or when their son scraped himself up falling out of a tree. She kept extra gauze and antiseptic she got from the hospital. Anything other than drugs. She wasn't like some of her counterparts there. She never stole the meds.

Solomon, Donnell, and the other Hester Boys had gotten to Cedrick, and she was running out of time to get him away from them. The guys helped her carry grocery bags, and the ones with cars would give her a ride from Deadford if she was on a day shift and they drove by and saw her standing at the bus stop, but Cedrick they'd ply with cognac, or Donnell would ask Cedrick to "hold" things for him, which were often guns or plastic bags filled with expensive street poison. The older Cedrick got, the more he was lost to her. So she skipped meals to save cash and never bought anything unless it was half off and she had a coupon. She already had her eye on an apartment in Sebastian Hills. She'd need a cosigner, but her boyfriend would do it.

When she saw a large white garbage bag sitting out front of her unit, she wanted to track down and shake her brother. Cedrick was supposed to take their refuse to the dumpster but instead had left it out in the open where it could attract rats and opossums. She was angry enough to cuss. He knew she was afraid of Hester Gardens' alleys. They were dark and hidden, and folks shot up smack, turned tricks, and settled scores in them. The garbage men rarely emptied the dumpsters, and the smell and sight made her so depressed. Of all the things she hated about living in Hester Gardens, the mountain of weeks-old trash was the worst part. Detroit had abandoned homes, Flint had poisonous water, and Medford's projects had sky-high trash.

A breeze rustled the garbage bag. She couldn't bring herself to pick it up. What was worse? The waste attracting rodents to their home or Kiandra braving the alley? She settled on going there and back quickly—the mere idea of rats made her skin crawl.

She snatched up the plastic sack. Bottles clanked together inside, and the heaviness altered her gait. She leaned to the left to support the weight on her right.

Problem was, when she was young, she'd read *The Rats* by James Herbert and could never shake the image of the rats attacking and gobbling both a baby and the family dog who tried to save the infant. Unable to finish the text, she swore off horror books and scary movies after, but ever since, everywhere she went, she thought she heard rat squeaks, and she'd even passed on the fear to her cousin Gretchen.

A tagged elm tree, dead and leaning but never cut down, cast jagged shadows that resembled claws on the ground beside her.

Curtains flapped behind open windows, but no lights were on in the units. A bike rested against a leafless bush. A blue ball sat at the edge of the alley.

She slowed her stride. She felt eyes on her. Someone was watching her as she moved. Where were they?

Her neighbor Ms. Lawson wasn't out, and she wished the woman had been. Stomach butterflies weren't a feeling Kiandra experienced with any frequency, but she had them now. Her shallow breaths escaped into the damp air as she checked every shadow, every doorway, peered into each window for whoever might have been lurking in the darkness, perhaps ready to pounce.

On shuffling, reluctant feet, she moved into the alley, which was lit only by the moon. She approached the dumpsters, the bag in front of her for protection. She tightened her grip on her backpack's strap, considering what she had that could serve as a weapon. Her keys? Her stainless-steel water bottle?

She caught movement in her peripheral vision, but no one was there. Was someone trying to scare her? Was the person trying to conceal himself from her? And she knew it was a "him" because no girl or woman would hide out near the dumpsters.

In the middle of the alley, where the gap between the brick row houses let in more light, she stopped, letting the summer-night breeze pass over her skin and lift strands of her hair from her ponytail.

A figure shrouded in darkness stood near the dumpsters, his back to Kiandra as he swayed from side to side, staring at the bins. She should run, but he might chase her, and she wasn't going to allow herself to get jumped from behind by some pervert, so she waited.

A chill passed through her because, as she inched closer, she realized he was the right size and shape to be Kendall. She had seen Kendall the evening after his funeral, but everyone told her it was just her grief. At the time, she knew it hadn't been, though.

She'd been in her living room, crying and staring out the front window, when she saw Kendall walk by, seemingly headed to his own home just as nonchalantly as he had every day before he'd been killed. She'd been so sure back then, but with time, she came to agree with the others. Grief had gotten the best of her.

Kiandra didn't pray often, but as she squinted and crept even closer, she asked God to not let her see Kendall again, to free her from the ghost of the man she loved. She was angry with Kendall. That's where her heartache came from. She was certain of it. He'd listened to his mother and stayed in Hester Gardens to help with his younger brothers when she and Kendall had already made a wonderful plan to get out after their graduation, and that decision he'd made—choosing his mother over his girlfriend—had cost him his life. And she was bitter about it because without his help, she was now stuck in the very place that had consumed him.

When Kiandra was close enough to the dumpster to see the figure's face, she dropped the garbage bag next to her feet, and her body seemed to be floating.

Kendall turned slowly and extended his hand the way he used to ask her for a dance. She froze in place as he pivoted and tucked his hands into the pocket of his denim shorts, his white T-shirt pasted to his body with sweat. He had what appeared to be a fresh edge on his haircut.

The smell of rot and weeks-old garbage intensified as their eyes met.

"Kendall?" She couldn't move. Couldn't breathe. Couldn't think beyond these seconds when time had stopped for her.

His clean-shaven face took on a monstrous, evil look she'd never seen on him when he'd been alive. His skin sagged the way a person's would when they were in their sixties or seventies. Worry lines tore across his forehead, and his mouth was bunched into an expression one might bring out at a burial, of anger, disbelief, intense sadness.

Pastor Davis often talked about demons walking the earth, and in that moment, arrested there with her breath frozen in her chest and the hairs standing on her forearms and tears forming in the outer corners of her eyes, Kiandra couldn't be seeing Kendall—it must have been a fiend from hell.

He narrowed his eyes and rushed toward her. She backed up quickly, tripped over a blue ball, and crashed onto her bottom. Her backpack slipped from her shoulders as she raised her hand to protect herself. A piercing pain tore across her wrist as Kendall touched her. She drew back her injured forearm, but there was no Kendall. She was panting but couldn't catch her breath.

The figure was at the dumpster again, with the back of his freshly cut hair and the span of his shoulders exactly as they had been when she'd first spotted him. He swayed. Who was he? Was there really someone there? Was it Kendall? Was it someone else? An addict?

A squeak echoed in the night, and a rat scurried over her thigh. A second. A third. Every muscle in her body tightened as the creatures pressed their weight into her legs, brushed their stiff fur against her hands, and clawed along her wrists, their muscular, veinlike tales coiling and uncoiling across her middle as they scrambled along her body. She screamed.

For several torturous seconds, she shouted up every fear she'd ever had in a blood-curdling, piercing cry for help that burned her throat.

"Kiki?" Suddenly, Donnell was beside her. He set down his own trash bag and lifted her to standing. She caught sight of a long tail disappearing between two buildings as the creatures scampered away.

"What happened?" Donnell brushed off her pants and placed her bag on her shoulder again.

She glanced at him, then back at the dumpsters. Kendall, or the demon or whoever, was gone.

"You all right?" Donnell followed her gaze.

"Did you see?" Kiandra asked, voice hoarse from her screams.

Donnell scanned the ground around them. "See what? The rats? Is that what scared you? 'Cause you were yelling like someone was attacking you."

So he'd seen the rats but not the figure near the dumpsters. Of course he hadn't. What was she even thinking? If Donnell had thought she was really being attacked or had seen someone creeping around in the dark, he'd have drawn his gun and shot the guy. Donnell's voice was tender, which meant he was worried about her but not actually alarmed by anything he'd seen in that narrow space. She turned and rushed from the alley toward her front door.

"Kiki?" Donnell called after her.

She couldn't think straight. Had the figure been in her head?

"Kiki? What's wrong? Talk to me." Donnell followed her.

"It's fine. Leave me alone, Nell." She stumbled forward on weak and wobbly legs, more unsettled now than when she didn't know who was lurking around back there.

Kiandra got inside her home and locked the front door. She caught her breath. Flicked on the lights. The couch sagged, the lamps were dim, the rug worn, but she was safe now at least.

She'd imagined him. That was all. She'd fallen, had come into contact with gross rats, and all because . . . Why? Fear. Fear had created the entire thing. Obviously. Hauntings weren't real. They were just expressions of grief, and that's what seeing Kendall had been. Grief.

Her wrist burned. And when she raised it to the light, three thin lacerations appeared. Something had torn her flesh. Had the cuts come from the rats or from Kendall's touch?

Pastor: Hello, you.
Nona: Hey.

Pastor: Any more fuss from the boys after yesterday?
Nona: All is quiet. Hasn't stopped me from worrying.
Pastor: I figured. I'm fasting this morning for Marcus. Why don't you join me?
Nona: Until what time?
Pastor: Let's say until 1 p.m. We'll fast and pray. Our intention will be that God will keep all hurt, harm, and danger away from Marcus and Lance, and that the workers of iniquity will not gain entry to them.
Nona: Okay. I can do that.
Pastor: It was good seeing you last night.
Nona: Same. Thank you again for such an elegant party. I'm sorry the boys ruined it.
Pastor: They didn't ruin anything. And it was my pleasure. I hope to drop by and see you this afternoon. I'll be at a meeting near the Gardens.
Nona: Near the Gardens? I'm afraid to ask what business would bring you to these parts.
Pastor: LOL. God's reach is far and wide. Maybe I can bring you a bite to eat. We can break our fast together.
Nona: I'd like that, Pastor.
Pastor: Timothy.
Nona: Timothy.
Pastor: Fantastic. Until then, I'll be thinking of you.

Five

It was rare that Lance was home alone, but he'd skipped summer school to kick it with Donnell and now found himself in the house late in the day, practically starving and playing video games in his bedroom, with his mother and Marcus still on their way home.

He would just play one game before eating leftovers. He powered on the console Pastor had bought for Marcus, but he was distracted.

Lance was nervous about the job Donnell wanted him to do. He'd originally thought Donnell would tell him to pick some pockets or shoplift, something that, if caught, he could get out of with fines or community service. Instead, Donnell told him the job was at a house in the suburbs, to steal some oxycodone and electronics, which sounded like a major case if they were caught. After Marcus and Peter got into it at the party, deep down Lance was pissed Donnell hadn't stepped between them when Marcus first pushed Peter. Peter had a lot of nerve showing up with Kendall's watch. And how had he gotten it? Lance couldn't say any of this without risking the crew turning on him. Maybe even roughing him up.

Outside the bedroom, the front door opened and banged shut. Lance barely noticed.

On the television, the icon of a game popped up among the array of logos installed on their system. Between the racecar and the basketball was the symbol of a long rifle. He'd never seen it before. The game was titled *Carnage Master*, and a message scrolled beneath the thumbnail image like breaking-news ticker tape: *Wicked, Marcus! Congratulations for winning all levels and becoming a "Master Assassin."*

What the hell?

Whatever Marcus had installed did not resemble anything Lance had seen on their console before.

He listened for his mom or Marcus at the front of the house. Had he heard correctly? Had they entered?

Lance stared at the screen, squinting to ensure he was seeing correctly, focusing on the words "Master Assassin." Evil Marcus had obviously gotten into some strange shit. Lance had only ever played basketball and racing games with Marcus and wondered when and why Marcus had started playing shooting games. And where did he even get something like this?

He glanced at the MP3 player on Marcus's bed. Just that morning, he'd noticed Marcus playing music their mother would never allow in the house if she knew about it. Stuff with lyrics about shooting, and killing, and maiming, and living life "on the edge" and "out of control." Weren't those the very things Marcus had warned against in his graduation speech?

He opened his phone. He wanted to check Marcus's online activity, but he hesitated—his mom had been on his case about his data overage charges. The previous day, he'd gotten a warning message from their carrier that he was running low on data and would be charged if he went over the limit. His thumb hovered over all of the social media apps he and Marcus were allowed on.

Ah, fuck it.

He pressed one of the icons and scanned Marcus's recent posts: smiling pics from graduation, news articles about Brown University, a quote from James Baldwin. As usual, Marcus was one way in public and another way in private. He eyed the game console and the MP3 player again. This recent stuff was all kinds of bizarre.

Lance considered opening *Carnage Master,* but he instead went to his own *Race for the Babe* game, the one with the women who stood trackside, half-dressed and leaning forward to show their cleavage. Whenever he won a race, he got a babe. The prizes were *digital* ladies, sure, but their round breasts and bottoms still made him throb below. This brought him much shame.

The lock on the front door clicked loud enough for him to hear over the game. Usually, his mom and Marcus would shout "It's me!" when they entered. His dad and Kendall used to do the same. It was just something they all did to let one another know they'd arrived. This time, they didn't say anything.

"Marcus?" he called out, but he was more focused on babe number three, Cherry. She was the only Black girl in the lineup, and she was wearing a bikini with a thong bottom.

He was finishing lap one of his game when the footsteps crossed the kitchen and the living room, then entered the hallway.

"Mom?" On to lap two, and Cherry was twerking on the screen.

The steps echoed down the hall, more of a stomp than a tread, but he was only half listening. He was seconds from finishing the race, and if he won, he'd get first dibs on the girls. Last time he'd played, he'd come in second and had to settle for Bunny, who gave his character a lap dance for his win. He could only imagine what Cherry would do for the winner. A hand job? Blowjob?

The footfalls continued down the hall to his mom's bedroom, where she immediately turned on the television.

Sound blasted from her TV loud enough to drown out the cheering crowd on his game. A local news report about a school shooting blared from the speakers, the volume loud enough for him to hear every word clearly from behind his closed door.

"Police say a suspect is in custody after the early-morning shooting Monday at Sebastian Hills High School that claimed three lives and rocked the wealthy suburb. Shortly after nine a.m., a student shot and killed two classmates and a teacher before fleeing and sending authorities on a daylong manhunt. A fourth victim remains in critical condition at Ford Hospital."

He finished second in his race. *Damn.* He paused the game. "Mom?" he shouted. "You might want to turn that down."

She didn't answer. Probably because she couldn't hear over the volume.

He hit *play* long enough for Bunny, his second choice, to give his avatar a lap dance. He was unimpressed. Was he ever going to win Cherry?

In a huff, he set down the controller and shut off the game. He stood, opened his bedroom door, and leaned into the hallway. His mom's room was mostly hidden behind her half-open door, where blue light flickered from the screen.

"Mom?" He raised his voice that time. She halved the volume, but the sound played on. Was she still angry about the fight at the graduation party?

"Sebastian Hills police say the slain students, whose identities have not been released, were both fifteen years old. If you have any information about . . ."

Lance shook his head as he went to the kitchen, opened the fridge, and heated up leftover chicken and mashed potatoes in the microwave. Just as the gadget beeped that his food was ready, his mother's television volume went up to blaring again, this time a report about a shooting at a birthday party.

"A celebration turned to tragedy Saturday night on a tree-lined street in Seabury Falls when shots rang out at a child's birthday party, killing two and injuring five. Residents of this typically quiet neighborhood in the affluent section of Genesee County say they were shocked that gun violence could strike in their peaceful enclave."

He removed his food, set it on the counter, and went to the edge of the hall.

"Mom?" He tried not to have a disrespectful tone as he yelled loud enough for her to hear. "Can you turn it down?"

She snapped the volume off that time. He imagined the blue light dancing across the walls but with no sound. Had she turned on closed captioning? Why wasn't she answering him? She must have been angrier than he'd thought.

Relieved to be rid of the noise, he returned to the counter and took a bite of the chicken. Flavor exploded in his mouth as a key turned in the front door, and Marcus and his mother opened the bars and entered the kitchen.

Lance choked on the chicken.

He spit most of it across the counter as he took in his mother, in jeans and T-shirt, hanging her purse on the back of the chair at the breakfast table.

"Were you calling me?" she asked as she removed her sneakers and set her backpack near the closet.

Lance coughed out every bit of food in his mouth, but he didn't answer. Gooseflesh sprouted on his arms, and he bolted down the narrow path to his mother's room.

"Lance?" his mother called after him.

"Dude, what's wrong?" Marcus asked.

Lance didn't speak. Imagining the man from his peripheral vision, always just out of sight, Lance threw open the door to his mother's bedroom and rushed to her dresser, his bare feet rumpling the area rug in his haste. He blinked several times trying to process what he was seeing or what he wasn't seeing. No flickering blue light. The television screen was black. The remote was resting neatly beside it. He snatched it up. Surely if someone had used it, the device would be warm in his hand. It was cold, and Lance couldn't be certain, but from the corner of his eye, he thought he saw that man from his peripheral vision take shape, large and looming, as if rising to the ceiling. He mustered the courage to face the shadow, but the room was empty, the only movement a curtain flapping in the breeze.

Six

The next day, Nona handed the grocery list to Lance, but Marcus dis- cussed it with her.

"You want collards, Mom? Or mustards and turnips?" Ever since his behavior at the graduation party, Marcus had been attentive and polite.

He hadn't said sorry again, but every time he held a door for her or pulled the chair out for her or wiped down the counter or took a dirty dish from her and washed it himself, he was apologizing, telling her he was remorseful for being rude and for embarrassing her. She was always stunned at how Marcus and Lance took after different sides of their father.

"Collards. And get a few bags because I'm going to freeze some."

Marcus took the list from Lance. "I'll hang onto this so we don't lose it." He tucked it in his pocket, smirked at Nona, then winked.

"Lose it? You really need to stop acting like I'm five." Lance whined like a five-year-old when he said it but didn't seem to realize he'd done so. Lance had seemed rattled when they'd entered the previous day. Checking her bedroom, their closets, under the beds. She and Marcus asked him what was wrong, but Lance wouldn't admit what had shaken him. He just kept repeating, "Nothing. I'm trippin'." She wanted to keep pressing him—perhaps she wasn't alone in her feelings about their home—but Lance grew sullen for the rest of the evening. She was just happy he was up and moving about today. Whatever it had been, he seemed to have put it behind him.

She smiled as they stepped into their sneakers and headed out the door, the smell of cologne, bubble gum, and roll-on deodorant traveling with them. When her boys made it across the courtyard and disappeared onto Prescott Road, her foot bumped the tied-up garbage bags near the door. Neither son had taken out the trash.

Ever since Marcus's fight with Peter, she kept Marcus and Lance away from the Gardens as much as possible, with errands and odd jobs around the church. It was Memorial Day, and the last thing she wanted to do on her day off was complete chores she'd assigned her sons, but since Marcus and Lance could only manage one task at a time, sending them to the grocery store meant she had to take over trash duty.

Standing before Hester Gardens' overflowing dumpsters, Nona retied the garbage bags as gray clouds gathered overhead. Hester Gardens had two main alleys. One was on the eastern side of the projects, where Vance had attacked NaDarius. The one where she stood now was on the western side. Neither set of dumpsters was emptied with any consistency, but Nona only ever came to the western alley, where there were no memories waiting for her.

Rats and opossums made their home behind the units and had ripped open bags bound with yellow twists. Some had no ties at all. Loose garbage was strewn about the concrete, and the mixed stench of soiled tissue, scraps of food, and used diapers wafted as the piles gathered heat in the sunlight.

Bass-heavy rap floated in the distance from oversized speakers a group of young men blasted at the front of the Gardens. Near Nona, four older men burned more trash in metal drums.

Nona coughed so loudly that Mable Cleveland poked her head out from behind a mound of filth and shouted, "Who's making all that damn noise?"

People who lived outside the Gardens typically picked up, fixed up, and resold bulky items like the unwanted recliners, mattresses, and threadbare area rugs wedged between the dumpsters. Dragging a discarded bathroom cabinet that seemed entirely constructed of splinters, Mable huffed and gasped. Behind Mable and scattered about the entryway to her home were jars of pink liquid that sloshed up and down the sides of the containers as if roused by an invisible finger.

When she saw Nona, the woman smiled. "Whatcha know good?"

"Hey, Mable." Nona couldn't help but think of Mable's son Donnell, who had been completely useless during Marcus's dustup with Peter at the graduation party. Whose side were Mable and Donnell on?

Mable opened her mouth but paused before speaking. "I sure am tired of lugging this stuff onto the bus for the market. Any word on my application?"

Nona mentally kicked herself for forgetting yet again to check on whether her boss was still considering Mable for the position. "They are usually pretty slow."

Mable nodded and averted her eyes. She forced a smile but grunted as she dragged the wooden fixture into her home.

Brakes squeaked on Prescott Road, and a U-Haul pulled up. An elderly woman got out and directed three young men who were the spitting image of her to lift furniture from the curb to the truck. More tenants leaving, and who could blame them?

Vega Lawson, who sat in her white plastic chair on the patch of grass outside her unit holding her mug of coffee, shouted, "Turn down that music! Hooligans. All of you!"

The young men lowered the volume.

As Vega's voice echoed off the brick homes, Nona averted her eyes, as did every other person tossing their trash and heading up to the main drag to catch the bus.

One winter a few years back, Vega's kids Solomon and Esmé had to drag Vega out of a snowstorm, during which the woman had been sitting in her lawn chair, sipping from her mug, wearing only her white-and-blue housedress. Rumor was the woman had frostbite on her toes that never got better.

A group of five children played hopscotch twenty feet away. The clouds darkened the sky, and a cord of dread crept up Nona's back.

When she set the garbage bags on top of the dumpster, one fell and landed alongside the other white, black, and brown ones littering the ground. Flies buzzed above her. She swatted them away, but that only attracted more.

"Hi, Sister McKinley." Seven-year-old Jocelyn attended youth service at church. Nona waved.

The girl whispered to her playmates as if Nona couldn't hear, "Mrs. McKinley's place faces north."

Her friend whispered, "So what?"

And Jocelyn whispered back, "Means she's got somebody dead living there. They all got somebody dead living there."

Nona paused, surprised that the girl who seemed to know her Bible so well at church was sharing an iniquitous story at home. Nona blamed the child's parents for this.

"Jocelyn, you stupid," her playmate teased. "The dead don't *live* anywhere. They're dead. You're just dumb."

"Am not."

"Are too."

"No need to argue," Nona chimed in. The kids scurried away.

A few of them had used a rock darkened with a broken printer-ink cartridge to write on the concrete "Beware the Garbage Goblin. Do Not Cross This Line."

Her phone buzzed: Pastor calling for the second time that day. She let it go to voicemail.

Despite the gang of flies still humming near her head, Nona lingered at the dumpster because Marcus and Lance were suddenly at the front of the Gardens, shouting and wagging fingers at each other. She inched closer. Marcus took out his cell phone and made a call. She squinted. They trudged along the concrete path through Hester Gardens with nary a grocery bag nor the fold-up shopping basket she'd asked them to use.

Lance held his nose, where blood rushed out and spilled down his arm. A purple bruise had formed on Marcus's jaw. Pinpricks crossed Nona's scalp. Heat gathered in her chest. She rushed forward, tripping over a blue ball that rolled into her path seemingly of its own power.

As she sprinted, her phone fell from her hand. She picked up the device and locked eyes with Marcus. She wasn't seeing him, really. She was seeing Kendall the month before he died, when he came home with that swollen right hand. She reached for Marcus and Lance. The panic coursing through her body was fresh, but it was also two years old.

"Who did this?" She ripped a piece of her T-shirt sleeve and pressed it against Lance's nose. No one was behind them. Neither at the front of the Gardens nor on Prescott outside the complex's threshold. The only people milling about were Mable Cleveland, who was now headed for the bus stop with a plastic bottle of pink water, and Vega Lawson, sipping from her coffee mug, laughing to herself.

Marcus ended his call, stuffed the mobile in his pocket, and had the nerve to roll his eyes toward the sky as if she were causing a problem. "Mom. It's no big deal. Don't get—"

"Don't tell me how to get. He's bleeding." She pulled Lance against her chest, but he pushed her away.

"I jus nee somb ice, Mob." Lance's injured nose distorted his words.

"I said, who did this?"

"Some guys." Marcus was doing the talking. The oldest was always the spokesperson for group lies. "Robbed us. Took the groceries."

"The groceries?"

Marcus nodded and averted his eyes.

"Get in this house right now." She raced ahead of them, threw open the squeaking iron door, and guided Lance in by his forearms.

She grabbed a towel from the drawer and an ice pack from the freezer. The refrigerator photos of her boys taunted her. Back then, they smiled deeply, eyes nearly closed they were so happy. Back then they still shared their dreams with her, and told her the truth.

When she turned to hand the ice pack to Lance, her boys were eyeing each other, likely trying to get their story straight.

"Sit down. Put this on your jaw and this on your nose to absorb the blood. Start talking. Both of you."

With a huff, Marcus sat at the kitchen table and iced the bruise, which had become a black lump.

"Some guys wanted our groceries," Marcus said. "We tried to fight them off because we knew you wanted to make us a nice dinner. That it was important to you."

Important to her? They always made her sound desperate and clingy, but she couldn't get distracted.

"You didn't recognize them?"

They both shook their heads no.

"Where did this happen?"

"Right, uh . . ." Lance began. "At the front of the—"

"At the bus stop." Marcus cut him off. "Looked like some silly kids."

"Silly kids?"

"Yep." Marcus nodded, averting his eyes.

"So, not Peter?"

"Peter? No." Marcus eyed her briefly.

Lance watched Marcus, probably trying to memorize these fake details.

Peter falling to the floor and taking the gift table with him flashed in her mind, as did the way Marcus's back seemed to grow in size to match his anger. In a matter of a couple of days, Marcus had been in two fights, and he must think her a fool if he was trying to play them off as unrelated.

She rose, put her hands on her hips. Her body went from hot to cold. This was how it unfolded with Kendall. His bruised fist. The fight he wouldn't tell her about. This was how it unfolded with Vance. The lies. The downplaying.

She sensed a shadow in her peripheral vision, but when she scanned the hallway, it was gone. Why did this keep happening? Was this anxiety? Grief? She certainly had both, but the feelings weren't new.

Her boys seemed nervous, the way they used to when they were twelve and eight and they'd broken a lamp in the house. She touched her forehead, and the movement made them shift in their seats.

"As surely as I'm standing here, you're both lying."

"Ah, Mom!" Marcus's voice had gone from annoyed to angry.

"Don't 'ah, Mom' me. You must think I'm stupid. Muggings are crimes of opportunity. And crimes of opportunity around here don't involve injuries like these—bruised knuckles on both hands, swollen jaws, black eyes, a busted nose. If someone wanted a car, they'd take it at gunpoint. A purse, they'd snatch. Same for sneakers and cell phones. Especially here in the Gardens. Speed is key—in and out." She slapped her fist in her opposite palm for emphasis and waited for them to roll their eyes. They didn't. Perhaps she was getting through to them. "I don't know anybody who would stick around long enough to duke it out with their victims. And, in all my forty-two years on God's green earth, I've never heard of anyone in Medford getting jumped for groceries. I never thought I'd see the day when my sons, my remaining sons, would fix their lips to lie to me in my own house, where I pay the bills."

"Like you ever tell us the truth." Venom burned in Marcus's tone. He met her gaze, his eyes piercing hers. At his side, his hand trembled. Would he try to hit her? Her boy? Who until recently had never made a snide remark to her? Had never raised his voice? Had never questioned her? The same boy who sang "I'll Always Love My Mama" on the phone with her? Her Marcus wouldn't do that. Who was this other Marcus? First, that odd stare during his graduation speech, then the punch at Peter, and now this different Marcus, the one so obviously lying to her?

Marcus rose and stepped forward. Their eyes remained locked. He might have been taller than she was now, but she wasn't an easy win. She took three steps forward, ready to go upside his head with her house slipper if he looked like he was going to raise a hand to her.

The stench from the dumpsters, like innards and death, filled the room. She wondered whether the muggers were the lie. Whether it was Marcus and Lance who actually fought.

"Excuse me, Marcus? You want to run that by me again? Like I ever . . . what did you say to me?"

"Listen, Mom." Lance's head swiveled between Nona and Marcus. "We're telling you the—"

"No, you're not!" She slapped her open hand on the kitchen table. Her palm throbbed as the wood shook beneath it.

They closed their mouths, but their eyes remained wide. Their demeanors shifted, as if they were twelve and eight again.

"Can we go now?" Marcus asked with a more respectful tone that did not match his pursed lip.

"Not until you tell me the truth."

Marcus held his ice pack against Lance's face and walked his brother toward their bedroom.

"Get back here right now, and tell me what really happened!"

Marcus continued through the threshold of their room and slammed the door.

The sound of his defiance and disrespect reverberated down the hall.

She stormed to their bedroom door, ready to throw it open and whoop Marcus's behind, but she heard their whispers and caught the name "Peter" in their hushed back-and-forth.

She knew it! Peter was somehow involved with this fistfight. Probably a continuation of what had happened at Marcus's graduation party.

Her arms trembled at her sides, and at some point, she'd come out of her shoes, having subconsciously prepared herself to use them as a weapon. A weapon to defend herself against her own son. A son she no longer knew, who was transforming into a version of himself she didn't like. When did he ever pick fights and lie about them to her face? And that step, as if he were on the verge of striking her?

She glanced across the hall and into the kitchen, where the photos of her boys stared back at her. She must have been imagining the smell of trash in the room. The odor was now faint, barely noticeable. Those dumpsters were rarely emptied. That must have been the reason the stench had come and gone so abruptly.

She put her hand on the knob. It was locked. "Marcus. Lance. Open this door right now."

This was her house. These were her boys. They would open this door and tell her what happened, and they would all solve this problem together.

Then music blared in the bedroom, a rap song the boys played to shield their whispered conversation. She pounded on the door until her fists ached, and shame seeped into her heart that she remained shut out of their room and out of their lives.

❖

Nona: Marcus and Lance got into a fistfight.

Harlan: What?

Nona: They won't tell me the specifics, but I have reason to believe Peter was involved.

Harlan: Do you know where it happened?

Nona: They said at the bus stop, but I think it was here at the Gardens. They were supposed to be buying groceries. Can you talk to Marcus? See if you can get some information out of him. He listens to you.

Harlan: He definitely doesn't listen to me. LOL. But I'll do some digging. I'm working on two shootings right now. A shooting at a birthday party and an unrelated school shooting. Both in the suburbs. Tight deadlines. You know how it goes. But I will make time. This is important.

Nona: Are these new stories? Not the one you were covering the other day? You cover so many shootings. I can't keep track.

Harlan: Yep. These two are new. But I was planning to take the boys to a talk about economic oppression at the university. Maybe I can ask them about the fight then?

Nona: Thank you! I've been worried sick.

Harlan: Don't. I'll keep you posted. They are good kids. I'm sure it was just boys being boys.

Seven

By the time Pastor dropped in, the boys were gone. Harlan had stopped by to take them out, but that calmed Nona only a bit. She still wanted answers. Maybe Harlan could get through to them.

"You look frazzled, Nona. What's wrong?" Pastor carried a bag of fried shrimp, French fries, and coleslaw. She was starving and guessed he must have been as well, since he'd said he was bringing "a bite to eat" and instead had gotten a meal for at least four people.

When he emptied the contents of his pockets on her counter like he lived there—wallet, phone, keys, lip balm, receipts—she noticed a tall stack of cash. Mistrust rose in her as she remembered the unaccounted-for money Vance carried around, but she pushed it down. Pastor was a man of God. These bills were probably from the collection plate.

She realized he was now staring at her, awaiting her answer.

"The boys were in a fight." Outside, someone bounced a basketball. It was probably Solomon, Vega's son. She didn't peek out the window. Sometimes seeing Solomon was too painful. Solomon had grown up with Kendall, and his presence reminded her that her oldest would never again be able to walk out the front door to play a pickup game with Solomon like he used to.

"Another fight?" He placed the bags on the counter. "With Peter?"

"They won't say. Claim they were jumped for groceries, but—"

"For groceries? Well, that's obviously a lie."

"Thank you! It's like I've lost control of both of them, and—"

"Nona." He took her in his arms, his chest firm against hers, his body feeling strong enough to lift her and carry her away from her troubles. "Breathe. Just take some deep breaths with me."

He pulled air in his nose and out his mouth, and she kept her eyes on the narrow gold chain buried just beneath the collar of his shirt. She followed his lead. He bent and kissed her forehead. That tiny gesture melted all the tension from her body.

"I got into so many fistfights when I was young. Over any and every little thing. Somebody stepped on my shoe? Somebody looked at me the wrong way? Somebody accidentally bumped into me as we were walking through a door?" He chuckled, and she grinned in spite of herself. "Boys can be this way sometimes. We just . . . Any little thing can set us off. We're like animals marking our territory. Letting people know they can't step to us the wrong way. My mother was worried half to death all the time when I was young."

He stroked her hair, her cheek, his other hand never breaking their embrace. He was often affectionate with her, but recently, the closer they got to Marcus leaving home, the more Pastor's affection felt like courting, like he was preparing to move into her life as soon as Marcus moved out. She shouldn't have allowed him, a married man and the pastor of her church, to carry on this way, but she enjoyed the physical touch, the companionship, the undivided attention.

"Things are different nowadays," Nona said. Marcus's trembling hand came to mind. She couldn't tell Pastor that Marcus had been on the verge of hitting her, because then she'd have to admit that to herself. "These boys around here, the Hester Boys? They have guns. And vendettas. And turf. They— I've already lost one of my babies."

Kendall's smiling face and dimples came to her. Tears burned her eyes.

"And God is not going to let this place take another." Pastor's grin was warm, calm, all-knowing. His certainty eased her worries. "I promise you, Nona. Marcus will be fine. I'll talk to him."

"That would mean so much to me. Will you?"

Concern washed over his face. He moved his free hand from her hair to her mouth and gently caressed her lips. She cleared her throat.

"You never have to question me when it comes to you. I would do anything for you." He hugged her, his hands stroking her hair, and her arms wrapped around his waist. He grew firm against her body, and she broke their embrace.

"We better eat." She chuckled, motioning to the bags on the counter growing soggy and damp. "Before the food gets cold."

Gretchen moved her baby away from the bathroom window and closer to the sink, but now that was too close to the open drywall. She relocated the bouncer again, this time away from the spot where her father had taped cling wrap over the tennis ball–sized gap. The housing authority had neither fixed the original leak nor replaced the sheetrock the plumber had removed, so the plastic served as a structural bandage. She had run out of suitable spaces in the bathroom for her baby. This constant repositioning was an old habit that developed after losing her twin Grace to a stray bullet.

Usually, her dead sister appeared to her in a flash. In the corner of a room. At the foot of her bed. Walking down the hall. Lying beside her when she woke in the morning. Each time, Grace was holding her doll, the one in a gingham dress that matched Gretchen's doll, both of which also matched the dresses she and Grace had been wearing when the bullet took Grace forever.

Gretchen had come to accept that these flashes were all in her mind.

Her son cooed and giggled in his bouncy seat as she dragged the base across the bathroom's tile floor, closer to the tub. Between diaper changes, breastfeeding, laundry, and cramming two pieces of toast into her own mouth for breakfast, she was managing to get a shower in before work and daycare drop-off. This was a real treat, but as she stepped into the stream and picked up the pine-scented soap, something felt off.

Along with the hot water, the memory of Grace's final moments washed over her. Eight years old, she and her identical twin sitting cross-legged on their townhome's front lawn, playing with their dolls, when a bullet from a gun in a hand passing by in a slow-moving car entered Grace's forehead, and she fell back on the grass and never sat back up.

Because of the blood spray, the gingham dress on Gretchen's doll was covered in Grace's blood. Gretchen often wondered why Grace had been the one to go and not herself. They'd chosen their spots in the grass randomly, but Gretchen had been the one to complain the sun was in her eyes, and Grace had shrugged and offered to trade places with her. Had Gretchen not complained, had Grace not been such a sweet and accommodating sister, Gretchen would have been the one hit, Grace's doll soaked in blood.

Gretchen had continued going to church with her mother, but she was still living and Grace was not, and the unfairness of that tore at her. She wondered what her life was supposed to mean, exactly. Secretly, she believed God was actually a lottery—a random drawing of numerical symbols—and when your number was called, your life came to an end.

She peeked again at the wall cavity where the plastic rustled from the bathroom steam. The hole seemed larger this time. About the size of a basketball now.

Once, a rat had appeared in that opening, and she wanted the drywall closed. Her father was not handy, and when Peter suspected she was seeing anybody else, he would argue with her and give her the third degree when he came to help her with Grayson, so getting him to pitch in for repairs was a no-go.

That morning, Gretchen had seen a news story on television about a toddler in the soon-to-be-shuttered Dempsey Woods projects being struck in the head by a bullet while sitting at home watching television on his couch. She'd searched for the story on the internet at work because she needed to know whether the parents had done something careless or dumb to get the kid killed. Like maybe the couch had been near the window (it hadn't been) or maybe the parents hadn't been home to tell the child to take shelter (they had been) or perhaps they'd never taught the toddler to get on the floor behind a large piece of furniture if they heard someone arguing (there had been no warning argument) or they probably sold drugs and their home had been targeted (they didn't sell drugs).

Her anxiety brought out hives on her neck and chest. The parents had done everything right and they still lost their baby. Well, they'd done everything right except for living in the projects. Poverty was their original sin.

None of that explained her strange feeling. She wasn't dehydrated. She was sleep-deprived, yes, but that wasn't it. Her heart rate had picked up and her body went ice cold.

She watched Grayson through the partially open shower curtain, the gap just wide enough so she could see him when she leaned forward but not gaping to the point she'd catch a breeze. Why'd she feel cold? It wasn't the season for it at all, and Grayson burbled happily in front of her. His entire fist was in his mouth; as the steam rose around him, he grinned.

Yet her heart rate sped up. She checked the movement near the hole, which had seemingly grown again to the size of a dodgeball. Lots of rustling, but the taped-up cling wrap held. Surely there couldn't be any rodent activity there.

Why did the crevice seem larger? Was that her imagination, or was the shower steam chipping away at the edges of the hole?

Would she faint? She'd argued with Peter that morning because he was supposed to take the baby to daycare and watch him after pickup, but he was refusing unless she told him where she was going. Only she couldn't tell him, since she was actually going to meet Marcus. That would set Peter off.

A flash of red appeared at the edge of the curtain. She blinked away shower water, held her breath. She willed the memory of her long-dead sister to disappear, but the color was still there. Her "survivor's guilt," her high school's counselor had called it, but this appearance, this blood, this red, this flash was lasting longer than usual.

She eased back the curtain, and the doll was sitting in Grayson's lap, blood dripping from the pink-and-white fabric onto his chubby thigh. He was crying now. It was a doll, only a doll, but even he knew something about it was wrong.

She snapped off the water, and with soap and moisture still dripping down her front and back, she leapt from the shower, reached down, and snatched up the toy. Gooseflesh spread across her skin as icy air pricked her body. Her teeth chattered from the cold but also from the object before her eyes.

When she got a grip on the doll's cloth-covered arm, movement appeared in the drywall hole and Grace's face filled the opening—bullet hole in her forehead, surprised eyes, mouth bunched up in pain, mottled deep brown skin, and hair still in pigtails.

Gretchen blinked repeatedly, hoping the image would disappear as usual, but it didn't.

Grace's shoulders jerked up and down in a repetitive shrug. The girl peeked her head through the gash in the wall.

"No." Gretchen startled back, lost her balance, and regained it by grabbing the shower curtain. The white material snapped off the rods and fell down, but it had been just enough to prevent her fall. Her baby cried louder.

Grace slithered her tiny body through the wall's divide, tearing it apart like a baby ripping from its mother's body. Grace hopped down to the floor next to Grayson. Shoulders shrugged and shrugged and shrugged. The girl leaned her bloody face down directly in front of his.

He screamed, eyes wide, and he jerked back and threw his arms out in front of him. The girl snatched him up, gripped him against her side like a football, and darted toward the large hole, his feet limply flopping behind them. His shrieks grew manic.

"No!" Gretchen dropped the doll and rushed across the wet tile, bare feet sliding as she went. She was on Grace's heels as the girl tried to stuff Grayson into the hole.

Gretchen reached out and snatched back her baby. Grace released him but reached up and scratched Gretchen, creating a sting like fire on Gretchen's right cheek.

"Don't you ever touch him!" Gretchen shouted, and her dead sister, still a decade younger, stuck out her tongue. Shoulders shrugged, again and again and again. Grayson's hysterical cries continued.

"Gretchen?" Peter appeared in the bathroom doorway. He removed his Tigers baseball cap and sunglasses and set them on the shelf. "What the fuck?"

Grace was gone. The plasterboard crevice was larger than it had been at the start of Gretchen's shower. She pulled Grayson's tiny feet away from the opening. Cling wrap and masking tape dangled down its front. Smears of blood ran along the wall, the tile floor, tub, shower curtain, and Grayson's bouncy seat. The doll was gone too.

Panting, Gretchen stood naked, holding their son, covered in soap, water, and blood. Grayson reached for his father, his screams desperate.

"It was Grace." She choked down a sob, shivering and panting.

Peter grabbed a towel from the rack, draped it around her shoulders, and took their baby. He bounced and kissed Grayson, shushing the boy, whose cries slowly calmed. "What you mean 'it was Grace?' What was Grace?"

"I—" What else could she say? She checked the wall, then the floor, where blood streamed from her own body.

What had she done? How had she done this? From Peter's perspective, she had cut herself and tried to stick their baby into the open wall.

She had no explanation for how her son got over to that hole, but now she could see the blood had a real-world cause: Gretchen's period had come back. She'd been nursing and hadn't had her cycle since before her pregnancy, but that's where all of the blood was coming from. Her period, heavy flow filled with red-tinted black clumps. "What are you doing here, Peter?"

"You said you wanted me to help with little man today." He continued to rock and bounce their son, who had finally stopped crying but clung to Peter's shirt for dear life.

"But you said—"

"You gon' tell me what you were doing just now when I got here?"

She didn't have an answer for him. Grace obviously hadn't been there. She'd imagined her, but Peter and other folks at the Gardens believed in ghosts. Would he believe her if she told the truth? Peter had told her he thought the ghost Carlotta, a dead prostitute who attacked johns, was really trying to protect sex workers from the folks who might hurt them. Gretchen didn't know what to believe, and now her imagination might have caused her to hurt her own baby.

"I don't know. I think I just need more sleep. I was . . . confused."

"About what?" Peter kissed their son again, and the baby nestled his face in Peter's neck.

Gretchen sobbed. Peter nodded. He obviously didn't believe her, but he probably could sense she was too upset right now to explain. With their son in his arms, he turned and walked away. She was so relieved to not have him stare at her any longer, accusations on his face.

She closed the door behind them and faced the bathroom. Her heart still raced. Water dripped in the shower, the sound rhythmic yet ominous. She shivered under the towel. She scanned every corner, every shadow. In that dark orifice, something darted by and shrieked.

She crept to the yawning space and leaned forward just enough to see inside. No one was there. The plastic rustled along the bottom, and cold wind brushed against her face, reminding her of that stinging pain on her cheek.

Gretchen rushed to the mirror, and sure enough, the flesh there was cut. The tiny, jagged slash, the size of a small fingernail, had drawn blood.

Eight

The bus took Nona past the home on Willowbrook, where two blond boys played basketball in the driveway. Their hair flapped in the breeze as one dribbled to the basket and the shorter one slapped at the ball. She imagined her boys living in this home, her dream home, on a street safe enough for them to remain outside without stray bullets striking them or drug dealers recruiting them.

She texted Harlan: Did the boys tell you anything about that fight? She hoped Harlan would respond soon.

She dismounted the Medford DOT bus at the Prescott stop and headed straight for Mother Lincoln's. She hadn't heard from Mother since Marcus punched Peter at the graduation party, even though she'd tried the woman's phone a few times.

A young couple rolled a couch up the ramp of a moving truck. She hadn't gotten a chance to introduce herself to them yet, to perhaps take over a pie or fruit basket, and they were already moving out.

Vega sat in her lawn chair sipping from her mug, leaning forward as if eager to chat. Nona waved but did not break her stride.

At Mother's unit, leaves had piled against the front door, and Nona cursed Peter for not sweeping them up. It wasn't even fall. There weren't even that many.

Nona usually rushed inside to escape the stench from the dumpsters, but this time, she took a few seconds to scoop out the squished foliage, soggy from recent rain, and shake out Mother's welcome mat.

She knocked on the door loud enough for Mother to hear even if the woman was in the bathroom. No answer. The door budged when she took away her hand. It was unlocked.

Nona pushed open the creaking screen door. Mother's home was mostly set up like Nona's, with the kitchen, dining area, and living room to the left. Instead of Mother's bedroom hall being straight ahead, hers was to the right of the front door.

Pictures of Peter as a baby and young boy—rarely smiling—lined the walls and filled the counters and side tables. Nona remembered the way he crinkled his nose with glee whenever he saw Kendall or Nona kissed his forehead.

It was unlike Mother to leave her home open. Nona's ears perked up when she heard something being dragged across the floor. She thought of Vance and NaDarius in that alley.

She tossed the leaves in Mother's kitchen trash bin and removed her shoes so she wouldn't track the outside in.

Mother's home smelled of black-eyed peas. A dingy chair leaned against the wall, and although Nona swept it often, crumbs littered the area rug already stained from Peter spilling food and God knows what else on it. Hoping to keep out the stench from the dumpsters, Nona closed the door again even though it was sweltering inside.

"Mother?"

On a bookcase between the living room and kitchen, a radio played "The Question Is" by the Winans. The gospel song took her back to Kendall's funeral, where the singers repeatedly crooning "no" sent the congregation into a series of sobs.

"Nona?" Mother's voice sounded weak, confused. Nona rushed down the narrow hallway to where Mother lay on her side, one house slipper off, one on, and a dirty sneaker between the woman's feet.

"Didn't see Peter's gym shoe."

Nona knelt and checked the woman's face and head. "Anything feel broken? Did you hit your head?"

"I'm fine, baby."

"You're lying on the floor, Mother." Nona wanted to go upside Peter's head. She'd told him several times that since his grandmother was on and off blood pressure and cholesterol medication, he had to keep the floors clear. The senior was off-balance half the time, and this was the second fall Nona knew of.

"Tripped right before you came in. Was getting back up. I didn't hit my head."

If Mother tripped just before Nona arrived, then the woman had been avoiding her. And it must have been because of the fight at the graduation party. This wasn't the first time Mother had pulled away from her—she'd done it when Peter started selling drugs, when Kendall was killed, when Peter dropped out of high school, when Gretchen became pregnant by Peter—and each time it angered Nona. Mother always took up for Peter and condoned so much of his reckless behavior when she needed to put him out, let street justice take care of him instead of allowing him to wreak havoc within the Gardens. Nona could never say any of this to her. Nona loved the woman and knew life had dealt her a bad hand.

Nona helped Mother up, adjusted her ankle-length skirt, and eased the house slipper back onto Mother's foot.

"But you haven't been answering my calls."

"Sorry, baby. Back and forth to these doctors. Told them they need to change my pressure medication. Shouldn't be dizzy all the time. And you know they want the insurance money, which is why they had me come in person for something they could've done over the phone."

Nona wasn't buying it. As she got Mother comfortable in front of the television and found the woman didn't appear bruised, she went to gather Mother's laundry, avoiding a talk Mother obviously didn't want to have.

Mother's unit was at the back corner of the Gardens. The alley behind it was the same place where Nona had found Vance holding that bloody gun, but Mother's hearing was bad, and Nona figured the woman had no idea it was a perfect eavesdropping spot.

Someone was in the alley, and when Nona peeked out the edge of the blinds, she saw fast-tail Gretchen whispering in Brother Taylor's ear, and he had his hand in the back pocket of the teen's denim shorts. There'd been rumors that sweet, gap-toothed Sister Taylor's husband was cheating on his wife with the eighteen-year-old, and that the encounters had begun when the girl was underage, but Nona had never really believed those stories until now. She scanned the ground behind the giggling pair and backed away—she could have sworn she saw NaDarius's blood.

She blinked. The blood was gone. Anxiety. Grief. Nothing more.

When she was back in the kitchen cooking a pot of penne with marinara sauce, she told Mother about Brother Taylor.

"That girl is so nasty. I've warned Peter about her time and time again," Mother said, shaking her head and wagging her finger.

"Gretchen is just a kid. Brother Taylor's the one who's nasty." Brother and Sister Taylor had seemed so happy when they'd cut up the dance floor doing the bop at Marcus's graduation party.

"They'll both get theirs eventually. Where's your plate, baby?"

Nona placed the serving tray on Mother's lap and put a glass of water with a coaster on the side table next to her.

"Eating your food is like spending your money. I won't do it."

"You're too good to me."

"Make sure you drink plenty of water. You can't get dehydrated on top of everything else."

"I'd rather have some sweet tea."

"You know I'm not giving you sweet tea." At the sink, Nona washed dishes.

"You're awful. Get out." Mother chuckled. Nona did too. They had the same conversation whenever Nona looked after the woman. It made Nona think of what it might have been like if her own mother were still alive.

"Baby, why you look so worried?"

Nona finished scrubbing the plates. "Have a lot on my mind."

"About our boys?"

She was relieved Mother brought it up first.

"Neither one of mine will tell me what it was about. And Marcus and Lance were in another fight, and I'm worried they fought Peter again."

"Another fight? Oh, Lord, give me strength. Peter wouldn't tell me anything either. And you know I lit into him when we got home. Told him I don't know what it was about, but I better not ever catch him carrying on with any of your sons like that ever again. I know I can't spank him anymore, but I have other ways to keep him in check."

"I've been worried that—"

"Don't worry, baby. Not one bit. Peter said he wouldn't do anything to upset me. That it was just silly boy stuff. And I believe him."

That was the problem. Mother always believed what Peter said. That he'd been expelled from school because of racism, when everyone knew he'd dropped out because his grades were poor and the school was threatening to expel him for fighting. That he had a job at the hospital working with Kiandra, which had been true for about a week until his boss rubbed him the wrong way and he'd given the man a black eye. That there was no such thing as the Hester Boys, it was just the name of their fantasy football group. Nona was somewhat relieved that Mother had at least chastised Peter. Maybe the woman had gotten through to him and he'd leave Marcus and Lance alone.

"Is there something else, baby? You still seem bothered. You take such good care of me and everybody else. Let me share your burdens." Mother spoke between bites of pasta and steamed broccoli. Nona was relieved she'd cooked. Maybe not getting enough food and water had contributed to Mother's fall.

"I just . . ." Nona dried her hands and sat at Mother's feet. She didn't know if she could talk to Mother about the changes she was seeing in Marcus. Mother was a devout Christian and was on the church's board of trustees. When Pastor had a major decision, he called Mother. Mother "rebuked" every crime at Hester Gardens and said sin caused people to get killed, that their iniquity was overtaking them. So she couldn't exactly tell Mother about her odd feelings, about the May 28 anniversary that came and went, about Marcus's hurtful statement—*You're the one imagining things*—about the voice she'd imagined in her home. "Do you believe in curses, Mother?"

"I believe the Enemy has all sorts of powers. But do I think a person can curse another? They can sure try, but my God is more powerful than that."

"What about the dead? Can the dead . . . ?" She didn't know how to ask the question because she hadn't fully accepted the idea.

"Can the dead what?"

"Nothing. It's silly talk." And it was. She had been through so much in the past four years, and the overwhelming grief was probably all just catching up to her, making her see and feel things that weren't really there.

"I'll tell you what I do know. Your mama prayed protection over you."

"What?"

"Did your mama ever tell you about how you were born?"

"No, ma'am."

"Well, you wouldn't wait the final two weeks of her pregnancy. The membranes started leaking when your mama was thirty-eight weeks and brushing her teeth in the bathroom mirror. By the time she called the nurse at the hospital, blood was pouring out with the clear fluid, and when she called the auto plant where your daddy worked, she had him paged between contractions. She had no idea the pressure she was feeling in her bottom was the urge to push you out. She just thought she needed a bowel movement." Mother chuckled. Nona loved imagining her parents young and full of hope.

"By the time your daddy jumped in his red Monte Carlo and sped up the Rodgers Freeway to get to Dempsey Woods, your mama was already on the floor with her legs spread and her hand out to catch you. You were born just as he entered the bathroom, and your mama was worried about you for the first five minutes because you would not stop screaming. The cries were high-pitched like you were wailing for all the sorrows of your life at the beginning to get them out of the way. Since you were born on September ninth, they decided to name you Nona. She prayed that God would continue to watch over you, guide you the way he'd ushered you into this world in the palm of his hand."

"Can't say that it's worked so far." She knew the story should have made her feel better, but it didn't. It highlighted how much promise she and her sons had at the moments of their births, and how the reality of their lives slowly chipped away at the quality of their futures. She wished she had her mother around to discuss her problems with. Her mother would have stroked the back of Nona's hand and said, *We'll figure this thing out together.*

"Have you heard from your husband, baby?"

"He wrote me another letter."

"Isn't he getting out soon?"

"Says with good behavior, maybe less than a year, but I'm not keeping track. Got too much to deal with, and he's not here to help."

"It's not like he's on vacation. You should write back. Or accept his calls. I'm surprised the boys haven't tried to visit him."

"They know I'd be furious."

"You gon' stay mad at him forever? What did Pastor say on Sunday?"

Game-show lights blinked on the television, but the volume was muted. With no closed captioning, Nona imagined the grinning faces on the screen were laughing at her. She remembered Pastor's body pressed against hers, his fingers on her lips, him growing firm against her middle.

"Pastor talked of forgiveness, but forgiveness isn't the problem. I want to be rid of Vance."

"That's probably why you're feeling cursed."

"Who said I was feeling cursed, Mother?"

Nona shifted against the front of the couch next to Mother's legs, where a pale bruise was forming near the woman's ankle.

"I thought you did, baby. You were about to say you thought the dead had cursed you, right? Making you feel strange?"

"No, Mother. I think it's just vertigo."

"Well, you know your vertigo comes right before something . . ." Mother paused.

Nona was back at that day, remembering Kendall's final kiss on her cheek. How he'd smiled and waved on his way out the door. "See you later, Mom." Only, he didn't. When he hadn't shown up for dinner at the time she'd expected him, it felt like the entire room was on rollers.

Nona kissed Mother's forehead. Beating back tears, she stood and grabbed her purse.

"If you're having vertigo, baby, you should take something for it. It will help with the dizziness."

"I will, Mother."

"And if you're feeling cursed, rebuke it. Because whatever it is, it's from the Enemy."

Nine

Pastor: Hello, you.
Nona: Hey.
Pastor: I spoke to Marcus. He said it wasn't Peter. It was some random guys. Thought maybe it was gang members from the Dempsey projects coming by to start trouble.
Nona: The Dempsey Boys? Nope. They only come around when they have an actual beef with a specific person. And they aren't going to randomly jump Marcus and Lance. I've known the DBs to actually help the Hester Boys when a dirty cop comes around. And they left me flowers when Kendall was killed, because real recognize real. They aren't that kind of gang.
Pastor: Are you sure? It seems to me a gang is a gang.
Nona: That's what a lot of folks would like you to believe, but the DBs look after folks too. Security, protection, crime-solving, justice, reconciliation. They give out loans, get folks jobs, take on dirty cops and bad landlords. Like I said. They are not like Peter and these troublemakers in Hester Gardens.

Pastor: Okay. I believe you. But Marcus didn't seem to know the people. It could have been a case of mistaken identity.
Nona: It was a case of Peter. I just know it.
Pastor: Have you spoken to Mother Lincoln?
Nona: I did. She said she talked to Peter and told him to leave Marcus and Lance alone.
Pastor: Okay. And if I know Mother, she didn't mince words. I bet this will all blow over in a day or two.
Nona: We'll see. Thanks for checking.
Pastor: When can I see you again, Nona?
Nona: I have work today. But I'll text you when I'm free.
Pastor: I hope I'm not out of line by saying I miss you whenever we're apart.
Nona: Not out of line. Same.

Jen

Nona trudged toward the Prescott Road bus stop, shielding her nose from the smell of trash oozing from the overflowing garbage dumpsters. Waste management still hadn't emptied the bins.

Her nephew Harlan finally texted her back: They didn't say much about the fight. Said something about the Dempsey Boys? I'll keep digging. In the meantime, need to talk to you about Lance.

Even with their beloved cousin, Marcus and Lance were deflecting. There was just no way they fought the Dempsey Boys. Nona had grown up in Dempsey Woods, and that gang was splintering because the housing project was shuttering. Those boys weren't going to waste what little time and energy they had left to come rough up some folks in Hester Gardens who weren't even in the Hester Boys.

And what could Harlan want to tell her about Lance? She texted him back: It wasn't the Dempsey Boys. Let me know when you want to talk about Lance. Is it bad?

Harlan responded: It ain't good.

As much as it pained her, important information always came from Harlan because, as with Kendall's murder, the police were no help. Harlan was the one to fill in the gaps.

Kendall had been blocks away from Kitledge High when he was gunned down. He'd attended senior day at the lake, the bus had brought them back to school, and he'd eaten nearby at Gus and Sam's Barbecue with his classmates, and then, as he waited alone in the dark at the covered stop to come home, someone shot him through the heart and killed him. Coroner said he'd died instantly. The streets had been busy, and passengers in a car driving by saw his lifeless body crumpled on the sidewalk and called 911. Harlan had told Nona back then that he'd listened to the call to see if he recognized the voice, but he didn't, and the caller was white, which was zero help.

No surveillance cameras were installed at the location, and the people who'd called for paramedics had not been there when the shooting happened. Medford Church of God in Christ had raised a ten-thousand-dollar reward for whomever had information, but no witnesses came forward.

Why couldn't she catch a break? What had Lance done now? He'd obviously been drinking at the graduation party. And he'd been hanging around Donnell a lot lately, and anyone related to Mable Cleveland couldn't be up to anything good. Had Lance moved on to weed? Something stronger? Had the mystery fight been related to Lance? Had he joined the gang?

Her mind went to Marcus: the way he glared at her. The tone of his voice. That hand that seemed it was itching to hit her.

Gray clouds hung over the Gardens, and the air portended rain. Vega Lawson sat in her rickety white lawn chair, sipping from her white mug, which gossip said was filled with coffee and Canadian Club whiskey. Nona had never smelled alcohol on Vega, and the woman referred to drugs and liquor as poison.

Nona waved.

"Hey, church lady."

Nona didn't mind the nickname because Vega always said it with a smile. Since Vega's home was at the front of the Gardens, she was like a sentinel for the community. She knew everyone's comings and goings, and also seemed to read minds.

When Nona first met Vega, she'd been told the woman used to work as a scientist at the bottling plant but was fired because she'd lost her mind when she lost her husband. Gang members often tried to ply the gangly brunette with drugs, but Vega would spit at them for even suggesting it.

"Tell Marcus I said congrats on his graduation." Vega winced.

"Will do." Nona tried to read Vega's facial expression. Was her pain owing to her son Solomon finishing high school but never making it out of the Gardens?

Old-school rap blared out of a speaker, a Bone Thugs cut about the crossroad between life and death. Nona tried to ignore the song and the hoots and hollers of her jobless neighbors drinking and smoking.

Men huddled together and whispered. Twenty yards ahead of her, women with laundry bags also headed for the bus.

A basketball bounced against the pavement, and Vega's son Solomon emerged from the alley. With a drop in her stomach, Nona searched the concrete and brick space behind him, where she'd discovered the truth of her husband, where he'd made her a part of his sin.

The former Kitledge High center towered over her. She'd been so disappointed when he didn't get recruited to play in college and instead joined the Hester Boys. The sounds of his ball bouncing around the Gardens morphed, the rhythm gone, the contact with the ground both timid and frustrated.

One thing never changed: He dribbled the orange sphere so often it seemed the ball was attached to his arm. With narrowed eyes, he waved to her, the spitting image of his mother Vega. She returned the gesture and continued to the Prescott stop. Tears stung her eyes. Her oldest, a point guard, used to dunk on Solomon. Back then, Kendall seemed to float on air.

The Metro riders wore jeans, shorts, T-shirts, or uniforms for their janitor or CNA jobs.

As she made her way to the final row, she nodded at Mable Cleveland. Across the woman's body was a bag likely filled with junk pilfered from their dumpsters. The woman pressed her palms against either side of a glass vase of pink water, and her holstered pistol bulged from beneath her shirt. Churchgoers who lived at the Gardens had always warned Nona to stay away from Mable. Had told her that Mable practiced some form of "witchcraft."

"Any word from the plant?" Mable shouted over the crush of people jockeying for seats between them.

Nona shook her head. "I'll let you know as soon as I hear."

Mable nodded, then hung her head. Nona sensed her foreman was dragging his feet in hiring Mable, and when she returned to work, she would ask him why. She hoped Mable's record wasn't standing in the way.

Too perturbed to continue with small talk, Nona sat and stared down at her phone. When she saw she had no new messages, she rested her palm on the bus's window, hoping the cool glass would steady her, calm the swaying in her head, but the day got worse.

Up the bus steps crept Peter Lincoln, typing feverishly on his phone, his shoulders hunched like a cat's, his eyes shaded by gold-rimmed sunglasses, and his beard stretching to his chest. He pushed aside a woman carrying a laundry basket, knocking her against a seat occupied by a man in a Stetson. Peter reached past the payment slot and tossed his coins at the driver before flopping in the first seat, which had a handicap symbol too large to miss. Noticing Nona, he nodded as if doing her a favor by acknowledging her.

She did not nod, smile, nor raise her hand. Where was he headed? It wasn't like he had a job. She checked behind him for his grandmother, but Mother Lincoln wasn't there.

When he turned his attention to the front of the bus, where the woman in a gold head wrap boarded with a bag of laundry and smacked her lips at him for his rudeness, Nona stared out the window at the place where she lived.

Grimy red brick, busted streetlights, bullet holes in doors, boarded-up windows, and tags on every building reading "HB" or "Hester Boys," some of which had been spray-painted by Peter.

Once, her cousin Jackie visited from down south and remarked how the town was gray and flat, and every corner had a liquor store on one side and a church on the other. The putdown had made Nona defensive with its implication that Medford had no culture and its people lacked sophistication.

The bus slammed its doors, and the rickety vehicle crept away from the curb like an old man rising with his cane. Everything was either old or falling apart. Maybe Jackie had been right after all.

Once they were moving, they passed the police precinct and the morgue with a revolving door that never came to rest. She peered through the windows, which were shored up with bars like the ones at her home.

Suddenly, she was under those fluorescent lights again. The tile squeaking beneath her shoes. The coolness of the medical examiner's lab surrounding her, freezing and numbing her flesh. Kendall's wide-open eyes. That shocked expression on his face. The mottled, icy flesh of his forehead. His missing gold watch.

She was at his funeral, where she'd spotted that smug-faced newspaper reporter who'd referred to Kendall's shooting as "gang-related" when her baby had hardly been in a gang. She'd cornered the man, made him think she was going to give him the statement he'd been leaving her voicemails about, and instead, she slapped him hard enough to draw blood from his lip, tears from his eyes, and stares from the crowd.

"You need to get your facts straight before you write articles, or don't

you know how to be a reporter? My boy wasn't in a gang. There's your statement, you vile pig."

She hadn't regretted what she'd done, but it got her no closer to what she really wanted, and that was to have him write a second article in which he told the truth about Kendall. That her boy was college-bound and churchgoing and never had want for the Hester Boys.

"Wake up, Mrs. McKinley." Peter stood over her. When she looked at him, he grinned wide enough for her to get a flash of his gold tooth. She stared at her own reflection in the black lenses of his sunglasses. He smelled of whiskey. His hand was on her shoulder. She slapped it away, stood, and brushed tears from her eyes. She couldn't believe she used to hug and feed this boy like he was one of her own.

"I wasn't asleep. Move, Peter."

She thought of Lance's bloody nose. Marcus's bruised cheek. Peter seemed to have a few fading welts on his chin as well.

He stepped back to let her exit, then returned to typing on his phone as he followed her out. She nodded at the woman with the laundry bag and gathered strength from the woman's smile. She wouldn't let anything ruin this summer, the summer she'd see Marcus off. Not Solomon's listless ball bouncing. Not Peter following her off the bus. She would pull herself together. She wouldn't dwell on the devastating night at the morgue. Nor the grim memories in the alley. She had been to hell and back, and, with faith in God, she was getting through.

Before dismounting, she patted the driver on the shoulder, hoping to atone for Peter's rudeness earlier. With each step down, she gained fortitude, and, thinking of Marcus in the fall, walking across his university's grassy lawn, she even mustered some joy. The devil wouldn't win this one.

❖

Peter: I'm free later today. Let me know a good time to come get Little Man.
Gretchen: Hell no. 'Cause every time you get him you question me about what I'm doing or where I'm going and I'm not doing that any more.
Peter: You was stressed AF in that bathroom the other morning and you still won't tell me what you was doing with Grayson and that wall. There was blood everywhere. You obviously need help. I'm trying to help.
Gretchen: I don't need your kind of help.
Peter: I won't ask you about anything you doing. I just wanna make sure my son is straight, and he can't be straight if you ain't straight. So we need a regular schedule of me taking him so you can calm the fuck down.
Gretchen: You half the reason I'm stressed to begin with! And you know how I worry about your bullshit in the streets catching up to you when he's with you.
Peter: My bullshit buys his diapers and daycare. Didn't hear you complaining about my bullshit when you needed cash for Grayson's clothes. Point is, we gon have to do better for him.
Gretchen: Yeah okay.
Peter: I'm serious, Gretchen. We owe it to him. We owe him everything.
Gretchen: I said okay.
Peter: I'm gon be there today. And I'm patching up that damn wall.
Gretchen: Fine.
Peter: Fine.

The closer Harlan got to Medford, the bumpier the freeway surface became. The grass on the side of the interstate was no longer trimmed, and the trees became sparser and more unkempt.

He parked along Prescott Road and stared out at Hester Gardens' buildings, which, in the gray daylight, appeared as haunted as folks said they were. The windows all had metal awnings above them that darkened the glass, making the openings look like eyes on the verge of tears.

He jotted a line in his notepad: *Feature story on youth violence, particularly guns. Tie in to gun violence as a public health crisis.* He would pitch this soon. He'd sent ideas to *U.S. News Daily* exactly twenty-three times before, but he'd never gotten a buy.

He pocketed his notebook, got out, and removed his collared shirt, as the day was heating up. His white T-shirt felt more appropriate for a walk through the Gardens.

Not much had changed since he lived here with his late mother and imprisoned father. No one was expecting him, but that's because he'd held his arrival for when his aunt was at work and Marcus was at his summer job. He wanted to talk to Lance. That boy had gotten himself mixed into some illegal shit, and Harlan was angry enough to go upside his head.

No one was out as he crossed the grounds. No birds singing like when he was young, because the trees were all dead, with leafless branches baking in the sun. The lifeless elm in the middle of the courtyard reminded him of the black eye he'd gotten just in front of its gnarled trunk. As a kid, he got roughed up a lot by the Hester Boys. The gang members were angry, and being mean to helpless people was the extent of their power.

He knocked on his aunt's door. He waited, noticing that the flowers she'd planted had all died. Footsteps clomped hurriedly on the other side and stopped right before the entrance. He expected Lance to answer—he knew his cousin often skipped summer school and hung out at the Gardens all day with Donnell—but the door didn't open.

"Lance. Open up. It's Harlan. We need to talk." He checked his phone. Ten a.m. He didn't have a lot of time. He had an interview scheduled for eleven across town. He knocked again. Texted Lance, Where are you?

He imagined Lance watching him through the peephole, not expecting Harlan but knowing that Harlan was probably here to reprimand him.

"They're all gone," Vega Lawson called from across the courtyard, her voice echoing off the brick. She hadn't been there moments before, but she now sat in her white lawn chair, back straight, hand covering her eyes since the sun had finally come out. Ms. Lawson hadn't changed a bit since he was a boy, back when she used to point upward and tell the kids that she was named for the fifth brightest star in the sky.

Harlan yelled back, "Somebody's home. I can hear them."

Ms. Lawson chuckled and sipped her coffee. "I said bye to each one of them myself."

Harlan nodded and faced the door again. He had a key. He never used it, but his aunt had given it to him for emergencies. Should he use it now? Did Lance behaving like a knucklehead qualify as an emergency? He fiddled with his keychain but stopped. If no one was home, then who was inside? A thought popped in his head: *What if it's Kendall?*

He imagined his late cousin's smiling face. The way Kendall would pop up at his home unexpectedly and demand that Harlan play a game of pickup with him. All the times Kendall asked to hang out with Harlan but Harlan begged off because of his deadlines. Nope. The noise inside the house didn't come from Kendall. Harlan's grief had gotten to him, as had his guilt and shame for assuming he'd had more time with Kendall and squandering the little he had. This was why he was here to talk to Lance. He feared what might happen if he neglected his younger cousins. He wouldn't fail them again.

His phone rang. Lance was calling.

"Hey, man. I'm out here. Don't you hear me knocking? Open up."

"What? I'm at summer school." Lance's voice cracked, reminding Harlan that Lance was still young, probably felt invincible, and was stupid merely because he had no life experience. "Everything okay?"

Harlan pressed the phone to his ear. Voices, young voices, spoke in the background of Lance's call. His cousin was definitely not calling from inside the house. He knew his aunt and Marcus weren't inside because he'd received texts from both of them this morning as they were heading out. And Ms. Lawson said she'd offered goodbyes to everyone already.

"We need to talk at some point, Lance." He jiggled the keys again. He had obviously imagined the noise.

"All right. I'll call you later today."

"I'm serious, Lance. No bullshit. You better call me."

"No bullshit. I'll call you. I gotta go." And Lance hung up.

"Told you," Ms. Lawson called out, giggling.

Harlan backed up but still stared at his aunt's home. Was the stress from work getting to him? Maybe that was it, because imagining things was a first.

He returned his phone to his pocket and pivoted to go. Something caught his eye in the kitchen window. He couldn't be certain, but he thought it was movement. Maybe a flash of light, a swipe of the curtain, a closing of the glass in the frame. Unease crept up his spine. He slowly, cautiously peered through the glass.

Kendall?

The image threw him off-balance and he stumbled back but managed to stay upright. He squinted, but the only face reflected in that glass was his own.

❖

With a mere fifteen-minute break to use the ladies' room, tend to her mail, and return to the floor before her foreman could dock her pay for tardiness, Nona padded through the glass-enclosed atrium. From this high vantage point, the bottle machine stretching across the assembly room resembled a snake.

The soles of her shoes clicking along the tiled floor sounded like her malfunctioning stove. That morning, the ticking had woken her up and produced a flame higher than the last time. Her worry afterward had kept her awake.

Today, the Up North Tea promotional team escorted a busload of kids from the parking lot through the front doors. When Nona was in fifth grade, the company opened the 180,000-square-foot plant. Her summer camp had taken her on one of the first tours of the facility, where she'd learned about its fifty dock positions and guard shack with more advanced technology than the state penitentiary.

The company marketed to kids, teens, poor folks, and Black people. Nona was familiar with the routine by now: Summer campers sampled all fifteen flavors, including regional favorite "Berry Berry Quite Con-Trerry." The drink was sugary as syrup, and anyone worried about their blood sugar levels would have been wise to avoid it, but it was the sort of thing that got a ten-year-old excited.

These kids oohed and aahed. She wanted to shout: *Run. Go to college. Don't fall for their tricks. Don't end up stuck here like me, with aching ankles, throbbing knees, and knotted neck muscles hard as rocks.*

"Looking good, Nona." Her fellow inspector's collarbone protruded from her shirt. The woman's face seemed gaunter than it had the previous day.

"Aw. You're so sweet, Lena."

It was Lena's job to inspect the tea before it hit the bottles, and Nona checked a group from each batch, ensuring labels and caps were properly affixed and the glass bore no blemishes.

Their jobs used to be automated, but the upkeep for machines was costlier than the eight bucks an hour Nona and Lena were paid.

"What you put in your hair?" Lena asked. Lena smoked weed several times a day and another co-worker said the woman's joints were laced with crack. Nona never confirmed that was true, but she'd spent several years silently judging the woman. Then Lena had been the first to visit Nona after Vance was locked up. And Nona in turn had brought Lena into the women's ministry, which put her in direct contact with a Narcotics Anonymous program. Now that Nona was actually paying attention to the woman's appearance, she worried her co-worker was using again.

"I add a little shea butter to my oil before I blow-dry it. Keeps my hair soft."

"Okay. I'ma try that. You really need your own website or something. Share your beauty tips."

Nona chuckled as she entered the locker area, and she waved as Lena headed outside to smoke. The woman's cigarette use was a telltale sign that Nona's suspicions were valid. Usually, she'd invite the woman back to church, ask how she was doing—how she was *really* doing—but Nona had enough to deal with without taking on Lena's problems again.

She did appreciate Lena's kind remarks. She certainly didn't feel beautiful, but she had in her youth. Before Vance.

The overhead intercom screeched on, and someone bleated out: "Mason Walterson, call on line twenty." Then, "All techs report to conference room seven."

She retrieved the mail from her backpack, flipping through envelopes she'd tucked inside after breakfast. The one on top, stamped with "This letter is from a prisoner at Medford Penitentiary," was from Vance.

She typically read Vance's letters but never responded. If anyone asked, she'd have said he was a bad example for their boys or that she resented him for getting locked up when he promised to always stay and take care of her. Truth was, her resentment began much earlier, with NaDarius. She'd told Vance she'd forgiven him, but really, she hadn't.

Dear Nona,

I hope the money I've been sending has helped with Marcus's graduation, bills, and getting Lance new sneakers. I know that boy's feet are probably bigger than mine now.

She wanted to shout at the paper trembling in her hand. "*Yeah. Both of our remaining sons' feet are bigger than yours now, and you haven't helped me buy nary a shoe, mofo.*"

You haven't answered my letters or calls, and I don't hold that against you.

Hold it against her? The nerve. The effing king-sized nerve. As if he had a right to hold anything against anyone ever again.

I promised you this wouldn't happen, and it's happening. You haven't divorced me either, so I'm praying you expect me to come home when my time at the country club is over.

There were so many things wrong with that last sentence that she tamped down the urge to rip apart the letter before finishing it.

Either way, want you to know I love you and our boys always. I'm dying inside every day that Kendall is gone. I enclosed a sketch I drew of him flying his kite. Remember how he used to do that?

You are my forever.

Vance

First of all, his bit about the "country club" was not cute. Something stirred inside her each time he put it in a letter. Vance downplayed everything and never took responsibility for his actions.

Second of all, she didn't have time during the day to make art. Did he think she wanted to see that the fruits of her husband's labor were now the equivalent of an eight-year-old's afternoon in day camp?

Third of all, even in her anger she could see that the sketch was gorgeous. He'd used pencil to draw the park near Kitledge High, with the elm tree where they used to spot cardinals, and Kendall, his sneakers untied, holding a string that floated toward the sky where it was attached to a dragon kite. As a preschooler, Kendall used to pretend to be a dragon stomping through their living room and breathing "fire" on his toys. In Vance's drawing, the kite was pulling Kendall into the air, one untied sneaker dangling from his airborne foot. Her throat clenched and tears burned the corners of her eyes.

Vance had used color only on Kendall, the kite, and a cardinal flying past a cloud, so those three figures were the bright ones on the page. He'd signed his name at the bottom and titled the piece "Flight."

Her stomach knotted as she folded the papers and shoved them into her bag. She wanted to sever the tie between her and Vance, to get rid of his hold on her. Each letter was his way of strumming the cord they shared. She hated him and wished she could hate him more. Her mind strayed to NaDarius. *Focus.* She took a deep breath and reached in for the next set of letters.

The water company had sent a shutoff notice. The thirty dollars Vance wired into her credit union account each month should have cleared already and would have to go toward this bill. She didn't know the source of Vance's money other than it came from a company in Florida and always sent on the fifteenth.

The next letter was from Brown University. It was addressed to Marcus, and she must have accidentally picked it up along with her mail. She flipped it over. He'd already opened it. She pulled out the paper and saw he'd been late with a registration fee.

The figure was a thousand dollars. The number on the page sent a painful wave through her. She continued reading and discovered he could have waived the amount due to hardship, but that deadline had already passed. The message also said they'd issued this statement to Marcus in early spring and had given him an extension, but could not allow him to register for classes without it.

She. Could. Scream!

She checked the clock. Five minutes left. Hands shaking, she phoned him, imagining his accomplishment slipping away, imagining him trapped in Hester Gardens forever.

A text from Pastor: I saw a beautiful red rose and it made me think of you. Hoping I can see you again soon. She'd have to respond to him later.

At this time of day, Marcus would be at their church helping with the youth ministry, probably holding some kid's hand as they went from basketball to morning snack on the back lawn.

"Everything okay?"

Since Kendall had died, that's how Marcus and Lance answered whenever she phoned them at an odd time.

Her voice wasn't exactly a whisper, but it was low enough that folks standing near the lockers couldn't hear. "Why didn't you tell me about this fee you owe for college?"

"You're going through my mail?"

"You better thank God I did." She'd bragged to anyone at work, church, and Hester Gardens who'd listen that Marcus was going to an Ivy League school on a full ride, and, other than a few fees here and there, she owed nothing. She'd thought "a few fees here and there" would be twenty or thirty dollars, not a thousand.

"Hold on." Kids shrieked in the background of Marcus's line. One yelled, "You're it!" Then a creaking noise, a whoosh and thump, and suddenly the kids' voices were far away. "There's always a catch, Mom."

That was Vance in his voice. Marcus probably had that same frustrated gaze, shoulders slumped as if life was consistently conspiring against him. If Vance were still around, Marcus never would have doubted their ability to pay that fee. Vance always found a way. Same if Kendall had still been alive. When she had help, Marcus and Lance never doubted her.

"Mom?"

"Yes. I'm here." She took a deep breath to stop herself from crying. "They offered an entire process to get this fee waived, but since you didn't tell me in time to actually *do* anything about it, we now owe the money. Do you realize what this means? You were about to give up on your future for something that is actually surmountable. Why would you do this?"

"I don't know. Maybe because we're always struggling for money. And this didn't seem surmountable to me. This seemed like something that would mean no food in the fridge. So, I figured, why bring it up to you? You have enough to worry about."

"I have enough to . . . ? Well, you know what I think? I think you no longer want to go."

"What?"

"I think you're scared."

"I'm not scared."

"You haven't been acting at all like somebody who is on his way to college. You haven't checked on housing. Haven't researched anything. You're getting into fights and lying to me about it—"

"I haven't—"

"And now you conveniently neglect to tell me about a fee for school when you are a summer away from a better future."

"A better future? Well, when stuff like this happens, I think a better future isn't in the cards for us."

"Are you listening to yourself right now? You sound like . . ." She didn't want to tell him he sounded like his father. She didn't want to invoke Vance's name in this conversation at all. And she knew when he said "stuff like this," he wasn't just talking about the fee. He was talking about Vance's imprisonment and Kendall's murder. "You can't give up so easily, Marcus."

Her eyes focused on the clock. She now had two minutes.

"We can't get a thousand dollars by the end of the month."

"You let me worry about that. You should've told me when you first got this. I could've been working on it. And what was your plan? Let the clock run out and not register? Ignoring problems won't make them disappear."

Silence on his end. He probably had those sad-puppy eyes that always melted her heart. She hated he'd been carrying this burden silently and alone. Maybe this was the real reason for the recent changes in his behavior.

"One person not going to college never hurt anybody."

"I don't have time for this foolishness. Figure out what classes you want to register for."

"Okay, Mom." His smile came through the phone. "You know I love you."

"You better. After all I do for you." And she would keep doing for him, but she had no idea how she was going to get that money.

When she returned to the machine, she inspected bottles quickly. She glanced up at the overhead offices where her foreman Ashford sat at his desk, hunched over his computer, squinting. A hi-lo rumbled and beeped as it transported the crates to the dock.

Marcus. Her middle baby. She had to get him out of Medford. He was special. Had God's anointing upon him. Labor had been nine hours from start to finish, and he'd been in such a hurry to come, she got the urge to push before her water broke, and Marcus was born with the amniotic sac fully intact.

The doctor had to pierce the membranes to release the water and pull him out. He was eight ounces heavier than Kendall had been at birth but was still under seven pounds. When she held him for the first time, his face pulled into a frown, his lips almost closed as he howled, his cries sounding like "Mama" from birth.

The doctor told her and Vance that babies born with a full or partial caul were so rare, Marcus was the doctor's first "veiled" delivery. One in every eighty thousand births. And Vance, holding Marcus for the first time, said, "You know this means he will be able to see things we can't."

She had laughed and said, "I thought it meant he would have good luck or couldn't drown or something."

And Vance responded, "It means that too."

Vance had been right about the clairvoyance: Whenever she'd go to Marcus's crib to check on him at night or in the morning, his eyes would already be open, his smile expectant.

The beeping in her ears pulled her out of the memory. Lena had fallen asleep at the machine and accidentally flipped a switch that started a repeated beep.

Where would Nona get the money? Even if she got a cash advance, her paycheck wasn't large enough to cover the fee and her bills too. Donating at the plasma center didn't get her anywhere near a thousand dollars. No one at work or Hester Gardens had that kind of cash, and if they did, they weren't in the habit of letting people know about it because they wanted to avoid folks like Nona coming to them for help.

Nona walked to the switch, powered everything down, and roused Lena. The woman hiccupped and flashed Nona a wan smile.

Nona returned to her station. There was always her nephew Harlan. He lived in Sebastian Hills and drove a car, but the last time she'd gone to him for cash, he told her he wouldn't be able to keep fronting her rent money because he was saving for grad school. She sensed he'd made up the grad school part to not loan her money anymore.

There was only one place she could get it.

When she headed home hours later, she finally responded to Pastor: Thinking of you as well. Can we meet?

Within seconds, he replied: Of course. When?

Nona arrived in her church's parking lot on foot to find First Lady Davis tiptoeing in four-inch heels across the concrete, the diamond studs in the woman's ears catching sunlight.

Medford Church of God in Christ sat on the corner of Lockheed and Cass, framed by an auto body shop, a McDonald's, a payday advance spot, and a liquor store. The four-story building was the largest on the street, with double doors, stained-glass windows, and an iron gate that wrapped around the manicured grass.

The half-acre lawn boasted two water fountains and a digital billboard announcing Sunday services at eight a.m., eleven a.m., and four p.m., and Bible study on Wednesdays at seven p.m. To maintain the gourmet kitchen, on-site gym, and business center, it took three collections per service: one for the scripture-mandated tithes and offerings, one for the deacon board, and one for the building fund.

First Lady Davis waved to Nona with a dazzling smile, then bent, sat in her teal Jaguar, and folded her ankle-length skirt into her lap.

The woman's hair had been neatly flat-ironed down to her shoulders, and her red lips and blush were impeccable. She wasn't much of a "looker" otherwise. Her face was not at all symmetrical, but she worked wonders with what she had.

The first lady typically stopped and talked to all her congregants, but as she backed out of her labeled parking space and burned rubber to the end of the lot, she eyed Nona in her sideview mirror. Nona waited patiently and smiled until the woman was out of sight.

She knows.

Everyone knows.

And everyone blamed her. Because she was the woman. The woman got the blame for her behavior and for the man's.

It was impossible for her and Pastor Davis to be around each other without the two of them smiling brightly. She'd noticed it. He'd noticed it. He often said to her, "I think we managed to find our soulmate at the wrong time." And she'd correct, "More like our kindred spirit."

Nona pushed open the double doors and entered the corridor. Even the air smelled better when she was away from Hester Gardens with that rotten trash odor wafting out of its dumpsters.

Donnie McClurkin's "Speak to My Heart" played on the overhead speakers. Maybe God sent her that song to tell her to stop. To turn around. To go home. To come up with a different plan.

In a nearby rehearsal room, the choir practiced a lively, fast-paced song in preparation for the midsummer festival. The floor shook as they held notes, clapped, stomped, and swayed.

The soloist waved and winked when she saw Nona. The musical director, who'd been the first lady's college roommate, glared over her shoulder at Nona. The woman slowly faced the singers again, her movements stiffer that time.

Nona kept her head down and eyes low as she moved through the window-filled halls on a day when she really had no business, literal or figurative, at the church, but as she passed the kitchen, the sous-chef shouted, "Nona!" He removed a rack of buns from the oven. "You better grab one of these on your way out or you won't get one all summer."

"I promise," she mouthed, avoiding eye contact with the folks filing through the hall with gowns and sheet music.

The young man from Marcus's graduation party who seemed like *security? A gruff assistant? A nephew Pastor was mentoring?* stood just outside Pastor's office, but he did not look up from his phone at Nona's arrival. Pastor's gray-haired receptionist said he was finishing up a conference call with a city council member.

Pastor reiterated this fact to Nona when he opened his door and kissed her on the cheek right next to her lips. He seemed upset.

"Everything okay?" She entered behind him, and he firmly closed his office door.

The phone rang. He backed up to his desk to check the caller ID, picked up the receiver, pressed the "end" button, and returned it to the base.

He let out a long, loud sigh. "It's . . . Things have been rough around here."

She noticed three stacks of cash on his desk next to his phone. The church had accountants. Why did he always have so much money with him? She talked down the voice. Pastor was not Vance. Pastor was a man of God.

"Rough how? You want to talk about it?" They always spent their time together discussing her problems, with Pastor helping her sort through them. She rarely asked him about his life, but he must have had his own worries.

He grinned. "I wish I could tell you everything. But I worry you . . ."

He appeared sheepish.

"I . . . what?"

He grinned and held up his hands in surrender. "One day I'll come clean."

Come clean? She didn't like the sound of that. Vance had come clean one day, and look at where that had gotten her.

Pastor hugged her and motioned to the chair. He was sixteen years her senior, a fact that seemed to bother him. The first time he'd flirted with her, he'd said, "I can't believe I was already sixteen when you were born. I feel like you get me. Like we're the same age." She agreed, though she wasn't sure it was a good thing.

At fifty-eight, he was gray at the temples and sideburns, which was the only way you could tell he was older. His skin was supple; he lifted weights and jogged three miles every morning, and it showed in the way his chest and biceps filled out his shirts. And his smile! It was like the sun had risen in the room. No wrinkles on his face, and no sagging on any part of his body.

All the women and some of the men in the congregation wanted him, but he wasn't a flirt and never did anything untoward with any of the other people at the church, though many of them wished he would. Lust was not his sin. Ambition was. With the daily phone calls, sometimes twice a day, and the text messages in between, it was obvious he held a special place in his heart for her, but she really didn't know what he saw in her. Maybe he liked having someone broken to fix.

Back up, Nona. Turn around. Run from this church.

She sat in one of two chairs in front of his desk, and he wedged between her and the work surface to take the seat next to her. He grinned as their knees touched. He smelled of fresh linen. He licked his lips, and her eyes went to his mouth.

He appeared more sun-kissed than usual, his muscles more defined than she remembered. Why couldn't he be a sloppy older pastor, hunched over in suits that were too loose? That was half the reason she never told Pastor no. The man was beautiful, intelligent, well-spoken, and charming.

"Is everything okay?"

"I'm still just worried about Marcus."

"When I talked to him, he said he was gathering a list of things he'll need for college."

"He is."

"See? That boy is going to make all of us proud. I never had kids, but your boys are like my own." When he laughed, his eyes became wet in the corners. "God's favor is upon Marcus."

She forced a smile. She'd rushed home and put on a full face of makeup and was wearing a cleavage-bearing blouse. Oh, God. She was definitely going to hell. She knew exactly what she was doing. Knew exactly what Pastor wanted her to do. It had been growing for months, for years, really. Ever since Vance was out of her life. It was like Pastor saw an opening and filled it. "You make me want to be a better man. And you make me smile, Nona." That's what he'd always say. And he'd pair it with, "You make me do other things too, but let's just focus on the smile." And he'd chuckle. And she'd giggle. She loved it more every time he made the joke.

"You still seem unhappy, Nona. Are you having second thoughts about him going away?"

"It's not that, Pastor."

"Timothy." He grinned, then grew concerned again.

The first time he'd asked her to call him Timothy, he'd told her how Timothy was a disciple of St. Paul who traveled with him to spread the message of Jesus. He'd told the story with great mirth, as if telling of his own works.

"Is it Lance?"

"No. Lance is . . ." She couldn't exactly say Lance was fine, since she and Pastor both knew that of all her sons, Lance was the trouble. And she and Harlan had yet to find a time for him to tell her what he knew of Lance. She'd been avoiding thinking about it. "Lance is Lance."

She chuckled awkwardly. Pastor's eyes landed on her chest and returned to her face. "I came to tell you that Marcus can't register for his college classes after all."

Her grandmother had told her to never ask for money outright, but rather to state the problem and ask for advice. She was likelier to get the cash that way.

"Why not?" His voice deepened. He pursed his lips. "His financial aid package is—"

"They have an enrollment fee that he told me about too late

for us to waive before the fall. And he can't register for classes without paying it."

She removed the letter from her pocketbook and opened it near her breasts to draw his attention there. She'd have to say an extra Our Father that night before bed.

"I even called the registrar's office." She remembered the woman's kind voice on the phone. A sista. The one who'd whispered, "Girl, let me give you a little inside tip since you sound sweet. It looks like a mistake that Marcus received the letter. I can put in the request to waive the fee and even put a rush on it, but by the time your request goes through the system and makes it back to you, we might be weeks into the semester already and he might not get the classes he wants because they are filling up as we speak. You'll save him and you the headache if you just figure out how to pay it now, and I can get it reimbursed later."

Pastor took the letter from her, held it away from his face, and squinted. His eyes scanned the page and came to rest on the thousand dollars before the "sincerely."

"This can't . . . What about the Brown Promise? A hundred percent of tuition for students who are in need. No loans. All through grants and work-study. Marcus is exactly . . ."

"They have been so generous. And I believe them when they say they will reimburse the money, but his ability to enroll is currently locked, and this will put him behind on everything. It's just the kind of setback that would make him give up completely. I think that's what he's done. Given up. So I came to tell you. I felt bad because you've been so excited for him. You threw him that amazing party. You've been counseling him. You asked him about the fight, and you've been encouraging him. And I just . . ."

She cried. At first it was fake, but when he took her in his arms, her tears became real. Their bodies stayed that way for longer than either of them would have been able to say was appropriate. Longer than when he'd held her in her kitchen.

He rubbed her back, ran his fingers through her hair, smelled her scalp, and as he pulled her closer, he pressed his knee along her thigh and into her warm dampness.

She gasped into his ear and put her arms around his neck, letting her hands caress his shoulders as she very gently rocked herself against his knee. Spirals of pleasure moved up her thighs to her stomach.

As she grew wetter and warmer against his leg, neither of them could deny the physical interaction they were having. He reached a hand under her skirt and gripped her thigh. His other hand found the inside of her blouse, where his thumb stroked her nipple. She brought her hands down, one on his bicep, the other on his erection. He drew in a quick, sharp breath. The hand under her skirt moved farther back and found her bottom. He squeezed and brought her against his knee even harder, the rhythm of her rocking building an even deeper tension there.

Time passed with them groping and petting, their breaths growing quicker, shallower. When he brought his mouth next to her ear so his lips caressed her lobe without kissing the curved flesh there, she climaxed, exploding moisture through her panties and onto his pants. He moaned in her ear, "Nona."

The phone on his desk rang quietly. Even the device knew something was happening in the office. She had not had sexual contact with anyone in the four years since Vance had been gone, and hadn't exactly meant to climax on Pastor's clothing like this. Her cheeks burned, and even though they hadn't kissed or fully undressed, a deep shame took hold of her.

She let go of him and rose. "This— I should go." Goosebumps crept along her flesh, and she had the sudden urge to shower, to scrub herself clean. She could still stop this thing between them. They hadn't had sexual intercourse, so they weren't really having an affair. She just had to tell him no. She would tell him no.

"Wait." He rose too, a wet stain on his pants leg at the knee.

His phone continued to ring.

"No. You have to get that." She realized the moisture on his pants was from her, and she was mortified.

He lightly touched her elbow. Not grabbing her, but also making sure she didn't run off.

"I'll give you the money." Red splotches crept up his neck and across his cheeks. He was usually such a confident man, preaching and counseling. She'd never seen him so vulnerable.

"You can't. I can't, Pasto— Timothy. It's too much money, and I'll never be able to pay you back."

"It's not a loan. It's a gift. Tell Marcus it's a . . . a grant . . . from his church if he promises to remain a member even when he's away."

She hung her head. With his left hand still on her elbow, he took his right hand and raised her chin.

"You must take it, Nona."

She nodded, pulled away, and headed toward the door. He was on her heels, his heat on her back, making her legs unsteady.

"Nona, I . . ." He turned her toward him, pulled her body flush against his so she could feel his erection, and gave her a full body hug. "I've wanted this . . ." He cleared his throat but didn't let her go. "I'll call you in the morning. Usual time."

The next morning, the aroma from Nona's cooking brought out three roaches that scurried along the floor underneath the sink as if invited and looking for their own plates of food. Pastor had phoned her, but she hadn't picked up. She couldn't talk to him yet. Not after what they'd done.

She reached inside the drawer near the stove, pulled out her fly swatter, and slapped each bug dead. Images of her in Pastor's embrace flashed in her mind: the feeling of his breath against her ear, his erection throbbing in her hand. She hated seeing insect guts on the mesh contraption but figured the bugs were punishment for her sins—past and present.

Seated at the breakfast table, Lance snatched up the toast and sausage like someone who hadn't eaten in a week. She and her youngest were a few feet away from each other, but as usual, they coexisted in awkward silence. She still hadn't found a time to talk to Harlan to learn what he knew about Lance.

As she wrapped the squashed roaches in paper towel and stuffed them in the trash, she listened for Marcus down the hall, where water hissed as it flowed from the shower head. The soundtrack of Marcus preparing to leave for his summer job at church filled their home. She needed to tell him about the money before he bumped into Pastor at work and the elder brought it up.

Minutes later, Marcus's electric razor buzzed, and his cell phone vibrated across the back of the toilet. She could even make out the clicking of the roll-on deodorant as he slid it beneath his underarms.

The toilet bubbled, likely filling with black water from the backed-up sewer line. The housing authority had promised they'd add sewage clean-outs to the property, but their vow had been months ago and nothing had changed.

At eight thirty, when gray-covered daylight peeked through the windows to heat up their home, Marcus emerged from the bathroom in knee-length shorts and a T-shirt, and he sized up Lance, who wore a similar get-up. "Why are you dressed so early?"

She could already sense the budding argument between the two of them.

"I'm coming with you right now, that's why I'm dressed so early." Too proud to just ask Marcus if he could tag along, Lance mimicked his brother's voice.

"I can't babysit you at work."

"Lucky for you, I'm not a baby. Don't need sitting."

"Fine. Whatever, Lance. I ain't got time to deal with you."

"Ain't?" Nona cut in. "I hope you don't say 'ain't' at work." She was smiling, hoping to cut the tension with a joke. Sweat gathered above her lip and about her temples. She reached over the kitchen sink to open the windows, but the locks were stuck again. After using her full body weight to pull on them, they budged, but only a smidgeon.

"If my beautiful mother wants me to say 'don't have' instead of 'ain't got,' I think I can manage that." Phone in hand, Marcus strode over and kissed her cheek. He was the Sweet Marcus. Maybe the one who'd fought Peter and had that trembling hand at his side was gone now that he had her help with that outstanding college fee.

She caught movement in the hallway. A shadow grew against the wall, but there was no shift in the daylight outside the window. A shape took form in the shadow, somehow embedded in the darkness. The figure of a thin man emerged.

The silhouette sent a creeping sensation along her arms. Her ears rang. Her head swayed. She placed a steadying hand on the counter. She waited for Marcus and Lance to notice as well, but they didn't seem to. She wanted to ask, but Marcus's comment—*You're the one imagining things*—made her keep the vision to herself.

What if it was Kendall? Watching over them? If the things she saw, heard, and felt were her eldest, would she recognize his presence? Would she sense him even in death?

"You okay, Mom?" Marcus patted her shoulder. She offered a weak smile.

"I . . . Yes. I have news to share."

Marcus sat opposite his brother, snatched up sausage and pancakes from the serving dishes, and removed a hunk of eggs from Lance's plate, putting it on his own.

"Hey!" Lance said, grinning, with crumbs around his mouth.

"Your eyes are bigger than your stomach." Marcus was grinning as well. "When I eat this, it's like I'm helping you out."

"Whatever." Lance stared at his plate, and both her boys chuckled.

This moment made her heart burst with glee. She hated to ruin it. "I got the thousand dollars for you to register!" She forced a smile so big her cheeks trembled. She hoped they'd cheer like when they were little and thought she was amazing. Lance furrowed his brow, and Marcus contorted his face into an expression that seemed more angry than relieved.

In her peripheral vision, the shadow from the hall seemed to slither along the floor and under Marcus's chair, but when she checked, there was nothing there. Marcus's voice brought her eyes back up.

"What? From where?" Ire crept into the way Marcus enunciated each syllable. Perhaps it wasn't anger; rather, perhaps he was afraid to get excited, afraid to hope, afraid to allow his blessings and success to come to him. Her boys were so used to pain, disappointment, and trauma. Joy was scary.

"The church."

Marcus leaned back, his shoulders seeming to grow with the gesture. He dropped his fork on his plate with a clank. He searched Lance's face. Lance shrugged.

She did not like the silent conversation they were having.

"You say 'from the church,' but you really mean from Pastor." Marcus held her gaze. Kendall never would have taken that tone with her.

She glanced at Lance, but he averted his eyes. He had a mouth full of food, and he chewed in silence, his hands resting on either side of his placemat. The remaining eggs wobbled at the edge of his plate, untouched.

"*Pastor* gave you the money, right?" The tilt of Marcus's head reminded her of Vance whenever he argued with her. "Not the church. Not the first lady."

It was not lost on her that Marcus had picked up on this change in her relationship with Pastor. She'd told herself that the boys were so caught up in their own lives that they wouldn't notice how she and the man talked incessantly and spent a lot of time together. Marcus, apparently, knew better.

Marcus's hair was still wet from the shower; he had missed some soap at his hairline. Same as when he was a toddler, when he feared getting shampoo in his eyes and would never let her fully rinse it out. She reached over to wipe off the white residue, but he leaned away, his lip curling. Did he just snarl at her?

"Whatever, Mom."

"Point is, you are going to college."

"Point is, loans have to be repaid."

"He said it was a grant from the church if you promise to remain a member even when you're away."

"Yeah, I bet. Did he use the word 'promise?' You know, like a *vow?*"

"What's that supposed to mean? He cares about you, Marcus."

"This doesn't have anything to do with me." He raised his voice. Her shame deepened, and she let his tone slide.

"It has everything to do with you."

"If I were going to give someone a grant"—he finger-quoted the word "grant"—"I think I'd talk to them about it."

"But I was the one who went to him."

"Exactly. That's my point!"

He rose, bumping into the breakfast table and tipping his cup of juice onto its side. Marcus was a bear again; the shadow in her peripheral vision slid back from beneath Marcus's chair and retreated into the hallway. She tracked it with her eyes but couldn't be certain it had been there at all.

The orange liquid spread across the table, and Lance hopped up and grabbed a dish towel to absorb the mess before it made it to the floor. Marcus stormed out the front door, letting the screen bang against the frame, and Lance went right behind him.

Blood rushed to her cheeks as she backed up and gained her balance by leaning against the refrigerator. She bumped the photos of her boys, and the prints fell to the floor.

The stench of garbage and the din of rap lyrics flowed in as she watched Lance, a sausage jammed into his mouth and another in his palm, rush across the courtyard to remain at the heels of his older brother.

At the main drag that ran along the northern perimeter of Hester Gardens, Marcus and Lance entered the bus stop shelter. She could no longer see them through the window. Tears stung her eyes. She was the world's worst mother. She couldn't win. Not for winning, not for losing, not for anything.

She fastened the deadbolt on her front door and locked the irons, and when she scooped the images of her boys from the floor and returned them to the refrigerator door, she noticed the photo of Kendall was missing. Only the pictures of Marcus and Lance remained. She searched the floor around her. No photo, but the shadow reappeared near her foot and slithered away into the darkness of the hallway. As she followed it, she caught a whiff of something awful. It was more than just the dumpster smell. The odor of innards and musk filled her nostrils. She stopped.

Her anxiety and grief could make her see things, she'd told herself, but the smell? Could her mind make that up too?

Her home closed in around her. She hugged herself as the room grew dimmer and the air became redolent of death. The squeak of knobs in the bathroom as the faucet suddenly sprayed water into the sink. The toilet bubbled. She tiptoed into the hall, trying to sense the being there. Was it Kendall? Shouldn't his presence make her feel calm, protected?

No one was in the bathroom. Black, backed-up sewage filled the toilet bowl. She flushed it and turned off the sink water. The knob was wet, as if a ghostly hand had left water there. Back in the kitchen, the stove started up, and the *tick tick tick* echoed throughout her home.

Part Two

Eleven

May 28, 2014

It was a fifteen-minute ride in the back of a squad car for Nona to arrive at the morgue. Her shoes squeaked on the tile. The overhead fluorescent lights cast a surreal effect on the hallway, where she hesitated and stalled. The place smelled of bleach, as if the dead needed purification from their earthly scum before going in the ground.

Death was familiar. Nona had attended more funerals than weddings. Her mother's hand she'd gripped until the bony grasp stopped squeezing back. Her father's burial suit she'd purchased secondhand with the last forty dollars in her savings account. She'd chosen the singer for both her parents' funerals, where the baritone of "Nobody Knows" crept into her soul, but her child? Her firstborn? This was different.

The door moaned open. The frigid air of the medical examiner's lab enveloped her. She'd checked her phone several times on the way in, hoping there had been a mistake. Praying he'd text and say, *Mom, I'm running late. Sorry. On my way*. It was now after eleven p.m. This body was going to be Kendall's.

She would break in two. Or she would turn into an animal and scream and claw at her skin to stop the pain.

Beside him as he lay on that metal slab, she heaved. They hadn't even bothered to close his eyes. Her chest tightened. Her cheeks and eyebrows ached as her face pulled into a wail. She gazed upon her baby as her drool slipped onto his cheek. His face bore an expression of surprise, which bothered her the most. As bad as their neighborhood was, as many young people had been shot down, as often as she'd warned him and prayed over him and tried to get him to see he should be worried too, in his final moment, death had still stunned him.

She put her forehead to his, the way she had so many times after giving him a hug. His flesh was already colder than she'd ever felt it, and when she pulled back to view him again, she wondered whether Marcus and Lance could survive without her, because she was certain she would die.

The first time she'd held Kendall, he was so tiny she worried his wrinkled body would slip from her grip. His first laugh had been so soft she thought it had been gas escaping his mouth. The first time he said "Mama," he'd watched her with eagerness, awaiting her smile, her squeal.

This was her fault.

She'd never gotten her boys out of Hester Gardens.

She'd stayed with Vance.

She'd not encouraged Kendall to leave Hester Gardens the day he finished high school and became an adult.

She was to blame. She'd brought him into an impoverished world and had not made a way for him beyond Hester Gardens' bullet-riddled walls. And now their home had devoured him.

She gave a positive identification for Kendall.

She felt unreal.

She wanted to die.

"Where is his watch?" She didn't recognize her own voice. Her mouth was speaking, but her mind was screaming.

Field Sergeant Victoria Prager held up a clipboard with a stack of papers attached to it. She quickly flipped through the pages. "We don't have a record of a watch."

"It's gold. It's his father's. He had it on this morning when he left. Everything is there except for his watch. He never takes it off. Not for anything. I want to know where the watch is."

Sgt. Prager checked the files again. She rifled through the documents, removed the cap from the pen with her teeth, and frantically scrawled on the sheet in front of her. "A watch wasn't recorded here, but we're still investigating, and we'll definitely look into it."

Outside a glass window, Gretchen and Kiki waited on a bench, pressed into each other so tightly the cousins seemed sewn together. They made eye contact with her, their faces pulled into an expression that asked, *Is it him?*

She nodded. Kiki screamed. Gretchen pulled Kiki's face into her bosom, and she rocked her older cousin, muttering words, a prayer perhaps, that Nona couldn't hear.

Kendall's surprised expression flashed in her mind. What if he'd been shocked by who had pulled the trigger? Who would do this to him?

Sgt. Prager hugged Nona, but Nona was numb to the gesture. As Sgt. Prager ushered her out of the morgue, Nona stared back at the door that separated her from Kendall's body. She wanted to place a blanket over him, to keep him warm, to tuck him in. She wanted to rock him to sleep and lie beside him until he woke again.

She wanted to be placed in a casket with him and lowered six feet under the earth, where the cold could seep in and envelop her. She was his mother, the person who'd brought him into this world. She should take his place in death. That replacement, that atonement for her sins . . . It only seemed right. It only seemed fair.

Twelve

June 6, 2016

She rode three buses to get to her nephew's Sebastian Hills home. She agreed to this lengthy trip because Harlan was still covering a shooting at the suburban high school in his neighborhood as well as a mass shooting at a birthday party. He was on deadline to file follow-up stories with his editor at eight a.m. It was now seven.

When she arrived on Harlan's porch, he threw open his front door and forced a smile. The odor of booze greeted her. Red-eyed and unshaven, he hugged her fiercely, and it reminded her of the way Kendall used to embrace her.

Inside, Harlan powered off the rap music he'd been playing when she arrived—she recognized it as "Lord Knows" by Meek Mill because Lance listened to the song on repeat.

"You don't have to turn it off because of me."

He grinned, but his eyes remained distant. "Explicit lyrics. Too much for your holy ears."

Nona figured he was still shaken from the shootings he'd been covering.

"How bad are these latest ones?"

As Harlan closed the door, his shoulders slumped. She caught sight of the framed photo of him with his on-again, off-again girlfriend Trina. In the image, Trina smiled. Harlan did not. No longer hanging on the nail on the wall like on Nona's previous visit, the picture was instead lying face up on a console table. The couple must have been off again.

Harlan shook his head as he led her through his foyer. His entryway was larger than Nona's entire living room.

"For the *school* shooting, kid shot two girls and a teacher. I think the only reason he didn't kill more is because they'd just had their active shooter drill the previous week, and the rules were fresh in the kids' minds. You know: Hide. Be silent. Keep the doors locked. For the *mass* shooting, that kid had killed a bunch of boys on his street before driving to the party and spraying up folks in the yard."

"Oh my God. Did either of the shooters survive?"

"School shooter eventually killed himself. Mass shooter? They took him into custody."

She didn't need to ask any more questions about the mass shooter. In her previous conversations with Harlan, "taken into custody" was code for "the killer wasn't Black." According to Harlan, police typically killed Black shooters. If someone was "taken into custody," they were likely white or a white-looking person of color.

"I met my deadlines, but each story gets tougher and tougher because when the shooters are white, the write-ups are all about how they came from a wonderful family and no one can believe that he would do this. He was a great student, he was an athlete, he liked to help little old ladies across the fucking street. Sorry. Language."

"It's okay. I know you're—"

"But let that same shooter be Black. He's just a criminal. Honestly, when I cover shootings and the victim is Black, they act like the dead child deserved it. 'He was no angel' and that bullshit."

"That's what they did with Kendall. They acted like he was a gang leader."

"And it's messed up." Harlan passed his wet bar and picked up a lowball filled with liquor. He carried it down the hall but did not drink. "Anyway . . . I'm just . . ."

"I don't know how you keep doing this. Covering death and killings all the time."

"I'm starting to wonder the same thing. I can't get any traction on these stories. I just sent off another pitch to *U.S. News Daily*. It looks at how these young shooters, whether inner-city, school, or mass shooters, are in some form of crisis. And be they in a gang or a lovely suburban household, they've either been victimized or traumatized or they've seen violence happen to someone they care about. They have access to guns, and while the majority of the shooters are white, still somewhere around sixty percent, there's a growing number of people of color committing these crimes. They all still get better treatment in the media than Black folks, of course. I'm saying that these killings are all connected, but my pitch will probably get rejected like the others. The shootings are becoming common enough that folks don't seem to care anymore."

"Folks do care, Harlan. Especially mothers. We care."

He shrugged. "Yeah. I'm hoping to tie it into a larger multi-part feature about gun violence as a public health crisis like how cigarettes and car accidents were tackled in the past, but shit ain't changing. Gun laws are . . . Look. I have coffee if you want. I need some."

She nodded and followed him into the kitchen, where he went to the sink and poured that lowball down the drain. She was unsettled by his abrupt change in subject.

Every time she visited Harlan's home, she was in awe of how spacious it was. She could stretch her arms to her sides if she wanted without touching furniture or walls. Sophisticated things he probably took for granted filled his home: real wooden floors that echoed when she walked across them, subway tile in the kitchen, marble counters, sturdy cast-iron cookware.

She once asked him how it felt to be in such a beautiful home in a safe neighborhood, and he'd responded, "Safe for whom? I'm surrounded by white folks. If I jog around the block at dusk, I have to worry they'll call the police or shoot my ass."

When she sat at the table and he started up a stainless steel and black machine on the counter that looked like it belonged in a fancy coffee shop, her hands trembled. She hoped whatever he had to tell her about Lance wouldn't break her heart.

"Heard from Uncle Vance recently?" Harlan's deadpan voice offered no trace of the jovial young man he used to be. That version of him died with Kendall.

"I try not to hear from your Uncle Vance."

"He misses you."

"I know. He writes me letters."

"Well, I still go out to see him . . . and my dad."

"I know. He writes me letters."

Harlan chuckled. "And he looks good. Taking care of himself. Thinks he's going to come back to a life with you after he gets out."

"I know." She actually managed a grin. "He writes me—"

"Not budging, Auntie?"

"You already know I'm not budging."

He gave a sad smile. "I want to tell you about Lance."

"Okay." The room shrank. The air shifted with her nephew's change in tone.

"I've been trying to get him to call me back, but he's avoiding me. He's been hanging out with Donnell."

"I know."

"Police think Donnell and Lance robbed a house out this way with a lady inside."

"What?" She cleared her throat, let that information wash over her. Robbed a house? Lance wouldn't rob a house. Wouldn't have any need to rob a house. They weren't living in the lap of luxury, but they made ends meet. And they certainly had more things recently with Pastor's help: fridge stocked with food, heat, television, video games, no more bill collectors breathing down their necks. All of the little extras that Vance used to provide. No. This was Donnell's influence. "When you say 'out this way,' you mean here in Sebastian Hills?"

Harlan nodded.

"I thought you were going to tell me they'd smoked weed together or something."

"I wish it were just weed smoking."

Her baby couldn't rob a house, could he? She wanted to show up to his summer school and whip his tail into next week. After everything they'd been through with Vance going to prison and losing Kendall, Lance had the nerve to pull some mess like this? "They're planning to arrest them?"

"Don't think they have enough evidence. Donnell was there at some point hooking up satellite, and police think he chose that house because the folks had recently moved in and didn't have any cameras or alarms. Sounds like Donnell was going to hurt the lady inside, but Lance roughed Donnell up and forced him to leave. So, if they're caught, it won't just be some sort of burglary–property crime thing. Donnell threatened her, so this would be more serious. So far, lady won't I.D. them."

"Won't I.D . . . ? She's scared?"

"She's Black. Doesn't want police coming after them, I guess."

"Lord, have mercy." God's grace was the only thing keeping that woman quiet. "Then how can they finger Donnell and Lance if the lady won't talk?"

"Donnell running his big mouth, and it must have made it to an informant. I'm telling you so you can get those two away from each other."

"Okay." She was grateful her baby didn't want to hurt anyone, but how long would that instinct last? At some point early in life, Vance probably hadn't been capable of hurting anyone either.

She rose to go. She had to find a way to get her boys out of Hester Gardens. If she thought Harlan would agree, she would send both of them to live in this beautiful home with her nephew. Only ten miles away and they'd be living in a completely different world, but Harlan had enough problems, starting with the booze.

She patted his shoulder and kissed his forehead, and on her way to the door, she picked up the framed photo of Harlan and Trina. She nodded at him to make sure he saw as she hung the wooden square back on the wall.

The gunshot woke Nona. A single blast, so loud it sounded like it was coming from inside her home. Silence after. She jumped out of bed, knocking over the Bible, lamp, and cell phone on her nightstand as she rushed into the dark hallway.

A shadow stood at the other end in the moonlit bathroom doorway. A figure too tall to be Marcus or Lance. The way the shape held its head, tilted to the side as if thinking, reminded her of Kendall. Same height as Kendall. She remembered the voice in her home. *It's me.* Had it been Kendall all along?

She snapped on the hall light, but no one was there. Could Kendall's spirit visit them? Did she really believe that could happen?

She rushed to the boys' bedroom, threw open their door, and clicked on their overhead light.

They both were in their beds, hair misshapen from their pillows, red eyes, faces swollen from sleep. They squinted against the light.

"Mom? What's wrong?" Marcus put his hand in front of his eyes as he sat up.

"You didn't hear that gunshot?"

Lance rose as well. "Was it close? I didn't hear anything."

They both exchanged glances and then searched her face. Lance yawned. Marcus rubbed his eyes. Their silence shifted something inside her; she was losing her grip on reality.

"Never mind." She backed up, reached for their light switch. "Yes. It was far off. Probably not even at the Gardens."

They sighed out of frustration and were each already lying back down when she turned off their light and closed the door.

A presence moved beside her in the hallway, its motion creating a breeze on her skin. Was Kendall really there beside her? Was he not at peace? Was he protecting them? Warning them? Or something else?

Or was the entire episode just her imagination? Maybe she'd still been dreaming.

She checked the front of her home, and the doors and windows were locked. The stove wasn't malfunctioning. Even the refrigerator's hum was quieter than usual. She peered outside and no one was milling about her unit or in the courtyard. Silence and calm enveloped the Gardens.

So she'd imagined both the gunshot and the figure in the hall? What was happening to her?

She returned to her room, replaced the lamp and cell phone on her milk crate nightstand, climbed into bed, and pulled her Bible next to her, holding it like one of her sons when they were babies.

A floorboard creaked in the hall, but the boys' bedroom door hadn't opened. The noise was probably the house settling, but she rebuked whatever was out there just in case.

Could Kendall have been the shadow she'd seen in the hall? Both this night and previously during the day? Could he have been the voice she'd heard that morning of the graduation? She told herself she couldn't think it. Wouldn't think it. But with each encounter, her resolve was waning. She rebuked it all: the fear, the tortuous memories, the thought that Kendall wasn't at peace and had returned home for purposes unclear to her. The thoughts swirled, and she was unable to sleep until hours later, when the sun had risen again.

Thirteen

Nona waited until she saw Mable step off the bus. She wanted to confront her in front of a lot of people in case the conversation went south.

Mable trudged across the courtyard, her head sunk low. Her hands rested in the pocket of her cargo pants, and her T-shirt swung about her loosely, likely to hide her pistol.

"Hey, Nona. Whatcha know good?" The woman's face brightened and then grew concerned when she saw Nona's expression.

"Need to talk to you for a second."

The two of them stepped into the shade of a dead elm tree, red-tagged but never hauled away. Mable sucked her teeth.

"Everything okay?" Mable was tough, but her face still got that nervous, bracing-for-heartache expression. Nona was familiar with that look. All the mothers she knew got it from time to time.

"Police think Donnell and Lance robbed a house out in Sebastian Hills."

"Donnell ain't do it." Mable's lips curled. Vega watched them from her white lawn chair.

"Donnell told somebody he did it, and it made its way to police."

"He ain't told nobody nothing because he ain't did nothing." Mable folded her arms across her chest.

"Okay, Mable." She wanted to shake the woman.

"Don't 'okay' me. He ain't do it." Mable flared her nostrils.

"Well, I don't want him and Lance around each other again."

"Sounds like a conversation you need to have with Lance."

Vega kept her eyes on them as she rose from her chair, likely figuring out whether she needed to intervene.

"I plan to have a conversation with Lance, but I was hoping you'd tell Donnell the same."

"I don't tell my grown-ass son a got-damn thing. He's an adult."

"But he still lives at home. And if you tell him, as a favor to me—"

"A favor to you?" Mable said. "Who is you? I asked you for a favor, and I don't even know if you took my application to that plant."

"Are you really serious right now? I am trying, Mable. And you know I am, but my boss is taking forever to get back to me, and I can't lose my job trying to press the issue for you."

"Ain't nobody losing they job trying to get somebody hired. Bottom line is, you think you better than me. You think you better than everybody around here."

"Better than you?"

"Yes. Better than me. I heard you and ol' church biddy Mother Lincoln whispering about how I stay strapped."

"What are you talking about?"

"Don't play dumb with me, Nona. You made Vance get rid of his guns. You judge me for my guns."

"You're saying this to someone whose son was shot to death?"

"I'm saying this to someone who acts like she don't know what the fuck it takes to survive on these streets. In this country. I didn't just wake up one day and decide to be strapped for shits and giggles. None of us do."

"You're joking."

"Joking? I come from a long line of bad Negroes. That's what they called my ancestors, 'bad Negroes,' because my family owned land in the south. We weren't sharecroppers. We were landowners. We belonged to trade unions, fraternal orders, we farmed, hunted, fished, we owned guns and knew how to use them. And we had to protect the land and the little we had. We never backed down, and we did not kowtow to white folks. I was raised to be that way. And I am raising Donnell to be that way."

Nona scoffed and felt justified in doing so. "You think you're following in some long and heroic Black family legacy by having a holstered gun? By sifting through trash and letting Donnell rob folks?"

"It's called survival." Mable lowered her voice, which was more frightening than if she'd raised it.

"If your family fought so hard for all of their land, then why are you here?"

"Why do you think I'm here, Nona? Why are any of us here? Why are any of us separated from our land, generation after generation, starting over? Pick up a history book after you read your Bible." Tears filled Mable's eyes. Nona knew she had struck something deep in the woman—she'd never seen Mable choke up. Not even when the woman attended Kendall's funeral. "I'm trying to dig myself out, but you don't know what I've been through. You don't know the choices I've faced."

"I've made tough choices too, but just as I told Vance time and time again, I know that guns aren't going to make those choices any easier. I'm trying to keep my boys, my remaining boys, from ending up killed or in prison. I want them to have a future. To move away from here. To not have to face the same tough choices you and I face. So excuse me if I don't want Lance and Donnell getting fingered for burglary and attempted murder."

"Attempted murder?" Mable's eyes grew wide. A blue ball rolled along the ground from behind them, but no one was there.

There was no real attempted murder, and no real witness, since the lady wasn't talking, but Nona had Mable's attention now.

"Who told you something about attempted murder?" Mable whispered. Her tears dried up.

"Did you know about the burglary?" Shaking Mable wouldn't be enough. She wanted to slap the woman, but she remembered that hidden pistol.

"This conversation is over." Mable stormed off. She kicked that blue ball toward the front of the complex and stomped across the courtyard past a wide-eyed Vega. When Mable entered her home, she slammed her front door.

Nona watched the ball roll to the edge of the Gardens. When it arrived at the threshold of Prescott, it disappeared. Nona blinked. Had she seen that correctly, or was this her stress playing tricks on her again? Vega was back in her chair reading a newspaper, so she hadn't seen.

Nona took a deep, calming breath and checked the time. Lance would be back soon, and she headed home so her face would be the first thing he saw when he entered.

Fourteen

"Mom! Calm down. I didn't go anywhere with Donnell." Lance's voice traveled across the kitchen. Nona had kept her windows closed for that very reason.

"You're drinking, probably doing drugs, getting into fistfights, now you're breaking into homes, and—"

"Who told you this?" Lance wasn't usually a hand-talker, but he was doing it now. The motion shook the breakfast table.

"Don't worry about who told me this. Did you do this?"

"No, Mom!"

"I want you to get your act together, you hear me? You want to end up like your father? Like Kendall?"

He put his head down. "You don't understand, Mom."

"What don't I understand?"

He stared into her eyes, perhaps debating whether to tell her anything. "You don't understand what it's like being a guy."

"I'm listening."

"We have to be tough. We have to . . . We can't be weak."

"What does that have to do with—"

"Okay. Remember when I was in preschool? How I used to hit the other kids all the time, was always in trouble, and you used to have to come up to the school and pick me up?"

She leaned forward, rested her arms on the breakfast table, remembering that awful period when her baby was constantly being suspended from school. "You weren't just hitting. You were biting and scratching too."

"Right. And it continued until, like, second grade? And I was always in trouble?"

"Yes." She had no clue where he was going with this, but she was relieved he was opening up to her. She didn't want to do anything to ruin this moment.

"Well, no one ever asked me what was going on. The teachers, you, the principal. Everyone saw me hitting or scratching or whatever, and they listened to the other kid saying what happened. And the other kid would always tell the story like I just up and decided to hit them. And that was never it." His eyes grew wet in the corners. Pink splotches appeared on his cheeks.

"It was always the same two or three boys. I got along with everybody else, remember? At home, I got along with Marcus and Kendall. I got along with the boys here at the Gardens. And at all my after-school activities. It was only ever at school. Those boys were picking on me. They picked with everybody in the class, actually. And I was the only one who fought back."

"I never knew you were fighting back." Her anger wasn't as sharp. She had the urge to hug him.

"You never asked. No one ever asked. They just thought I was bad." He got those puppy-dog eyes and folded his arms across his chest. He was three years old again.

"What does that have to do with you and Donnell?"

"Donnell isn't the problem, Mom. What I'm saying is that boys can't be weak. It's different with girls. If we let somebody take our lunch and we don't do anything, they will take our lunch every day and we'll be hungry. But if we go upside their head, then they eventually learn to leave us alone, and we can eat our lunch." He leaned back in the chair as if satisfied that he had made his point.

"I know this. Are you saying that the boys around here are bullying you?"

"I'm saying that in order for me to survive around here, I can't be soft." His voice was exasperated now, as if she were the problem.

"I'm not asking you to be soft, Lance. I haven't raised any of my boys to be soft. I am asking you to . . . gee . . . I don't know . . . not break into houses. Not hang out with boys you know are good-for-nothings. There are plenty of young people at the church for you to hang out with. I have you signed up for basketball camp. You skip it. You skip school. You skip summer school. There are enrichment classes in the church's after-school program."

"All of those things are lame and have lame folks in them." His rude teen tone had returned.

She rose.

"I am done with your excuses. You're choosing to be around folks headed in the wrong direction. So let me be clear, Lance. Stay. Away. From. Donnell. If I find out you've been around him or are texting with him, you will be in a world of trouble with me."

He sighed and seemed ready to make another point, but she was done with the conversation.

She turned to go. Sitting atop Lance's backpack were his copies of *Monster* by Walter Dean Myers that Marcus had given him and *Soledad Brother* from Harlan. She called over her shoulder. "And you need to actually read these books instead of just carrying them around for show."

Pastor: Is Marcus angry with me?

Nona: With me, really. Why?

Pastor: I don't know. He seemed distant. He thanked me for the money, but . . . there was something else there in his eyes.

Nona: He's angry that I went to you for the money.

Pastor: Why?

Nona: He didn't say, but I suspect it has to do with his father. And him not wanting another man around the house, helping me.

Pastor: I see. And what do you think of that?

Nona: I don't know.

Pastor: Well, I know. I want to see you again. To feel you again.

Nona: We should stop.

Pastor: We should. I know we should, but I don't think I can. Can you?

Nona: No. I guess not.

Sixteen

Nona had just opened her Bible to the book of Revelation when the scream rang out. The shriek echoed across the courtyard, piercing the evening air billowing out her drapes. As she rose from the foot of her bed, her knees cracked. She placed the leather book on the milk crate nightstand, and, throat dry and feet heavy, she crept to the window to listen.

The streetlight above the walkway at the back of her home was busted again, so she squinted but only saw darkness. A light breeze brushed her face. Another wail. This one louder. Someone pumping Tupac's "Hail Mary" from their car's speakers lowered the volume until the rap song died.

Shouts in the black of night weren't unusual, but for survival, she had to concentrate on what followed. The screech of tires meant drop to the floor, brace for gunfire. Shouted curses required a fastening of her windows and a prayer to calm the anger simmering outside the glass. A long scream followed by wails? Meant someone was already dead.

Marcus had gone to a school-sponsored bonfire and dance party on the outskirts of Medford for the Kitledge High graduates. It was the same event Kendall had attended the day he'd died, only back then it had been on May 28. She hated to foist her anxiety onto Marcus, but she had asked him not to go. Had pleaded with him, actually, but he'd told her she was overreacting. He would be home by ten. "Eleven at the latest." She'd only agreed because it was related to his graduation.

She removed her nightgown. With thick, trembling fingers, she fished the T-shirt and jeans she'd worn to work that day out of the hamper and pulled them on. She needed to account for her boys.

She'd been seconds from reading the verse about overcoming iniquity by the blood of the Lamb, and she whispered a prayer that her boys would remain covered by that blood.

Her cell phone was not on the dresser top. The wall clock said eleven fifteen p.m. She rushed from her room into the hall and eased open the door to her boys' bedroom. The loud drone of their rectangular fan—on full blast and oscillating from the middle of the floor—drowned out the noise from outside. When she saw Lance asleep, his shirtless back exposed to the house's eighty-degree temperature, it served to ratchet up her anxiety about Marcus.

She watched the curve of Lance's spine as his bones rose and fell in rhythm with his delicate snores. On the other side of the room, the sheets on the twin bed remained tucked beneath the mattress, the pillow fluffed. She closed the bedroom door, muffling the roar of the spinning blades, and another scream tore through the air. A knot grew in her stomach.

She moved to her kitchen. Outside those windows, the high-pitched voice roared in agony again. She squinted, trying to see across the courtyard, but all she could make out were shadows darting through pale light.

Another wail from outside. She was familiar with that pain. As she searched for her cell phone, she accidentally bumped the breakfast table, pushing it tightly against the chairs and sending the bowl of plastic apples crashing to the floor. She'd accidentally left her phone on her kitchen counter again. She quickly texted Marcus: Still at the lake?

She held her breath.

Thirty seconds.

Forty seconds.

She blinked and stared at the refrigerator and the smiling photos of her boys she kept there. Kendall's photo had never reappeared, though she'd searched her entire home for it. She couldn't fret about that now. Marcus should have been home already.

Sixty seconds.

He'd said "eleven at the latest." Why did she let him go? She should have trusted her gut.

The stove ticked, but the knobs were all set to off. She readied herself for the flames to rise up, but when the fire arrived, it was tiny enough to blow out like a birthday candle. Why did the stove keep malfunctioning?

Two minutes.

She returned to the window and peered out. More silhouettes. Some rushing around, others standing still, watching. She couldn't make out any faces. Where was he? What if he had been walking back from the bus and was caught up in whatever was happening outside?

Another scream.

This one longer than the last.

This one with less panic and more despair.

The person was not calling for help, and Nona knew the body lying on the ground out there had either suffered a stab wound or been riddled with bullets. If she had to put her money on one of the two, she'd guess the gun. It was usually a gun, but she hadn't heard any shooting, had she? The music outside had been loud, but she would have heard gunshots over it.

Three minutes.

Her phone's screen displayed a photo she'd taken of all three of her sons flying a kite in the park with their father, their final outing together, all five of them as a family. She took in the image, willing Marcus's response to pop up, but the sigh of relief never arrived.

Not again, Lord. Please. Not again.

She couldn't wait any longer. She called him.

As she stared out the window, hoping she could make out a face, any face, in the gathering crowd, her breaths grew shallow and sped up. She beat back the tears stinging her eyes.

His line rang four times and went to voicemail. "Be smart. Hang up and send me a text."

Kendall used to have the same outgoing message. The laughter in Marcus's voice made her insides scream. She wouldn't relax until he turned his key in the front door.

Another scream outside, and this time the voice of a man shouting, "Everybody, get back!"

She would have to risk her safety to go outside. There was no other way for her to know where Marcus was.

She dialed him one last time, and again his voicemail picked up. She cleared her throat, hoping to sound matter-of-fact and light. "It's me. Did you forget you'd be home by eleven at the latest? Call me."

She texted him: Where are you???

She pocketed her phone and rushed across the kitchen to the front door. The lock on the iron should have popped up as soon as she pushed in the key and turned, but it wouldn't budge. She pounded on the part containing the metal slider with the back of her fist and tried her key again. Still didn't work. She shook the iron door until it clicked, and then tried her key once more. It opened that time. Her heart pounded as she stepped into the chaotic night to search for her son.

The moon passed in and out of view, and she was grateful for the little light at the corners of the clouds. She wouldn't look at the alley. She wouldn't think of NaDarius. Not now.

The zinnias she'd planted had all shriveled, grown deep brown, and died. No matter how well she cared for the things she loved, she struggled to keep them alive.

Vega Lawson sat in her lopsided chair as police lights strobed across her face. The woman typically sipped coffee from a mug with clear lip gloss smeared across the rim, but not tonight.

Vega stared at the people gathered on the concrete walkway, her feet wedged between blades of grass, her toes curling up and down, her hands folded into her lap where her red-and-white housedress bunched at the top of her thighs. Her eyes peered out of a gaunt face, watching the scene around her like the witness to a drama she was not a part of.

Vega's daughter Esmé was the screaming one, doubled over in pain, baring her teeth, her shrieks giving way to a growl.

The police officers spoke to Mable Cleveland. With one hand on a hip and the other struggling with two gallon-sized plastic bags filled with pink water, the stout woman shook her head and shouted, "Oh, we know exactly who did this shit."

The hum of the gathered crowd echoed and bounced off the courtyard brick. Hester Gardens' residents stood shoulder to shoulder in various states of dress, jockeying for position behind the police tape, mesmerized like people peering into an open grave, lamenting the deceased, thanking God it wasn't their turn yet.

Though the sun had long since set, some of the kids' swimsuits were slick with water from the local rec center's pool. A man coming from work at the bottling plant carried a backpack; another held a lunch sack and a plastic water bottle filled with a purple drink. A woman still in her CNA scrubs chatted quietly and frantically with a man cursing through lips half pursed around a cigarette, and tweens and teens lucky enough to own phones snapped pictures. They behaved like the audience of a show and not bystanders encroaching upon a crime scene.

The paramedics radioed for a longer stretcher and bigger body bag. The second ambulance arrived and loaded the remains into a sack that, under the moonlight, glistened not unlike those bags sitting atop the garbage receptacles.

No longer talking to the police officer, Mable Cleveland nodded at Nona, exposing the bulge in her shirt where the woman kept her pistol. Mable crossed over to Nona, the woman's face softer than it had been the last time they'd spoken. Mable must have checked with Donnell about the burglary and perhaps discovered that Nona's information about their boys had been correct.

"Solomon," Mable said. Nona glanced back at Vega, understanding now why the woman's cup was shattered on the ground.

"When?" Nona thought of Solomon's dribbling, slow and methodical, like he'd merely been biding his time on earth. She'd think of him every time a ball bounced, but thank God it wasn't Marcus or Lance.

"Hour ago. She . . ." Mable lowered her voice when she saw Vega watching them. "Says she saw the shooter."

"I didn't say I saw the shooter." Vega's voice was a machete cutting through the night. Heads swiveled and eyes rested on the woman.

"That's your problem, Mable," she said. "You're always jaw-jacking and never know what you're talking about. I didn't say anything about seeing a shooter."

"Sorry." Mable's cheeks flushed red. Mable would have gotten huffy with anybody else for being rude, but Vega seemed to have a hold on Mable that no one else did. A neighbor had once gossiped that Vega got Mable out of prison and helped get her back on her feet, and rumor had it that Vega had taken the heat for Mable on a crime Mable committed after being released. Vega never served time, though, because the judge thought the woman was too "crazy" to know what she'd done but not crazy enough to be institutionalized. So Mable owed her.

"What was it you said, Vega?" Mable's voice was high-pitched and sweet.

"I said I saw a figure."

"A figure?" Mable spoke like a parent humoring a toddler.

Nona leaned in closer, but Vega rose. Mable tried to hug her, but Vega pushed Mable away.

Vega grabbed Esmé's arm and guided her hysterical daughter inside their home. Nona and Mable stood with their mouths open. Nona's heart was heavy. That night on the way to the morgue for Kendall, she'd wondered whether a person could die from grief.

Watching Esmé barely able to walk, it hit Nona that she still didn't know where Marcus was.

"Talking 'bout she saw a figure," Mable said, rolling her eyes, sucking her teeth, and shifting the gallon freezer bags to cradle them against her chest. Nona remembered how she'd invited Mable to church, but the woman had said she couldn't go because she loved to gamble and wasn't going to be acting "all familiar like that with the Lord."

The water sloshed around the bags violently, as if it had its own source of movement unrelated to Mable's fidgeting. Police and residents alike glanced at Mable.

"This wasn't nothing but them boys from over at Dempsey. Ain't none of us heard shit. But it wasn't no figure. He was shot. There was a shooter. But you know how Vega is. Half out her mind."

"Half out her mind or not, she's calmer than I was when . . ." She couldn't bring herself to say *when I lost Kendall.*

Mable winced, seemingly caught in a rare moment of speechlessness.

"I don't think the Dempsey Boys would do this. They get blamed for everything, but you know they're about to close that whole place down. The gang that was there when I was growing up is barely there now."

"Well, who else then?"

Nona thought of Peter. "Probably someone a little closer to home." Despair took hold of Nona. "Have you seen Marcus?"

Mable screwed up her face, and then an eyebrow slowly rose. "Saw him earlier, headed out with Gretchen and them. They were going to the lake."

"Gretchen back yet?"

"Her baby's been crying since she left and is still going, so I'd say no. They probably having too much fun and don't know what time it is. Don't worry, Nona."

It was impossible for Nona to be carefree in this situation. Mable must have sensed Nona's thoughts. The woman shifted the bags to free her hand and touched Nona's shoulder.

"I'll text you if I hear anything."

"I'd really appreciate that."

Mable hesitated, perhaps considering their previous disagreement. She turned to go, and then broke her stride.

"I talked to him."

"To Donnell?"

Mable nodded.

"I talked to Lance too."

"And I thought about what you said, Nona. About your boys and what you want for them. And I guess I always thought by now you all woulda made it out." Mable offered a weak smile. When Nona first met Mable, the woman had a gold tooth in the front of her mouth. The gold and the tooth had since fallen out, but Nona still imagined a twinkle each time Mable showed off the black gap in her smile.

"Yeah? Made it out with whose money?" Nona asked.

"Girl, I heard that." The bags in Mable's hands bulged as she shouted and laughed, and it seemed the water was alive. It pressed against the bag as if trying to get out.

Nona squinted and thought she saw a water-shaped finger push against one of the sacks, but she didn't want to be caught staring, so she quickly looked away. What did Mable have in those bags? Not only was it odd, it also seemed otherworldly.

"Guess it's got to be your own money, Nona."

"I guess so. I still haven't given up on your application, by the way."

Mable nodded but didn't seem convinced. Nona vowed to change that.

On the way back to her unit, Nona's phone vibrated in her hand. A text from Marcus: Bus late. On my way back now.

She could breathe again. She choked down a sob until she couldn't, and she let the sting in her eyes become a stream of tears down her face. She was trembling again, but this time from the pent-up fear leaving her body.

She resisted the urge to send him an all-caps text letting him know A) There was no way the bus was this late, and B) If the bus were, by some astonishing phenomenon, this late, he should have texted her the minute he knew he wouldn't make it on time. She simply returned her phone to her pocket and entered her front door.

Back in her bedroom, she went to her closet and pulled down the shirt her firstborn had worn the day before he was killed. There was nothing particularly special about the Detroit Lions T-shirt nor the day he'd worn it, but it had become the center of her quiet time since he'd died. She'd preserved it in a plastic freezer bag with his baseball cap and belt. And after placing it in the plastic, she never washed it because she wanted to hold on to Kendall's smell.

She returned to her knees at the foot of her bed and held the bag to her chest, grateful that for one more night, her remaining boys were safe. They were covered, she thanked God, by the blood of the Lamb.

Almost out of earshot, a sound traveled to her from the kitchen and down the dark hall. The stove had come to life. The burner ticked, and seconds later, she smelled smoke.

Pastor: I'm hiring someone to fix the stove.
Nona: Thank you.
Pastor: Anything for you. If it doesn't work, I'm getting you a new one. And don't say it's too much.
Nona: Okay. I won't say a thing.

Seventeen

It was her day to visit Kendall. On her way out the door, she could smell Lance from down the hall. He reeked of weed; the skunky odor burned her throat. She should confront him, but since losing Kendall she could only deal with one major problem at a time. Right now, she felt her focus should be on Marcus.

Outside, her eyes accidentally went to the alley behind Mother Lincoln's, where she imagined a thick streak of blood on the ground.

She forced herself to look away, to feel the morning's growing heat, to take in a deep, calming breath, but the stench of garbage enveloped her and interrupted her thoughts.

Long ago, she'd found out by pestering Harlan that trash collection for the city of Medford had been outsourced to a private company.

Midwestern Waste Systems made most of its money not from its suburban customers but through municipal contracts in places like Medford, where its agreements weren't with residents but with the city's public works department, which used taxpayers' money to pay Midwestern Waste for once-weekly collection. Only, consistent collection did not extend to Medford public housing. Nona and other Gardens residents often complained to the public works department that two or three weeks would go by with no pickup.

She passed Vega's rickety white lawn chair. It was empty. She heard Solomon's ghostly ball dribbling as she picked up the shards of Vega's broken coffee mug. Nona ripped down the forgotten crime-scene tape still outlining Vega's unit and placed a casserole of macaroni and cheese outside the woman's front door. Her handwritten note read, *I know your pain. I'm praying for you.*

Mable had left a store-bought rotisserie chicken with a note that said, *We'll get the motherfuckers.* Nona shook her head, removed Mable's note, and tucked it into her purse. More violence was exactly what they didn't need.

Every bus that arrived at her stop was packed with commuters pressed together like body bags. She was lucky to eventually get one with enough space for her to sit alone in the row.

The pothole-filled gray streets near Hester Gardens gave way to smooth black pavement. Stout brick houses with lopsided front doors became two-story homes bedecked in pastel-colored wood siding.

The Metro drove past Willowbrook, the street where the home with the white pillars waited for her. One day she'd be able to afford the down payment, and it would come on the market just in time, and she'd get a cosigner, and it would all go so smoothly, and she'd spend her mornings tending to the daffodils in the front yard. In the summers, she'd water the grass, and in the spring, she'd paint the picket fence white, so its color could always be bright.

The bus circled back through the rougher parts of Medford to her first stop of the morning, which was Prescott Cemetery, known locally as "Bum Graves" because most of its dead had lived poor, lived on the streets, or barely lived at all.

The rusted iron gates screeched as she entered, and nary a living soul stalked the grounds as she carried the carnations to Kendall's headstone at the back of the one-acre graveyard.

She'd always imagined herself and her boys far in the future buried at her church's cemetery, where the grass was bright green and even the mayor had a plot, but Kendall's life had been cut short so abruptly she'd buried him in this place, a double-lot, dandelion-lined churchyard run by a Dominican order of nuns.

Pastor had offered to get him a plot at Medford C.O.G.I.C., but back then she'd been too proud to accept. She'd used her savings to pay for Kendall's headstone at this place, and it was the only one with color and a multiline epitaph: *Kendall Gene McKinley. Beloved son, brother, friend. Sunrise: 1996. Sunset: 2014.*

She knelt before the stone, caressed the letters of his name, felt along the indentations the way she used to touch the contours of his face, his dimples.

"Hate to start off with bad news, baby, but somebody killed Solomon. Vega's too proud to show how hurt she is, but she's got a tremor now, and she probably won't be sitting out front anymore with that coffee cup. Actually, she broke the cup. You know I know that pain. Everybody thinks it's the Dempsey Boys, but I don't think so. Seems like a lot of trouble when they're about to get shut down. And why Solomon, you know?"

She sat cross-legged in front of Kendall's headstone, the way she used to sit across from him in the living room and roll a ball back and forth between them when he was a toddler. He'd always squeal when the red sphere made it back to him, and the memory of it sent a wave of pain through her chest. Some days were better than others for her grief. Today was a bad day.

"Marcus was something else at his graduation. You'd be so surprised at how he's changed. When I saw him in that cap and gown, it's like I was looking at you."

It unnerved Nona the way she could imagine Kendall responding to her. She could see a smile spread across his face at the idea of Marcus's speech, and could even hear Kendall say *Well, we have such a wonderful mom.*

"At the end, it was like something went wrong. I've never seen him like that. Not even after you were . . ." She could never say "killed" to Kendall. If he was really listening, he'd obviously know he'd passed to the other side, but there was something about acknowledging the intentional way he was removed from his life that she could never say out loud. "Killed" sounded like defeat.

"This might sound wild, but I was wondering if you visited us at the graduation. When he got to the end of his speech, was he seeing you?"

Kendall usually gave her an answer through some sign. A cardinal would fly down and plod across the top of his headstone or a squirrel would scurry by and drop an acorn near her feet. The red bird in particular let her know that Kendall was communicating with her from above. Vance used to always tell the boys that in ancient folklore, a visit from a cardinal was a signal from a loved one who had passed.

"Or have you been visiting us at home? I feel like something is there. Haunting me. I'd feel a whole lot better if I knew it was you."

Actually, that wasn't entirely true either, she realized. Second Corinthians had taught her that in death the saints would prefer "*to be absent from the body and to be present with the Lord.*" Her entire faith was built on this idea. Church had taught her that any spirits walking the earth were not with the Lord and therefore were not *of* the Lord. Until recently, when Kendall communicated with her, she'd imagined it had been from above. Among the clouds. And, most importantly, with God.

She searched the brown grass near her, the elms that marked the edge of the burial place, and even the groundskeeper who pulled up weeds near the entry booth, but this time Kendall didn't seem to be saying anything at all.

Then the wind picked up, gave her a whiff of petrol from the gas station next door, and a shadow passed over the top of Kendall's tomb, as if someone were approaching from behind. A chill tore through the middle of her body. When she checked over her shoulder, no one was there.

You're the one imagining things.

She returned her gaze to his grave, and the shadow continued its passage across the stone and disappeared. She thought of the voice she'd imagined in her home, the broadening of Marcus's back, the shadowy figure in the hall, the way Marcus had snapped at her recently.

She suddenly felt watched. She didn't think Kendall had anything to do with it, but she sensed that at any moment a hand would reach from the shadow, press its clammy fingers to her throat, and squeeze.

"I love you, Kendall."

She stood, grabbed her bag, and headed for the bus stop. It was usually difficult to leave, but today, staying was hard.

No way in hell that basketball should be bouncing like that outside Donnell's window. Sounded like Solomon's ball bouncing. Same rhythm and everything. Was somebody playing games with Donnell? Toying with his mind? His emotions?

He wished a motherfucker would test him like this. The way he was feeling, whoever was out there with the *thump, thump, thump* would be on his last day. Solomon hadn't even been dead a week, and already some mofo was out here showing they ass.

Donnell grabbed his Glock 17, added the magazine, and removed the safety. He'd loaded Grave Digger multiple times before, just like his moms had shown him as a kid, just like he did at target practice again and again, but this time the gun felt foreign in his hands, like it was his first time at that range, back when the pistol seemed heavy in his palm.

At the window, the lock was stuck as usual, and opening the thing would take all of his strength to push it up. His moms had asked for all of their windows to be repaired, but no one ever fixed shit in this hellhole.

Eventually he got the grubby panes up, and he peered outside. If Donnell knew the nigga well, he wasn't gon' actually cap him, but this would be the warning: *Don't. Play. With. My. Muhfuckin feelings.*

Donnell was suddenly sick to his stomach. Grave Digger's grooves dug into his skin like they did when he was younger and afraid to pull the trigger. Shame radiated up his chest along with burning acid from his breakfast burrito. His weapon wouldn't protect him from his guilt. He'd stepped aside when Peter went for Solomon, and that shit had cut him deep. Solomon had been his brother. Why didn't Solomon listen when Donnell told him? *Just let Peter do what he gon' do. The product. The cash. The girls. The turf. Stop offering your opinions. Stop arguing with him.*

Donnell knew Solomon couldn't stop with the animosity if he wanted to. Solomon had been angry about Kendall's killing, because Solomon had stepped aside and let Peter go after Kendall. Was the same going to happen to Donnell? If his time was gon' be up eventually, who would stand back and watch it unfold? Cedrick? Red? Rayvon? Lance?

The bouncing continued and even grew louder as Donnell stuck his head out. "Ay. Yo. Who the fuck is . . ."

Nobody was there. The bouncing hadn't let up. The sound of it. The vibration of it against his chest.

His mind went to Little Lonnie. And the dead hooker Carlotta. What if the ball bouncing wasn't a person playing a trick on him but was actually Solomon?

Donnell scanned the concrete just below the window. The bouncing stopped. Cold air passed up his spine. Above him, the window dislodged and slammed down on his neck.

He dropped Grave Digger onto the concrete below. The gun went off as soon as she hit the pavement. His throat slammed down on the ledge as a piercing pain shot through his skull under the weight of the window. His right hand dangled free outside, and something tore through the flesh of his palm.

His breath left his body as the frame crushed the base of his head and the nape of his neck. He wanted to scream for help, but his throat was constricted. He managed a cough. Sneakers squeaked on the ground nearby, but he couldn't move his head to look up.

"The fuck is you doing, Nell?" He heard Peter drag over an abandoned stool and climb on it to reach the window. He lifted the frame off of Donnell.

Donnell's breath returned, and he searched the area behind Peter. Red and Cedrick stood gaping at him like they were ready to help but confused on what to do.

"Was y'all out here bouncing a fucking ball?" Donnell coughed again. Rubbed his neck, and the movement smeared blood all down the front of his shirt. He held up his hand. The bullet from Grave Digger had ricocheted and cut across his skin. A chunk of flesh the shape of a snake was missing from the middle of his palm. It stung like hell, but he'd live. "Man. Fuck. This gon' need stitches."

"Were we bouncing a ball?" That was Red, hiding a smirk and two seconds from cracking up laughing. "What ball?"

"You bet' not laugh. I heard somebody bouncing a fucking ball!"

"Okay. And you was gon' shoot 'em?" That was Cedrick. Donnell knew then, Cedrick would be the one to turn on him if the time came. He filed away that thought.

"Just answer the fucking question. Did y'all see who was bouncing the ball?"

"Wasn't no ball bouncing." Peter returned Grave Digger to Donnell, moved the stool back to its original spot, and backed up. He shook his head, and Red and Cedrick exchanged glances.

Peter cleared his throat and motioned the other two to follow him as he walked off, shaking his head. "Man, Nell. You need to lay off that lean."

As Nona stood in the break room at work, she noticed a text from Pastor: Still thinking of you. Thinking of holding you again.

And she also noticed that her nephew Harlan had sent her an audio file. His accompanying text said, I know you were worried about the boys. Listen to this.

The break room seemingly went silent as she opened the file and drew in a deep breath. The audio loaded, and a woman's voice poured out of the phone so clearly, it sounded like she was beside Nona. She scanned the area. The space was empty, but she took the audio off of speaker anyway and pressed the phone to her ear.

"Medford 911. This is Bernie. What is your emergency?"

"My brother and I were just assaulted."

A jolt ran through her at the sound of Marcus's voice. Nona remembered rushing toward Marcus and Lance and discovering their bloody and swollen faces. Marcus had hung up the phone as soon as she'd arrived. This call had been the reason.

The woman's voice continued.

"Where are you?"

"Outside our home. We live in the Gardens."

"Hester Gardens?"

"Yes, ma'am."

"Are you still in danger?"

"We are always in danger."

"Who assaulted you?"

"Some guys we know. We live with them."

A piercing coldness snaked up her chest to her throat. Her eyes burned, and a prickle spread across her scalp. The very thing she feared had indeed come true.

"Okay. I'm sending help to you. Are you related to the people who assaulted you? They live in the home with you?"

"You could say that. The Gardens is my home. Our attackers live in the Gardens."

"So you have been assaulted by another resident?"

"Yes. Assaulted and threatened. They also confessed to a murder."

A tremble took over her hands. Lena entered the break room and said, "Hey, girl," but immediately quieted down when her eyes met Nona's. Nona held up a hand to let her know she was on the phone.

Lena mouthed, "Everything okay?" and when Nona nodded, Lena grabbed a pack of cigarettes from her locker and left again.

"Can you go inside your unit?"

"Yes."

"What is your unit number?"

"We're at the end, facing north."

"Okay. Please tell me when you're inside and safe. I'll stay on the line."

"Let's go, Lance."

By that point, her youngest had a bloody nose and swollen lips and was probably staring at his older brother in disbelief because she didn't allow her boys to call the police. She'd instructed them to call her. Always.

Marcus coughed on the recording.

He coughed again.

"We . . . uh . . . can't go inside yet."

The reason he'd not gone inside was because she'd been home, and he likely saw her that day taking out the trash.

"Okay. Well, can you at least tell me what happened?"

"Someone killed my older brother two years ago. They confessed. And they are after me and my little brother now."

Marcus coughed again, and Nona pressed the phone to her ear even harder, feeling her heart would burst from her chest.

"Who confessed?"

"The Hester Boys."

"And gang members threatened you?"

"And assaulted us."

"What are their names?"

"Just told you their names. The Hester Boys."

"Yes. I'm hoping you can identify the person or people who attacked you."

"I don't understand the question."

"Okay. Can you tell me what happened? Exactly. Did they have a weapon?"

"They always have a weapon."

"What kind of weapon did they assault you with?"

"Their fists."

"So you were in a fistfight?"

"Are you listening to me?"

"Yes. Of course. I'm trying to understand what is happening right now so I can determine how to best help you stay safe. What is your name?"

"I was not in a fistfight. A fistfight would imply my attacker and I decided to fight one another, and that's not what happened. I was simply attacked. And threatened. By a gang."

"Are they still there now?"

"They're here all the time. Are you going to send someone to arrest them?"

"Help is already on the way. I have to collect as much information as I can to guide you until the officers arrive. Can you tell me—"

"I need them to be arrested."

"Officers are on their way to help you, okay?"

No response.

"Hello?"

No response.

"Hello?"

No response.

"Can you hear me?"

No response.

"Are you still there, young man?"

The audio file had reached its end. She closed her hand around the device imagining it was Peter's neck.

Marcus always knew. One night not long after Kendall was killed, Marcus had come to her and said, "Mom, we should tell the police." And Nona had known exactly what he was talking about, but she pretended to not know because she knew they'd do no such thing. And she said, "Tell them what?" And he said, "That we think it was Peter who did it."

And at that time, she pulled Marcus to her, and he was still young enough to rest his head on her shoulder, but she remembered his body was stiff in the hug as if holding his ground for Kendall. She said, "We don't really know who did it. And I'm not going to get Mother all upset when we might be wrong."

Truth was, Kendall had gotten into a fistfight, and he hadn't told her the truth about what had happened. Told her it was just "guy stuff." After he was killed, she asked Harlan to snoop around, and she found out that Kendall had gotten into a fight with Peter because Peter had been trying to recruit Marcus to the gang. And Kendall told Peter to lay off Marcus and Lance.

Tears spilled down to her mouth. She'd felt powerless after Kendall's death and still felt powerless now. Peter had been wearing Kendall's watch when he arrived at the funeral. The watch was gold and platinum with diamonds on the hour and minute hands. It had been a gift from Vance. Although Vance had probably stolen it himself, Kendall wouldn't pawn it for rent money when she had asked.

Kendall wore it to bed and only took it off to shower, and even then, he made sure it sat in the original box on the counter next to the tub while he was washing behind the curtain. He wouldn't even let his own brothers touch it, and he'd fought Marcus and Lance more than once when one of them tried to borrow it. She'd noticed it was missing when she went to ID Kendall's body. And there was no way Kendall gave a watch so precious to him to, of all people, Peter Lincoln, someone Kendall couldn't stand.

Nona exited the break room and headed to the front of the plant. She stared out the double doors, ignoring the gaggle of local kids shrieking and chatting in the lobby.

Outside the glass, she noticed a red-breasted bird that waddled across the branch of an elm tree. It resembled the cardinal from Vance's sketch.

In the weeks after Kendall had died, she'd confronted Peter about the watch. He'd said he'd found it. When she asked for it back, he'd said he'd lost it. She wanted to strangle the boy, but instead, she'd had Sgt. Prager question Peter about the watch. And Peter told the police he'd found it in the alley. The same alley where NaDarius had lost his life.

Sgt. Prager had told her that Peter's alibi checked out. His story about finding the watch couldn't be proven or disproven, really, and either way, possession of the watch did not equal murder. So Nona had to drop the accusation.

The watch never made an appearance again after that.

It hit her—Marcus punching Peter in the chest at the graduation party. And Marcus shouting something like "I'll get back what's mine." And Lance had said, "Peter stole something from Marcus."

Had that good-for-nothing boy resurfaced the watch at the graduation party to antagonize Marcus? Is that what had happened? Had he been so envious of Marcus's success that he triggered Marcus with the one thing that would cut him deeply: Kendall?

She wanted to scream. She thought back to the 911 call. It was odd the way Marcus didn't answer the emergency operator's questions.

He didn't give his own name. He didn't say Peter's name. He wanted the police to come out, but it was like he was still protecting the Hester Boys.

Why did he call the police in the first place?

He must have been devastated and traumatized from the fight and then realized what he'd done and changed his mind. It was clear to her that Marcus had been protecting Peter during that call, but was Marcus protecting Peter because he planned to go after Peter himself? She put that thought away. Marcus had become a lot of things recently, but he was not a strike-first type of person. Or was he?

If Marcus would just talk to her! Tell her the truth. But he wouldn't say anything. Lance wouldn't say anything. Not together. Not separately. And she didn't know what started this latest dustup with Peter. It could have been about Kendall. It could have been about the watch. It could have been about anything.

She called Sgt. Prager. The line seemed to take forever to connect and ring.

That was the thing no one understood. Never mind what the news media wanted folks to believe, most murders were committed by people who knew the victim, often by people who knew them well. So, in a closed community like Hester Gardens, if her son was murdered, of course he would know his killer. She'd babysat his killer. Had fed his killer. Had sat him on her lap and kissed his sweaty little forehead multiple times. Had played him his favorite *Sesame Street* episode when he was still a preschooler. If she couldn't get an arrest and conviction of Peter, she was stuck living beside him and his grandmother. She couldn't accuse him or else he might attack her or her remaining boys. And Mother Lincoln relied on Nona, and Nona relied on Mother Lincoln. And short of prison, how could Nona get justice for her son without killing for him? And as much as she'd grown to hate Peter, she couldn't kill him herself—where would that leave her boys?

Sgt. Prager didn't answer. Nona got her voicemail. "This is Nona McKinley. Peter Lincoln confessed to killing my boy. Call me."

She felt lightheaded. She waited for the room to start spinning like it had the day Vance had been carted off to jail, the day Kendall had been killed, but the disorientation didn't arrive. No ringing in her ears either. She would be able to hold on this time.

She would just stick to her plan for Marcus. She would hold it together long enough to see Marcus out of their neighborhood and off to school.

As she crossed the lobby, snaked through the crush of summer camp tour groups, and headed to the bottling floor for the remainder of her shift, another thought occurred to her. Marcus had said the person who confessed was "after" him and his brother. Had Peter just roughed them up, or had he threatened to finish the job?

She played the recording for Marcus and Lance, both of whom sat and listened wide-eyed and sheepish. When it was over, Marcus rose from the breakfast table and Lance leaned forward and rubbed his head.

"In the call, you say, 'Someone killed my older brother two years ago. They confessed. And they are after me and my little brother now.'" She wasn't shouting, but it took all her strength not to.

"No one confessed to a killing." Marcus's voice was calm, but he breathed deliberately, perhaps struggling to stay that way. Lance stared at Marcus. "We'd just gotten jumped. I was angry." Marcus paced. "I just said whatever I could to get the police to come out and make an arrest."

"You named the Hester Boys in the call. Did you make this entire thing up? Did you and Lance fight each other and you pinned it on the Hester Boys out of revenge against Peter?"

"What? No. We were jumped."

"Who jumped you?"

"We don't know!" Marcus shouted, then seemed to realize he'd done so and lowered his voice. "Why is it so difficult for you to understand that we live in a bad neighborhood? Stuff just happens sometimes. I made the 911 call because I wanted the police to come out, and I thought if they had a confession, they'd be more likely to show up."

She was reliving all the moments in which Vance had lied to her. The complete ridiculousness of his stories. How the end products contained so many nonsensical twists and turns that she grew angrier the longer they went on.

"Why won't you two tell me the truth?"

"We are telling you the truth!" Marcus said.

"Lance?" She studied her youngest, knowing he was the most likely to crack. Lance stared at the table.

"Look at me, Lance." She softened her voice and moved closer to him. "Tell me what happened."

Lance glanced up at Marcus.

"Don't look at him. Look at me." She stepped even closer to Lance.

Lance met her gaze with tears in his eyes. She couldn't be certain, but she thought she saw fear in his expression.

"Some mangey kids, Mom. We didn't know them. That's why Marcus and I were angry with each other by the time you saw us, because I was wondering why he called the police. We never call the police. That's what you taught us, anyway."

Marcus jammed his hands in his pockets; a nearly imperceptible smirk appeared on his face and disappeared. "See, Mom? There's no confession. It wasn't Peter. Or any of the Hester Boys. Are you satisfied now?"

"Am I satisfied?" She stormed over to the hall closets, where the boys had dropped their backpacks and dingy sneakers. She snatched up Lance's copy of *Soledad Brother*. "I don't know whether you two actually read this book, but it makes clear that our country is nefarious. It has a place for Black people, particularly Black men."

They both were silent, glancing at the text in her hand and up at her face.

"They never intended for us to be citizens. They never intended for us to be American. We were meant to work to enrich them, and if we're not working to enrich them, they really want us in prison or in the ground. Look around you. Where is your father right now? In prison. Where is your brother right now? In the ground."

"Mom." Lance was choked up and trying his best not to cry. "We get it."

"No, you don't get it! And that is my point. You. Don't. Get. It. Neither of you. Because if you got it, you would tell me the truth. If you got it, you wouldn't have fought with Peter at your graduation party. You wouldn't have fought with Peter again and called 911."

Marcus was choked up as well. "I told you—"

"Shut your mouth. Both of you." She slapped the book in her hand for emphasis. They remained silent. "I know you two think I'm out of touch. I know you two think all I do is work, make life hard for you, and read books and go to church. But I grew up in Dempsey Woods. You know why I never take you two to Dempsey? Why I tell you to stay away from Dempsey? Because it was worse than Hester Gardens. You know who used to keep me safe? The Dempsey Boys. You know how your father and I got together? The first night that your father and I started dating was because I was coming home from the bus after a long shift at the plant, no DBs were around, and some no-good mofo rolled up on me at the bus stop and attacked me. I knew how to fight. And I fought back. But the guy had a knife and eventually, in our struggle, he took a fist to my face and knocked me unconscious."

"Mom—?" Marcus's eyes were wide, and he moved closer to Lance, who had tears streaming down his cheeks. Marcus rubbed Lance's back. She hadn't seen him in that protective older-brother role in a long time.

"The man would have raped me, probably killed me, but your father was visiting your uncle, Harlan's dad, who also lived at Dempsey, and your father saw the entire thing unfold and stopped it. You know how he stopped it? He shot the man, and in the process he saved my life.

"This book. The other book you're both reading . . . *Monster.* Let them be warnings to you. My rules. My prying. My wanting to know where you are and what you're doing and who you're with, my focus on college and getting out of Hester Gardens—they're all because I want better for you than what I had and what your father had. To a certain degree, I have sheltered you. As much as I could. But you're older now, and you both are going to have to help me. Help me keep you out of prison and out of the ground."

She tossed the book on the table, where it landed with a *thwack* that made both of her boys flinch.

"Curfew."

"Aw, Mom!" Marcus shouted.

"You both will be home by dinner each night, and I must know your whereabouts before you leave."

Lance was staring at the book, tears still streaming down his face.

"Come on, Mom." Marcus was still rubbing his brother's back but was growing angry again. "I've got lots of—"

"I don't give a damn what you've got."

Silence filled the room again. The boys had never heard a curse word leave her mouth before. Yet this was also one of a handful of times they'd openly disobeyed and lied to her.

"I want you both to remember that I am your mother and this is my house, no matter how old you get. I do not like being lied to, and as you so eloquently put it, Marcus—we live in a bad neighborhood. Need I remind you Solomon was just killed? Even if we go along with your BS story, you two were allegedly jumped for groceries. So that means you will have your behinds in this house by dinner every night. If you can't abide by my rules, find someplace else to live."

She grabbed her purse and stormed out. She could feel her boys staring at her back as she slammed the front door. She did not feel triumphant. She was losing her grip on her boys, and in another neighborhood, that would be a mere rite of passage, but not for her. Not for her.

Eighteen

Sgt. Prager called Nona for the second time in twenty-four hours. "We went through this already, Nona. And I am so sorry. I have seen cases like this before. I just questioned Marcus, Lance, Peter, Donnell, and Cedrick, and none of them will admit anything. Marcus said there wasn't a confession from Peter. He said they were just in a silly squabble at his party, and they were all mad, and that was that."

"What about the watch? I know—"

"No one will admit anything about the watch. I can try to get a search warrant for it, but, again, it doesn't prove murder. I will say that Peter's latest story doesn't match his first. When I asked him about it two years ago, he said he'd found the watch. This time, he said Kendall gave him the watch."

"That's a lie. Kendall would never—"

"I know. I'm saying maybe we have cause to search for it, but I honestly don't think it will lead anywhere even if we find it."

"You know what? Forget it."

"I mean, if—"

"No. I got it. I'm on my own. You all couldn't help me back then. Can't help me now."

"That's not—"

Nona hung up. She stuffed the phone in her pocket and crossed to her kitchen counter. She picked up the gift bag she'd put together and stormed out her front door.

She locked up and scanned the courtyard all the way across to Vega's unit. Still fuming from her call with Sgt. Prager, she arrived outside her grieving neighbor's home. The casserole and chicken Nona and Mable had put out for Vega were gone, but the woman's white lawn chair still sat empty. A bouquet of roses rested against Vega's doorframe. Even from several feet away, Nona could tell the flowers were from the church. Vega wasn't a member, was an atheist in fact, and would likely cuss and toss them in the trash.

Nona placed a white coffee mug on Vega's porch with a card attached that read *I'm here to talk if you need.*

Nona marched over to Mother Lincoln's, with Marcus's 911 call on loop in her mind, the echo of his voice shifting her insides: *We are always in danger.*

Mother's bedroom was sweltering. Nona opened the window and stared at the spot in the alley that haunted her. Externally, this visit to Mother's was no different than any before. Internally, Nona's stomach was in knots. She'd prayed about it, had spoken to Pastor about it, and she couldn't see how talking to Mother again and having the woman talk to Peter . . . again . . . would help the Marcus–Peter beef at all.

So, as Mother sat in her recliner, legs elevated, Nona planned to talk to Peter herself. Tell him to leave her babies alone or go to prison.

She turned away from the screen, where dead flies hung from the mesh, deciding she'd add "clean Mother's windows" to her to-do list. She gathered the sheets and pillowcases from Mother's mattress, pulled the additional linens from the closet, and made Mother's bed.

She glanced out to the living room, where Mother watched television and rubbed her knees. Her legs seemed uncomfortable, but she wouldn't take Nona's advice and have a doctor examine them.

Nona listened for signs of Peter in his bedroom. Would he be on the phone or perhaps playing video games? She'd chosen this time because he was usually eating Nona's leftovers before heading out for the evening.

Outside the window, two young women giggled and a Rihanna tune played at low volume.

The voices belonged to Kiki and Gretchen. Nona wasn't interested. Whenever those girls were in the alley, perched on the low concrete wall like a pair of birds, they flitted hurriedly among conversation topics that pertained only to themselves, like who was going to babysit Grayson and which store had the best deal on a pound of chicken breast.

This time, they mentioned Marcus's name.

Nona peeked into the living room, where Mother had fallen asleep in her chair. She dumped Mother's clean clothes on the freshly made bed and folded while she listened.

"You know, Marcus was acting strange at our date." Gretchen was directly next to the window. Nona was glad she'd left the blinds closed and prayed the wind didn't show up and blow them open; otherwise, they'd see her a few feet away.

"Said he had something to tell me," Gretchen continued. "Thought I was going to scream because you know how I am about Marcus."

"Uh, yeah. Everybody does."

Nona was furious that Marcus had anything to do with this girl.

"We went on a hike, and—"

"A hike? Where, Gretchen? Medford is flat."

"Well, it was more a long walk around the lake."

"You really need to stop exaggerating."

"You gon' let me finish?"

Kiki didn't answer, and the older cousin was probably rolling her eyes.

"So Marcus had a plastic pouch of apples and a large shoulder bag draped all down the side of his body. He was grinning. And I could see the swelling from his fight with Peter had gone down."

Tears burned Nona's eyes. Gretchen and Kiki knew more about her sons than she did.

"We went down to that wooded area with all the pink rhododendrons."

"Ohhhh. I love that place." Kiki's voice remained flat even when she expressed emotion. Was this grief from losing Kendall or was she just weathered for a twenty-year-old? "It looks like you're not even in Medford down there."

Nona put stacks of clothes in Mother's dresser drawers and returned to folding the rest. It sounded like Marcus had been trying to impress Gretchen by taking her to that spot. Nona didn't like it one bit.

"I know," Gretchen said. "And it's so romantic. Well, this squirrel showed up and was chomping on some acorns. But it gets weird. We sat together on a picnic blanket, then Marcus opened his backpack, pulled out a rifle, unfolded it, and rested his hands on these front and back handles."

Nona stopped folding. Her pulse quickened. What did Gretchen mean he took out a rifle? Marcus had gotten a gun?

"A rifle?" Kiki shouted, then gasped.

"Shhhhhh." Gretchen lowered her voice, so Nona stepped closer to the window. "Yes, girl. It was straight out of an action movie. It's just like one Peter has. That thang scared me half to death, and I dropped my phone."

"What? I hope you didn't break it, because you know you don't have any money to get it fixed."

"Shut up, Kiki. It was fine."

Images flashed in Nona's mind: Marcus's hand itching to hit her when she confronted him about the fight, him saying *You're the one imagining things* while glaring at her, his back seeming to grow in size when he punched Peter. The Marcus she thought she'd raised was capable of much more than she'd been willing to admit.

"Sister McKinley would kill him if she knew."

"I know!" Gretchen whisper-shouted. "That's what I told him. And he was smiling all weird and stroking it like his dick. And he was like, 'I know.'"

Why would he have a gun? For protection? Was he afraid Peter would hurt them? Or was he planning to avenge his brother's murder? Was Marcus even capable of that?

"Noooo, girl," Kiki said. "This is crazy."

Nona was sweating now, profusely. She needed water.

"I asked him where he got it, and he was like, 'Guy I know.' Then I asked why he had it, and he was like, 'You wanna hold it?' I made him put it away."

"This whole story is crazy, Gretchen."

"I know. But this isn't even the craziest part! Marcus had made a trail on the ground with those apples and the squirrel comes back to nibble on them, which was weird, too, because I thought they only ate nuts, and Marcus stands up, raises the rifle."

Nona's stomach churned.

"You should have left, Gretchen. What if he had shot you?"

"Marcus?" Gretchen scoffed.

"I mean, what if he shot Solomon?"

Nona's mind went to Vega's son dribbling his ball. Solomon was Kendall's friend, despite being Peter's fellow gang member. What beef would Marcus have had with Solomon? And Marcus wasn't capable of shooting anyone.

"What? No. Marcus would never shoot me or Solomon or anybody else."

This was the one time Nona agreed with Gretchen.

"Before this conversation I would have said Marcus would never buy a gun either, so—"

"You're a prude, Kiki. Can I finish? Anyway, he shoots the thing, I start screaming and packing up to leave, he apologizes, and then we start making out."

"Making out? After he killed the squirrel?"

Nona couldn't believe what she was hearing. She beat back tears. She crept to the bedroom door to see if Mother was still asleep. The old woman's mouth was open, and she was snoring, so Nona returned to the window.

"He didn't kill the squirrel, Kiki. Just grazed it. And you don't understand. I'd been waiting for this moment, like, my entire life."

"So you're both crazy."

"Anyway." Gretchen cleared her throat. "We start messing around, next thing I know, we're both naked."

Nona wanted to rip the linens to shreds. Everything she'd done for this boy, the road she'd paved for him, and he was, step-by-step, throwing it all away.

"He put on a rubber, but before we got started, he heard a noise, only I didn't hear shit."

"Like at your graduation."

"I thought the same thing! Like, there's nobody there. The fuck is he looking at?"

Nona held her breath and leaned in.

"So we got up and dressed and hurried out of there. It was like he was scared. I asked him what was up, and he was like, 'Nothing.'"

"What do you think he saw?"

"Didn't you say you saw Kendall after he died?"

Kiki paused.

Nona hadn't known anyone had seen Kendall after he died. The thought made goosebumps sprout on her arms and neck. She thought of the shadowy figure in the hall.

"Yeah. Walked right past my window the night after his funeral like he was headed home. Thought I'd imagined him because I missed him so much, but it happened more than once, so . . ."

"More than once?"

"Yeah. Recently. Thought I saw him down there." Kiki paused again.

"By the dumpsters?" Gretchen whispered.

"Yeah. I didn't know what to think. I mean, everybody talks about Hester Gardens having ghosts. *'The homes that face north are haunted.' 'If you get murdered here, your spirit stays.'* Yada yada. But I never believed any of that stuff. Until . . . Well, this time when I saw Kendall or whatever I saw, I got so scared I tripped over a toy and got scratched by some gross rats."

"Rats? Oh my God."

"I know. I got some shots at the hospital just in case. In the end, I think I just imagined him. I must have."

"I think the same thing might have . . ." Gretchen said but paused for several seconds. "I don't know. I think I saw Grace."

"What? When? That must have been . . . Are you okay?"

"I can't talk about it, Kiki. Like at all."

"I'm sorry. I'm so sorry. I mean, I miss Grace. I can only—"

"You think Marcus could be seeing Kendall too?" Gretchen asked. "Maybe that's who he saw when we were at the lake? Do you think when we see spirits, they can make us do stuff?"

"Stuff like what?"

"I don't know. Weird stuff. I feel like Grace made me . . . I can't say it."

"Kendall hasn't made me do anything. I mean, if it were really him I saw, he frightened me. I guess he made me fall and get scratched up by rats. What did Grace make you do?"

Gretchen didn't answer right away. "I just wonder if Grace is like making me act . . . a certain way . . . because she's angry with me."

"Cedrick and I have told you a thousand times. Grace isn't angry with you because you switched places with her in the grass before she got shot."

"But what if she is? What if she wants revenge? And Kendall too. What if Kendall wants revenge against whoever shot him? If Grace is making me do things, could Kendall do the same with Marcus?"

Sweat soaked Nona's shirt, and her heartbeat pulsed at her temples. She had slowly come around to the idea that Kendall could be present in their lives, but even when she stretched her mind to accept that, she imagined him helping them, maybe protecting them. What if that wasn't true? What if she was blinded by her love for him? He'd been kind in life and unwilling to harm anyone. Only in self-defense. Could he be angry in death? Vengeful? Could he be making Marcus do things?

"Maybe. I don't know, Gretchen. I really didn't believe in any of this stuff until it happened to me."

Nona felt the same way. Months ago, she'd have said even entertaining these thoughts was an abomination of Christ.

"Something isn't right, I guess." Kiki sounded defeated.

"Yeah. Between the gun, the graduation speech, and him not getting busy with me because he saw something that wasn't even there. And you know he won that fight with Peter."

"I didn't know because I haven't seen Marcus. Lance looked pretty bad, and I offered to get him into my department for X-rays."

"Yeah, but you didn't see Peter's face. Marcus fucked Peter up. Peter's right eye was swollen shut for a few days."

"So did Marcus ever tell you the other part? What he wanted to ask you or whatever?"

"Oh, right. Yeah. He did. We'd walked a long way to get to the far side of the park. So far away, we needed to take the bus back home. When we got to the bench, he sat next to me and asked me to look after Lance when he's gone."

Nona struggled to breathe.

"And I was like, 'Look after him how, Marcus?' And he was like, 'I'm not going to be around much longer.' And I was like, 'You going away to college doesn't mean you can't keep tabs on Lance.' Then he had the nerve to raise his voice at me and say, 'Are you going to help me or not?'"

"No, he didn't."

"Yes, he did, girl. And you know I was done. So I told him to leave me alone. And then he was like, 'I think we know better than that.' And he kissed me again."

"I really don't understand you two. You sneak around like you're both married to other people and you have these unnecessarily passionate talks."

"It's because all the mothers around here tell their boys to stay away from me, and I'm sure Sister McKinley is no different, so he has to sneak around to see me. But this is the crazy part, Kiki."

"You haven't told me the crazy part yet?"

"When the bus arrived, I pulled away from him and got on. He stayed at the stop. When the bus got to the end of the block, I checked to see whether he was still staring at me, and, I kid you not, I leapt up in my seat and crashed back down at what I saw."

"Why?"

"I still get goosebumps thinking about it."

"You're so dramatic. What did you see, Gretchen?"

"I don't know how to say it."

"Say it."

"Okay." Gretchen paused for a long time, and every muscle in Nona's body was stiff. Her throat and lips were dry.

"When Marcus was staring at me through the bus window, over his right shoulder, there was another figure, which wasn't really there."

A figure. It was always a figure. A shadow. Someone lurking. Some*thing* lurking. What was it and what did it want? She couldn't let herself believe it was Kendall, a vengeful Kendall. Could she?

Nona was hyperventilating and closed her eyes to calm her breathing. Her stomach pulled into knots. What if it was all connected? The voice she'd imagined in her home. The smell of garbage and death that kept showing up. The shadow in the hall. Marcus's behavior. And now Gretchen and Kiki mentioning the figure was evidence that maybe it wasn't all in Nona's head. Because they had seen something too.

"We should tell Sister McKinley."

"No, Kiki. Don't. You can't say anything. She will kill him and then he will kill me."

As Gretchen and Kiki turned their conversation to Kiki's new boyfriend and her work at the hospital, Nona gathered the laundry quickly, thoughts of the rifle, the fistfight, the figure, Solomon's murder, and Kendall's spirit out for revenge swirling in her mind.

On her way down the hall, she noticed that the door to Peter's room was ajar. He usually kept it closed, so seeing it open, his dresser on full display with papers and shiny objects glistening atop it, made her slow down. The items were practically calling to her.

She peeked inside. He wasn't home. *Shoot!* Defeat replaced the nervous energy that had been building in her gut.

She glanced down the hall. Mother's mouth was still spread wide, though her snores were lighter. Nona didn't think she should risk going into his room, but she really couldn't help herself.

She kept the laundry basket in her hand as an excuse in case Mother Lincoln did wake and find her there, or worse, in case Peter showed up.

To her surprise, Peter had a picture of drooling, chubby-cheeked Grayson printed out and sitting on the dresser top beside an empty four-by-six frame. Grayson's face looked exactly like Peter's when Peter was a baby, back when Peter used to sit on her lap and pull her pearl necklace into his mouth to soothe his sore gums. How could he be so tender to Mother and Grayson and so violent with practically everyone else, including Gretchen, the mother of his child?

Peter had a wad of cash rolled in a rubber band, a square-shaped glass tray with ashes sitting in the middle, and two joints resting in an open rectangular box.

Nona leaned in. The container held three bullets as well. There was no way Mother knew of the bullets and drugs. Nona scanned the bed, neatly made with tucked-in blue linens and a stack of folded shirts and shorts on the end of the mattress. So he did his own laundry and made his own bed but didn't help Mother around the house? Bastard.

Forgive, Lord. Language.

She turned to go and spotted a toy soldier, the kind one would see at Christmastime. It stood six inches high and on guard at the back of the dresser. Its mouth hung open, and beneath the soldier was a picture someone had taken of Peter, Donnell, Marcus, and Lance at Marcus's graduation party.

She lifted the photo and stared at Marcus smiling, Lance also beaming, Donnell with a goofy grin on his face, and, of course, Peter, who appeared angry. With Peter's glasses removed from his face, his inner machinations leaped out at her—he was plotting how to spoil the event, how to upset Marcus, how to set Marcus up to fail the same way he was failing.

Nona took the photo and tucked it in her pocket. It was not Peter's to keep. Why would he get a print of a photo that was likely on his phone? Why would he want a photo from an event he tried to destroy? He was one vile person, and every time she thought of him, she hated him more.

Back in the living room, Nona made enough noise to gently rouse Mother.

"Oh, baby, I see I fell asleep." Mother slowly rose from her recliner, put on her shoes, and plodded to the bathroom.

"It's okay, Mother. Just finished."

When the woman had flushed and washed and was making her way back to the living room, she asked, "Any updates on Vance?"

"He wrote again. Said he started having dreams about Kendall. Sent another sketch to go with the dream."

"What did he dream?"

"That Kendall was still alive."

"I dream about Sylvester being alive. Happens at least once a week still after nearly thirty years of him being gone. I'll dream he's lying beside me in bed, and everything is normal. Then I wake up and remember he had a heart attack and died. Those are the worst because it's like you lose the person all over again in the morning."

That happened to Nona every morning the entire first year after losing Kendall.

"Do you want to stay for dinner? I was gonna make that baked chicken you put on my menu. Peter should be home by then, and—"

"No, that's okay, Mother. You make dinner and get some rest. I'll be back around with your laundry when it's finished."

Nona closed Mother's door and saw Gretchen and Kiki head out of the alley. The girls waved to Nona as if they hadn't just spent the last twenty minutes gossiping about her son. Nona returned the smile, but under her breath she whispered, "Lord, have mercy."

Nineteen

Pastor: Nona. First Marcus, now you're being distant. I can feel you pulling away from me. I don't think my heart can take that.
Nona: I'm not pulling away from you. Not on purpose, anyway. These boys are just putting me in a frenzy.
Pastor: What is it now?
Nona: I'll tell you when I see you. It's too long for text. I just . . . I'm at my wit's end.
Pastor: You know I'm here for you. Why won't you let me help you?
Nona: I will. I mean, you have. I'm just trying to figure out a few things right now on my own.
Pastor: Okay. You know I care about you, right?
Nona: I know you care.
Pastor: Then when are you going to tell me this in person?
Nona: Soon.
Pastor: Please don't make me wait too long to see you again.

Twenty

She flung open the boys' bedroom door, letting the knob crash into the side of Marcus's desk. Having fretted the entire day over whether to enter while they were out, she now moved like she was running out of time.

She couldn't rid her mind of Gretchen describing that figure over Marcus's shoulder and saying Marcus had a rifle. If the gun was in his room, Nona would find it and get rid of it.

An MP3 player was set to heavy metal that flowed from the speakers. Must have been Marcus's. He listened to all types of music. Lance only listened to rap and Beyoncé.

The lyrics shouted something about the dead, with the drums, guitars, and those guttural utterances all coming together to make Nona feel she'd arrived in hell.

Folks at church would call this "the devil's music." She shut it off, relieved to be rid of it but unhappy Marcus listened to this sort of thing.

The room smelled of unwashed socks, sweaty sneakers, and an overabundance of sandalwood cologne. Her boys' choices for wall decor told of their differences. Posters of James Baldwin, Malcolm X, Shirley Chisholm, and Barack Obama adorned the wall above Marcus's twin bed and desk. Only one poster hung from the wall on Lance's side of the room: Beyoncé, barely clothed and shaking her hips. With Lance, it was always Beyoncé.

She pulled open Marcus's dresser drawers. Fished through shirts, shorts, socks. Searched under their beds. Found clumps of dust and lint but nothing else. She opened the closet. Top shelf held boxes of shoes. She checked each one. Floor had various balls—for soccer, hoops, and batting practice. No duffle bags.

On the desk, she found a notebook with Marcus's handwriting inside. On one page, he'd sketched three red-breasted birds, and the small creatures jolted her. *Cardinals.* He'd taken the time to detail the plumage, and when she squinted, she noticed he'd written the names *Kendall, Marcus,* and *Lance* in tiny letters between the feathers. The image reminded her of Vance's sketch of the cardinal, the kite, and Kendall.

Tears stung her eyes. When the boys were little, Vance would wake them early on spring weekends to listen to the songbirds in the trees, back when the elms were alive and still bore leaves. He'd gotten them binoculars to peer out the window with him, and the image of all of their curved backs and scrunched-up shoulders in T-shirts came to her in a strong wave of grief. Vance and Marcus were on opposite sides of the state and hadn't spoken in years, yet they both had sketched those cardinals. She turned the page, shame building that she'd continued to keep her boys from their father, whom they so obviously missed.

On the next page, Marcus had started a letter to Gretchen.

Dear Gretchen,

I know you don't agree with me.

She made a mental note to find out from fast-tail Gretchen what she and Marcus didn't see eye to eye on.

There was a separate black-and-white checkered notebook on which he'd scrawled some unfinished thoughts:

I am stuck on this one fact: The number of urban homicides versus the number of mass and/or school shootings in the state over the previous few years. Even with all of the think tanks and not-for-profits with bloated executive director salaries and fundraisers and "talks," not one of them has thought to compare the stats.

Thirteen kids die every day in America by homicide, most of them killed by guns, and yet no one looks at white and Black killers as one group. They section them off as mass shooters, school shooters, and urban criminals when they're all a by-product of the same violent country.

The current state of gun violence in America didn't begin with heavy metal, rap music, and video games. If so, what of duel culture from the eighteenth and nineteenth centuries?

Current youth violence mimics duel culture in that the latter practice was about protecting one's personal "honor," which the young men I've grown up around call "respect."

In a duel, the "gentlemen"—sometimes politicians, slave holders, and businessmen—set a time to settle their differences, meet, and even their score with bullets. The most famous victim was Alexander Hamilton, who was shot to death by Aaron Burr, a man who had been a senator and vice president of the United States.

Nona found the passage odd. It seemed he'd pressed the pen into the paper hard enough to make indentations, and the words were slanted, angular, not sitting on the line properly. Had he been dozing off or perhaps angry?

She spotted an essay he'd written titled "The Proliferation of Guns in the Inner City" about how poor Black and brown people suffered the most at the hands of legislation designed and lobbied for by the National Rifle Association. Each time "rifle" appeared in the piece—more than thirty times—Marcus had underlined it with red ink.

The way the paper was indented from him pressing into it with the pen sent a jolt through her. In some places, the tip had cut through the sheet, leaving holes and slashes beneath the letters.

She phoned Harlan. He didn't answer. She texted. Need to talk. Again. Sorry.

She called Pastor.

"Nona." He sounded relieved to hear from her.

"Has Marcus ever mentioned any writing to you? About youth violence?"

"Marcus? No. Not at all. Why?"

She told him about the essay in her hand.

"Why don't I talk to him again, Nona?"

"I don't think that's a good idea."

"He seems to have warmed up to me again. I think if I can get some one-on-one time with him to see how he's doing, I'll be able to put your mind at ease."

"I don't know." She couldn't imagine Marcus opening up to Pastor at this point, but who else did she have, really?

"Think about it."

"Shoot. I hear the boys coming back."

She hung up abruptly and realized she'd misjudged the sound: They were already outside their bedroom door. She panicked, tiptoed across the carpet, and ducked inside their closet to avoid getting caught.

She was a fool. This was her house. And these were her sons. She could have come up with the excuse that she was searching for something, or cleaning because they were pigs, or leaving a gift for them, but there she was, silencing her phone in the dark and staring at them through the slats in their closet door. What was her plan if they opened it? She was an idiot, she reminded herself. This was why she could never make it on her own.

The essay she'd dropped haphazardly on Marcus's desk rustled as the boys burst into the room. It caught Lance's eye. The black-and-white checkered notebook was open to the NRA page, and Nona wished she'd grabbed it when she hid. When Lance picked up the journal, Marcus snatched it from him.

"Don't read my work."

"What? I always read your work."

"Not anymore."

"Why not?"

"Because you've obviously been snooping through my stuff." Marcus pointed to the mess she'd made while rifling through his papers. And as he picked up a stack of pages, he revealed a metal lockbox, about the size of a lunch pail, resting in the middle of the desk. "These pages are only for Kendall to read."

The hair on Nona's forearms stood on end, and the frisson brought tears to her eyes.

Lance shot Marcus a look. Had he noticed Marcus's present-tense mention of Kendall as well? "Man, whatever. I didn't go through your stuff."

Marcus closed the notebook and stuffed it inside the box. He locked the container with a silver key the size of a marble. He tucked the case under his bed, which used to be Kendall's bed.

"And what you mean, 'for Kendall to read'? Kendall's dead." Lance's voice was cautious, almost a whisper.

She'd heard Marcus correctly: ". . . for Kendall to read." Present tense. As if Kendall still shared the room with the two of them, as if Kendall had been away on a trip for the past two years and would return any moment.

"Exactly." Marcus stared at him, one eye squinting. Would he strike his younger brother? "And what does that tell you?"

"That he can't read it."

"That nobody can read my stuff. You know what? I'm splitting our room in two. This will be my side. That will be your side. You stay on your side, and I'll stay on mine. I won't read your stuff, and you don't read my stuff."

"The room ain't big enough, Marcus."

She thought of emerging from the closet and intervening, since it was her snooping that had caused this disagreement. She wanted to defend Lance, who looked five again, wanting to play with the older brother who was locking him out, toughening him up.

Marcus exited their room and returned with the box from the kitchen labeled *tools,* along with a white bedsheet. He opened the cardboard flaps and pulled out a hammer. Panic rushed through her. The way Marcus gripped the handle—tight jaw, eyes narrowed, canines visible through his grimace—she worried he might wield that hammer against his younger brother.

The closet filled with the stench of garbage. Marcus's back seemed to grow again like Vance in that alley; his shoulder muscles appeared to tighten. With bangs that reverberated like he'd break through the drywall, he nailed the sheet to the ceiling in two places so it divided the space like a hospital room.

"Why you acting like this?" Lance said, his voice on the verge of cracking.

Nona missed Kendall even more. Marcus never would've treated Lance like this if Kendall were still alive. Kendall used to play ball and video games with Lance, taught him about girls when he thought Nona wasn't listening, helped him with his homework.

Lance huffed back tears and blurted out, "That's why Pacman is always fucking with you. Because you act like a moody bitch."

Pacman. A.k.a. Peter. Was it possible to hate a kid? Because she hated Peter. Mother certainly didn't deserve such an awful grandchild.

The phone lit up in Nona's hand, and the light must have flashed in Marcus's peripheral vision, because he squinted and glanced at the closet. There was an evil quality to his expression, as if at any moment he'd sink his teeth into someone. Her ears rang.

He crept to the door, the stench of garbage increased, his shoulders broadened, and his face was inches from hers on the other side of those slats, so close she could smell the onions on his breath.

She covered the phone screen with her palm, closed her eyes, and braced for the opening of the door, the shock, and the accusations of snooping.

The moment never arrived. She opened her eyes and saw the back of Marcus's head through those slats.

"Don't mention Peter to me ever again." Marcus stormed back across the room. He hammered so hard the walls shook.

Lance sat on his bed, his head down, staring at the gray metal box under Marcus's bed. She needed to get to that box before Marcus hid it and before Lance got to it.

Nona didn't know how she was going to get out of the situation she was in, but, whenever she reemerged as their mother, who was legitimately at home and not crouching in their closet, she would rip down that divider.

Argument over, Marcus and Lance changed clothes and reorganized their backpacks for afternoon sports in complete silence.

Someone was in the closet with her.

Pulsating breath, hot, damp, emanated from the darkness behind her and spread across her nape and back. Someone was standing behind her, exhaling warm air down her spine. The exhalation meant she couldn't chalk this up to her imagination. Someone, some*thing* was really there, moving wisps of her hair with its quiet panting.

Kendall?

No. Not Kendall. Never Kendall.

Too afraid to face the entity, she stood stock-still. She couldn't leave the closet. She couldn't stay in the closet. She held her breath as whatever it was crouched low to her ankles and snaked a warm finger along the skin on her foot.

She bit back her scream. Hot tears leaked down her cheeks. Fear shot through her stomach, making her grip a shirt on a hanger next to her to steady herself. Snot gathered above her top lip as she brought her fist to her mouth and bit down.

Darkness bathed the closet as Marcus and Lance snapped off the light, slammed the door, clomped down the hallway, and left the house as abruptly as they'd arrived.

She threw open the closet door and ran from the room before anything could snatch her. She rushed to the front door, hoping to follow the boys outside. Perhaps she could pretend she'd been in her bedroom the whole time, but when she snatched up her house keys from the counter and made it to the iron that Marcus and Lance had locked, the bolt wouldn't budge.

She refused to look into the hall. She checked the kitchen window, remembering how her boys said no one could fit through it. She needed to know whether she could open it. She needed to be able to open something, some path out of her home.

It wouldn't slide up. The wooden frame squeaked but stayed put, seeming to laugh at her attempts.

She had nowhere to run. She smelled smoke, and the burner on the stove started up. *Tick, tick, tick.*

Twenty-One

Nona prayed. The anointing oil sloshed around a glass jar that fit snugly in Pastor's fist, reminding Nona of a flask of whiskey. When she'd told him about Lance and Donnell, about Solomon getting killed, about Gretchen's mention of a gun, Pastor came right over. She hadn't told him about Gretchen's talk of the figure nor about the closet. She hadn't reconciled in her own mind what had happened in the boys' room, but she now firmly believed what she'd been experiencing was more than anxiety and grief.

He handed another container to her. She already had one under her pillow and yet another in the dresser drawer. He'd given her so many, and so far, they hadn't done a thing.

The entity in the closet flashed in her mind. The heat of it. The contact it had made with her body.

Pastor covered the bottle top with a finger and shook the oil at the walls, doorframes, and windows. He prayed that God would "bind the enemy" and "bless Nona's home." He even hummed "Standing in the Need of a Blessing," and, in her mind, she could hear Kendall singing the lyrics the way he used to when he was in the church's youth choir.

In her bedroom, she pressed her back against the window, getting as far from Pastor as possible. She caught his reflection in the blank screen of the seventeen-inch television sitting atop her late mother's chest-high dresser with missing pulls. She tried not to stare at him as he moved near her bed.

In the kitchen, the stove ticked. She'd experienced it so often, she didn't rush over to it this time, though Pastor did.

"Can't believe this is still happening, Nona." He stood in front of the range, hands ready to fix a problem he didn't have a clue how to.

"Your service guy came out," she explained. "Tinkered, but couldn't fix it. I left another message for the housing authority."

The burner lit itself, but it remained on the lowest setting, as if a small pot were boiling on top of it.

She pointed to the dish towel on the counter near him.

"I thought it was fixed." He snatched up the red towel, wet it in the sink, and threw it over the flame. "I'm guessing it's the pilot? Something is making it . . . I don't know."

He poured blessing oil in his right hand and rubbed it along the stove's surface. When the flames were completely gone and the ticking had abated, he draped the towel over the faucet handle and stared at her.

"Have you told me everything, Nona?"

"The housing authority isn't good about giving me an answer unless it is 'no.'"

"That's not what I'm talking about. This doesn't seem like a repair-person kind of fix." His voice was kind, but his eyes were firm, concerned.

"That part. Yeah." She might as well have been naked, because she was definitely exposed.

Pastor guided her to the kitchen table, sat across from her, and took her hands in his for prayer. His touch was a safe haven, reminding her that the shadows were really her imagination after all.

"You know how at church, you talk about the devil going after the saints, using the ones we love to get to us?"

"Yes. It's something I see all the time." Pastor caressed the back of her hands with his thumbs, and each stroke sent a wave of desire through her body. "The enemy is always at war with God's people. It's quite possible the devil's making life difficult for you by using this neighborhood to go after your boys."

"I'm starting to think this isn't a general devil thing." Her throat was raspy from crying and praying. She was so tired. She wanted to go to sleep, but she wouldn't be able to since she was up at night now, listening to floorboards creak, staring at shadows in the hall.

"God is strong enough to drive out any spirit, Nona."

"What if God doesn't want to help me drive out this spirit?"

Pastor stopped stroking her hand with his thumbs. "You are . . . familiar with this entity?"

Her cheeks grew warm. Her voice was trapped in her throat. It had been the moment in the closet, when the thing's finger had swiped her ankle. She couldn't be certain, but she'd connected it then with that bloody hand reaching for her in the alley. How could she tell Pastor she thought something had cursed her from the grave?

"You're seeing Kendall?"

Kendall's dimpled smile flashed in her mind. Then his bruised fist.

Tears filled her eyes and her hands trembled in Pastor's. He gripped her tightly, but it didn't stop her nerves from taking over. The tears fell and she lowered her head, letting them splash on her table.

"I thought maybe, at first, but no. I don't think this is Kendall."

"Is it the boy who you said was just shot the other . . . What was his name?"

"Solomon? No."

"Who, then?"

She couldn't tell him. She couldn't tell anyone. She wanted to utter the name NaDarius, but the word wouldn't leave her mouth.

She stood, motioning toward the door for him to go. He appeared surprised.

"Why won't you tell me, Nona?"

"Because . . . I can't."

"Why not?"

"I mean, you don't tell me everything, do you?"

"What do you mean?"

"I mean . . . your problems. Your worries. Your troubles. Something is bothering you, and you haven't told me. You said—"

"The church is in financial trouble." He put his hands in his pockets and rocked back on his heels. "Membership is down. Collection plates aren't filled the way they used to be. First Lady blames me, that I can't draw a crowd like I used to. I think the church wouldn't be in this trouble if she didn't overspend. When you were there in my office and the phone kept ringing? Bill collectors."

"Yet you've been helping me with money?"

"Helping you hasn't been an issue. Hasn't contributed to this problem."

"What are you going to do about the church?"

"I . . ." He scratched his head, averted his eyes.

He was hiding something from her. She knew that look.

"I have a few irons in the fire."

"You're not going to tell me? This is my point. There are things I can't tell you. There are things you can't tell me."

"I will tell you eventually, Nona. I just can't right now, but I don't think these things are the same. I trust you. I think perhaps you don't trust me."

"I trust you as much as I'm capable of trusting another person."

"Then you know you can tell me, Nona. You can tell me what's frightening you."

"I know." She walked to the door. "But one thing at a time."

Before she grabbed the wooden knob, he gripped her shoulders, turned her to him, took her cheeks in his hands, leaned down, and brought her lips to his, gently. One peck, his mouth slightly open. The kiss was slow and long enough that she had time to wrap her arms around his back to brace herself.

He kissed her again, letting his tongue linger on her lips. His hands raised her skirt, his thigh opened her legs, and he pressed her back against the door. He pushed his firmness against her. She unbuckled his pants and reached inside. He let out a gasp as her hand closed around him. His mouth covered hers, and all of her problems faded away as he lifted her, removed her panties, and entered her.

For a few seconds, they were still, not moving or even breathing. He throbbed inside of her and she pulsed around him. He stared into her eyes.

"Nona," he whispered as his mouth found hers again, and he slowly rocked inside of her again and again and again. Her home was silent. Outside her unit, every noise seemed to fade. Their breaths were rhythmic as his hands cupped her bottom, his body pressed into hers, faster and harder, sending throbs through her back as it banged into the door behind her.

Tears stung her eyes as his thrusts grew erratic and his breath turned to grunts just beside her ear. Sweat dripped from his face and dampened her neck. She tasted the salt as her tongue found his cheek, his chin. As they both climaxed, he whispered her name again and again. He remained with her legs tight around his waist and her back against the door as his slowing breaths blew her hair away from her shoulders.

"Nona. I'm undone by you," he whimpered, his face buried in her hair.

Her phone vibrated on the counter. A call, not a text. She pushed him away, shame growing inside of her as she pulled up her moisture-soaked panties, adjusted her bra. He didn't make eye contact with her as he buttoned his shirt, pulled up his pants, and buckled his belt.

Her legs were like jelly. She wanted more. She wanted to take him to her bed and spend the rest of the day wrapped in his arms, but she stepped away without meeting his eyes and turned the lock on the front gate.

"Nona. We have to talk."

Her phone vibrated again. A text this time.

"Later. I can't . . . The boys will be home."

He nodded, and she tried her front gate again.

The iron did not budge. She wiggled and banged on it, and it still didn't work. Pastor pounded on the compartment where the key should go, and the lock popped up, releasing the door.

"What are we going to do, Nona?" He pulled her close, put his forehead to hers, where their perspiration mixed.

"Pray about it." She kissed him gently. One peck. She grinned, and he managed a small smirk as she playfully pushed him out and closed the door.

She missed the call. Minutes later, it started ringing again. No one was on the other end when she answered. No voicemail. No actual message in the text. The call log showed a private number. She caught her breath, feeling the ache in her middle where Pastor had been. She returned her phone to the counter and immediately sensed someone behind her. She faced the dark hallway, where a floorboard creaked.

Her heart pounded against her ribs. Could one of the boys have been home this entire time? Did they see or hear what she'd just done?

Another floorboard creak gave way to footsteps, steady, heavy, and moving down the hall toward the boys' room.

"Lance? Marcus?" She didn't dare move from her spot near the front door.

The footsteps stopped. *"It's me."* It was that voice again. The one she'd heard the morning of the graduation, old, deadpan, evil. *"It's me."*

She snatched up her cell phone and the anointing oil Pastor had left behind as she turned to exit. Only the iron door was stuck again. She tugged at the bars, screaming, crying, hysterical in her fright as the voice, closer and closer behind her, repeated, *"It's me. It's me. It's me. It's me."*

Mother Lincoln appeared in the doorway, managed to unstick the lock, and let Nona outside. "What is going on, baby?"

Nona fell into the woman's arms, sobbing, unable to speak.

Mother checked inside of Nona's open unit. Nothing and no one were there. The woman prayed as she patted Nona's back, "Heavenly Father, I come to you in prayer for my baby Nona . . ." and she held and shushed Nona's sobbing the way she had after Kendall's funeral.

The next morning, Nona returned to the boys' room before getting on the bus, crouched near Marcus's bed that used to be Kendall's bed, and reached underneath for the box filled with Marcus's writings. It was gone.

During the ride to work, she fretted about the boys, about what she'd done with Pastor, about the finger swiping her foot in the closet, the voice in her home. She distracted herself by catching up on her missed messages. At some point during the night, Mable Cleveland had called to ask again about that open position at the plant.

Later at work, Nona used the beginning of her fifteen-minute break to check in with her foreman about her neighbor's job application.

"I found somebody else."

"But Mable's a really dependable, hardworking—"

"Ex-con."

"Who paid her debt to society and—"

"It's not going to work."

Nona stormed out of his office and went to the break room. She and Mable had just squashed the tension between them, and Nona wasn't looking forward to breaking the news to her. She'd have to do that later; she would spend the rest of her break phoning Gretchen.

She stood near her locker and watched another busload of summer camp kids file off and into the lobby on a tour of Up North. She scrolled through the numbers in her phone searching for Gretchen's, figuring out what she'd say to the eighteen-year-old. It was so rare she spoke to the fast-tail girl.

The overhead pager blared on: "Ashford, you have a call on line one." She hoped her foreman's phone call lasted a while in case Nona's ran long, but after his nonsense about Mable's application, a part of her didn't care whether he noticed her absence on the floor.

Gretchen answered on the second ring.

"Sister McKinley?"

"Hey, Gretchen."

"What a pleasant surprise."

Gretchen knew good and well she and Nona didn't get along. The girl should have known if Nona called, it was for a reason, and it wasn't going to be pleasant.

"I'm sorry to bother you, Gretchen, but I'm at work, so I'm going to cut to the chase."

"Okay, ma'am."

The promotional team led the children and their camp counselors to the glass wall to show them the snake of a bottling machine. As usual, the kids all oohed, aahed, and jostled to be up front.

"Have you spoken to Marcus recently?"

"Um, yes." Gretchen paused and cleared her throat. "He and I . . . uh . . . talk pretty regularly. Is everything okay?"

"I don't know if everything's okay. I know he . . . hasn't been himself recently. And he won't talk to me. Do you know anything?"

Gretchen was a chatty thing. Nona used to hate babysitting the girl because Gretchen would enter the house, talk nonstop for four or five hours, and then continue to flap her jaws on the way out the door. Nona tried to have compassion for her—at eight, the girl had lost her identical twin to a stray bullet, was often home alone, and didn't have anyone to talk to—but Nona was used to boys, who could spend an entire rainy Saturday in the living room together and not utter a word. So, when Gretchen paused on the phone call and didn't have a ready answer, Nona knew the girl was about to lie.

"Hasn't been himself? No, ma'am. I don't know anything about that."

"Right. Okay, Gretchen. Are you aware of Marcus purchasing a gun?"

"What?"

"A gun. I overheard you tell Kiki that Marcus purchased a gun. Is that true, Gretchen?"

"I— No, ma'am."

"Don't lie to me."

"I'm not, ma'am."

"Then why did you say it?"

"I don't know . . ." Gretchen's voice cracked.

The promotional team led the field trip group toward the entrance to the factory floor. A girl with afro puffs at the end of the line smiled at Nona as she passed. Nona couldn't return the gesture.

"Have you and Marcus had any disagreements recently?"

"Ma'am, I think you should talk to Marcus."

"About what? I've already tried to talk to him, and he clammed up. I found a letter he was about to write to you. He started it with something like, 'Dear Gretchen, I know you don't agree with me,' and then he didn't finish it."

"I don't feel comfortable sharing our conversations like this, though."

"You're a mother now, Gretchen. Imagine if Grayson grew up to be an eighteen-year-old man about to head off to college and he got into a fistfight and wouldn't tell you anything beyond that. And then you overheard a girl he knows telling someone else that he got a gun. Wouldn't you do everything in your power to find out what was going on?"

"Yes, ma'am."

"Do you have any information you can share with me about this fight? About this gun you may or may not have made up?"

"No, ma'am."

"Where is the gun, Gretchen?"

"There is no gun, Sister McKinley." Gretchen was full-on crying now.

The heavy factory doors creaked open and slammed shut as the group disappeared behind them.

"Then do you have anything you can share with me that will help me understand what is going on with him right now?"

"Shadows, ma'am."

The intercom crackled on again.

"Shadows?"

"Yes, ma'am."

"Say more."

"Marcus is . . ." Grayson whined in the background. It'd only be a few seconds before his tiny protests became wails.

"He's what, Gretchen? Spit it out."

"I don't know how to say it. He's . . . not himself. It's like he's possessed sometimes."

Nona's stomach dropped. The plant doubled in size, and the lights suddenly seemed dim.

"What do you mean, 'possessed sometimes?'" A headache arrived and pounded at her temples. "How? Who's possessing him?"

"I don't know. Maybe he should see a therapist? That's all I can share, and I've already shared too much."

"But who—"

Grayson started wailing.

"I have to go, Sister McKinley. Please don't tell Marcus I told you. He'd kill me."

And the girl hung up.

Gretchen had been careless when she'd said "he'd kill me" to the mother of a young man who'd been killed, but Nona was more concerned with how frightened Gretchen sounded when she uttered the words—whispered, as if jeopardizing more than her friendship with Marcus by betraying his secrets.

Recalling the way Marcus wielded that hammer in the bedroom with Lance, Nona put away her phone and closed her locker, turning over the word "possessed" in her mind. Without articulating it, Nona had been worried about that very idea. Then and now, that same fear crept into her heart.

Twenty-Two

Before she arrived at church, Nona ensured Pastor was not scheduled to be there, and she wore a hat and sunglasses, hoping to slip in and out of the business center unnoticed. The space had two things she didn't have at home: a computer and Wi-Fi. Lance had surpassed his phone's monthly data allowance twice over already, costing her an additional forty dollars for the month—money she didn't have—so as much as she wanted to research this on her phone, she was out of luck. Church business center it was, and she couldn't believe what she was about to do.

She entered, and the entire place was abuzz with staff readying everything for a visiting pastor from New York. The cleaning crew stood on ladders to wipe dust from the chandeliers. Kitchen workers folded white linens and rolled them into gold-plated napkin rings. The first lady conducted a dress rehearsal with the musical director. The two women glared over their shoulders at Nona and exchanged a look as Nona headed for the stairwell.

The church's basement housed the ballroom where Marcus's graduation party had been, an auditorium, two conference rooms, and the business center with five computer stations, a printer, a copy machine, and a landline.

A woman with a purple buzz cut sat at the station farthest from the door. She noticed Nona, nodded, and then went back to staring at the computer, the blue light from the screen glowing on her face.

"God is good," Nona said, expecting the woman to respond *All the time.*

She instead gave Nona a side-eye, whispered, "Ooookay," and returned her eyes to the screen.

Nona chose the station nearest the door so the young woman wouldn't see what she was researching. She didn't know what she was looking for, exactly, but after adjusting her chair and logging in, she searched the words "curse" and "how to get rid of curses." This was an abomination of Christ. She sensed her late mother, the church elders, and Mother Lincoln all standing over her shoulder, muttering *tsk tsk tsk,* and calling her research "witchcraft" and "voodoo."

How had she gotten to the point in her life in which she was searching for answers outside of God and the Word, all from inside her church? Even Pastor would tell her this was sacrilegious. *Giving the devil glory.* She couldn't care about their judgment right now. And Pastor had slept with her, after all. Who was he to judge anybody?

She found some famous curses. The curse of Tippecanoe, which she'd learned about in grade school, was blamed on the Shawnee chief Tecumseh, who, after losing a battle, placed a curse on the future President Harrison and later presidents. Between Harrison and John F. Kennedy, the country elected a president every twenty years who died in office. Taylor was the exception.

She hadn't believed the curse in grade school, and she still didn't believe it now. She assumed being president was stressful and that's what killed the men.

There was the supposed curse of King Tut's tomb by the archaeologists who opened it.

The Hope Diamond curse. Another tomb. That time the burial place of a Polish king that cursed the archaeologists who opened it. Tombs apparently shouldn't be opened.

She combed through endless web pages, many describing the same lethal hexes, others claiming outlandish outcomes like enlarged lips or backsides. She decided to scrap the entire search. As she hovered her mouse over the x at the top of the screen, she noticed the title of an article by a self-proclaimed medium: *How to tell if you've been cursed.*

She fully believed it was meant for her to find that article. She clicked the link. Her pulse quickened. She had no clue whether this medium knew what he was talking about, but she read it anyway.

Do you feel everything is going wrong in your life?

Yes. She could attest to that fact. The raid. Vance imprisoned. Kendall killed. Marcus and Peter fighting, and the shadow in her home.

Does everything around you seem to die—flowers, plants, pets, loved ones?

Definitely. Even her zinnias were dead.

Do you or a loved one exhibit odd or dangerous behavior at times, as if possessed?

She thought back to her call with Gretchen. "Possessed" is how the girl had described Marcus. Did Nona believe that? She mentally ticked off his recent behavior: his anger, his fight with Peter, his possible purchase of a gun. Lance drinking alcohol, smoking weed, breaking into homes. This was all new behavior for both of them. Pastor said they were acting out because of all the loss and grief, but that couldn't explain everything, could it?

Does it seem that nothing ever works out, even on minor occasions and when you expect it to?

Yes. Yes. Yes. The thousand-dollar fee for Marcus's registration that came out of nowhere, which she had to sin to get from Pastor. The faulty stove. Mable's job application.

Do you have strange physical ailments and unexplained bodily dysfunction?

Yes. The feelings of vertigo she sometimes experienced. The foul smells.

From the other end of the business center, Purple Hair moved in her seat, and the squeaking made Nona jump.

With a notebook in hand, the young woman rifled through her shoulder bag, which was well-worn leather and seemed expensive. "You got a pen?"

Nona grabbed the one she'd packed in her own purse, and the woman came over to retrieve it.

Noticing Nona's screen, Purple Hair glared. "See? That's why I don't be talking to half the saints in this place."

"Excuse me?"

"Y'all be walking around talking 'bout 'God is good' and 'let the church say amen,' then you get behind closed doors and be looking up hoodoo."

Nona snatched the pen back from the woman and said, "I hope you never lose a son. I hope you never have to fight something you don't understand."

Purple Hair's eyes widened; she padded back to her chair with a lot less spunk that time.

The article on Nona's screen went on to say she needed a spiritual cleansing to counter the hex. Nona didn't even know what a spiritual cleansing was but imagined it was different than the blessing oil Pastor had used.

Only a medium can guide you, the article continued. *Someone with access to water.*

Water? She kept reading, and it said the medium would use *nature's liquid* to create a connection to the spirit realm.

Nona pressed *print* on the screen and stood to retrieve the paper from the machine. The door behind her thumped, then creaked open. A golden church hat appeared in the entryway. It rose slowly and revealed thick black sunglasses like those typically worn by Hollywood starlets. The dark frames eased down a pointed and powdered nose.

"Hello, Sister Carter. I've been praying for your job search."

"Hi, First Lady," Purple Hair said. "I sent three resumes out. I hope the bottling plant calls me back. I live right by the bus line."

"God is good, Sister Carter."

"All the time, ma'am."

So purple-haired Sister Carter knew how to be respectful, but she hadn't been that way to Nona? *Heifer.*

"Sister McKinley," First Lady said, nearly whispering. "A word."

The woman raised her hand and waved Nona over, gesturing for Nona to come to her, but she'd snapped her fingers and flicked her thumb the way a person would call their dog.

Nona picked up her paper from the printer, folded it to hide its contents, and slowly made her way to the first lady, pinpricks spreading across her scalp. She sensed Sister Carter staring at her back, waiting for some gossip-worthy conversation to unfold.

"Why is it that every time I see Tim on the phone, he's talking to you?"

First Lady Davis stood in the doorframe with her hand on her hip. Between the heels and the church hat, the woman looked like a golden tree. Her eyes pierced Nona's soul, and when the woman spoke, she exposed her canines like a Doberman.

Nona felt two feet tall in her stained jeans, sneakers, and T-shirt, her hair falling loosely at her shoulders. She was a caterpillar to the first lady's butterfly. She caught a glimpse of the first lady's flawless three-carat wedding ring. Dead caterpillar was a better description for Nona.

"Marcus and Lance have gotten into a bit of trouble. Pastor has been helping with—"

"I figured you'd say that."

In the hallway, two church administrators walked by with their eyes low, but they peeked over the first lady's shoulder to catch a glimpse of Nona and then whispered to one another as they continued down the corridor.

Nona wished Pastor would show up at this very moment. He'd have found a way to protect her.

"I knew you'd say this was about your boys, and I know that is not the case."

"I'm not following." She was following and had the rapid heartbeat to prove it. She didn't want to have this conversation. Being confronted about sneaking around with Pastor made their interactions real. She could no longer pretend.

"Well, maybe you can follow this. Do you know Arthur Reynolds?"

"The guy who owns the bottling plant?"

"Yes."

"Yes. I know him. He owns the plant."

"Does he come to your home? Has he invited you to his home?"

"Arthur Reynolds? No. I just work there."

"Right. My point exactly. You cannot say you know him. You merely work at his company. So you can say you know *of* him. Art and I attended the same college. Same year. Many of the same classes. He invites Tim and me to his home, and he is always welcome at ours."

"Why are you telling me this?"

"Because your husband is in prison and you need your job."

Nona's breathing picked up. Heat crept up her collar, past her cheeks, and onto her scalp.

"I will not speak to you about this again." First Lady Davis raised her voice that time, which brought out the security-looking guy who had been at Marcus's graduation party. The man stood in the hallway and trained his eyes on Nona. Nona couldn't tell whether the young man was security for Pastor, the first lady, the church, or perhaps he wasn't even security, but she remembered him seeming out of place at Marcus's graduation. Despite his suit, something sinister in his face made him seem out of place here as well.

And with that, First Lady Davis sauntered off, strutting in her heels, waving off the security guy as she passed.

Nona returned to her seat at the computer, swiveling the chair left and right as she caught her breath. Tears burned her eyes.

Purple-haired Sister Carter cleared her throat. "If she all buddy-buddy with dude who own the bottling plant, why she got me out here submitting my resume through they website?"

Nona wasn't sure whether Sister Carter was speaking to her or thinking out loud.

"I mean, why she ain't hand my application directly to him?"

Nona rose, packed her belongings, and said, "Because that would be too much like right. I work there. Give me your resume. I'll give it to my foreman."

The woman sheepishly handed over the paper, and Nona placed it inside the folder beside the curse research articles.

"You ain't gotta do that. But thank you. I live at Dempsey."

"I grew up at Dempsey. I'm at Hester Gardens now."

"You heard they closing us down? Few more months and Dempsey will be a memory."

"I heard."

"I'm trying to get me some work so I ain't gotta go into public housing again after I leave. I want . . ."

The young woman seemed pained, but Nona didn't need her to finish the sentence to know what she was thinking.

"I'll see what my foreman can get you. I'll call you."

Nona headed to the door. Marcus's future was disappearing before her.

"Hey," Sister Carter said. "If you need help with a curse or something, you got a neighbor over there in the Gardens who can help you. She's my mom's cousin. More like my auntie."

Nona turned, a jolt running through her. Talking about the curse was like talking about her affair with Pastor: The words made the thing real and, in the case of her curse, for the first time, surmountable.

"A neighbor?"

"Yeah. She's real secretive about it, but you can tell her Tahleasy told you to come. I don't think she follows a religion or anything, but she definitely knows how to deal with the spirits and such. I've seen her do it. Her name is Mable."

"Mable Cleveland?"

"Yeah. You know her?"

She'd left a message for Mable to call her but hadn't heard back, which wasn't unusual—Mable sometimes went silent when bill collectors were after her for overdue payment. Nona remembered those days well, of screening calls, not answering the door when the postal worker wanted her to sign for certified mail, getting her paycheck and discovering her wages had been garnished. Pastor had freed her from that, but the trauma remained, and she understood exactly what Mable was going through. So, when her cell phone rang and she saw Mable's face on the screen, she answered on the second ring.

"Mable. So glad to hear from you."

Silence on the other end.

"Mable?"

"Mrs. McKinley, it's Donnell."

Nona's heart shot into her throat. Her body became erect in the chair at her kitchen table. "Donnell?" Something horrific must have happened for Donnell to call from his mother's phone. "Is Mother okay?"

"Mother's okay. My moms is okay. Everybody's all right. But I . . . I don't know."

"Do you want to speak to Marcus?" She didn't offer up Lance, because she wanted Donnell to stay away from her youngest.

"No. I meant to call you. I tried everybody, and for some reason you the only person I could reach quickly. Everybody must be out. And my moms left behind her phone."

"Okay. Slow down. You're talking kind of fast. Are *you* okay?"

"I'm straight." He sounded like the little boy she used to babysit after school, who used to play jacks with Kendall. She could see the two of them on her living room floor, baseball caps on, sitting cross-legged, bouncing the ball, picking up the metal pieces, and shouting "Ah, man!" when they lost.

"I just . . . I need for you to look out at my house right now."

"Look at your house?"

"Yeah. I keep hearing something and I don't know what it is, but—"

"Something like what?"

Nona concluded Donnell was high. Or that he'd experimented with a hallucinogen, which was not unusual for him.

"Okay. Look. It's not gon' make no sense what I'm finna tell you."

"Then maybe you shouldn't tell me, Donnell. Where's your mother?"

"She's at . . . I don't know." He was lying. He knew where his mother was. "Please, Mrs. McKinley."

She thought of the night Mable and Vega sat with Marcus and Lance when Nona went to I.D. Kendall's body. Mable had been there for her even though Nona didn't really deserve Mable's help. Even though Nona hadn't gotten her the job at the plant. Even though Nona judged the woman. And she still needed a favor from Mable. She told herself to listen to Mable's son. Help him. By doing so, she was helping Mable.

"Okay, Donnell. Tell me what happened."

"Me and Wiggly was watching TV."

Wiggly was Mable's nephew who stayed with her and Donnell from time to time. He wasn't in the HBs, or any gang for that matter, but he was just as street as Donnell. Maybe worse.

"And it was getting dark out, but something kept going *thump, thump, thump* out the window, like a basketball bouncing."

She thought of Solomon.

"This wasn't the first time either. Last time I heard the bouncing, nobody was there. So, this time, I was already nervous, but I looked out the window, and there was this thing standing there, but it for sure wasn't bouncing no ball. Then it was kind of pacing there. I told Wiggly to come see, but when he got there, it was gone."

Nona waited for Donnell to crack up laughing and say *syke!* But the more he spoke, the more frightened his voice became.

"A thing?" She sat up straight. Here was another person seeing something. Hearing something. Knowing something was wrong. "What was it?"

"I don't know. Like a creature."

"A creature?"

"More like a shape. Something. A figure."

A figure.

"And did you see it again?"

"No. And I didn't hear the ball bouncing anymore either. I know, Mrs. McKinley. It's . . ."

"Could it have been a person?"

"Maybe."

"And maybe they walked away? Did you follow them?"

"Hell no! It's like this thing is directed at me. This shit is personal. Language. Sorry, Mrs. McKinley. No disrespect. I'm just saying, the last time I went looking for it, the thing crashed the window down on my neck."

"Donnell." Anger rose in her stomach. He'd had her for a minute, but Gretchen had probably told Donnell about their call. She found it hard to believe the same person who carried a pistol everywhere, broke into houses, and had no issue with roughing up their owners was suddenly scared. And she definitely didn't believe that Donnell would admit something had hurt him with a window. "Stop playing on my phone. I'm about to hang up."

"No. No. No. No. No. I'm not playing on your phone, Mrs. McKinley. On my life. On my mama's life. You know me, Mrs. McKinley. I know I'm not like Kendall, but you know I have never disrespected you. Ever. I'm . . . I'm losing it right now, and—"

"Okay. Okay. Okay. Donnell. It's okay." These young men were so big and bad all the time with their tattoos and guns and foul language, but when it really got down to it, they were scared boys seeking out their mothers. "What do you want me to do?"

"Can you just go out and look at my unit? You don't have to walk all the way over. Look from the courtyard. I mean, I guess. I don't know. I just want to make sure the thing isn't still—"

"Donnell. Are you high?"

"No, ma'am." Donnell answered Nona's question as if under oath.

Nona tried to imagine a silhouette bouncing a ball outside Donnell's unit, only with no basketball. And then a thought popped in her head, and fear, like a cold, dead finger, slid up her spine. What if Donnell was telling the truth? What if it was her curse? Or the figure Vega saw when Solomon was killed? She glanced at the hallway, remembering the shadow that had looked like Kendall.

"Why can't you look outside for yourself? I heard you aren't scared of anything. That you break into homes in Sebastian Hills with folks inside."

Long pause. She imagined him with those puppy-dog eyes her boys often got.

"This is different, Mrs. McKinley. This is . . . I don't know what this is."

"Okay. I'll take a look. I'll call you when I'm outside."

"Thank you, Mrs. McKinley. And I swear. If you don't see anything, I'm going to church. I'll have Pastor anoint me or something. I'll go to counseling. Anything."

She locked up, and with only her cell phone, she crept along the courtyard just far enough to see the Clevelands' unit. Dusk had settled on the Gardens. Televisions blared from most homes. The clink of dishes and the sound of running sink water came from most windows. Vega wasn't outside, and Nona wished she were.

Nona squinted past the dead trees with bikes and hula hoops resting against the trunks. No one was near the door or windows of the Clevelands' home. She called Mable's phone back.

"What you see, Mrs. McKinley?"

"Looks like I'll be seeing you at church on Sunday."

"You sure?"

"I'm sure."

"Man. Okay. I'm trippin' again." Donnell's voice still trembled. He didn't seem convinced.

"Have a good night, Donnell."

She hung up. And as she headed home, from the corner of her eye, she caught movement in the darkness. She stopped. A band of light had fallen on the Clevelands' home. Near the front door, a shadowy figure crouched low, watching her. An icy cord spread from her scalp down her spine. Her breath hitched in her throat. She took an unsteady step forward to get a better view, and the crouching figure's eyes glowed. She must be confused. Was she seeing a cat? A large one? Or some other creature? A coyote?

She moved two steps closer, and to remove all doubt, the figure slowly rose like a man, standing tall on two legs and staring at her with the eyes of a night creature. She held her breath and didn't dare blink—she didn't want the figure to go away without her knowing what she was seeing.

Her phone rang, and it frightened her so much she dropped it on the ground. It rang again and again. She finally managed to grab it, stand, and answer.

"Mrs. McKinley." It was Donnell, frantic again. "What you see? I see you out my window still staring. What is it?"

There was nothing near his door. "Nothing, Donnell." She was panting and her voice trembled. He wouldn't believe her if she didn't calm down again. "Nothing is there. I think sometimes our minds just play tricks on us."

He was going to speak again, but she hung up. This thing near the door, this was someone else. Some*thing* else. The figure in her hallway had tipped its head like Kendall. The entity in the boys' closet had swiped at her foot, pointing to NaDarius, but the eyes. The glowing eyes.

She took one final glimpse of Donnell's unit. Nothing was there. Even the band of moonlight had disappeared.

Part Three

Twenty-Three

Nona couldn't get Mable to return her calls. So Nona went to Vega. She was overdue to pay the woman a visit after Solomon was killed.

Nona knocked on Vega's door, and the gangly woman let her in with a "Hey, church lady."

Nona had never been inside Vega Lawson's home. She'd always imagined the woman's unit would be filled with black lights, incense, and dragon statues, but that ended up not being the case.

The furniture was sparse: a couch, a coffee table, and a kitchen dining set with one chair. The place looked as if Vega spent all her time scrubbing it. And when Janis Joplin's voice came flowing from a tabletop speaker, the space felt familiar.

Vega offered her a shot of bourbon and lowered the volume of the music but left it high enough for the speakers to pump out Joplin's screeching mezzo-soprano. Nona accepted the drink, surprised to also see Vega joining in. The alcohol burned Nona's tongue as she sipped it on Vega's firm-cushioned couch. The last time she'd had alcohol, Vance had made it for her. As the buzz took hold of her body, Nona was grateful the woman hadn't turned her away.

"Haven't seen you much since . . ." Nona paused, unable to finish the sentence. She hated it when people didn't say the words

Kendall was killed, and yet she found herself struggling to do the same about Solomon.

"My grief's like a straitjacket. Can't take it off, and it's hard to move around with it on. But you've come because you're worried about Marcus."

Nona was always taken aback at Vega's ability to know what everyone was thinking.

"You read my mind again."

"I don't read minds. I read intentions." Vega's smile was warm even though it was pained.

"Intentions. I guess I don't know what to do. Or who to talk to."

"So you came to me. You must be desperate." Vega let out a belly-quivering cackle that made Nona jump. Nona tried to find the humor in Vega's self-deprecating words and forced a smile. "You know everyone calls me the mad scientist? Oh, they don't say it to my face, but they say it."

"People can be judgmental." Nona was aware she was also referring to herself.

"Tell me what the trouble is, and start at the beginning."

Nona let out a sigh that raised her bangs. "I'm . . . seeing and hearing things that aren't real. And I'm not the only one around here that it's happening to." She thought of Donnell, Kiki, and Gretchen. "But it seems Marcus might be seeing them too, only he won't admit it."

"Seeing and hearing what things?"

Between sips of bourbon and Vega's multiple shots of the drink, Nona told her about the voice in her home. Marcus's odd graduation speech. The fight with Peter. Peter's confession. Marcus's essay. The secrets he shared with Gretchen. The gun. She left out the part about Donnell and the ball bouncing. She didn't want the thought of Solomon lurking around to unsettle Vega the way the idea of Kendall being spotted hurt her.

"Nona, I told you to start at the beginning." With a deadpan face, Vega's eyes bore into Nona's. "And what you did was start at the first time you noticed the thing, but that's not the beginning. You can't bullshit me, Nona. Nobody can." With a raised eyebrow and a smirk, Vega daintily lifted her cup and sipped.

Everything stopped for Nona. She couldn't be angry with Vega, because this was what she needed: clarity, help, a way out.

"The thing in your home is specific to you. Like the figure I saw after my Solomon was killed is specific to me."

"What did it look like?"

"A shadow. An outline. A shape. Someone there, but also someone unseen. It was my curse. And I know why my curse is here. Why is yours? What have you done?"

Yes. Nona was cursed, but she couldn't say exactly where her curse was from. NaDarius had haunted her mind every day since the alley, but could she say with certainty that he was also haunting her home and her boys? How did she know it wasn't Kendall using Marcus to get back at Peter? She hated to let her mind go there, but maybe Gretchen was right and Kendall was as angry as she was that Peter was walking around free, growing older, having his own child, while Kendall's future had abruptly ended. Yet NaDarius was brutally beaten to death. He'd have just as much right to be angry.

"I don't really know, but I fear it's not something I've done." Nona reached over to the coffee table and poured herself a full shot of bourbon. She didn't sip it this time. She downed it and appreciated Vega for letting her sit in silence as the drink relaxed her muscles. The final drink Vance had mixed for her had been a martini. Extra dirty. And he'd placed each olive in her mouth, followed by a kiss. "It might be something I didn't do. Something I let happen."

"As long as you know what it is. But listen. Violence is like an infection. These government experts will sit around and come up with plans to fix a public health crisis like cigarettes or car accidents, but they won't do shit for violence. We have an epidemic of violence, no different than if a virus ran through here. It gets into one of these young men's bodies, and it takes over everything. The way they walk, talk, think, the people they hang around, the music they listen to. You can smell the violence on them. It's like they're possessed."

Exactly what Gretchen had said.

"That violence makes them pick up a gun and fire that bullet. And then that violence passes to the next person who cared about that victim. And then they keep passing it along like the damn flu, only deadlier."

"So what do I do?"

"My boy is dead, Nona. If I knew, he'd still be here. Why don't you ask that pastor who's been running up behind you every five seconds?"

"I did. That's where I got the blessing oil."

"Why you think you always need a man, Nona?"

"Vance stopped someone from attacking me at the beginning of our relationship, and I . . ." She remembered the man who jumped out of the shadows at the bus stop late that night. The one who grabbed her, dragged her to the ground.

"Solomon and Esmé's father saved me too, in a way."

"You've never mentioned him before."

"I know. And that's by design. The kids never even knew who he was. Esmé asked me while we were getting dressed for Solomon's burial, and I still didn't tell her."

"Where is he?"

"Where . . . ? Well, he's dead, of course. So I'd been hoping he was in hell." Vega cackled again.

Nona was floored. She'd heard the gossip. That he was in prison or ran off with some woman or was in the military and Vega got tired of waiting for him to come back. At no point had Nona considered the man could be dead.

"That was the figure I saw when my boy was shot. It was that good-for-nothing man, back from the grave to destroy me. Because he knew, they all know, a loving mother would rather leave this earth than watch her child die. Anybody who gets killed here, you know they stay."

"You saw him? And he's in your home?"

"Not just him, and not just in my home. In yours. In Mable's. Mother Lincoln's. All the others too."

"In my home?"

"Before you and Vance moved in, your unit kept the smiths at Medford Door and Key busy. They were always called out to re-key locks, no matter the tenant. Doors and windows were always fastening shut and none of the keys would turn the deadbolts."

"The same thing happens with my door and windows sometimes."

"The lady just before y'all moved in had a three-year-old who wandered out of the house, and when Mom went to the front door to bring the toddler back inside, she was locked inside her home with her baby headed to Prescott Road."

"Oh my God."

"I had to pick up the toddler to keep him from making it into street traffic. I told her that no matter how many locksmiths she called, the doors and windows would always close up on her. It's why they gave us the 'no bars' rule. I told her, but she didn't listen. She eventually put bars on like everybody else."

Nona thought about her irons, her windows, grateful her boys were older now. "You never told me about this before."

"Because it seemed things were fine in that unit after you arrived. But you see? Spirits walk the same grounds our feet are resting on."

She thought back to the figure outside Mable and Donnell's unit. Was it different than the one in her home?

"Ask me? It's because they stole this land from Black folks a long time ago. Trumped-up charges for the Black people who owned it—the Hester family. Locked them up in prison and took the land. Land seizures weren't only in the south and weren't only done by lynchings. No-good suckas drove all the Black owners right off the land, and now they're renting it back to us like it belongs to them.

"These Hollywood movies will have us thinking Native folk are the only ones to curse some land. They love to throw that in when their imaginations and research fall short, but it's bullshit."

"If your theory is correct, and Black folks cursed the land, why are Black folks the ones dying?"

"Land curses are like bullets. They ain't got no name on 'em. And we *weren't* the only ones. Poor white folks used to live here in the beginning too. They were getting killed, and their spirits stuck around just like the others. There's one dead white man lurking around who I heard would beat his wife until his brother-in-law found out and strangled him to death in his living room."

"Oh my God."

"Things are heating up around here too. Spirits are unsettled because they're shutting down Dempsey and we're eventually going to be next."

"What?" It had been Nona's dream to leave Hester Gardens, but she'd always imagined leaving on her own, not being forced out because the place was shut down.

"Yep. That's what I heard. Shutting us down too. Anyway, back to you. My guess is since the evil you're facing is not of this world, the solution isn't either. What did you use to get better after Kendall was killed?"

"I didn't get better. I just kept going."

"How?"

"Prayer. My Bible. Going to church. My blessing oil."

"My guess is you are wise to start there. I don't have those things at my disposal. You know I think religion is no different than magic, but if it worked for you before, maybe it will work now. And more than that, I think you have to figure out what the curse needs."

"What it needs?"

"Yep. It needs something from you. So you have to stop bullshitting yourself about what caused it."

Nona thought back to Vance in the alley with the bloody gun in his hand, the body slithering across the ground with its outstretched hand—*Don't let him kill me.* Was it NaDarius? And, if so, what did he need? Did she really have the power to give it to him?

"And that's it, church lady. See Marcus off to college. Make sure he gets out of town without a hitch. That's really it at this point, right?"

Nona nodded. Was that a real solution? Violence and curses had no regard for geography. What if the curse could follow Marcus anywhere? She couldn't think that now. She stood. And Vega did not like physical contact, but she allowed Nona to hug her. She did not hug Nona back, but she at least did not push Nona away.

Nona stepped outside. "One last thing, Vega."

Vega kept her door open; perhaps she didn't want their visit to end.

"I think Mable might be able to help me. Don't you think so too?"

Vega paused. Stared long and hard at Nona, seeming to weigh whether or not to answer.

"You'd have to ask her yourself, church lady."

"She's not returning my calls. I tried to get her a job out at the—"

"Knock on her door. If she gives you a hard time, let me know." Vega closed her screen door and clicked the lock. She stared at Nona through the mesh. "I hope your god will forgive you for whatever it is you've not done. Maybe that will help too. Because these spiteful ones really want vengeance. And when they want revenge, they stop at nothing to get it."

Pastor: Are you avoiding me? I wanted to see you again, but you haven't answered my calls or texts. Is everything okay? Are you having second thoughts because of the other day? I miss you. Being away from you is killing me.

As she crossed the courtyard, she started a text to Pastor: Your wife confronted me.

She was going to tell him about how the first lady had threatened her job, but Vega's words echoed in her mind: *Why you think you always need a man, Nona?*

She deleted the text and put away her phone. A blue ball rolled into her path as she crossed the courtyard. Why did this toy keep appearing out of nowhere? Last time she'd seen it, the thing had even disappeared. Looking for the ball's owner, she scanned the center of Hester Gardens, but there were no children there.

Nona knocked on the screen door to Mable Cleveland's home, banging the rusted rectangle against the frame. The main door was open, but the lights were off inside except for the pale fluorescent above the stove and a dim pendant barely illuminating the breakfast nook. At eye level, a hole the size of a bullet had punctured the middle of the screen's dusty mesh. A bass-heavy rap song unfamiliar to Nona flowed from the unit.

"Hey, Nona. Whatcha know good?" Seated at her dining table, Mable clicked on the lamp that rested on her nearby buffet. The stout woman was drinking and playing a card game with Donnell.

"What up, Mrs. McKinley?" A cigarette hung from Donnell's mouth. His eyes were frantic, and even through the screen, she could tell he had a tremor. That was new; she wondered if it was related to the thing that had frightened him.

Nona got a mental image of the figure near the Clevelands' door, and a shudder passed through her.

Mable and Donnell were still listening to that rap song, and when the track seemed to get too loud, Mable said to Donnell, "Cut that shit down."

"Ah, Ma. I thought you like The Game."

"Yeah, boy, but we got company."

Donnell reached over to a bookcase behind them and turned off the music; he and Mable seemed more like friends than a mother and son. Nona never allowed her boys to get familiar with her like this. She came close with Kendall, but there was still a threshold she never crossed.

"I was hoping I could talk to you, Mable."

"Me?" Mable smiled, exposing the gap where that gold tooth used to be, and she exchanged a look with Donnell, who shrugged, his eyes darting between his mother and Nona.

Mable shifted in her seat. Was the woman thinking Nona was about to bring up Donnell staying away from Lance again?

"It's personal," Nona said, smiling, letting them both know Nona hadn't arrived to stir up any trouble. "Woman stuff."

Mable's shoulders relaxed, and she tilted her head at Donnell. A dismissal.

"Catch y'all later." He shuffled off quickly, taking puffs of his cigarette as he went.

Mable watched him go and took a sip from her glass.

"Wanna come in, Nona?"

Nona drew back the screen and crossed the doorway of a home she'd never entered before. The place crowded in on her. Baskets of unwashed jeans and T-shirts waited to be carted to the laundromat. Cans of black beans and sweet corn littered the counter, begging to be put away. And it seemed the woman had not been to her stall at the flea market in weeks, for she'd placed six rows of costume jewelry on her coffee table; lamps, throw pillows, two winter coats, and a prom dress filled the corner. Nona hated she couldn't get Mable hired at the plant.

"I checked in with my foreman again, and he said no."

"My record?"

"Your record. I'm sorry, Mable."

"Don't mention it. You tried."

Mable wasn't an "it's okay" or "thank you" kind of person. "Don't mention it" was about as soft as the woman got.

"You could have texted about my application. Seems that ain't why you're here."

"I'll cut to the chase, Mable."

"That's how I like it, Nona."

Mable also wasn't the hostess kind, so she didn't gesture for Nona to sit. Nona stood next to the chair Donnell had vacated, shifting from foot to foot, self-conscious as Mable's concerned eyes took her in.

"I think I've been cursed."

Mable's face was hard to read, but she did not seem happy. "Cursed?"

"Like a hex."

With a hint of mirth on her mouth, Mable stared up at Nona from her spot at the table. "The woman of God thinks she's been cursed." Mable caressed her glass of brown liquid. "What you know about curses?"

"Not much." She removed the curse research article from her pocket and handed it to Mable. The woman squinted, skimmed it, then dropped it on the table.

"Sometimes folk'll speak a curse over somebody, and the victim believes it, then goes around making their own curse happen by acting a fool or being careless. They create their own suffering."

"That's not what's happening to me."

"How you know?"

"Because I believe I'm meant to suffer by watching those I love die, and as surely as I'm standing here, that is happening. It only struck me recently that this is what's going on, but it's been unfolding for years. And I'm worried about Marcus. It's coming for Marcus."

"Why you telling me? Why don't you tell your . . . pastor?" Mable smirked on that final word.

"I need something other than blessing oil."

"And you think I can do something about this?"

"I heard you might be able to help."

Mable leaned back in her chair, her shoulders square, the life force seemingly sucked from her body. Had Nona offended Mable?

"Have a seat, Nona."

Nona took Donnell's spot.

"What you want me to do for you?"

"I need you to stop the curse."

"I can help you do a smudge. It's where you walk through the house with some burning sage and—"

"I've already done that." She hadn't, but it sounded too much like the blessing oil to make a bit of difference. "Do you have anything more powerful?"

"You don't want that. I won't do that."

"Why not? Whatever it is, I want it."

"Because you believe different things. This won't work if you think your expensive church makes your faith stronger than mine."

"What can I do to make you do it?"

"Nothing."

Nona texted Vega: Help!

Mable glanced at a nearby shelf, where a pistol rested silently within arm's reach. A threat. "You should go."

"But—"

"If you know what's good for you." The woman flared her nostrils.

Before Nona could respond, Vega was at Mable's door, coffee

mug in hand. Vega slammed open Mable's screen and stood in the living room.

"Ah, shit." Mable rubbed her forehead. "This the last time I leave my door unguarded."

"Nona said she needed your help?" Vega took a sip from her coffee.

"Yeah, but Nona also don't know what the fuck she's poking at."

"That's the thing"—Nona hadn't meant to raise her voice—"I'm already in it. I've already lost one of my sons."

That line sucked the air from the room. As Mable's gaze went from Nona's face to Vega's, the woman went from anger to tears. "Don't do this to me, Nona. You know I love all these boys around here like they my own."

Vega nodded and matter-of-factly added, "She ain't lying about the curse."

"Then let me do the smudge, Nona. The other thing is . . . iffy. It can get . . . dangerous." Mable was pleading, and Nona had never seen this side of the woman.

Nona folded her arms across her chest and said, "Things are already dangerous."

Mable brought the glass to her mouth, noticed it was empty, slammed it on the table, and whispered to herself, "Damn."

"You don't know what it's like," Vega said, her voice low and near a whisper. "To lose your child. You don't know that pain. Because if you did—"

"Look, the thing you need, Nona, it can make things worse."

"I have to try."

"What I do—it's not what you might have heard about me on the streets." Mable cut an angry glance at Vega, who smirked and averted her eyes. "I don't do counter-hexes and anti-jinxes or none of that bullshit."

"Then what do you do?"

Mable massaged her browbone. "Listen. I know you think I don't believe in God—"

"You told me you don't believe in God."

"No. What I told you is I don't go to church, and you took that to mean I don't believe in God. But you and I worship the same god. Difference is, I don't go directly to him for help. I'm too lowly for that. I go through my ancestors. I help others do the same."

"That doesn't sound risky at all." Hopeful, Nona peeked at Vega and searched the woman's face, but Vega did not seem to share the same optimism.

"Because that ain't all. Asking the spirit realm to communicate with someone else in the spirit realm is basically like praying with a little extra stuff thrown in, but what you're asking for . . . I mean . . . When the spirit world gets mixed into the real world, when the spirit must manifest itself in the real world, I conjure."

"Conjure?" Again, Nona looked at Vega, who was stoic. "Demons?"

"De . . . ? No, Nona. Why the fuck would I conjure a demon?" Mable shot a look at Vega as if to say *Talk some sense into this fool.* Vega shrugged.

"I conjure ancestors." Mable's voice was soft, but her face was anything but. "For good. For protection. If someone needs to be shielded from the spiritual realm, I conjure their ancestors to guard them."

"Okay."

"You can't tell nobody about this. Ain't many of us around anymore. I've been called all kinds of witches and had some folks say I'm schizophrenic, I was hallucinating or had psychosis. I had to look that last one up. I don't need no trouble behind all this."

"I won't tell anybody. Let's do that. Let's conjure."

"There's a catch."

Mable unfolded a chair that had been resting against the wall and motioned for Vega to take a seat. Nona felt safer with Vega at her side.

"I create a path, a portal, but it is never a guarantee which spirit gets brought forth."

Nona's world shifted around her. What was she doing? She was stepping outside of her faith. A conjuring would cross yet another threshold she wouldn't have mere months before. Her world was undone. She was undoing it, but she couldn't turn back now. She wouldn't.

She had the urge to sip Donnell's brown drink, but Vega, seemingly reading her intentions again, reached over and poured the liquid into her coffee mug.

"What are my options, Mable?"

"Your options? This ain't a fucking buffet."

"Well, Nona obviously doesn't know how this works, Mable." Vega stirred the contents of her cup with her pinky finger, her enunciation of her friend's name dripping with frustration. "Which ancestors are you talking?"

"I conjure one of the spirits that are with you." Mable stared deeply into Nona's eyes. The woman seemed younger, vulnerable.

"The spirits that are with me?"

"Yes. The ones you're . . . let's say . . . rolling with."

"How will we know which ones I'm rolling with?"

Mable's eyes did not leave Nona's face, but they took on the vacant quality of someone talking on the phone.

"Well, I see you have a lot."

"You can see them?"

"Yes."

"Right now?"

"Yes."

"Who are they?"

"I see Kendall."

Nona didn't know whether to cry, scream, or laugh, so she did all three. She checked over her shoulder and around the room. She tried to sense him near her, but she couldn't feel anything. Why was he here? She'd spent the past two years praying he was at peace, but Kiki had seen him after his death, and now Mable said he was here, perhaps just over her shoulder. She was both happy he was near and saddened that his spirit wasn't with the Lord.

"This is why I didn't want . . ." Mable leaned back, seemed to brace for Nona to fall from her chair.

"Just give her a minute." Vega sipped from her mug, but she eyed Nona cautiously as well.

Nona wiped her eyes, but the tears kept streaming. "It's fine. Kendall can protect Marcus and Lance. He was already doing that when he was alive."

"There are others."

"Who?"

"I'm guessing your parents. They are older and they both look like you. Some aunts, maybe. Heavyset, tall women who smile at you, but without all the worry that a mother would have. And ones even older. Four of them. Two men. Two women. Grandparents, perhaps."

"Any one of them would be good. I need this, Mable. Something awful is going to happen if I don't."

"Something awful might happen if you do." Mable tightened her jaw, and Nona got the feeling the conversation was over.

Vega crossed over to the sink and placed her cup inside with a clunk. She squeezed detergent in the dish and scrubbed it with a sponge. "You know, Mable, I heard Donnell was there when Peter and Marcus fought at the graduation party at the church. Heard he was there when the boys all got into a fistfight here at the Gardens. Is that what you heard? That Donnell has been standing idly by while there's a beef between the Hester Boys and Nona's sons?"

What air remained in the room was definitely gone. Mable didn't speak, and she slowly turned toward Vega. Nona could have had answers a long time ago if she had sought Vega's help sooner.

"What are you saying, Vega?" Mable kept her voice steady, but her face was sheepish.

"I'm saying I think you can do this for Nona."

Mable rubbed her eyebrows and temples and fixed her gaze on Nona. "Fine. Get a keepsake from the one you want to call forth. Bring it to Medford Lake. I'll meet you there in an hour."

"Can Vega come?" Nona checked Vega's face, ensuring the invitation was okay. Vega nodded.

Mable rose, ushered both of them out her front door, closed it, and spoke to them from behind the screen. "Like I got a choice."

Pastor: Nona, I need to talk to you. I need you. Are you ever going to answer me?

Nona had never seen Vega in anything other than those housedresses, but her neighbor had changed into a pair of shorts and a T-shirt that seemed borrowed from Esmé. The clothes made the woman seem younger, somehow happier.

"Don't tell me you're afraid of the dark, Nona."

Nona chuckled but offered no comeback. She was afraid of more than the darkness.

A coyote barked in the distance. Mosquitoes nipped at the flesh above Nona's socks.

From the shadows, Mable appeared in pants wet from the knees down. She palmed a flashlight, the beam trembling. An animal carcass with blood-covered fur lay at Mable's feet. It stank of guts, its blood on Mable's hands.

"What is that?" Nona stepped back and avoided looking at the tangle of furry flesh.

"Coyote."

"How did you . . . ?" She couldn't manage much more than that because the stench was strong and she wanted to vomit.

"There are . . . suppliers . . . for this sort of thing. In other words, I know a guy."

Nona thought of Mable's bags of water. Did she get those from her supplier too?

"Back here." Mable grabbed the remains, turned, and lit their path with the pale white light. Nona stared at the dangling guts and fur-covered backside of the sliced-open coyote. The distant barks became all the more eerie. "This the best time to do this. Nobody around to bother us."

Mable moved at a quick pace, and anytime a twig snapped, she'd pause and shine the light in that direction. "Never do get used to this."

"Why do we need to be at the lake?" Nona wished they could have used some other water. A bathtub, maybe.

"Maybe we don't need to be, but this is how my great-uncle taught me to do this."

"Your great-uncle?" Vega asked. "Not your great-aunt?"

"My family had conjurers in all genders, not just the women, and it skipped some generations. So I was taught by a male family member, but he was taught by his mother."

"I didn't know this was something a person could teach." Nona hoped she didn't sound judgmental.

"Guess I should say he explained to me what I was already capable of. We all have conjuring in our religions, our cultures. They even tell us in church, 'Just call on the name of Jesus.' Or the pastor will lay his hands on a sick person and heal them. That's all a form of conjuring. Some folks call on Allah. Jehovah. Olodumare. Or Catholics will ask the Holy Spirit to intercede for them. Practitioners of Vodou, Santéria, and Candomblé bring faith healing to their people. Even now, folks are walking around every day doing their own little conjurings of protection—blessing people after they sneeze, knocking on wood when they say something they don't want to come true, throwing salt over their shoulders—but what I'm capable of is like a more specific form of that. I've been conjuring from the time I could walk. I'd see somebody, invite them to play ball with me, and next thing I knew, their spirit would be unleashed in the house.

"They're usually harmless. My parents just thought I had imaginary friends, but my great-uncle visited us one day from down south, and I was out front running through the opened fire hydrant. He watched me with excitement because he knew I was conjuring."

"Did his faith grow out of any one religion?" Vega asked as she sniffled and cleared her throat, likely from the night air growing thick and humid.

"Not that I'm aware of, but he taught me all religions. Put symbols of the Yoruba orishas and the Catholic guardian angels and patron saints all throughout our house—Oshun, Yemaya, Michael the Archangel, and St. Francis of Assisi. Taught me the rituals of both my Black and Muscogee ancestors, placing symbols of Bondye and Esaugeta Emissee beside each other on our altar. He wanted me to respect all faith traditions. Modern and traditional. And I do, but what he taught me, it is specific to me, specific to the Cleveland family. Our gift is . . . different. Then one day, he brought me here to the lake. Showed me how to use the gift the right way."

"Is there a wrong way?" Nona had been lulled by her friends' voices, but her fear slowly returned.

"Yep. I'm worried that's what we're about to do."

With Mable's voice and Vega's soft laughter carried on a breeze, they managed to make the half-mile trek to the lake in under fifteen minutes. Surrounded by an embankment of elms, the water stretched out before them like an endless bath. The moon shone down on the surface, its image appearing in full as if someone had drawn it on the ripples.

This was where she'd had her first night with Vance, where he'd parked below the tree canopy, where the smell of their bodies mixed with the scent of the water, and where the leather seat squeaked beneath them as the car rocked gently. Back then, she couldn't believe a bad choice could make her feel so good.

"Spirits are like us," Mable said, her voice sounding far away, the sound absorbed by the brush. "They get stuck sometimes in the same place, doing the same thing, never learning their lesson because they don't know how to grow and go. If I conjure them, I'm sometimes able to get them unstuck. Usually, a living person will have one, maybe two spirits with them. I can conjure them and release one of them."

"How can you tell if you're seeing a spirit or someone living?" Vega's voice was strong, steady.

"Focus. Spirits focus on one person or one object, a house maybe. They'll stare at that thing and won't take their eyes off of it. Living folk are too self-centered for that." Barefoot and sloshing around, Mable moved to the edge of the water. She checked over her shoulders, seemingly expecting someone. They were alone. If anyone was around, they were hidden by the trees.

"Remove your shoes." Mable's voice was calm and commanding, nothing like how she'd been back at home.

Nona took off her socks and sneakers and left them on the gravel. She'd done the same at her baptism. God was probably angry with her right now. Angry that her faith was weak. That she wasn't relying on him. Pastor's face flashed in her mind. Within a summer she had broken so many commandments.

Vega picked up Nona's shoes and held them. "I'll make sure no bugs get in them."

Nona squeezed Vega's shoulder. The pair nodded and nervously grinned at each other.

The gravel was warm as it pricked Nona's toes. She inched down to Mable's side and reached for the woman's shoulder to balance herself. She'd expected for them to do the conjuring right there between the canopies of two trees, but Mable pulled Nona's arm, and the two of them kept going until their feet met the water.

It was like stepping onto bricks of ice. She didn't understand how a night as hot as this could coexist with a lake so frigid. Mable dropped the carcass in the water between her and Nona's legs, and Nona jumped when the fur brushed against her shin. She took a breath, told herself she was doing this for Marcus.

"What did you bring?" Mable dipped her hands into the water, swished them around, brought them out, and clapped them together.

Nona removed the Pistons T-shirt from the oversized purse hanging across her torso.

"Kendall's?" Mable asked, her voice tender.

Nona nodded, tears stinging her eyes. Now that the shirt was out of the plastic, Kendall's scent would be lost forever.

Water slapped Nona's calves as Mable shifted her stance. Vega moved slowly to the water's edge.

Nona could no longer feel her toes. She marched in place to warm them, to keep the blood circulating, and the lump of animal remains bobbed as she splashed around.

Mable retrieved a red candle from a pocket, lit it, and let the smoke pass through the threads of Kendall's shirt. Mable handed the memento back to Nona, and Nona handed it off to Vega, who held it with reverence as if it belonged to Solomon.

From her hip pack, Mable retrieved an open notebook and a white sachet, the sides of which were stained by oil. "This will be like a baptism. You've been baptized, right?"

"Yes." Nona had been dunked at seven. Would she be submerged like that this time?

"This flame is a force of nature, as is this water we stand in, as are these remains. Together, they create thresholds between our world and the spirit world. Hold the candle."

Nona held the stick with both hands, heat against her palm and melted wax on her fingers.

"Come forward, spirit." Mable spoke to the area over Nona's left shoulder, and Nona resisted the urge to turn toward it. A ringing started up in Nona's ears.

Mable stopped. Her eyes grew wide. The woman heaved.

"What's wrong?" Nona spun around in spite of herself but only saw darkness and the rhododendron bushes. The ringing grew louder.

"I see one here that wasn't with you before." Mable eyed Nona suspiciously, her gaze going between Nona and the spirit she was watching.

"What do they look like?"

Mable shook her head. "We can't do this."

"We have to!" Nona removed one hand from the candle and placed it on Mable's forearm.

"He . . . I didn't see him before, Nona. He's . . ."

"He's what?"

A pungent smell of burnt plastic drifted up from the pouch's fabric as she unwound the packet's cord of cowrie shells and placed the sachet around her neck. She closed the notebook. "He's covered in blood."

From her feet to her head, the freezing cold rushed up Nona's body. The ringing in her ears muffled the sound of the wind rustling the trees.

"We have to go, Nona." Mable tucked the notebook in her pants pocket and waded through the water toward Vega, who was backing up.

"We have to try," Nona screamed, knowing who Mable was seeing and praying Kendall was faster, stronger. The ringing was higher-pitched now, sending a pounding pain across her head. "For Marcus. For Kendall. For Solomon."

Mable swiveled and stared at Nona, pain in the set of her mouth. The woman jerked away from Nona's hand, water sloshing with the movement. She returned Nona's fingers to the candle and raised both of her arms in the air so her palms were facing the top of Nona's head without touching it. "We must be quick."

"What do I need to—"

"Spirit of protection, come forward." Mable's voice thundered across the lake, echoing in the spaces between the trees. "Step forward. Walk forward ahead of the others. We need you to guard . . ." Mable didn't finish the sentence. Panting, staring behind Nona, she shouted, "No!"

A blow came down on Nona's head. She was certain it had cracked her skull. As she went down, she took in a mouthful of water. A force grabbed her neck. Jerked her farther away from the surface. She lost the candle. Freezing liquid rushed into her ears. Up her nose. Burned her eyes. She closed her lids. The water bubbled around her. A hand held her head under. The ringing continued.

Nona thrashed and ducked in an attempt to free her head from the grasp, but she could not rid her hair of the clawed fingers digging into her scalp. She shook her body. Tried to rise. Tried to remember her swimming lessons from thirty years before at the local Y. The lake was forty-five feet deep. How far was she from the surface? Panic was overtaking her. *Think!*

She got her arms and legs out in front of her and reached for the wrists to remove the hands from her, but when she opened her eyes again, she couldn't see anything. Her chest was caving in. She couldn't take in a breath. Two hands gripped hers. Another squeezed her throat. A fourth grabbed her waist. A palm wrapped itself around her left ankle. Another around her right. They all dragged her down.

Down. Down. Deeper into the watery depths, where the ringing grew even louder. Voices deadened by the water spoke above her. She kicked at the hands that were struggling to get a grip on her ankles again. She clawed her way up and bumped against something she thought would be Mable's hand.

An arm closed around her waist, pulling her down, deeper into the blackness. She remembered holding the newspaper clipping, her hand trembling as she stared into the photo of the smiling young man, the caption underneath stating *NaDarius Rucker. Missing.* His smile. He had once posed for a photo. He had once grinned.

She needed to breathe. One breath or she'd lose consciousness. She was slipping into a vastness blacker than the water surrounding her.

Her cheeks bulged as she twisted and flailed and tried to push herself up. She would die in Medford Lake, and she would no longer be able to protect Marcus and Lance. The ringing was steady, drowning out the sounds of the rippling water.

A claw thrashed down beside her, slicing her ear and making contact with her collarbone. She was going up now, and when her face broke through the surface of the water, she took in a breath so violently she vomited. Icy water leaked from her nose and mouth, poured from her ears, and she didn't have the energy to paddle herself over to the gravel shore.

"Cough it all up." Vega grunted as she pulled Nona free of the water's edge, dragging Nona by her armpits onto the dirt and twigs and dropping her in a patch of brush next to her shoes, her socks, and her cross-body bag of mementos.

"Who the fuck was that?" Mable yelled at Nona.

Vega was bent at the waist, inches from Nona's face, the coffee strong on the woman's breath.

Vega glared at Mable, and Mable shook her head. Nona didn't like it. Their exchange reminded her of Marcus and Lance, and of Marcus's accusation: *You're the one imagining things.*

Nona remembered the crack across her scalp, the force that shoved her under so quickly it made her swallow water.

"Who was that, Nona?" Mable finally stepped onto the gravel. She had a jar of pink water, and, as she moved closer to Nona, she screwed a golden lid onto it. "He wouldn't let Kendall or anyone else through."

"We brought you up," Vega panted. Mable was panting too. The hand on Nona's collar, the force pulling her up, had been one of them.

"It had black eyes," Mable said. "Completely black. A twisted mouth. Bloated hands with long claws, looked to be sharp as knives."

Nona stared from one to the other, feeling deep shame, embarrassment, fear, anger.

"Mable doesn't even know how to swim, but she waded deep into that water, under the surface, searching for you." Vega's voice was steady, but her anger was just under the surface. "By the end, I had to grab you both because she reached you but was going under herself."

The earth shifted around Nona. The danger, the power of the curse enveloped her like needles scraping along her skin. She checked the water, expecting to see NaDarius's hand reaching for her.

"What does this mean?" Nona shivered. Her chest ached. Her ear burned where the fingernail had caught her skin. She still wasn't ready to tell them about NaDarius, about how big a fool she'd been for Vance. "It didn't work? At all?"

"It means you're in worse danger now than before. Are you going to tell us who that was?"

Beating back tears, she squinted at the sky. The trees. The ground. If they knew what she'd done, they would hate her for dragging them into this.

"Fine. Here." Mable handed off the jar. "I would advise you to take this."

"What is it?"

"It's the treated water. It's what I used to open the passage. Keep this at home."

"By my door, like you do? It will bring me protection?"

Mable shook her head and looked over at Vega again.

"Protection? Not against the one that passed through."

"Then let's do the ritual again. We can bring Kendall out this time."

"Bitch, you almost died. Almost took my ass with you."

"But if we—"

"Hell no. I don't trust you. We rushed things. That's why I was nervous. I didn't have time to fully vet you. So I don't know who or what else you got around you, but I know I want no part of it. You better take that water and get gone."

"What will the water actually do?"

"After what I just saw, probably nothing, but I'm hoping it will buy you enough time to see Marcus off to school."

Twenty-Four

Nona placed the jar of water at the threshold as soon as she entered her front door. She couldn't shake the feeling of NaDarius clawing at her flesh. When she'd checked her ear in her pocketbook mirror, her skin was intact. She was grateful Mable had seen him too. At least now she knew she wasn't imagining him.

Then a knock at the door.

Nona didn't run the kind of house where people could show up at all odd hours of the night. If no one was expecting company, no one answered. So, especially after the botched conjuring, she knew this unexpected ten p.m. visitor was something evil.

On the second knock, Nona made sure her cell phone was in her pocket. She waited and listened. The third knock was slightly louder, and she expected the person to get a clue and get gone. But the fourth knock was police-officer loud; the person knew she was home. Perhaps they'd watched her return moments ago.

She backed away from the window so if they peeked through the gap between the fabric and the wall, they wouldn't see her.

The fifth knock sounded like someone was trying to kick in the door. She stormed over to the irons and shouted "Who is it?"

in a voice that would let the person know not only that she was home, but also that she wasn't an easy win.

She eyed her knife holder on the kitchen counter, slid it closer to where she stood.

"Mrs. McKinley? It's Peter."

Her insides churned. Goosebumps spread down her forearms. When the boys were young teens, she and Vance had banned Peter from their home after he flipped over her coffee table because he'd lost a game of UNO he'd been playing with Marcus, Gretchen, and Kiki's younger brother Cedrick. This was the first time he'd knocked since.

"What do you want, Peter?"

"Need to talk to you."

"Is Mother okay?" She imagined the woman taking a fall or being hospitalized for another stroke, her high blood pressure winning this time.

Peter didn't answer, but he made a noise behind the door. Was he crying? She unlocked the iron, removed the deadbolt and chain from the main door, and threw them both open.

"I said, is Mother okay?" Through the screen door she saw her home reflected back at her in Peter's sunglasses, the lenses even darker in the nighttime. He kept a cigarette behind his right ear and wore a crimson T-shirt, gold chains around his neck, baggy shorts, and red sneakers, their tongues sticking straight up like rabbit ears. He slowly grinned and stroked his long, unkempt beard as he stared at her.

"My grandmother's fine, Mrs. McKinley." He enunciated every syllable, sounding rehearsed and formal.

"Then what do you want?" Her phone vibrated in her hand. She glanced down to see whether it was the boys, and when she looked up, Peter was opening the screen door that separated the two of them.

"Excuse me?" she shouted and, without hesitation, reached for the knife on the counter, drew it against Peter's throat, and watched as he put both hands up and backed away from her, but not far enough. He was still inside the screen door, inches from the tip of her blade.

He did not appear bothered by the weapon and even smiled brighter, seeming to draw pleasure from frightening her.

"You gon' cut me, Mrs. McKinley?"

"You gon' come up in my house without an invitation, Peter? Notice my hand is not trembling."

"My bad, Mrs. McKinley. I thought you were inviting me in."

"I made no move that would lead you to believe I was inviting you in."

"True. Well, I thought I was welcome."

"You haven't been welcome here in years."

"I thought bygones would be bygones."

"Bygones are definitely not bygones. Why are you here?"

"Can you put the knife down, Mrs. McKinley?"

"I'll put the knife down when you leave. Why are you here?"

"Why you hate me?" And with that, he slowly, carefully raised his right hand and removed his glasses. Both of his eyes were trained on her, and he seemed to be really asking the question. "We used to be—"

"Cut the shit, Peter."

"Language, Mrs. McKinley. I'm surprised to hear a woman of God, who is so close to a man of God like Pastor Davis, use that kind of language. You'd expect something like that from me, I guess, but not you."

"You finished?"

"I was going to ask you the same thing. Whether you were finished with me."

His smile faded, and his eyes became distant. He stepped forward, pressing his neck against the blade once more. "You might not know this, but when I was a little boy, my parents were both shot to death point-blank in front of me in my living room over at Dempsey Woods."

"I already know this, Peter."

"But what you don't know, Mrs. McKinley, is that it was Christmas Eve. My grandmother came to pick me up, and when she did, she took me to the store, bought me a toy soldier. I was scared, seeing as how I was only five years old, but she told me to keep the wooden nutcracker. He would protect me. And my grandmother knows I kept the gift, but what she doesn't know is that I keep a camera in my bedroom, right inside of the soldier's mouth. I always have a view of my room, and that camera sends the footage to my phone, so I know what's going on in there. That's why I have no problem leaving cash out. Leaving my product out. Because my grandmother doesn't snoop around my room, and if anyone else comes in, well, I'm able to see them."

A surge of adrenaline tore through Nona's chest, and panic flooded her middle.

"I have a lot of things in my bedroom that people might like to take. Even photos. Oh. I see your hand is trembling now, Mrs. McKinley." He smiled wide, his teeth like those of an animal. She wanted to slash his throat for every bit of grief he caused her and for being smug about it right now.

Behind her, floorboards creaked. She heard something being dragged across the floor. She could not risk turning around even though the sound drew closer.

Something alighted on her shoulders and snaked down to the backs of her thighs. Then a sharp pain, like giving birth but in reverse, and the something was inside her. Its separate thoughts joined to hers.

She dug the tip of the knife deeper into Peter's flesh. She thought of stabbing it in, tearing it downward. Ending all her problems right now. Marcus would safely go off to school, Lance would stop trying to impress the Hester Boys, even Mother's life would improve after she got over the initial shock. Could Nona do it? Could she take this young man's life? Given his record, everyone would believe any story she told about him.

Her ears rang, and a surge of anger like nothing she'd ever experienced overtook her. A stench, more wretched than the dumpsters, enveloped her, filling her nose and throat, and a deep voice resounded in her mind: *Do it. He deserves it. He took away my firstborn. My baby. He deserves to burn in hell. Send him there.*

Whose voice was it? She'd heard it before.

Her hand steadied. Heat entered her feet and rushed up her body until it came to rest on the crown of her head. The something inside her told her to do it. She would do it. Would kill him. The voice in her head was no longer deep. The voice was her own. *This no-good-piece-of-shit-murderous-devil-spawn-of-motherfucking-vileness does not deserve to live when my baby is dead.*

KILL.

HIM.

"Easy, Mrs. McKinley." His voice wasn't as steady. She sensed fear rising in him, and the corners of his eyes filled with tears. "Easy, ma'am. Forgive me if I . . ." His breath caught in his throat, he held it, and then it came out in huffs. "Ma'am?"

Could he see the change in her as well? She was going to kill him. She would pass the blade through his flesh and strike something deep within him. Muscle. Artery. Bone. The blood would flow hot from the wound and spread down her arm. The tiny part of her brain that was still the true Nona shouted down the other thing inside of her, but the true Nona was losing. The thing was winning. Peter was red-tinged; a haze of fiery gauze passed before her eyes.

"You must take it easy, Mrs. McKinley." He was whimpering now, backing up. Over his right shoulder, Nona caught movement. Vega Lawson was marching toward Nona's door, arms spread out at her hips, palms forward, ready to grab and pounce. Not even a second passed and Vega was standing next to Peter.

"Street justice," Vega said, peering into Nona's eyes. "The street always gets even. You aren't street, Nona."

Vega reached forward carefully, past Peter's stiff head and shoulders, and grabbed Nona's wrist. When Vega touched Nona's skin, whatever had entered Nona flew from her body with a painful ripping jolt. She scanned her legs and the floor, expecting to find blood and tissue, but all she saw were her bare feet, toenails unpolished.

Head spinning, she was nauseated. Vega eased the knife from Peter's flesh, where a pinprick of blood trembled. "You better be glad I saw your raggedy behind walk over here to Nona's or you might have gotten filleted."

Peter inhaled deeply.

He searched Vega's face, then looked back at Nona. "Mrs. McKinley, I . . ." He was polite, obsequious; she'd not seen him this well-mannered since he was six years old.

When Peter backed up, he let the thin door go. Vega released Nona's wrist, and the screen banged against the frame.

Nona did not release the knife.

Vega shoved Peter as he rushed away. "Get yourself on home to your grandmother before I cut you myself." Vega eyed the young man as he jogged up to Prescott, turned left, and disappeared into the night.

Twenty-Five

It had been a week since Peter came to her home. Marcus claimed he'd squashed the beef with Peter, but she'd had a hard time believing that, so she came to Mother Lincoln's to ensure it was true.

Nona accepted Mother Lincoln's offer of ginger tea because she sensed Mother wanted to talk to her about Nona pulling a knife on Peter. She didn't know what had happened, exactly. How had that thing gotten hold of her and made her think such awful things? Is this what was happening to Marcus and Lance? And what had Peter told his grandmother had happened?

Nona didn't like the drink at all. It was too sharp on her tongue and often made her sneeze when she brought the cup to her face.

She'd called in sick to work, and that wasn't far from the truth: This situation with Marcus and Peter and the thing at the lake was making her sick. On paper, things seemed fine because she'd gotten everything together: She'd sent the money to the university, she'd gone over the checklist of items Marcus would need to bring with him to campus. Once he received his housing assignment, packed, and got the airline ticket his coach had purchased for him, he'd be on his way.

And even though she was still avoiding Pastor, he'd ordered her a new stove. On the first night the appliance was in her home, she discovered that it suffered the same condition as the old one: The range lit itself.

The air inside Mother's home was lighter, smelled fresher. She sensed Peter's toxicity wasn't clouding the space, and she knew immediately he wasn't at home.

When Mother finally sat on the couch beside Nona, the older woman became choked up, and Nona could barely understand her.

"Mother, what's wrong?" She knew this cry. This was a *something is wrong with my child* kind of cry.

The woman sobbed. Mother had been upset before, like when Peter quit high school, but nothing like this.

"Take deep breaths, Mother."

Mother wailed, and the woman sounded like Esmé the night Solomon was killed. The anguish resembled the cry of an animal.

"Do it with me, Mother." Nona breathed in and out as she hurried into Mother's kitchen and opened the window. It was seven thirty a.m. The day was warming up already, and she wanted any breeze that might be outside to make it in, even if it brought the stench of trash with it.

On the television, the Clark Sisters sang "Is My Living in Vain?" The gospel song filled the silence, the question seeming directed at Nona.

Mother stared at the TV screen, seeming to focus on the song as well. After a couple of deep breaths, Mother finally stopped sobbing.

Nona returned to her side.

"Nona, baby. I'm so sorry. I don't mean to worry you with my problems. I've been praying the Lord makes your burden lighter. If anybody deserves some goodness, it's you, baby. Don't worry about me."

Nona's mind went to Kendall, which happened every time someone referred to her mother-of-a-homicide-victim status.

"It's okay, Mother. Tell me what's wrong."

"Peter's older now." The woman sniffled. "It's been so hard to keep up with him. Maybe I have too many rules. Maybe he's mad at me because I kept calling his favorite songs the devil's music."

So he hadn't told Mother about his encounter with Nona.

"I've never seen him mad at you," Nona said. "He adores you."

"So you don't think he'd ever get mad enough to move out without telling me?"

Her heart raced as she considered Mother's question. What outcome did Nona really want here?

"Of course he wouldn't move out without telling you. He wouldn't worry you like that."

"That's what I thought. It's how I know he's missing."

"Missing?"

"Yes. My grandbaby." Mother became choked up again.

Nona's shoulder and neck muscles tightened. She sipped the ginger tea, her mind immediately going to Marcus. The Marcus who may have gotten a gun. The Marcus who seemed ready to hit her. The Marcus who had fought Peter twice already.

"Week ago, he left and hasn't come home since."

Mother prattled on and Nona struggled to focus. Could Marcus have done something to Peter? She told herself that was a stretch, but NaDarius could make him do it. She had experienced that firsthand.

"I even called the police." Mother choked down a sob.

"What did they say?"

"They say they're . . . investigating"—Mother uttered the last word as if it tasted bad in her mouth—"but I don't believe them because they didn't talk to anybody I told them to. I told them to talk to Gretchen, and they still haven't."

"They may follow up with her still. I'm so sorry Peter's got you worried, Mother."

As horrible as it was, Nona began to calm down. Ever since Peter joined the Hester Boys, he was in trouble at least once a week. And if he were missing, he could be dead or in jail, and no one would suspect Marcus.

How could she think this? She sat up straight, drew her bottom lip into her mouth, and gnawed on it. What was she becoming? Was NaDarius doing this to her? Yes, the next weeks of her life in which Marcus prepared to leave for school would be a little less anxious with Peter gone, but this was the wrong reaction to have.

"Did he take his phone with him? His keys? His wallet?"

"You know, that's the same thing Mable asked me. He did. He took all those things."

"Well, that's a good sign. I'm sure he'll be back."

"Can you ask Marcus about Peter?"

"Ask him what?"

"Ask him where Peter went."

Nona blinked, feeling exposed.

"Oh, Mother. I don't think Marcus and Lance have seen Peter," other than the fistfight Peter started with them, but she didn't say that part. "I mean, I don't think Marcus and Lance hang out with him." She should have told Mother about the fistfight, about Peter entering her home, but Mother had enough to worry about. Nona finished her tea.

"Can you ask Marcus anyway? Whether he's seen Peter?"

"Sure, Mother, I'll check with him."

"Thank you, baby. I guess it is odd if they never hang out."

"What's odd, Mother? I don't think they have any of the same interests."

"Maybe that's the case, baby. But last time I saw Peter, he was going to meet Marcus."

❖

"Mom, you're acting like you don't believe me."

"I'm not acting." Nona didn't know what to believe, but she knew her boys got their lying gene from Vance.

Marcus was giving most of his shirts, jerseys, and pants to Lance. He was sorting through his closet, opening boxes, removing caps from the shelves, and dumping it all on Lance's bed. It was a good sign he was finally getting ready for school. She wished she could go back and force Kendall to pack and leave the day after he graduated.

"Can you really imagine me with a gun?"

NaDarius had nearly drowned her in Medford Lake. Had possessed her body. At this point, she could imagine anything. But even though there had been so many similarities between Kendall's final days and the last couple of months, Marcus was managing to live deeper into the year after his eighteenth birthday than Kendall had. That had to be worth something.

"Why would Gretchen make up a story like that?"

"You'd have to ask her. To impress Kiki? I don't know. Peter did start the fight with Lance and me, and I didn't tell you because I didn't want you to worry." He'd moved on to sneakers. Most of the ones Marcus was lining up by Lance's bed still fit him.

"They don't wear sneakers in Rhode Island?"

"I can't pack all these, and it will cost too much to ship."

"But you can wear these when you come back to visit. I don't want you and Lance fighting over shoes come Thanksgiving."

Marcus looked sheepish. "I don't think I'll be able to afford a plane ticket for Thanksgiving. And, you know, I'll have games."

She took a deep breath, encouraged he was planning for school.

"Did you meet Peter a week or so ago?"

"No. I haven't seen him." His back was to her; he was yanking shirts from his top drawer.

"Mother said Peter was planning to meet you."

"I did call him. I asked him to meet me in person so we could squash our beef, but he didn't show up. I figured my phone call had been enough."

"But he's missing."

"Missing?" His voice was deadpan. He still hadn't turned around. She wanted to scream *Did you kill Peter? Did you seek vengeance that belonged to God?* Her pulse quickened; she stifled a cough. The odor from the dumpsters seemed to grow. Was it actually the garbage she was smelling this time?

"Mother called the police and everything."

"Huh." He faced her finally, an eyebrow raised. "What'd they say?"

"I don't know. Not much, I don't think."

He glanced over at his desk. The metal box was there, lying open and empty.

"You been going through my stuff?"

"Have the cops questioned you about Peter?"

"The cops are pretty useless." Marcus walked over and kissed her cheek. "They haven't questioned me, and they probably won't. Stop worrying, Mom. Everything will be okay."

"Has anything strange been happening to you?"

"Uh . . . no. Strange like how?"

"Like you feel something inside of you? Inside of your thoughts?"

"What?"

"Just listen to me, Marcus. Have you been feeling angrier than usual? Or like your thoughts aren't your own? Like someone else's thoughts have gotten inside of you? Or someone else is inside, controlling you?"

Something shifted on his face. Recognition, perhaps, of what she'd said. Tears rose in his eyes. He opened his mouth to speak, but nothing came out. If he would admit it, she didn't know how she would help him, but she knew she would. They would fight this thing together.

"It's okay, Marcus. You can tell me. I've experi—"

"No, Mom." His eyes were dry again. His face muscles back to normal. "You think I'm losing my mind?"

"More like being influenced by somebody else's mind."

He grabbed his backpack and slung it over his shoulder. "I'm going to pretend we didn't have this conversation, okay?"

"Marcus, wait."

"Mom. Everything. Is. Fine. Nobody is controlling me. I'm good. I really just need for you to trust me."

He patted her shoulder and headed for the door.

"What time will you be back?" She wanted him to stay within sight. At least until he headed off to college.

"Before curfew. I'm making a quick stop."

"Where?"

"Just going here and there." Annoyance crept into his tone. "No big deal."

As they exited the room, she checked over her shoulder and examined the stacks of folded clothes sitting in the center of Lance's bed. Marcus had given away practically everything. What did he even have left to wear to school?

Pastor: Can I come see you today or tonight? Just to talk.

Nona: I need space.

Pastor: Why?

Nona: Because what we did was wrong.

Pastor: I don't see it that way. Please don't throw us away.

Twenty-Six

The news bureau where Nona's nephew worked was in a Medford office complex called Medford Commons that had been constructed in the late 1970s and seemingly had not been updated since. A man in a business suit nodded at her as he entered. A woman in jeans and three men in slacks and collared shirts filed in and out of the revolving doors, paper coffee cups and briefcases in hand. Law offices, accounting firms, medical practices, and bank branches were also on the premises. Everyone seemed so important, like their lives were filled with purpose.

She stood near the curb where the bus had pulled off and smoked a cigarette she'd bought loose from a neighbor on her way to the stop. She thought of her co-worker Lena. How she'd preached to the woman about giving up the "cancer sticks." And now look at Nona. Her fingers trembled as she brought the skinny paper to her lips and let the heat spread through her. She'd only smoked once before in her life—the first night with Vance at the lake—but this time, after a few minutes of coughing, she stuck to short pulls on the stick and slowly started to feel calm. Calm enough to keep going.

"You can buy the nicotine in a patch, you know."

Harlan was suddenly at her side with a wry smile. She'd been watching the revolving door, expecting him to come from inside the office building, but he instead exited the parking garage next door.

"I need the smoke to destroy my health in the process." She put out her cigarette, and they hugged. It was always difficult to get on his calendar because he was forever chasing a new story, so she was grateful when he'd told her to meet him at work. Today, he had an important meeting with a scientist from the CDC in town for a conference, who Harlan said he was interviewing for that story pitch about how gun violence was a public health crisis. "The boys miss you," she said.

"I know. I feel guilty too. I will—"

"No, you won't. You always say you're going to come around and then you get sent out on another story."

"Maybe I can video chat with them?"

"They'd like that. But make sure you're making time for something other than work, Harlan. Like that girlfriend you keep professing your love to, then neglecting."

"I didn't know you were here to get on my case." His smile never left his face.

"I know you're still grieving Kendall something awful, but I don't want you to use your work as an excuse to not connect with the people you love."

"Understood."

He motioned for her to enter the revolving doors with him, and, inside, they sat on a bench in a carpeted lobby across from the receptionist. The building was old, but the tile floors glistened. The entry rug, emblazoned with a cursive *MC,* was immaculate. Someone must have spent half the day vacuuming it to keep it so clean.

It was a big deal that Harlan worked for the paper, and it made him a quasi-celebrity in Medford. The newspaper employees were labor leaders in the town because, long ago, they had successfully run a strike against the company and won. Nona's parents and most everyone else in Medford stopped buying the "scab papers" when the journalists took to their picket lines. The daily received so many cancelations that it had to borrow money to keep its press running.

That had been in '87. Now, they were moving to digital-only, and Harlan said reporters would be hard-pressed to fight the owners again.

"At least today you're not interviewing frantic kids running from their school."

"You know, the suburban birthday party shooter is a juvenile. That story is so strange. He shot a bunch of boys in his neighborhood before he arrived at the party. It seemed improbable he was able to enter their homes, undetected, one after the other the way he did, but police say all evidence points to him acting alone. His lawyer got expert psychologists to testify that he didn't fully understand the repercussions of his actions or his mental health got in the way, yada yada, so he will likely go free one day."

"I can't."

"I know. I don't know how much longer I can stay on this beat. I'm still waiting to hear back from *U.S. News Daily* about my gun violence pitch. Anyway. What's going on with the boys now?" He looked like he wanted to give her another hug.

"I don't even know where to begin. I found a box with Marcus's writings, and I don't think I'll ever be able to sleep again unless I find out what is going on with him."

"Found?" He raised an eyebrow.

"I already feel guilty for snooping. Don't make me feel worse."

"Won't mention it again. What kind of writings?"

She told him about the essays and how he'd underlined the word "rifle" in red throughout.

"Marcus is an amazing kid," Harlan said. "But he's been through . . . a lot. And he's obviously stressed right now. You should have seen how stressed I was before going off to school."

"I did see, but your stress consisted of you drawing up a list of supplies and gear you'd need and then telling everyone so you could buy everything used. Spent the whole summer doing it."

They both smiled at the memory.

"That's not all," Nona said. "I overheard Gretchen and Kiki talking."

"Overheard?"

"I was at Mother's. They were talking near the window. Don't give me that look. I wasn't snooping again. Gretchen and Kiki are loud."

"Uh huh. You might want to leave the investigations to me." Harlan chuckled as he checked the clock on the wall above the receptionist. He'd told Nona he had fifteen minutes to chat with her before that meeting he couldn't miss.

"Gretchen said Marcus bought a gun."

"A gun?"

"That's what she told Kiki."

"Yeah, I don't see him doing that."

Sharing this burden with him was good for Nona, even if he was pressed for time and perhaps annoyed by her fretting.

"Pastor Davis has had his eye on Marcus all summer through that camp job, right?" Harlan asked. "And Marcus seems pretty regular to me. I just don't think he would ever purchase a gun. Now Lance? I'd be worried. But not Marcus."

"But Marcus isn't regular. He's been acting strange. He only recently focused on going to college in the fall. He's angry all the time."

"I was angry too. I'm still angry from growing up in that place. The trauma, the lack of resources and investment, it has a feeling to go along with it."

"How do you mean?"

"Think about the place. Do you enjoy waking up there? Do you look forward to being there after a long day of work? Having your garbage pile up and spill out of the dumpsters has a feeling attached to it. Having roaches crawl across your walls and floors has a feeling attached to it. Stray bullets pelting your front door, helicopters roaring overhead, leaky plumbing, peeling paint, faulty electrical, uneven hinges, overgrown grass, dry rot on wooden steps, and shoddy construction materials. All those things have a feeling attached to them. A feeling of hopelessness, despair, worthlessness, sadness, and sometimes, the anger is just a way to hide the hurt."

"Okay. But he has so little time left before he heads off to school, I just . . . And now Peter's missing."

"What?"

"You haven't heard?"

"I . . . No. Since when? What are folks saying about it?" Harlan drew back his shoulders, which raised his neck and made him seem several inches taller. He got that fire in his eye he always had whenever he flipped into journalist mode. She could see him piecing together the details in his mind. "Mother must be worried sick."

Nona told him everything Mother had told her. "And Marcus is denying everything. He said, 'No clue where Peter is.' And 'Don't be ridiculous, Mom! You know how Gretchen lies. Of course I don't have a gun.'"

"Gretchen *is* loose with the truth, so—"

"I'm worried Marcus might have . . ." She couldn't bring herself to say it.

"Have the police questioned Marcus?"

"I don't think so. But that—"

"I'm inclined to believe him."

"Well, I'm not." Of course he was inclined to believe Marcus. He didn't know about the thing that kept coming back to her house to get her boys. She wanted so badly to tell Harlan about the way Marcus changed when he was angry, the voices in her home, the botched conjuring, the thing that had made her almost slit Peter's throat, but Harlan checked the clock again and stood.

"I think you should view this as good news. You were worried Peter might hurt Marcus; now Peter is gone, doing God knows what, might even be in jail, and now you're worried that Marcus might have hurt Peter. I can see you being worried about Peter being violent, but it's a huge leap to worry about Marcus in the same way."

"Can you look into it?"

"Which part? The gun? Peter?"

"Both. Everything. I'm worried sick here. I mean, Harlan, come on. Have you ever seen me smoke a cigarette before?"

"There's no way for me to snoop on Marcus without him finding out, and . . ." He checked the clock. "Look. Let me do some digging on Peter. That kid's got a lot of enemies, so . . ."

Harlan leaned over and hugged Nona, planted a kiss on her cheek. He reached into his pocket and took out a five-dollar bill.

"No. That's okay. I have bus fare."

He pocketed the money and headed to the elevator bank.

"Before you go," Nona said, her stomach pulling into a knot, "Mother said the last time she saw Peter, he was headed out to see Marcus. That was the last time she heard from him."

Harlan paused. Turned. Cocked his head to the side.

"You ask Marcus about this?"

"I did. He said it wasn't true."

"You believe him?"

"I . . ." She didn't know what to say. She was having a hard time admitting she didn't.

"I'll ask Marcus myself." Harlan took a few extra seconds to stare at her. That last detail, about Peter meeting Marcus, had jostled something loose inside of Harlan. As he reached the elevator, it seemed he was still turning over the idea in his mind. He was perhaps starting to see she had every right to be worried.

The knock at Nona's door was an intrusion. She'd intended to spend the afternoon at church as an excuse to keep an eye on Marcus while he worked. The last thing Nona needed was a one-day furlough, but the plant did that from time to time, and she'd planned to make good use of it.

When she answered, Sgt. Prager stood in the doorway next to Lance. The officer was about ten pounds heavier than she'd been when Nona first met her the night Kendall had been killed. The woman wore her hair shorter now, and dark polish on her nails. Sgt. Prager looked sheepish. So did Lance.

"What's going on?"

"Mrs. McKinley, can I have a word with you?"

Lance trudged in, head still down.

"Where were you?" she snapped at Lance. "You were supposed to be at camp at the rec center."

Lance never met Nona's eyes as he slinked past her and into his bedroom.

Nona stepped outside the front door and closed it. The women huddled together, seeking shade from the gnarled and arid branches of a nearby elm tree. A blue ball rested at its base. Was it the same one she kept seeing? Would this one vanish as well?

"He was brought into the station along with a group of boys joyriding downtown in a stolen car."

"Downtown? Who were the boys?"

"I'm not at liberty to say, but I didn't let them officially arrest Lance. No fingerprinting. None of that. That's why I'm dropping him off here."

"Oh my God."

"You've been through a lot. So has he. I didn't want to add . . ."

"Thank you." She was feeling guilty for snapping at Sgt. Prager the last time they spoke.

"He doesn't have a record. Things will be so much easier for him if he doesn't get one. I told him this on the ride here, but I'm not sure whether I got through to him. He didn't seem scared. Which worries me."

"What do you mean?"

"When the boys I come across are still impressionable, they cry when they get into trouble. And they seem scared and nervous. Lance . . . He might have cried a year ago or so, but this time he wouldn't give a statement. He wouldn't say anything, really. And he . . . Like I say. He wasn't scared."

Nona thought back to her conversation with Lance. How he'd said boys weren't allowed to be soft. She glanced over at the elm. The blue ball was still there.

"Okay. I'm trying," she said. "I just don't know what will get through to him."

"I wondered if he visited his father . . ."

"In prison?"

"I know it's not ideal, but not only will he see the consequences of crime up close, but maybe having that relationship with—"

"Thank you for dropping Lance off." Nona opened her door and stepped back inside.

Sgt. Prager seemed flustered at being cut off, but she nodded. "Okay. Let me know if you ever need anything. I'd be—"

"No. Thanks. That won't be necessary. I really appreciate it, but you've done enough."

Nona closed the door and stood with her back to the wood. Down the hall, rap lyrics flowed from the speaker in Lance and Marcus's room. She was done trying to get through to him. Trying to get through to Marcus. She was done waiting and praying the curse didn't get her boys.

She peered through her kitchen window to where the dead elm tree stood. The ball was gone, but a few yards beyond where it had been resting, a boy about seven or eight years old skipped and kicked the sphere toward Prescott Road. A chill passed through her. His shirt and shorts were outdated; the striped print and formal collar had been more prevalent in her youth. Red stains covered the fabric. She knew all of the kids in the Gardens, but she didn't recognize him. She squinted and suddenly, the boy was gone.

Twenty-Seven

"Kendall, I need you."

Nona knelt before the gravestone, feeling the hard blades of grass, parched from lack of rainfall that week, digging into her flesh. It was Kendall's birthday, and she still couldn't believe they had to celebrate his birth at his grave site.

She watched as Pastor, Marcus, and Lance walked along the cement path to Pastor's Mercedes, her boys with their heads hung low, listening to Pastor's ongoing words of encouragement. As much as she hated to admit it, they looked like two boys being comforted by their father. She was still putting off her inevitable conversation with Pastor, and he seemed relieved to just be in contact with her again.

She spoke to Kendall.

"I haven't just been seeing things. Imagining things. We unleashed him. And I know now that it's not you. I don't know how I ever thought you were capable of this type of evil. I know exactly who he is. I helped create him. Your father and I. We are the reason he is angry. And he has every right to be. He died an awful death. But I can't let him . . ." She choked down a sob. "He's coming for your brothers. I need you to fight him."

Wind whispered through the trees. A bright green leaf blew near her and fell atop Kendall's headstone. She reached inside her shoulder bag and pulled out the jar of Mable's treated water. She poured it on the dirt. It had not protected her home. She hoped that placing the water near Kendall would bring him forward. Like a mini-conjuring.

"I know that's half my problem. I was always leaning on folks. Especially you. I leaned on you too much. Kiki wanted you and her to move away from Medford, and I stood in the way. Told you I needed your help with the boys since your father was gone. And I lost you. I won't make that same mistake with Marcus. I need you now, and I don't know where else to go. I need you to fight this curse. For Marcus and Lance. I need you to come home and get this thing out. His name is . . ." She feared if she said his name out loud, he'd appear. She leaned forward and put her lips close to the headstone as if speaking into Kendall's ear. "His name is NaDarius."

When they returned home, her kitchen and living room smelled of the pine cleanser she'd used earlier in the day.

She received a text from Mable.

Mable: Donnell been seeing things. And last night while I was sleeping, my bedroom door opened, but nobody was there. Scared the living shit out of me.
Nona: The curse is still after Marcus and Lance.
Mable: It's your curse, Nona. It's after you.
Nona: Has this happened to you before? In your home?
Mable: Not to me. I've seen it with other conjurers, but I've always been more careful.

Nona: I'm sorry, Mable. What should I do? I'm so scared for Marcus right now.
Mable: Can he go off to school early?

Before she could answer, Marcus's bedroom door opened slowly. He emerged from his room grinning. The ringing in her ears disappeared with his smile.

"Guess what, Mom." He beamed at her. It was a clear grin, with bright, dancing eyes. She hadn't seen him this happy since before Vance went away, and she checked behind him in the hallway. No shadows. Lance was there, wearing his basketball shorts and jersey, which meant Lance had actually attended the sports camp she'd signed him up for. Perhaps he'd also shown up to summer school.

"What, baby?" She returned the smile. It had been a while since she'd done so, and that simple gesture calmed her nerves.

"I finally registered for my classes. All of them. Mostly they were core courses. You know. That stuff all freshman have to take, but I had a couple of electives, and anyway, it's done."

Joy rushed through her so suddenly she became choked up. Could it be? Had Kendall heard her plea and saved them all? Even from the grave, Kendall was still taking care of her.

"Man, I'm hungry," Marcus said. He walked over and gave her a hug. A real hug. The kind of hug that made her want to sob in his arms, but she held it together. He kissed her cheek and made his way to the stove. "Haven't been this hungry in a while. I better grab some extra food on my way out."

She stared at her ceiling, mouthed *Thank you, Kendall,* and wished she'd asked her oldest for help sooner.

Twenty-Eight

Peter was still missing, and Harlan said he hadn't been arrested or spot-ted anywhere. Maybe he left town, Harlan had texted. The curse seemed to have left Nona's home, and the burden of keeping Marcus safe had been lifted. He was back to his old self. Finally, and in spite of herself, she believed Marcus when he told her, yet again, that he didn't own a gun. She stopped snooping on him.

She stood near the stove as Marcus got ready to leave the house to meet with "a dude out in Sebastian Hills," who was going to play basketball in the fall at Brown too, and "maybe we could be roommates."

The thick heat was a weight pressing against her skin. The humidity threatened to curl her hair, so she kept it in a taut bun, and it was tight about her ears and heavy on her crown.

The air conditioner she'd bought used—the air conditioner she wasn't supposed to own, according to the housing authority—was busted again, and she didn't have the money to get it repaired.

Cooking had sent the room temperature up ten more degrees, but she was grateful the pilot light worked properly when she turned on the burner. No extra flames shooting up this time.

The song "Don't Worry, Be Happy" played in her mind. The idea made her smile.

"Lance, how was summer school today?"

Her youngest was eating and not paying attention to her, so he grunted instead of answering.

"Come again?"

"Great." The mouthful of food puffed out his cheeks like a chipmunk.

"You know what?" She rolled her eyes at him. "Never mind."

How long could she put off the inevitable argument with Lance? In the past, she'd avoided important conversations with Vance, and that had gotten her all the problems she had today.

At nine p.m., Marcus appeared in the kitchen wearing denim shorts, a white polo shirt he'd gotten as a graduation gift from Mother Lincoln, and ankle socks that made the room seem hotter just looking at them. He tied up the trash bag from the bathroom, added it to the others he'd collected near the front door.

He tossed his cell phone and keys on the counter and sat for dinner. Nona joined them and was grinning so widely, so rapt that both her boys were sharing a meal with her, she didn't touch her food. Kendall's placemat remained on the rickety card table they used for meals, keeping his presence beside them in the now-empty chair, only his right wrist on the table, his left palm in his lap, modeling for the other two the proper way to sit when dining.

Taking a break from his pork chop, Lance burped, crumpled his napkin, and placed it on the table. Both arms rested beside his plate—Lance never sat properly at the table.

Wild laughter rose from the entrance of their complex and echoed off the concrete and brick. Vega shouted, "They used to call me the mad scientist!"

Nona, Marcus, and Lance all exchanged glances and then burst into laughter.

Nona said, "You know, Vega was here when your father and I first moved in. She hasn't changed a bit."

Marcus and Lance exchanged a look. Marcus had barely touched his food. He sipped water from a Mason jar he often used as a drinking glass. Maybe the heat was killing his appetite.

"Why did y'all move here in the first place?" Lance asked the question nonchalantly, which was his way when something had been eating him up inside.

"It's all we could afford."

"But did you, like, want to stay here this long?" Lance was hedging. When he looked over at Marcus, Marcus paused from his sipping and shook his head no, perhaps warning Lance he was taking the conversation someplace he shouldn't.

"Well, if you must know, we'd been living with your grandmother and grandfather, but when we got pregnant with Kendall, they told us they were done raising kids. We got on the waiting list here. And about a month before Kendall was born, our application was accepted." She smiled. Lance and Marcus did not.

"Our plan had been to buy a home in the good parts of Medford, with lawns and backyards. We were saving for it, at least, when your father got carted off."

"And was this place all messed up like this back then?"

"Chill, man." Marcus slammed his glass on the table. Nona's scalp prickled with anxiety at the abrupt change.

"I can't ask a question, man?" Lance had a mouth full of food when he spoke and didn't seem to care about the crumbs falling from his lips.

"Ask any question you want, but don't be disrespectful. I'd like to see you find a better place than this given the same meager resources Mom and Dad had back then." He pointed his finger at Lance, who seemed frightened even though he tried to come off as angry too. "You better learn some respect."

"Whatever, man."

"Whatever? Who you think you talking to?"

"It's fine, Marcus." Nona raised her voice and held up her palm. "And to answer your question, Lance, the place was brand new. Nice. Lots of families and working people. But things changed."

"Why?" Lance seemed embarrassed as he wiped his face. He'd gotten rid of the remaining crumbs, but grease from the meat lingered around his mouth.

"Because the system is set up to destroy us," Marcus interjected.

"Marcus!"

"Sorry, Mom, but there shouldn't even be such a thing as public housing unless everyone is living in it."

"This place isn't so bad, you two." She was lying. They exchanged their look again. At least they weren't still arguing.

"Listen. I gotta get going." Marcus rose, placed his picked-over plate of food on the counter, drained his water glass, and placed it in the sink. He jammed his feet inside the shoes and stared down at them, lifting each heel and admiring it. He paused, noticing Lance, who was staring at him, sullen and forlorn. "I'll take out the trash, Lance."

Marcus and Lance nodded at each other. She was relieved they'd gotten past their squabble.

"You barely touched your food." She lifted Marcus's plate, still filled with a pork chop, salad, cornbread, and macaroni and cheese. "You only have a couple weeks at home still. I was hoping we could have a real family meal again, like we used to." She was laying it on thick.

When she held the food up to Marcus, she recalled the memory of him as a one-year-old on her hip, trying his first bite of cornbread, which he'd snatched right out of her hand. When he'd gotten the bread into his mouth, he'd grinned and rested his head on her shoulder. It was one of the most adorable things she'd ever experienced as a mother.

"I'm sorry, Mom. I didn't know you'd . . ." He was sheepish. "It was . . . great. I'm just not that . . . I'm sure Lance will have at it."

He must have intended to stay out late, because he didn't say *I'll finish it later.*

Lance took a sip of grape pop, cleared his throat, and asked, "How you getting there, Marcky?"

Vega's shouts and laughter were interrupted by a police or ambulance siren—Nona could never tell the blaring sounds apart.

"You my daddy now, Lance?" And there was Marcus's harsh tone again.

She remembered that voice in her home. *It's me.*

"I want to know where you're going, Marcus."

He stopped at the door. "I already told you, Mom."

"And who exactly are you going to be with?"

"I already said." He half grinned, but irritation crept into his voice.

"Fine. Don't tell me."

"I always tell you where I'm going. Don't be like this." He walked over and kissed her on the cheek.

She stared at her remaining boys. How could she stop Marcus? Was she using her rational mind or her overprotective mother heart?

"And I'm not Daddy"—Lance's voice was firm as he reinserted himself in the conversation—"but I know you ain't got no car, Marcky."

Monster sat next to Lance's plate and was stacked on top of *Soledad Brother.* The edges were curled because within the last few days, when Lance didn't have his face stuck between the pages, he strolled around with the books folded into the back pocket of his jeans.

"We don't say 'ain't,' Lance," Nona said. She placed Marcus's plate in the microwave.

"Sorry, Mom. I know you don't got no car, Marcky."

"That's worse, honey."

"What, Mom?"

"Never mind."

"Dudes in the suburbs have cars, Lance." Marcus grabbed his keys and several quarters from the counter near the door.

Someone dribbled a basketball outside with a slow rhythm. Solomon's dribbling used to sound like this. She thought of Donnell, how frightened he was after hearing the ball bouncing. What if the sound really was Solomon bouncing his ball from the grave?

The kitchen smelled of the Thousand Island dressing on their salads, and the air was so stifling she worried she might overheat and faint. Perhaps a brief loss of consciousness would keep Marcus at home.

"What time will you be back?" She grinned and kept her tone light, hoping she sounded curious instead of desperate and mother-like.

Like Vance, Marcus didn't look her in the eye.

"Before curfew, Mom, but don't wait up." Marcus let the screen door snap against the frame. He padded beside the bed of dead zinnias and tossed the trash bags at the alley's edge, where white bags littered the ground around the overflowing dumpster.

She thought of guilt-tripping him by reminding him that Peter still hadn't shown up at Mother's, that Nona would fret all night until Marcus returned, but she sensed it would only further frustrate Marcus.

She inched to her home's threshold and found Marcus illuminated by the reddish-yellow streetlights that lined the courtyard. Brown's brochures had included pictures of students walking across the Rhode Island campus's tree-lined pathways and lush green lawns, where kids Marcus's age were free to play frisbee between classes. Marcus was getting out, and she had already practiced her church testimony for the Sunday after his departure: *God is good. He saw fit to send my middle baby to an Ivy League school this week. The Lord saw the pain and good intentions in my heart and had mercy on me.*

As Marcus strode toward Prescott Road, he raised his eyes toward the street and squinted at the cars whizzing by. He'd found a way out, even if it was without her. Hopefully his ambition would rub off on Lance, with his "ain't" and "don't got no" talk. Maybe that's why Marcus had given Lance the *Monster* book. Perhaps Marcus knew Lance was turning out streetwise and apathetic like Vance and the novel had been a warning.

From the darkness outside, there was more laughter from Vega; a pop can snapped and hissed. Nona waited for a breeze to flow to her, perhaps to cool the kitchen a bit, but none came. The crickets chirped, and the moist heat left a dewy layer of sweat on her skin.

Before Marcus stepped beyond the orange glow, she took in a final image of him—straining and in search of something. She scanned the darkness on Prescott Road beyond him to see what he was noticing. She watched him until his retreating back, then his legs, then the soles of his sneakers moved beyond the streetlights and became completely enveloped in darkness.

Harlan was in Medford at a family reunion where a shooting had broken out. Three young men dead after a beef over one of their girlfriends.

He was in the middle of an interview with the Medford Police Department's public information officer when his phone rang. He was waiting to hear back from *U.S. News Daily* about his gun violence pitch. Every phone call could be his big break. He checked the screen. Marcus was calling.

That boy had the worst timing. Harlan would call him back later that night after he filed his story.

Yet once Harlan returned to the office, the call from Marcus slipped his mind as he typed out the details of the latest fatal shooting. Marcus had not left a voicemail.

Nona couldn't bring herself to worry about Lance, even though he left shortly after. She was relieved to be alone. She wanted a moment to think of Kendall and to talk to him in her mind about all the things that had happened since visiting his grave.

She sang "I'll Always Love My Mama" as she wiped down the kitchen counter.

She actually smiled and was about to sing the next line when a voice from the hallway sang the opening lyrics to the song.

The closest weapon to her was the skillet on the drying rack. She grabbed it, spun around, and held it in front of her.

It was the same voice. The one that had said *It's me.*

The cast iron frying pan was heavy; she might as well have been holding a boulder in front of her. She gripped the handle with both hands as she approached the bathroom. She glanced inside.

Trapped air filled the pipes. The rusty cylinders moaned, high-pitched, like a woman in agony, in the early stages of labor, when her body was trying to stay closed, trying to prevent the bursting open of flesh and blood that she knew was to come. The bathroom was empty.

She went down the hall and stood outside the boys' bedroom. That's where the voice had come from.

She threw open their door. What did she expect to find? NaDarius, reaching for her, bleeding but smiling, perhaps because he'd frightened her again?

She stepped in and found no one there. Not under their beds; not in the closet. Same for her own room, and inside all the kitchen cabinets. Empty. Quiet. Undisturbed. She didn't even find mice this time.

Her phone buzzed. A text from Pastor: Haven't heard from you since the cemetery. You good?

Through tears, she responded: No. I'm not good. Not at all.

Twenty-Nine

She didn't tell Pastor about the voice. She didn't tell Pastor about the botched conjuring, nor about Peter coming to her home, nor about the fact that she'd felt possessed and maybe almost could have killed Peter. She needed to see Pastor. Needed to feel safe. So she told him she was worried about the stove.

"Honestly, Nona, if I can't get this to work, I think you should move." He rummaged around in the box of tools she kept in the kitchen cabinet below the counter.

The perspiration that stuck Pastor's shirt to his skin made Nona's cheeks flush. He checked the manual for the new stove and then the pilot light.

"Move?"

"That's what I said." He grunted as he pulled the thing forward, and the appliance gave a loud screech as its bottom scraped the floor.

"Move where?"

"I don't know. We'll just have to figure that part out."

We'll just have to figure that part out. We'll. We. She liked the sound of that but also didn't like the sound of that.

With her broom, her dustpan, and a garbage bag, he took care of the dead mice he found back there, then checked the outlet and plug.

She'd be lying if she said his presence hadn't eased her fear: Someone else dealing with one of her problems, looking after her, caring about her instead of her having to care for everybody else for a change. And after hearing that voice again, singing in her hallway, she was relieved to not be alone.

She'd thought Kendall had driven NaDarius away. She'd been wrong, but she was relieved that Marcus was going out with his future roommate. That part was at least working out.

Pastor slid the heavy monster back in and replaced the burner covers. "Hopefully, it's like a gadget—unplug it, fiddle with it, plug it back in, and it fixes itself."

She hoped so too.

"Who was the guy who gave you a ride here?"

"Security."

"I noticed him at Marcus's graduation party and . . ." She wanted to say 'and at the church when your wife threatened my job,' but then she'd have to tell him about the research. The confrontation. "Why do you need security?"

"I don't, really." His back to her, he washed his hands, his head tilted as he lathered. "Just a thing pastors do when we have big churches. There's a lot of money there."

She appreciated him wiping up the water he'd splashed on the counter. He was more conscientious and attentive than Vance had been, but there was something he still wasn't telling her. Did she have trust issues, or was he hiding something?

"And you keep a lot of money on you." She eyed the latest stack of cash next to his phone, wallet, and lip balm on her counter.

"What?" He chuckled nervously and followed her gaze. "Oh. That's just . . ." He took her hand and pulled her toward the breakfast table. "Just petty cash. Not a big deal."

It seemed like a big deal to her, but she talked down that worry.

As they sat, Pastor seemed uneasy. “Switching gears, I heard about Mable Cleveland’s son . . . What’s his name? Donnell?”

“Yes.”

“Police questioned him about robbing a house in Sebastian Hills.”

“I know. Donnell gets fired from every job because he uses them as an excuse to steal.”

“I heard Lance helped him with the job.”

“I talked to Lance and to Donnell’s mother about keeping the two of them away from each other. I can only pray that it works.”

“What’s your plan for Lance this fall? Do you want me to talk—”

“No. Don’t talk to him. And I don’t know what to do about him either. With everything going on with Marcus, I—”

“The deck is stacked against you, Nona. I feel bad because I’ve been meaning to get Lance more involved at the church, and here he—”

“Not your responsibility.”

“Not . . . not my—” Pastor seemed hurt. Angry, even. “Did you really say ‘not my responsibility’? I don’t do anything for you out of obligation.”

She wanted to ask: *Then why do you do all these things for me? What do you want in return?*

Everything above her neck was heavy, as though any minute, her forehead would land on the kitchen table with a thud. She rested her head in her hand and leaned forward. In the hallway, floorboards shifted.

Seemingly unaware of the sound, Pastor reached across the table, placed his palm against her cheek, and lifted her head again.

He took her hands and pulled her around the table and onto his lap, holding her against his chest. “I’ve been wanting to talk to you about us. Because there is an ‘us,’ Nona. You realize that, don’t you?”

His heart pumped rapidly against her breast. He pulled her mouth to his and kissed her gently. And he was gentle when he placed her on her bed, and tender when he entered her. Noticing tears on her cheeks, he licked them dry.

This time was different than in the kitchen. This was slow love, as if he wanted to crawl beneath her skin. The type of love-making a couple does when they are consummating a committed relationship.

He moaned; his body shivered; tears formed in his eyes, landed on her cheeks, and slid down to her ears. He held her like a precious thing. And his thrusts weren't forceful and animalistic like before. This time he was gentle, going deeper than he had before, and whenever she moaned, his breath hitched as well. Her arms and legs were entwined with his, and when they brought each other to climax, she felt she and Pastor had become one soul.

"Open your eyes," he whispered as they caught their breath. "Look at me." He stared into her eyes for a long time, gently kissing her lips until he was soft and naturally slipped out of her.

Afterward, when their breathing had returned to normal and their heart rates had calmed, he held her and tugged her hair between his fingers.

"We're separated." His voice was serious but hopeful.

She leaned away and stared into his eyes. He seemed nervous, vulnerable, the way he'd appeared in his office when he'd given her the money. She wasn't used to having his face so close, seeing the contours of his skin and the firmness of his jaw.

"When?"

"Weeks ago. I heard she'd threatened your job."

Nona was silent. Guilt filled her because she hadn't told him about that herself.

"Heard it from my security guy. Said she snapped at you in the business center."

Nona thought back to the guy in gold chains at Marcus's party and in the hallway of the church. His face had been hardened those times, but she'd noticed a smile from him this evening as he escorted Pastor to her door.

"Why didn't *you* tell me, Nona?"

"Because she's your wife, and I'm in the wrong. I wasn't going to tell you and have you come to my rescue against your wife."

"That's why you've been avoiding me?"

"Mostly. Yes."

"We've been married on paper only. She and I have been apart, honestly, for years. When I heard she threatened you, I confronted her about it."

"What? Oh my God. I'm mortified."

"Why? She had no right."

"I have no right."

"Well, it was the perfect opportunity for me to say what I'd been intending to say for the longest and had been putting off. I want a divorce."

"What did she do?"

"Nothing. She only threatened you because she was worried about losing the church. Not because she cares about me. I'm like one of her handbags, you know? And she's seeing somebody else too, so what could she really say?"

"What? Who? Arthur Reynolds?"

"Yeah. Guy who owns your plant. How'd you know?"

"That was how she threatened my job. Said she knew Arthur Reynolds."

"I can't believe her." He paused for a long time, turning that information over in his mind. "Yep. Him. So it's not like she could call me a cheater. It's all officially over now."

"Are you okay?"

"I am. Better than okay. I feel like a weight has been lifted. A bad marriage is a prison, you know? I'm sad I wasted so many good years of my life in a loveless union—isolated, lonely, no one to confide in. Until I became close to you, I was lost."

"Are you still in the house?"

"No. Been living out of my church office. We haven't told anyone yet because there's so much money tied up in the church. And the public image, you know? Pastor with a broken marriage. Not a good look, but she's the one who cares about the image."

"As bad as it is, divorce is a pretty common thing. I don't think any of the saints would judge you."

He chuckled. Then when he saw she was serious, his chuckle became a belly laugh, his stomach vibrating against hers. She loved the feeling of being held close and sharing intimate thoughts. The emotional intimacy was the best part of sex. With Vance gone, this was what she'd been missing.

"We're talking about the same saints, right?" He continued to chuckle, but there was sadness beneath the humor. "I will need to step down when I tell everyone."

"Why?"

"I honestly didn't want a big church anyway. This was her doing. I wanted a small congregation that ran a ministry in the streets. Community work. Active. Not crammed together in some stuffy house of prayer with plasma screens broadcasting the service into balconies. That church is her dream, so I say let her have it."

"What will you do?"

"I don't know yet. What do you think I should do?"

"Start a community service. Run it the way you always say you want to. A not-for-profit."

"I suppose." He stared at her ceiling. "I hope, whatever I do, I can spend more time with you."

She thought of Vance. It was wrong having her pastor in the bed she used to share with her husband, whom she was still married to, who used to hold her in the same spot. If Lance or Marcus returned and found her in bed with their pastor, they would disown her, and she would have no justification for her actions. She'd locked her bedroom door for that reason.

"I'm telling you all this stuff, Nona, because I don't want you to think I'm going around sleeping with all the ladies in the congregation. I've never done this before. And I know how awful this seems."

"I'm lying here with you."

"But . . . you know what I mean? I'm supposed to be a man of God, and I—"

"I wouldn't have made it through the last four years if it weren't for you. I know this doesn't fit neatly into anybody's rules about who we're allowed to be with, but I don't regret anything."

He kissed her gently on her forehead and pulled her in closer so her face was nestled against his neck. "Neither do I."

It was warm there against his skin, and her head fit perfectly. Perhaps that spot on him was made specifically for her.

"I really want you and the boys to make it out of this place."

"I do too."

He kissed her nose. "Is there someplace else you want to live?"

She couldn't tell him about the home on Willowbrook. That detail was too intimate. Some things she wanted to only exist in her mind.

"I don't know."

"Think about where you want to live with Lance after Marcus leaves. Let me know where that is. I could get you moved out of here and in there next month. Even a few miles away would put Lance in a much safer school district."

"I know."

"Deposit. Cosigner. Whatever you need. Let me know."

"I will." She wouldn't. She needed the help, but she also was smart enough to know not to have his name on her home. Nor to borrow too much money unless she was willing to be owned by him.

"You never mention Vance anymore."

Vance? Who she sensed was somehow able to see her in bed with another man. "That's because there's nothing to mention."

"What are your plans? He's going to get out at some point. I'm sure he's going to be expecting all of this." He caressed her backside. "I've never been incarcerated, but I can imagine he's thinking every night of his homecoming with you."

"Homecoming? Please. He can live with his parents until he gets on his feet." And she meant it.

His body became tense, the crook of his neck less welcoming.

He said, "I only ask because I've been interviewing lawyers, and when I was sitting in the office, it hit me that you hadn't gotten a divorce. And it's been four years."

"You were interviewing a lawyer for your divorce and thinking about me?"

His body became even more tense. If he stiffened any more, she'd be lying against a rock.

"I always think about you, Nona."

Was he thinking he was going to divorce his wife and be with her? Because if she ever got around to divorcing Vance, she wasn't going to get in a serious relationship with anyone else. She could count on Pastor for now, but she also knew he was a man capable of cheating on his wife.

"When you're thinking about me, you're really thinking about the idea of me. You don't really know me. Not the real me."

"I'd know you even more if you would stop keeping things from me." He playfully spanked her bottom. "I've known you for more than twenty years, Nona. The last four intimately."

"Yes, but that's not really me."

"I'm listening."

She couldn't tell him.

"I mean, I can't really talk about it. I'm just saying, I'm not who you think I am."

"To me? You can't talk about it . . . to me? Until recently, isn't that all we've been doing? Talking? Sharing? Being each other's confidant and companion?"

"Yes, but . . ."

"I've told you everything, Nona."

"You haven't."

"I . . ." He paused. Bit his bottom lip. "Yes. There are some things I can't tell you because I'm not proud of them and I don't think you're ready to hear them, but I will tell you eventually. Once I fix them. Once I correct those things. I mean, I'm not perfect, but I've been honest. About how I had been sleeping down the hall from my bedroom in my own house, by myself. About how I am tired of pastoring. About how I feel about you."

"I know, but . . ."

"Then why do you keep doing this?" Exasperation crept into his voice. "Why do you think you can't talk to me about something? After Kendall was killed, there were nights when I didn't think you would make it to the morning, and I listened to you. I honestly think those long nights are what drew me to you. Made me fall for you. You were vulnerable, honest; you needed me. And I, in my loneliness, needed you and felt wanted. Whatever it is, you know I'm not going to judge you, right?"

"I mean, I guess."

"You guess, Nona?"

She had to tell him. He was right, and it was obvious he wasn't going to let this go.

She closed her eyes and thought back to the spot in Hester Gardens where she'd found Vance with that bloody pistol in his hand. She let out a deep sigh and decided that, unlike her talk with Vega, this time she would share the entire truth.

May 28, 2002

"Help me get him back there." Vance pocketed the weapon and grabbed her, smearing red across her forearm. He pointed to the dumpsters.

Help Vance or help the man whose life was seeping from his body? How could Vance even utter the word "help"? When her feet remained rooted, Vance dragged the unconscious man by his legs to the back side of the receptacles, hiding his victim but leaving behind a trail of clotted blood.

Vance tugged on her red-smeared forearm, bringing her across Hester Gardens and over the threshold of their home. She needed to call an ambulance for the man behind the dumpster, but ambulance meant police. Police meant Vance would be cuffed, taken away. What would happen to her and the boys if Vance were gone? What if the police decided to lock her up too? They wouldn't know about *let* and her inability to prevent her husband from beating the man.

Inside, Vance set the fishing pole—the anniversary gift she'd bought for him—beside the front door. She hugged her torso, licking her top lip where salty snot threatened to enter her mouth. Her face muscles twitched as she watched him wrap the gun in newspaper, scrub blood from his hands in the kitchen sink, discard his soiled clothes, and replace them with a crisp tracksuit, seeming familiar with the routine.

"I want you to tell me the truth." She usually never questioned him about the unaccounted-for time in the evenings between the closure of his dad's body shop and when Vance got home, usually buttoned her lips and stared at the floor when he explained why he always had enough for new shoes, Christmas tree ornaments, science fair fees. But this wasn't usually.

"Nona, my forever—"

"I want you to tell me the truth."

He tried to cross from their hallway to the living room, but she blocked his path. They stood opposite each other beside the breakfast table where, that morning, they'd shared coffee and a kiss above their steamy mugs.

"Guy tried to rob me." He spoke with his hands. He never spoke with his hands.

"The truth."

"Just told you." He tried to get around her.

She slid to the left and stopped him, her nose coming to rest directly in front of his neck. She smelled the lavender from the hand soap.

"He called you by name."

"Must have been casing our house or something." He placed his hands in his pants pockets, hiding his palms like he was trying to hide the truth, and this simple gesture made her want to shove him to the floor.

"And you just happened to have a gun on you?" She glanced at the wad of newspaper dirtying up the kitchen counter she'd scrubbed for their anniversary.

"Carry it for protection." He returned to the counter, poured a cup of water from the faucet, and kept his back to her. The news-wrapped gun was inches from him, but he didn't acknowledge it.

She usually would have let up by now. Would have let him kiss her and caress away all her justified anxiety.

"Protection from what? I don't carry a gun."

"These streets." He didn't raise his voice, but exasperation crept into his tone.

"I want you to tell me the truth."

He sighed. Took a swig of water. Swirled the remaining liquid in the cup. Continued to sip while staring out their kitchen window.

She sensed Vance was figuring out the words to get out of this conversation, but that bloody hand reaching toward her slithered into her thoughts. The battered man dragging his lifeless legs, pleading. There weren't words enough in Vance's vocabulary to make this right with her.

"You should be happy I was strapped. So I could get home to you and the boys."

"Folks who are strapped for protection don't pistol-whip people who are pleading for their lives."

"Bet he'll think twice now before robbing anybody else."

"You're a damn lie!" Her throat burned. She knocked the cup from his hand, and it landed in the sink with a metallic bang. Water splashed across the counter, sprayed the lump of newspaper, and puddled on the floor.

It was impossible to lie to someone without also thinking they were stupid. That angered her the most. The liar had to believe the lied-to was unable to put together two and two.

Vance closed the kitchen window.

"I want you to tell me the truth!" Her throat was hoarse.

Vance took her by the arms and guided her to the living-room rug, where they often made love when the boys weren't home. He held her under the brightest ceiling light. He gripped her shoulders, perhaps considering shaking her, but he remained calm. "You don't want the truth."

She slapped him. When she drew back her hand, a red mark spread across his cheek. He grabbed her wrist and placed her palm against his chest, where his heart thudded rapidly. She snatched her hand away.

"I'm sick of you answering me with questions, kissing me instead of explaining. Tell the truth. For once!"

He took a step back and sat on the armrest of the couch—a leather sofa he'd shown up with one day but with no store delivery, tags, or a receipt. He hung his head like a crane.

"Got a guy that sells some stuff for me in a couple spots around here." His voice softened like when he held her at night. "The guy you just saw, name's NaDarius. He rolled up on my guy last week and stole my stuff. When I pulled up here, he had the nerve to be out there trying to sell my stuff to—"

"Stuff?"

He winced. "You know. Stuff. Nothing major. A little something."

"Say it." She closed the gap between them, towered over him, ready to slap him again.

"I did." He was nearly pleading now.

"Say what it is."

"Come on, baby."

She waited for his eyes to grow wet, for his face to become red with shame, but neither happened. "I want you to say it."

"I never bring it back here to you and the boys." He grabbed her hand lovingly. She snatched it away. "I keep everything away—"

"Oh, but you haven't. You kept the gun. You're selling dope. You beat this man, NaDarius, in a spot where the boys might have been able to see you do it."

"I'm doing the best I can."

"You were covered in blood!"

"Everything I do is for you and these boys."

"If you were really thinking of me and the boys, you would have gotten yourself together a long time ago."

"I am together."

"I want you to stop selling."

The air left the room. Silence enveloped them. He clenched his jaw. Narrowed his eyes. Pursed his lips. Raised his head in an expression that let her know what he'd done to NaDarius, he could do to her. If he were the hitting kind, this was the moment he would have smacked her.

"How we gon' eat, Nona?" He stood. He was a bear again. His voice a growl, his back and shoulders stretching to the ceiling.

"I work," she sputtered. "You work."

"We can't afford anything off that piddly money you get at the plant and I get from whatever my father decides to pay me each week." He'd finally raised his voice. "Between rent, medical bills when one of the boys gets a bellyache, utilities, and transportation, how we gon' afford food and water?"

"Stop exaggerating."

"I'm not!" He was full-on shouting and pacing now. A small voice inside her wondered whether he could ever hurt her and the boys the way he'd hurt that man. How could her love, who playfully nibbled her ear each night, also be a murderer? "Karate lessons, basketball camp, that fishing pole you know nobody around here can afford, my car note. Do the math." He slapped his fist into his palm. For the first time in their marriage, she flinched. "Don't act like you didn't know all this time."

"You told me you were getting the money from your dad's body shop." She was small. A mouse next to him.

"Do I ever come home with paint on my clothes?" Another slap of his fist into his palms. Another flinch from her, and he didn't seem to notice. "Are my hands ever dirty? I been keeping the specifics from you out of respect because I know you don't approve, but you not gon' stand here and act like you didn't know anything. At all. All these years."

"Get out!" She shoved him, and he didn't budge. She shoved him harder. She didn't need to worry whether he could harm her, because she wanted to kill him. Whatever rage had been growing in him dissipated as it seemed to dawn on him that she hadn't, in fact, known all along. In this fight—the only fight they'd ever had on the subject—she'd revealed herself not to be turning a blind eye, but rather to be just plain blind.

"Baby." A tear like a tiny diamond formed in the corner of his eye. "You really didn't know?"

Even when he'd told her the pistol was for protection, she suspected there was more, but suspecting while hoping your husband was telling you the truth was not the same as knowing outright. And now he'd managed to make her feel ashamed and stupid, and to make her feel like his accomplice.

"I want you to leave." She shoved him again, but this time he pulled her in for an embrace.

"I'm not leaving you, Nona. I'm not leaving our boys. I'm not trying to control you, but I'm also not going to be somewhere else watching you and the boys struggle to eat and have basics. You can hate me, but I do love you. I always will."

"You're not going to turn this around on me." She told herself that he could never hurt her or her boys. He must have reserved that part of himself for people like NaDarius. That had to be the case. Because, in spite of herself, she instantly felt safer in his embrace.

"I'm not trying to, baby." He grabbed her waist, rubbing the small of her back, the sandalwood cologne on his neck reminding her of their anniversary and the version of her husband that kissed the back of her hand before he held it. The version who called her his "forever," who had woken her that morning by nuzzling her neck and making love to her gently, quietly. She didn't cry. She wouldn't in front of him, but she did remain in his embrace.

"I'm doing the best I can to take care of you and the boys. I'm really careful. You know I'd never do anything to put you all in danger. The boys will never find out. It's really not enough stuff for anyone to notice at all. Give me some time. I'm so close to having enough money to buy into my dad's business, making some real money there instead of always going to him to beg for it. Enough for our house."

It was true his father never supported him. He'd once pointed out that most kids in families that owned businesses benefitted from nepotism, but his dad never let him own a stake. Wouldn't even let him manage the workers.

She remembered how the man on the ground—NaDarius—had pleaded, "I will pay you back." It was the last thing he'd uttered. So he must have stolen something from Vance. Or owed and come up short. Vance was probably telling the truth about that part.

"What about NaDarius? We have to—"

"If he's out here trying to take corners, he knows how to recover from an ass-whooping."

That night, Vance climbed into bed beside her, kissed her cheek, said, "Goodnight, my forever," and went straight to sleep. No guilty conscience, apparently.

She lay awake thinking of NaDarius. The way he'd reached for her like the victim in the Bible story of the Good Samaritan who asked for help and everyone passed him by, left him for dead in the road. And that was exactly what she'd done. She'd not been the Good Samaritan. She was the villain in NaDarius's story. She was Vance's accomplice, and everything inside of her was screaming, *Take your boys and leave!*

She did a mental calculation of the money she brought into the house versus the amount they spent, and Vance was right. Kendall's after-school computer classes and Marcus's basketball camp would vanish without Vance. And she couldn't bear to be the brokest person at church, if she was really being honest with herself. She was the one people came to when they needed extra cash, not the other way around.

Hot tears spilled down the sides of her face and crawled into her ears as she thought of Vance scooping up that gun-filled newspaper and heading out at sunset. He'd returned hours later without it.

He shifted in his sleep, and Nona finally allowed herself that cry. She inched to the edge of the bed, as far away from his body as she could get. The truth was heavy. She wished she could go back to not knowing, could go back to spooning him in the night to feel safe, desired, needed, loved.

And, in the moments before she dozed off, listening to the light snores of her three boys from down the hall, she doubted her decision to stay. What if NaDarius hadn't owed Vance? What if, when he said, "I will pay you back," he meant something altogether different? What if "I will pay you back" meant revenge?

August 9, 2016

Pastor was silent as she whispered her secrets in his ear.

"Our anniversary came and went, and the next day, while cleaning the kitchen and listening to the local news, I learned the family of eighteen-year-old NaDarius Rucker had reported the teen missing." It occurred to her that NaDarius had been eighteen when Vance killed him. That Kendall had been eighteen when he'd been killed. That Peter, missing, was eighteen. That her Marcus was eighteen. The pattern was only illuminated for her now that she'd said his age.

"So what did you do?" Pastor's voice came out in a whisper.

"I . . . I glanced at Vance, who was sitting at the table eating the meal I had finally cooked for him, and he finished his food, brought his plate to the sink, and told me to go rest my feet in the living room.

"'Don't worry about this mess, baby.' He didn't make eye contact with me. 'You relax. I'll take care of the rest.'"

In the seconds after the words left her mouth, she thought Pastor was going to get up, get dressed, and get the hell out of her home.

"I had no clue, Nona."

"You asked me about the spirit here. That's the spirit. It was a young man Vance beat in front of me. A teen. Somebody's baby. And I did nothing to save him. I stood there and watched Vance pistol-whip him. And the young man called out to me. He said, 'Don't let him kill me.' And he died because that's exactly what I did."

She thought back to NaDarius's age. At the time she'd been in that alley, her boys were young. Now that she'd raised her children to eighteen, the same age as NaDarius at his death, Vance's murder, her standing idly by, was even more vile than she'd thought.

"I could have stopped Vance. Could have shoved him or yelled at him or threatened to call the cops on him. And I've been cursed. That's why Vance went to prison. Why Kendall was killed. Why I can't get my boys out of Hester Gardens. That's why the thing is in my house now. An eye for an eye. And I don't know how to make it stop."

Pastor seemed horrified. She couldn't bear to have him stare at her that way. She faced the window and let her tears soak into the pillow.

The mattress shifted. She figured Pastor was getting up to leave, but he wrapped his arms around her, pulled her close to him, and whispered in her ear. "You did not kill that man. Nothing that has happened since then is because of what you witnessed. If Vance killed a man in front of you, you were victimized in that moment too. I suspect the curse you are experiencing here is you torturing yourself with guilt."

He kissed her neck and caressed her shoulder. For a moment, she closed her eyes and allowed herself to feel safe, free.

Part Four

Thirty

Kiandra knew something was wrong as soon as she finished her shift. The last text she'd received from her brother was On my way, Kiki, but Cedrick wasn't sitting in the lobby of Medford "Deadford" Hospital waiting to accompany her home, and Cedrick had never been late.

She stood in Deadford's entryway with her CNA scrubs hanging over her left arm; she was too tired to fold them properly and throw them in the overweight rucksack on her back. The bag was filled with two seven-hundred-page textbooks she'd gotten from her nursing program to help prepare her for the upcoming exam. That's the other thing Cedrick was supposed to help her with—the heavy bag! She texted him.

> **Kiandra:** Where are you? You were supposed to be here at 9:45 sharp. See how much help I am the next time you need me!

Every person who crossed the street between the bus stop and the sidewalk in front of Deadford seemed like they could have been Cedrick until they got close enough for her to see.

At ten thirty, when she should have been home already in the shower washing germs from her body, she left the air-conditioned lobby and went outside into the unrelenting heat. In the hospital's circular drive, frantic folks arrived and escorted sick or injured family members into the trauma unit's lobby or pulled up and asked the security guard where to park.

There were several signs explaining that the lot was behind the hospital, but frightened people could only see the large ER sign and its promise of healing, even if the hospital had the worst outcomes and highest death rate in the state of Michigan.

Her parents had asked her why she wanted to work there and have the hospital's name on her resume. There had been so many write-ups in the papers about physicians who had let their training lag, medication errors, neglect by care staff, mistakes in surgeries, and preventable deaths. And there was one sensational headline about how a stun gun had been used on a patient in the mental health division. Even with its reputation, medical residents came from around the region to learn to sew up gunshot and knife wounds. Her answer to her parents had been simple: "We don't have a car. What other hospital can I really get to every day?"

"It's too hot to be out here waiting," the security guard with a gold tooth said. It was rare these days for her to see a person with one gold tooth, especially the canine. She instantly wanted him to go away. "Your ride late?"

"Something like that." She was leery even of the guard. At twenty, she was at an age when Black women were prey to everyone. No one but her family would care if she went missing, and if something happened to her, she'd be blamed. *What was she doing out all alone at night? Where were her people? She was probably up to no good anyway.*

Likely sensing she didn't feel like talking, the security guard went back inside, and the opening and closing of those electric sliding doors sent a blast of cold air conditioning outside to remind her of how uncomfortable she was. She called and got Cedrick's voicemail.

"Call me as soon as you get this. You know I can't get on the bus by myself, punk."

It wasn't so much she couldn't get on the bus alone. She could, but she was still afraid. Her mind returned to the moment when she'd slammed her nursing text against that groper's head. Since she'd beaten the guy so badly, everyone assumed Kiandra was fine, but Cedrick knew how frightened she was. He was scared for her too, as well as overprotective, and one day he just said, "You get off at ten? I'ma be out there at ten." She didn't argue with him either. Just hugged him until he pushed her away. She'd been so pleased that he'd offered, because ever since he'd started hanging with the Hester Boys, he did stupid things.

At eleven p.m., she called Donnell, her hands trembling as she dialed. Where was Cedrick?

Once, when Cedrick needed cash for science and math fees, she took him to the plasma center. He didn't have a government ID, so she donated blood in his stead. With forty-five dollars and a couple pints less of blood, she came out of the donation room to find him missing. Pissed she had to search for him when she was already lightheaded, she smacked the goofy grin off his face when she found him. "You can be so ungrateful," she'd yelled at him.

He hadn't always been that way. When Cedrick was five, he wanted to be a veterinarian and would rescue stray animals from the courtyard or the alley, bring them home, and feed them left-over turkey and bread from the fridge.

Now, he rarely smiled. Not even video games made him excited, and he kept secrets about where he was going and who he was with. Their mother said he was just "growing up" and "being a teenager," but Kiandra knew the change was something more. And she later learned he hadn't gotten lost at the plasma center at all but had crept to a medicine supply room to steal codeine.

Donnell answered after one ring.

"Surprised you calling me so late." Sounded like he hadn't been drinking for once.

"Have you seen Cedrick?"

"Not since he went downtown with me and Lance yesterday."

Donnell knew good and damn well they had been up to no good the previous day, and likely nowhere near downtown.

"Is the light on in my house?"

"Wait a sec."

A muffled sound came through the receiver. She imagined Donnell with his sleeve of tattoos pulling back his bedroom curtain and looking across the alley at her unit. When they were all prepubescent and knew nothing of hormones, attraction, and sex, she actually used to hang out in Donnell's room watching WWE wrestling matches with him and his gaggle of cousins. Back then, she'd considered Donnell her best friend.

"Yep. They on. Want me to knock?"

"No. He probably fell asleep."

"In this heat? I don't see how. You at Deadford? You know, I can come get you."

"In what car, Nell?"

"Cedrick ain't got no car either."

"But it takes thirty minutes one way. I'm not waiting thirty more minutes for you to get here on the bus. I'll get a ride with somebody else."

"I told you before, Kiki, let me be the one to come walk you home. You wouldn't have to worry about anybody messing with you on the bus again, and you know I wouldn't keep you waiting like this."

"Nope. I don't want you walking me anywhere."

"It's like that now?"

"If you see Cedrick, tell him he better be gone when I get there or I'm going to beat his ass."

"Ay. Before you go. You seen Peter?"

She'd been ready to hang up, but the mention of Peter stopped her. Peter going missing bothered her. It bothered everyone. Hester Gardens folks didn't just go missing like that.

"No." She waited for Donnell to say more, but all she heard was a rap song playing softly in the background. "You?"

"Nah."

"Why'd you ask?" She wondered what Donnell wasn't saying. "You thought I saw him at the hospital? Like you think something happened to him?"

"Happened . . . like somebody got to him?" Donnell's voice got deeper as he suddenly grew angry.

"Yes."

"If I thought somebody had done something to Peter, I would be out hunting down the mothafucka . . . Sorry for the language."

"It's cool, Nell. Police found out anything?"

"Ain't nothing to find, really. His phone and wallet were with him. They told Mother Lincoln he ain't used the phone since he left."

She thought of Gretchen and her baby boy. Her cousin had been frantic since Peter had disappeared, and Kiki couldn't help but think Peter had just ducked out on his responsibilities. "Look, I gotta go."

"All right. Remember I'm here if you need me. We gotta look out for each other out here."

"Right, Nell."

"I'm serious, girl. I'm not trying to get ass. I'm saying. Something ain't right."

She hung up, her anxiety about Cedrick more pronounced. It wasn't like him to just not show up. If he were at home, why would he have on all the lights in this heat? Cedrick wasn't a lights-all-on kind of person anyway. He usually sat in front of the television in the dark, but she could imagine him falling asleep before their parents left and maybe oversleeping. Maybe her parents had left on all the lights?

She had the same sinking feeling the night she lost Kendall. *Calm down, Kiandra.*

She called her boyfriend, Selwin, who did not live in Hester Gardens. Selwin didn't even live in Medford. He didn't have a sleeve of tattoos, he never said "ain't" or "finna," and he knew how to conjugate verbs. She'd met him at the hospital when he'd visited his grandfather after heart surgery. She'd noticed right away he wore collared shirts and jeans with the proper fit, and leather shoes instead of sneakers, all of which made up for his too-lean body and too-small ears.

Within ten minutes, Selwin pulled up to the hospital and placed her heavy backpack in his trunk, and she got in. She was ashamed of him seeing where she lived, but she needed to get home to check on her brother. She pecked Selwin on the cheek. Every time he showed up, her burdens seemed lighter.

She called Cedrick again. No answer. She remembered him saying he was stopping by Gretchen's to help with the baby. She called Gretchen. Her cousin's phone didn't even ring. Gretchen's phone was shut off again, which was one of the reasons she wanted to get Cedrick out and leave their life and their backward family behind. She was tired of the not having—cars, phone service, trash pickup, reliable pest control. She wasn't wishing for a mansion and a yacht. She just wanted her day-to-day life to not be so difficult.

"Everything okay?" Selwin asked with a grin and raised eyebrow, seeming unsure whether to smile or offer sympathy.

She patted his thigh and looked out the window. "I think so." But inside she knew *I think so* was a lie.

Thirty-One

*Gretchen sat at the end of the couch as far away from the window as pos*sible, tucked in the corner where the two dingy walls met, as safe as she could make herself from stray bullets and from her dead twin Grace.

A car pulled up to the projects, and, at first, she didn't notice it. Grayson wasn't sleeping through the night consistently yet, so Gretchen was micro-sleeping. The blinkers flashed into her window and woke her fully.

Her parents' landline rang, which was unexpected because as far as she knew, they hadn't paid the bill in months. Grayson cried out once but drifted back off. She jumped up and answered it, but slammed it back down when she heard a bill collector's automated recording. She had been expecting a call from Peter. Or from Marcus. A call from either would do, but mostly she wanted to know where the hell Peter had disappeared to.

She needed Peter to come back. Their baby went through a lot of diapers, wipes, and bibs; WIC and her measly paychecks weren't cutting it, and her parents told her they weren't going to "finance" her "sins" beyond giving her a roof to stay under. Peter had patched up the hole in her bathroom wall, had helped a few times with the baby, and then she hadn't heard from him again. She was panicked—Peter would never leave Grayson like this.

When she hung up the cordless phone and picked it up again, she got a recording that the line was out of service. Of course it was. Nothing ever worked.

Those turn signals brought her to the window. Since she lived across from Vega Lawson's unit in one of the first homes near Prescott Road, whenever she stepped outside her door, she witnessed everything coming up and down Medford's main drag. She needed her windows to remain open so she could get some air, yet she also wanted the aggravating light to stop blinking. She crossed the area rug she had bought used to liven up the dreary room. She prayed the creaking floorboards didn't wake the baby.

In his diaper and nothing else, Grayson rested his tiny head on her shoulder, with his mouth open and a trail of drool sliding out and onto her arm. As she moved, she rubbed his sweat-soaked back, careful not to wake him. There was nothing more helpless than having a sweaty, miserable child and no a/c to cool them off.

Gretchen pulled back the window's sheer curtain. The light was coming from a white boy sitting in a car with his hazards on, squinting and staring across his empty passenger seat at the Gardens' front lawn. Who would be dumb enough to let a customer wait out front on busy-ass Prescott Road? This fool might as well have put out a sign saying, *I'm here for drugs and prostitutes. Arrest me.* Or worse, *I'm here for drugs and prostitutes. Rob me.*

After making a phone call, typing out what seemed like a text, and checking his blind spot in the side mirror, the white boy finally pulled off and disappeared down the near-empty six-lane road.

Gretchen heard a screen door snap to the left of her unit, but she couldn't see who it was.

A wave of queasiness flowed through her as the wind blew the stench from the piled-up trash into her living room.

Someone crossed directly in front of her window, inches from her face, in the darkness, but they were in profile, and she couldn't make out their face. She jumped back and tripped on the area rug, but balanced herself and Grayson by placing her free hand on the side chair across from the couch.

When she'd jumped, the sheers she'd been holding had fallen closed against the open window. She stood in the middle of her living room, holding Grayson and staring at the fabric as it caught the attention of the figure, who stopped and faced her window. The shadow raised what looked like a long rifle and pointed it at her.

Her mind went to her twin falling and blood splattering their dresses. At first, Gretchen hadn't even known anything had happened; one second her sister was playing and saying "So, Susie. Where are we going today in our fancy . . ." and then, in the next second, Grace was lying flat on her back, staring at the sky. Gretchen leaned into the memory until she could feel the anguish tightening her chest and burning her eyes.

She took two more steps back and bumped into her dining table, sending the legs screaming over the wooden floor. The noise woke her baby, who shrieked and wailed on her shoulder.

The figure outside lowered their gun but remained there, seemingly listening and deciding. Gretchen wasn't sure what possessed her, but since Grayson was fully awake and she didn't need to keep quiet, she drew closer to the curtain. She knew every family who lived in the Gardens. Hell, she'd slept with most of them—the sons and the married dads. If the person outside with the rifle lived there, she wanted to know why they were creeping around armed.

Just as the shape moved away from her window, she placed Grayson in his playpen in the kitchen. She opened her front door slowly and quietly, so it didn't make a sound.

When she clearly saw the figure, she brought her hand to her mouth to keep any sound from escaping. Her palms were clammy, and she had the urge to tiptoe back to the baby and shelter with him under the dining table.

The person seemed familiar as he stalked Prescott Road near Vega Lawson's unit. Was it Peter? Marcus? Was it her anxious mind making her imagine it was one of them? The rifle looked like the one Marcus had shown her at the lake, but Peter owned the same kind of gun. Peter kept his in his bedroom closet, but Marcus? She thought of him shooting the squirrel. She remembered the bloody animal darting away, Marcus's erection, and the way he pulled her to him as if she'd become his prey and he wanted to draw her blood.

Thirty-Two

"Yeah?" That was how Mother Lincoln answered Nona's phone call. Nona paused to ensure she'd heard correctly. Nona hadn't spoken to Mother since the woman had told her Peter was missing. She'd phoned Mother every day, but Mother never answered, and Nona no longer felt welcome to show up at her home uninvited.

"Mother?"

"Yeah?" There was that curt tone again.

"I was checking in to see how you're doing." Really, she was afraid of being home alone and wanted to hear someone's voice.

"Peter's still gone. That's how I'm doing."

"Is there anything I can—"

"No. You've done enough."

"Mother, you seem mad at me."

"Have the police visited you yet?"

"No. Why would they visit me?"

"Because somebody say they saw you pull a knife on my baby. And then right after that, he went missing."

"Who told you that?"

"Doesn't matter who told me. Is it true?"

"It's . . ." Nona couldn't believe how things were being twisted against her.

"Because if it wasn't true, you would have said so already."

"Peter threatened me, Mother. He tried to force his way into my house, and I—"

"If he did, he must have had a mighty good reason." Mother was nearly yelling now.

"Are you really serious? I honestly don't believe you. After what Peter did to Kendall?"

There was a long silence. Two years' worth of anguish hung between them, and Nona never thought this moment of truth would come.

"What Peter did to Kendall? What is that supposed to mean? My baby has never done anything to anybody. Folks are always messing with him. What are you trying to say?"

Nona took a deep breath. Did Mother really not know all this time that Peter had either killed Kendall or had him set up? Had the woman been acting all along, or had she been that oblivious? Something began churning in Nona's stomach. Was Nona also being naïve about Marcus? About the gun? About him harming Peter?

"This is not about my precious Peter. This is about your family. There is something evil over there festering and . . ."

"Something evil?" Nona's stomach pulled into knots. Tears stung her eyes, and she took a second to calm her breathing. "Look. I know you're worried sick about Peter, but my family—"

"I can see the entire alley, Nona. The entire alley. I've always been able to. Folks think I'm some deaf and blind old lady, but I always know what time it is. I know what you and Vance did out there in that alley when you asked me to watch your boys. I know what you're both capable of, and if the police haven't made it over to your house yet, I'll give them a call and make sure they get right on it."

And the line was dead.

Nona's mind swirled with thoughts and memories, panic, rage, and shame. Mother had seen? Mother had known all these years?

Would Mother really tell the police? Had Mother been secretly judging Nona all of these years? When Nona was feeling superior to Mother, had Mother furtively been feeling superior to Nona? She had half a mind to call Mother back, tell her the truth about Peter's drug dealing, the truth about his gangbanging, the truth that, just as Pastor had said, Nona was victimized in that moment alongside NaDarius. She couldn't bring herself to do it. Peter was gone. It was a tough row for Mother to hoe, but Nona would be relieved if he never returned.

Thirty-Three

Donnell sat on his bed, drinking a lowball of cognac with three cubes of ice. He smoked a joint, popped a Xanax, listened to Wiz Khalifa, and tried to forget his conversation with Kiki.

When did Kiki go out and get a boyfriend? It was bad enough Donnell had to watch her date Kendall for all those years. He didn't say anything about that when it happened, but then when he was trying to comfort her after, she pushed him away. Again. He hated feeling like he was never good enough for her. Then he considered the glass in his hand. Kiki was right about him. She was smart. Hardworking. A queen. She was actually going to get out of the Gardens one of these days.

An hour later, he was lying on his bed, shirt off, in his boxers, letting the stuff do its job in his body. He'd given up lean after he started seeing things, but this stuff, this regular stuff got him where he wanted to be. He was *cool, cool, cool. Mellow, mellow, mellow.* He wasn't thinking about his crabby mom, always on his case about getting a real job, becoming "legal." He didn't care about his loud and ragtag cousins, who thankfully were watching pornos in the front room and would leave him alone to rest.

He was still thinking about Kiki. When they were kids, Kiki used to call him Nelly Belly. He'd thought she'd love him forever.

But now? That girl would *never* give him no play. Always acted like she was too good for everybody and was always up under Kendall when he was alive, and some needle-dick from the suburbs now. He'd heard about the guy but thought it'd just been a rumor.

Donnell had thought if he fucked her younger cousin Gretchen, it would be almost the same, but it wasn't. Gretchen was bony and like a little kid when she was beneath him. She knew how to move—she'd been having sex since junior high—but he'd stopped things with her the previous year because he didn't like feeling he was some pervert in bed with her.

He knew Kiandra would have been full, though, thick, and would have felt like a woman if she had ever let him in. And he wasn't just trying to score with her. Kiki was the type of girl that could make him get his act together. Or was that just the weed talking?

He'd dozed completely when the scraping started up at his window. He opened his eyes and thought he was seeing a large hawk, no, a vulture, its wings spread. He vowed to stop drinking and smoking, a promise he often made when he found himself in a bind. This time he meant it.

He sat up. The room swayed. He tried to focus, but that was a struggle. A brown hand pushed the window in.

Donnell grabbed at his waistband, but Grave Digger wasn't there. Where had he left her? His desk? The nightstand? Near his shoes? Before he could search, two white sneakers jumped onto the windowsill. He tried to get a glimpse of the fool, but the butt of a gun smacked against his nose.

He fell back on his bed and stared up at the ceiling. The pain made his entire head heavy. A brick might as well have been lying in the middle of his face. A dark shadow rose in front of him, and as he touched his nose and drew back his bloody fingertips, those sneakers stomped down on his chest, rough on his skin. A figure, its face shadowed by a baseball cap, pointed a rifle at his head and waited.

The guy looked to be six feet tall. The full weight of his body rested on Donnell's ribcage and the bottom of his windpipe. Donnell couldn't breathe. Was Peter attacking him? Because Peter often got that wild look in his eyes when something else seemed to take hold of him, like the night he stormed into Donnell's room and told him he'd killed Kendall.

"Fuck. I . . . can't . . . breathe." Donnell coughed, gasped, tried to draw in air.

Donnell pushed on the dude's ankles with his hands and struggled to throw the guy off-balance, but the weight was too much, and he still couldn't breathe. He'd had nightmares like this many times since he was young. He'd read online they were sleep paralysis dreams, where the body can't move and a phantom sits square on your chest and you can't wake up and you can't stop it.

This time, someone was actually standing on Donnell's chest, stopping his breath, and he was so high and drunk he couldn't think straight either.

"I . . . can't . . . breathe." Where had he put Grave Digger? He scanned the desk, dresser, end of the bed. There she was. On the nightstand. Why couldn't his outstretched hand reach her?

"I . . . can't . . ."

The hat fell back and dude bent in close until Donnell and his enemy were nose to nose. The face was distorted, like a composite of more than one profile, filled with shadows. Its eyes were wide and glowing like a cat's, and its mouth twisted into a deranged smirk. Warm breath, thick with the smell of garbage, pressed into his face and filled his nostrils.

"I . . ."

The pressure on his chest changed as the figure stared into his eyes, and Donnell opened his mouth, finally feeling he could scream, but the entity pressed his palm to Donnell's lips, and with the other hand, he fired.

Thirty-Four

Nona received a text from Pastor: There are some things I want to ask of you, but I'm scared. She responded with a heart emoji, and he with two.

She knew what he would say, and she didn't want him to utter those words, because if he asked to be her man, his name would be on her new apartment, he'd buy her a car, which he'd mentioned several times before they'd even slept together, and she'd be trusting a man again. Then, the next thing out his mouth would be *When are you getting that divorce?*

Outside, someone was blasting Gnarls Barkley, a song about a coming storm. The fan she'd set on the dresser was loud as it spun around. With her every move, her bed creaked. She couldn't stop staring at the clock. The red glow of the digital numbers seemed brighter, as if screaming *midnight* from across the room.

Marcus had been gone for hours, and she had no idea when he'd be back or where he was exactly. At least Lance was in bed, so she wouldn't have to worry about him.

The fan muffled a thud in the kitchen. She sat up, peering into the dark hall, waiting for a trace of movement. Perhaps Marcus would tiptoe to his bedroom. A band of light shining on the hallway's analog wall clock reminded her yet again of the time.

The water faucet squeaked on in the bathroom, but Lance hadn't left his room since he'd returned.

She coughed. The faucet screeched off abruptly.

She grabbed the bottle of blessing oil. She trembled in the heat as her feet met the warm, splintery wood. She approached the bathroom door, and the water slowly groaned on again. Was this the moment the thing would finally get her?

Inside, black water bubbled up from the toilet basin. It didn't spill this time, and even if it did, she kept towels beneath to catch the sewage. She'd once told Vance about the rumors of ghosts that haunted the projects. He'd scoffed and said, "The only ghost here is poverty." And she thought of that line every time the bathroom flooded, every time trash day came and went without a pickup, every time the pipes moaned like a woman in labor.

She scanned the bathroom. Nothing was there. No spirits lurking in the shower or crouching beside the vanity.

Something caught her eye. The watch box sat on the counter in the same spot it had occupied when Kendall was alive. Her pulse quickened. She hadn't seen the wooden cube in four years, but she told herself Marcus was probably going through old things in preparation for heading to college. She needed to believe that. She opened the box and her breath caught in her throat.

Resting in the middle like a crown was the gold watch Kendall had been wearing when he'd died. The watch he'd gotten from Vance. The watch she'd asked Sgt. Prager about after identifying his body. The watch that Marcus had said he'd seen on—

The fight Marcus and Peter had at his graduation party—Marcus had snatched at Peter's wrist, but he hadn't gotten the watch then.

She texted Harlan: I need to talk to you. ASAP again.

How had the watch returned? It hadn't been there earlier in the evening. Did Marcus come back and leave it? Had he heard her and Pastor in the bed? Or could NaDarius have done it? She remembered NaDarius trying to drag her to the bottom of the lake. Was NaDarius powerful enough to kill Kendall, and Solomon, and Peter, and also leave behind this watch to terrorize her?

She closed the box, poured a dime-sized amount of blessing oil into her left palm, rubbed her hands together, and spread the liquid on the wood.

The anger in Mother's voice when the older woman said she'd seen her and Vance in the alley made Nona wonder: Would Mother really send the police after her and Marcus?

She usually turned the bathroom light off before exiting, but this was a night to not move in the darkness. She left it on.

Outside Marcus and Lance's room, she peeked in at Lance, sprawled on the bed in his boxers and nothing else, snoring and making the air thick with young boy musk. She used to hate that smell but had grown accustomed to it.

Lance's sweat had soaked his sheets. His mouth hung open the way it did when he was a baby.

An ugly thought crept into her mind—she wished Lance was still out for the evening instead of Marcus—and she tamped that nastiness down with a prayer. Because she knew why she struggled to put Lance on a pedestal the way she had Kendall and Marcus: Lance reminded her of Vance. *Give me a clean heart, Lord.*

Tick. Tick. Tick. The noise started up in the kitchen. She pounded down the hall, the hardness of the wood reverberating up her ankles and shins. In the kitchen, the flames were nearly licking the ceiling but shrank down as soon as she entered, like one of her sons caught in mischief.

She listened for any sound of Marcus putting his key in the lock and opening the door. The circular floor fans hummed as they blasted in every room because she refused to sleep with the doors and windows open.

The fans mostly blew around hot air. The stench from the dumpsters had made its way inside her home. She coughed.

She heated up Marcus's pork chop in the microwave, ate it standing at the stove, chased it with a glass of milk, and wiped down the counter with a worn dishrag. No roaches this time. The house was probably too hot for them.

When she brought the cloth to the spot on the counter closest to the door, her hand bumped against Marcus's sneaker polish and cell phone. Her heart skipped. Her throat tightened.

Wait. The watch was in the bathroom and his phone was on the counter. Was Marcus home? She stared into the darkness of her living room, imagining him sitting there watching her. She flipped on the light, but the room was empty. He hadn't been in his bedroom with Lance. Not in the bathroom, and obviously not in her room. She faced the hall. Would he be inside the closet? Hiding? If so, why? She crept toward those doors, imagining Marcus, possessed by NaDarius, waiting inside ready to . . . What? What would or could Marcus do to her? To Lance? What could NaDarius make him do?

She threw open the closet. It was filled with coats, bags, shoes, and nothing else.

Was Marcus just outside the front door? Maybe getting some fresh air. She opened the irons and the wooden entry. The zinnias were still dead. No Marcus.

She returned to the kitchen counter and stared at the phone. The room seemed to shrink in size.

So Marcus was gone and he'd not taken it? Typically, he carried his phone around like an extra arm, so when she'd seen him put his keys and loose change into his pocket before leaving, she'd assumed he had his cell too.

Marcus leaving behind his phone ratcheted up her worry a couple thousand more notches. How would she get in touch with him? How would he get in touch with her? Not only did she not know where he was, she also couldn't contact him now.

She stared at the screen. The phone case was personalized—a graduation gift from Pastor—and it contained a picture of Kendall, Marcus, and Lance two months before Kendall was killed.

Marcus and Lance had changed so much since then. It wasn't only their more defined jaw lines, thinner cheeks, and larger bodies. Back then, their eyes twinkled and their smiles sparkled. She was looking at their innocence. They didn't yet know what it was to have a sibling get killed, so they could smile and hug with abandon, thinking they still had all the time in the world together.

Nona hated being a snoop again, but she thought maybe, in some Freudian-slip way, Marcus had intended for her to do that.

The device requested a code she didn't have. She tried Kendall's birthday. Lance's birthday. Marcus's birthday. Her birthday. Their father's birthday. And then the device locked her out because she'd made too many login attempts.

Frustrated, she tossed the mobile back onto the counter. The phone buzzed and a preview of a missed text appeared at the top of the black screen. The name of the sender popped up—*Future Roommate*—as well as the timestamp. The text was three hours old, and the message appeared in three-word snippets:

hey, marcus! waiting
on prescott rd
where r u?

"Calm down, Auntie."

In a frantic phone call, Nona brought Harlan up to speed on everything with Marcus, including the watch. She had left out the part about the voice in her home and the stove that seemed to have a mind of its own.

"I can't reach him if he left his phone here."

"But he called me, Auntie."

"What? When?"

"A while ago now. I don't know. I didn't pick up. I was—"

"Did he leave a message?"

"No. No text either."

"He must have come back to the house then. He must have . . ." She stared at Marcus's phone. What if Marcus hadn't come back? What if the phone had called Harlan but Marcus hadn't been the one using it? At this point, she just wanted to know where he was. "And I know for a fact he didn't meet up with the boy he said he would. The one he's going to college with. Because that boy texted him wondering where Marcus was."

"You know the kid's name? The one he was supposed to meet?"

"I don't."

"And you think Marcus having the watch has to do with Peter being missing."

"I don't know." She had to consider the possibility. Was she a bad mother for doing so?

"Maybe he got the watch back in one of their fights, but . . ."

"At this point, I just want to know where he is, and I want him back home."

"Okay. I'll see what I can do."

Thirty-Five

It was well past midnight when Kiandra's boyfriend dropped her off on Prescott Road. Selwin waited with his hazards on as she entered the front lawn of the Hester Gardens housing complex.

She traversed grass and concrete. The first house on her left was where her cousin Gretchen lived. She knocked on Gretchen's door to see if Cedrick had mentioned where he was going after he ate dinner with Gretchen and Grayson, but the lights were off and there was no answer. Her irritation about her cousin's shut-off phone became more pronounced as she continued walking home.

Kiandra glanced back at Selwin, still in his car, and she smiled, which was her way of thanking him for being there for her yet again. The first time she knew she liked Selwin . . . really liked him, Cedrick had gotten caught by a Medford resident when he tried to steal the person's hubcaps. Everyone, her parents included, said it was no big deal, but Kiandra had been furious. Selwin had been the only person to agree with her that the theft was a bad omen. After dating him for six months, she realized he was what she needed. No, he wasn't Kendall, but he was going somewhere in life.

As she slid her key into the front door of her unit, queasiness rose in her middle. She scanned the dead elm tree behind her, the alley and its dented overflowing dumpsters, remembering when she'd seen Kendall there. She checked over her shoulder in the other direction to ensure Selwin was still waiting on Prescott in his car. He was, thank God.

She entered her home and waved, letting him know she was safe. He tapped his horn twice before pulling off. She wished she'd taken him up on his offer to walk her inside, but he lived on a quaint college campus and on weekends at his parents' mansion in Sebastian Hills. She hadn't wanted him to see her raggedy house.

Inside, the home was hot enough to melt the paint off the walls, and the lights were all off even though, a couple of hours before, Donnell had told her they were all on. Cedrick had closed all the windows she'd propped open with twelve-inch sticks of wood when she'd left. The nerve.

Her father had gone against the housing authority's "no irons" rule and installed bars on the doors and windows for hot nights just like this. They could leave the home's front windows open to let in cool air while keeping out the addicts and thieves.

She scratched at her braids and pinned them to the crown of her head. On top of being stuffy, the house was quiet. Odd. Cedrick was a snorer, so he couldn't have been asleep—there was no noise coming from back there.

She switched on the light in the kitchen; a mouse scurried from the windowsill, rushed across the counter, and darted behind the refrigerator, its tail the last thing she saw. A shiver passed through her. She would always fear those rodents. Cedrick had left his dinner plate in the sink with the ketchup still stuck to the center—she wasn't washing it for him either!—and his cup half-filled with pop. As if they didn't have a pest problem. He must have gotten the food from his visit to Gretchen's house, since he never cooked and never seemed interested in learning how.

Her cell phone buzzed in the pocket of her shorts. Selwin texted to check on her, but the vibration had frightened her. Something wasn't right in Cedrick's room. His window rattled whenever it slid open in there, which it did briefly now. His floor usually creaked with every step he took, but it was quiet now. The silence was the issue. No footsteps, but the window opened?

She stood in the hall, held her breath, and listened. She turned on the light, and one of the bulbs blew out, dimming the space, making it surreal, foreign.

She should text Selwin and ask him to return, or she should grab the pistol her father kept in his sock drawer, cleaned and loaded. She did neither because she was frozen. Was Cedrick standing on the other side of his bedroom door? If so, why? Was he listening too? To what?

She reached for the knob and uttered a quick prayer. To whom? Did she even believe in God still? Two muffled thumps sounded from the room. She threw open the bedroom door and flicked on the light. Cedrick was face down in his bed, his head buried between two pillows the way it usually was when she went in to wake him for school. The problem was the blood.

She stumbled back, into the hallway. She lost her balance and fell against the wall, banging her head but barely registering the pain. She reached forward and pulled herself back into his room. Yes, the problem was the blood.

There is too much blood.

She checked his pulse. No beat.

Cedrick used to cuddle with her on the couch in winter and play video games. He always made sure the raggedy blanket covered both of their knees and feet, and he'd jump down from the sofa and readjust it for her if ever it fell or became lopsided. She loved his bony elbows and knees against her thighs and waist as she shouted at the television, "Prepare to get clobbered!" She'd sometimes lose every game they played just so she could stare at the side of his face and watch it light up when he realized the round they were playing would go to him.

Too much blood.

Too much.

No.

No.

That isn't the only problem.

There is too much of Cedrick's blood.

His blood isn't supposed to be there.

Not Cedrick's.

It should be my blood there.

Not his.

Not Cedrick's.

He is too young to give his blood.

He doesn't even have a government ID.

Something told her to check the window. Her parents couldn't afford irons for the back windows, and Cedrick's led to one of the alleys behind the Gardens.

She squinted into the hot darkness outside and across at Donnell's unit. The lights were off, and the back window of Donnell's was open, but no one was in the narrow, concrete-filled space between their homes. The only sounds were crickets and a neighbor's television.

Kiandra fingered the glass of Cedrick's open window. The screen was not connected to the top. The mesh lay loosely in the frame as if removed and hastily propped back into place. Leaning into the darkness before her, Kiandra drew in a violently deep breath, and she screamed.

Thirty-Six

A scream cut through the darkness outside and entered Nona's window. She couldn't tell whether the person was shouting "no" or "go."

Her mind went to Marcus. The night Solomon was killed, she'd also heard screams. And this time Marcus didn't even have his phone.

She opened her front door. She could make out silhouettes in the distance, close to Prescott Road, but police had not arrived.

Another scream, and Nona's stomach pulled into knots.

Back inside, she checked Marcus's phone. Where was he if he wasn't with his future roommate? Was he involved with the screaming outside?

Down the hall, Lance's cell phone vibrated. He stopped snoring. His mattress squeaked. Seconds later, he bounded down the hallway, panic on his face.

Another scream outside.

"Mom." Lance didn't wait for her to speak. "Got a text from Wiggly." He stared at the phone's screen, eyes wide and tear-filled. It bothered her that Lance had any direct communication with Mable Cleveland's nephew. Wiggly was worse than Donnell.

"What's wrong?" She rushed to Lance's side. Another scream outside. Lance handed her his phone, and a surge coursed through her as she took the device. Her boys never gave over their cells.

> **Wiggly:** Somebody shot Donnell, Cedrick, and a bunch of other folks.
> **Lance:** What? Where?
> **Wiggly:** Right here. Point-blank. And we ain't heard nothing.
> **Lance:** They dead?
> **Wiggly:** Can you fucking believe this shit?
> **Lance:** Who?
> **Wiggly:** Don't know yet. Heard they got some other fools on the side near the Rodgers.
> **Lance:** They whole house or just them?
> **Wiggly:** Just them. And we were here at the time. Musta came through Donnell's window. We ain't letting it go, though. We working on a plan. You and Marcus straight?
> **Lance:** We good.

She gave the phone back to Lance. His hand shook when he took it.

Her mind returned to Marcus. The gun. His face when he pushed Peter. His trembling hand, ready to hit her. She was worried about Marcus, but also about what Marcus might do. What NaDarius might make him do.

"I tried to text Marcus to make sure he's all right, but he never—"

"That's because his phone is still here." She was unsteady on her feet. Adrenaline rushed up from her ankles. The ringing in her ears was louder. Her knees weak, she sat at the breakfast table.

The phone vibrated in Lance's hand, and she and Lance looked down to see two more texts from folks she didn't know but who claimed to live in the Gardens. The first speculated that the Dempsey Woods gang carried out the killings, and the second opined that it was Peter.

"I found Kendall's watch in the bathroom," Nona said.

Lance searched her eyes, then cast his gaze at the floor.

"I need you to tell me the truth, Lance."

Lance sat at the table opposite her. Tears appeared in the corners of his eyes. He was seven again, when she was still his safe zone, and he was finally ready to level with her about the trouble he and Marcus had gotten themselves into.

"Oh, man." He nodded and rubbed his head. He leaned forward and covered his eyes, presumably to stave off a flood of emotion.

"Tell me."

"The day of the fight, when we were walking back home from the grocery store . . ."

She could feel her heartbeat quicken.

"Peter confronted us."

She reached across the table and patted his hand.

"Donnell tried to help out, saying, 'Pacman, we ain't got time for this,' but Peter swung on Marcus, and we ended up in a fistfight. I know you don't like for us to fight, and I know I sometimes hang out with these fools, but Marcus is my flesh and blood, and I ain't finna let him go out like that."

She wanted to both hug and slap Lance. Marcus too. And Peter, for that matter. These boys. These ridiculous boys in this messed-up environment.

"So how did it end?"

"Marcus messed Peter up. Had him down on the ground."

Lance's account matched up with Gretchen's, with Marcus winning the fight.

"Lord Jesus."

"I know. I know. But when Peter got up, his face was bloody and he was foaming at the mouth, and instead of punching Marcus, he sucker-punched me in the nose when I wasn't paying attention, and I thought I was going to pass out. I landed on the ground, but the strange thing was, when I looked up at Marcus, it's like he wasn't himself anymore."

She leaned forward. This might be the first time either of her boys admitted they'd seen something supernatural.

"How do you mean?"

"He had the strangest face I'd ever seen. I mean, he was angry, but this was . . ." Lance glanced at the ceiling, searching for words. He met her eyes again.

"Say it."

"I don't know. It's like . . . You know those horror movies me and Marcus watch that you always want us to turn off? The ones where the people transform into werewolves. How they kind of grow? Their teeth get sharper or . . . I can't describe it. Like, for a second, Marcus was something else. Or he was himself still, I guess, but he . . . wasn't . . ."

She knew what Lance meant. The curse had taken hold of Marcus, just like when she'd pulled that knife on Peter. Gretchen had been telling the truth. Marcus had been possessed.

"And he frowned and got this V shape in his forehead."

"Does he have a gun, Lance?" She hated to interrupt, but it was like a window had opened and she had to get as much information as she could before it closed.

"No. I mean, I don't know. He's got some weird video games and music now."

"Weird like how?"

"Killing video games. Where he shoots people in them. And he just . . . That's not the games we used to play. We played race-car games and basketball, football games. And the music lyrics are all about death, killing, and hypocrisy. And lately, he just has an evil side that you don't know about."

"I know more than you think."

"Anyway, when I was down, Marcus let out this . . . I don't know . . . growl. And I didn't know what I was seeing, but it was like he shouted a spirit up from his chest. And the thing kind of stood behind him? Mom, I don't know."

"It's okay. Tell me what happened after that."

"Peter was scared. I mean, we all were scared. Everyone was like, 'Oh, shit!' Sorry. Language. Peter backed away without Donnell having to grab him or anything. And Peter shouted, 'You gon' end up like your brother. With some steel in your dome.' And we took that to mean Peter had actually killed Kendall."

"That was the confession?"

"Confession?"

"When Marcus called 911, he said someone had confessed to killing his brother. Was that the confession?"

"Yeah. That was it."

"That wouldn't hold up in court."

"Well, Marcus shot Peter a look that made Peter cut and run. And, honestly, Marcus was more concerned about my nose than anything else. Next thing I know, Marcus is walking me through the Gardens, pulling out his phone to call the police."

She was trying to process Lance's story as quickly as she could, to match it to the 911 call she'd listened to.

"So that watch that Marcus and Peter were arguing over at the graduation party . . ." She waited for Lance to nod, to show that he knew what she was talking about. For once, he didn't try to hide his knowledge of the watch. "When you two got into the fistfight with Peter, Marcus got the watch back then?"

"No."

"When, then?"

"They didn't really see each other again that I know of. I don't know when Marcus got the watch back."

"You're telling me the truth?"

He raised his hand. "On Kendall's grave."

She struggled to put together the pieces.

"Mom, what if Marcus did this?"

She shifted in her seat. It was one thing for her to worry that Marcus could shoot people, and a completely different thing for her to acknowledge it out loud. Especially to Lance.

She was back at the moment when Marcus came to her and said he thought Peter killed Kendall. Only this time, Lance was asking *What if Marcus killed . . .*

"If anyone is responsible for what's going on outside, it's Peter returning and ambushing everyone, or it's the Dempsey Boys." She couldn't believe she had joined the chorus scapegoating the Dempsey Boys, but she rose, letting him know that she wouldn't even entertain the thought of it being Marcus.

"Look, Mom. I think Peter killed Solomon. He didn't like having anyone around with as much clout as him. He's done a lot of messed-up stuff, but going house to house killing dudes where they lay their heads? This doesn't sound like Peter."

"This doesn't sound like Marcus!" She hadn't meant to shout. She took a deep breath. "Peter has always been a bit off. He disappeared and was probably lying in wait for this moment, when he would return to kill everyone who has ever challenged him."

"Then how did Marcus get the watch?"

"We need to figure out a way to get in touch with Marcus. To warn him to stay away from here until the police lock up Peter. I know Peter is responsible for this." She didn't really know that. She was resolute on the outside, but inside she was panicked. Terrified. Even Lance could see the facts.

Lance checked his phone. She paced the kitchen floor, the room getting tighter around her. She went to her front door, opened it, and stared out. The pale orange streetlights were off this time. Marcus was out there somewhere, and she prayed to God he'd return her boy this time.

Thirty-Seven

When the 911 calls started rolling in, Bernadette was training a young woman with bright blue hair to be on the lines. It was a perfect night for instruction. Wednesday night into Thursday morning was not a popular time for parties or drag races or lots of drinking or socializing. Folks who worked had to get up early the next day, and folks who didn't had few people to hang out with. Although it was hot out, rain was in the forecast, and downpours made everyone a little weird. Folks would be in their homes, asleep, or working an overnight at the plant.

A dispatcher a row behind her said, "Two-Adam Fifty-Four to Hester Gardens. One-eight-seven, but no report of shots fired." Because the dispatcher, a newbie with an obvious wig to whom Bernadette had not bothered to introduce herself, had spoken so loudly, it wasn't clear to Bernadette whether the dispatcher was hard of hearing or nervous. "Two-Adam Fifty-Six to Hester Gardens. Two-David Twelve, hang tight."

During a typical week, Bernadette fielded five or six shooting-related requests for police in Medford, most from Hester Gardens. Bernadette grew up in Hester Gardens, so she had an affinity for its residents, and her stomach dropped whenever dispatch sent units there.

"The lines are going crazy, Mrs. Huntley. I can't keep up." Seated next to Bernadette, Blue Hair stared at the computer screen and held her forehead. A few of the dispatchers stood at their desks, their headset cords dangling in front of them as they leaned forward. Their hands beside their computers, they peered into their screens, shouted to one another, then spoke calmly to the officers on the other end of the line.

"Medford 911. This is Bernie. What is your emergency?"

"Somebody shot my son!" The woman sobbed and panted. "Jesus."

"There's a shooting happening right now?"

"No. I just got home, and somebody shot my son. Oh, God."

"Okay. Don't hang up. What's the address?"

"The Gardens. Fourteen thirty-three Prescott Road, Medford."

"Okay. You're at Hester Gardens."

"Yeah.

"What building are you in? And what is your unit number?"

"Penobscot Building. Unit four."

"We have paramedics and police en route. Is there anyone else with you? Is the shooter present?"

"No. I just live with my son."

"Is he breathing?"

"There's a lot of blood. I don't know."

"Can you feel for a pulse or place a finger under his nose to check for breath? Do you know where on his body he's shot?"

"I— He ain't breathing. Oh, God! My baby!"

"I need you to stay calm for me. I need—"

"Wait a minute." Shrieking in the background. "I hear Mable screaming."

"What's going on?"

"My neighbor. Mable Cleveland. She's screaming."

"How many gunshots have you heard? Are you hearing gunshots now?"

"No. I haven't heard anything."

"Where are you right now?"

"In his bedroom."

"Can you stay inside and lock your front door?"

"It's locked."

"Stay away from your windows as well, ma'am. Can you get low, away from the windows and doors?"

"Oh, my God. Jesus. Jesus. Jesus. You think someone is still shooting? I don't hear anything. Just screaming."

"I just want you to stay low until officers arrive. We have help on the way."

"My boy. My baby. I can't—"

"What is your name, ma'am?"

"Carrie. My name's Carrie. I—I hear Sister Taylor screaming too. I need to go make sure she is okay."

"No, Carrie. Please. Listen to me. Police are on their way, and they are aware of the situation. Please continue to take cover. Try not to make too much noise, OK? Please try to stay calm and remain on the line with me until help arrives."

Ten minutes later, Blue Hair's training had completely stalled because Bernadette had taken seven calls, all from the Gardens and with an odd fact pattern.

"Stay calm, baby girl. Just do what you can." She touched Blue Hair's shoulder, and the girl nodded, but she still seemed seconds from screaming. Bernadette took a swig from her water bottle. The lukewarm liquid did little to wet her dry throat. The adrenaline flowing through her body had gotten rid of the pain in her back, shoulders, and wrists.

"Medford 911. This is Bernie. What is your emergency?"

"Somebody shot my brother!" The young woman let out three sharp screams. "They killed him."

"Your address?"

"I'm at the Gardens."

"Okay. Unit number?"

"Ten."

"Help is on the way. Are you near your brother?"

"Yes. Oh, God. Oh, God. Not my brother. Not Cedrick!"

"Is your front door locked? Windows closed?"

"Huh?"

"Your front door. Is it locked?"

"It's— Yes." The caller sniffled. "It's locked."

"How about your windows. Are they secure?"

"Not Cedrick's window. It's— The window is out of the frame."

"Can you close the window?"

"I can't leave him!"

"Okay. Okay. Is Cedrick breathing still?"

"No. He's not. I checked his pulse. Nothing. I'm performing CPR."

"You're trained in CPR?"

"Yes. I'm— My neighbors are screaming. Is the shooter still out there?"

"Have you heard gunshots?"

"No."

"Okay. Let's focus on Cedrick. The last time you checked, was there any breath coming from his nose or mouth?"

"No."

"Do you know where on his body he's shot?"

"There's so much blood— Oh, God!"

"Stay with me."

"I think they shot him in the back of his head while he was sleeping."

"He's in bed?"

"Yes. There's blood and he's not moving. What is happening? Oh, God! Cedrick!"

"Okay. Just stay low, if you can, please. I mean, continue the CPR until help arrives, but stay away from your windows and doors. And stay on the phone with me. What is your name?"

"Kiandra."

"Okay, Kiandra. I used to live in the Gardens. I know exactly where you are, which means I can tell the police exactly where to find you, okay? I just need for you to stay on the line. Don't leave, okay?"

"Yes, ma'am. I didn't see anybody, ma'am."

"Pardon?"

"Somebody was in my brother's room when I got home. I think they left just as I came in, but I didn't see their face."

"How did they get out?"

"Through the window, ma'am."

The panic continued for several more calls until police arrived and the callers were able to leave their units. On the lines, when Bernadette asked what the emergency was, each caller had a dead teenager inside their home. The photo of her son, taped to the right side of her monitor, seemed to grow in size as Bernadette asked each caller where the boy was located. "In his bed," many callers said.

Even though her Sebastian Hills home was several miles away from the Gardens, she still whipped out her cell phone and texted her husband to make sure her boy was okay.

The callers screamed and some were hysterical, yet most answered her questions as if she had the power to bring back their children. There were no suspects. There had been no fights. In several of the homes, there were no weapons present, so this wasn't some bizarre mass suicide.

"What's going on? Are we in danger?"

"Stay low. Stay calm," she told them all.

She didn't put down her cell phone until her husband responded, Yes. He's fine. Why?

When Bernadette checked the system records, all but one unit were either headed to the Gardens or already there. She switched computer screens. What were the other operators pulling in?

She asked the new, wig-wearing dispatcher, "You all right?"

Sweat-soaked, the woman nodded as she spoke on the line with officers.

"They know what it is?"

The woman's eyes became large as she shook her head no. "Two-Adam Fifty-Four. We have medical arriving at the Prescott entrance to the Gardens," the woman said.

Bernadette sighed when she realized officers and paramedics had actually arrived. The grid showed operators had taken another dozen calls, all from within the two acres of Hester Gardens.

She picked up the landline and called her boss, Herc. Like her nose, her hand was sweating. The receiver almost slipped from her hand.

Unlike Bernadette, her boss was a sworn officer. Captain Herc Wesley had trained her. He let her leave work early whenever her son got sick, and he'd given her extra shifts when her husband had been laid off from his construction job.

"I already know, Bernie."

She'd never heard Herc's voice take on this panic-stricken quality.

"Mass shooter?"

"I don't know. I don't know what the hell it is yet."

She imagined him pounding his fist on the desk beside his mug brimming with cold coffee. She heard his other phone line ring.

"Bernie, I've gotta take this."

Herc hung up, and about an hour later, the calls died down. One even came as a relief. There was no one screaming on the line, no one in the background shouting, "My baby!"

The person's query seemed pretty routine, reminded her of the "suspicious activity" calls that typically amounted to nothing from her suburban dispatch days. A slow-talking, fragile-voiced lady, who said she'd been startled awake, wanted to notify police that the lights were on in the auditorium of Kitledge High School, an odd occurrence after midnight.

Thirty-Eight

"Kiki?"

Lance's stomach jumped to his throat. He never received phone calls from Kiandra.

"No. It's Gretchen. I'm using Kiki's phone."

"Why are you whispering?"

"Listen. You heard about the killings?"

"Yep."

"Have you heard from Marcus?"

"Been trying to reach him."

"I need to tell you something. I'm worried sick about him. And I don't have anybody to tell."

"I'm listening."

"I . . ."

Lance rose from his mattress and paced. He knew Marcus slept with Gretchen. And even though Lance didn't like the way his mother judged Gretchen, he had to admit he had very little respect for Gretchen himself these days. Not because she slept with everybody and had a baby young, which was his mother's issue, but because Gretchen acted like she cared about Peter and then acted like she cared about Marcus. If she cared about either or both of them, she would have done something to stop the two of them from going at it all the time. She would have admitted that Peter had killed Kendall, and if she had a heart, she would have parted ways with Peter for that alone. Gretchen knew what it was to lose a sibling.

"Spit it out, Gretchen."

"Just . . . Can you go out and look for Marcus?"

"What do you know, Gretchen?"

"I heard he was supposed to be meeting a white dude that's going to play basketball with him at Brown. Is that true?"

"Yep."

"Well, I think I saw that guy in a car. I didn't know at the time that he was meeting Marcus, but Marcus ain't with him. The guy left without Marcus, I mean. And I think I saw something . . ."

"What did you see?"

"I saw a figure walking around out front near Prescott."

"Doing what?"

"Can you just look for Marcus? Then call Kiki's phone when you find him?"

"Where the fuck am I looking, Gretchen?"

She started crying. "I don't know, Lance. I just . . ."

Lance crossed to his dresser, grabbed his keys.

"Just try to find him. Please. I know Marcus has a gun."

"So that's true?"

"Yes. And I saw someone who looked like it could have been Peter or could have been Marcus, and I think . . ." Gretchen paused, then said in a strangled voice, "If it's Marcus, I think he's possessed."

Lance had to slip out without his mother noticing. He was able to do it only because she'd called Pastor and gone into her room, whispering as she went.

Lights from the police cars and ambulances strobed around the courtyard. A crowd of shell-shocked neighbors huddled together, whispering to one another, staring into their phones. Usually, his mother made him stay inside after a shooting. This was the first time he'd been outside in the aftermath, and he didn't like the eerie silence that hung over Hester Gardens. The place was never this quiet.

"Hey, Ms. Lawson. You seen Marcus?"

Sipping from the white mug with brown stains streaking down the sides, Vega Lawson put out her cigarette and sidled up to Lance with a wild look in her eyes. She smelled of liquor. He'd never known her to smoke or drink.

"Haven't seen him, but several folks are dead and nobody heard anything. All these gangsters. Every last one of them: Donnell, Rayvon, Cedrick. All of them. Dead. Nary a gunshot to be heard. I been out here all night and I haven't heard a thing. Silencer. Only explanation. Same as . . ."

Ms. Lawson's voice trailed off. She was probably going to say *same as my boy Solomon,* but she got that pained, distant expression his mom did whenever she started talking about Kendall.

Donnell's goofy face popped into Lance's mind. He knew what grief was. Knew that he'd never see Donnell's face in real life again, and the heaviness grew in the pit of his stomach.

"How many dead, Ms. Lawson?"

"At least half a dozen."

"Shit." Lance squinted and scanned the groups of people standing around, crying, leaning on one another's shoulders. He spotted a blue ball resting against the wall beside Donnell's front door. He thought about that ball in the alley and put the thought of Little Lonnie out of his mind. And the thought of the footsteps he'd heard in the hall when he'd been playing video games. As well as the thought of the man in his peripheral vision, always just over his shoulder, always just out of sight. Lance didn't know how it had happened, but he realized he was seriously haunted. He searched the faces of everyone milling about, hoping one of them would be Marcus.

"Tell me this, Lance. You know where Peter is?"

"Of course I don't." Why would Ms. Lawson ask him that? Was the woman thinking of his mother holding the knife to Peter's neck? His mother hadn't told him about it, but everyone knew. "You know I don't."

"Those motherfuckers aren't investigating anything." Ms. Lawson gave the police officers a long glare. "We need to find out where Peter is."

"You think Peter did this?" His "Peter or Marcus" conversations with his mom and Gretchen were both fresh in his mind.

"No. Peter didn't do this, because Peter is dead."

"How you know this?"

Ms. Lawson gave him a cold stare, pivoted, and returned to her porch.

Thirty-Nine

On a normal night, Sgt. Victoria Prager would be on traffic duty with her partner, dealing with DUIs and drag racers, but when dispatch needed someone at Kitledge High, the only unit left was on the opposite side of Medford handling a domestic call, so Sgt. Prager left her partner at the Gardens and went to answer the call at the school.

After hours, teens sometimes snuck into Kitledge to pull the fire alarm. At the school's rear parking lot, light peeked out of the gap from the gymnasium's double doors. They were ajar. This possible B&E was probably nothing, she told herself, but she drew her service weapon anyway.

Approaching slowly, her gun pointed at the ground, Sgt. Prager had the feeling a person might get heading to the basement to investigate a mysterious noise: wet eyes, goosebumps, and clammy hands.

The night had grown strange, from the heat to the moisture in the air portending rain. She hoped when that rainfall finally arrived, it would bring a breeze.

The air changed, and she checked over her shoulder. Her car was the only one in the lot. A streetlight flickered and blew out, plunging her into darkness. With a deep breath, she pushed the door. It moaned open, and the sound tightened her shoulders.

The auditorium was empty, but beyond the basketball court, beyond the folded-in bleachers, and up on the stage near the podium lay a dark lump. She squinted and crossed fifty feet of polished maple court, the sound of her leather shoes squeaking against the wood reminiscent of a basketball game.

A badge didn't block adrenaline, and hers was rushing through her body. Close up, the black lump was a bloody duffle bag and shirt.

Her radio was in her free hand before she could even speculate. She asked for backup and eased to the right of the podium with her weapon now pointed at the lump. That's where he lay, in his shorts, on his back, with a hole in his right temple. If not for the wound, he could have been a teen finishing yoga in resting pose, his toes upward, his hands by his sides with palms facing the ceiling, skin so spotless it seemed it'd never been dirty.

His weapon rested on the floor at the foot of the stage. Was this gun related to the slayings at Hester Gardens?

To her right, in the hallway, a door slammed. The sound made her breath catch in her throat. She rushed to the entrance separating the auditorium from the hall and listened before she pulled it open.

As she held her gun in front of her, her heart pulsed in her throat and goosebumps spread down her arms. She eased into the dark space, letting the light from the auditorium creep in. Her fingers glided along the cold cement wall until they found the light switch. Before she turned it on, the sound of shoes running down the hall made her want to retreat.

She snapped on the light just as a white-shirted young man rushed outside and into the school's south parking lot. She raced down the hallway and blasted through the doors as well, but no one was in the lot. No one was on the street either. There were no cars on the side of the building, so there was no way he was hiding out.

Sirens from approaching units cut through the night. She pivoted toward the building, and on the roof just above the south auditorium doors, a shadowy figure with glowing eyes stared down and reached a hand toward her.

Startled, she jumped back, tripping over her feet and landing square on her ass. When she got her bearings, she raised her pistol, but before she could shout *Freeze,* the dark shape had repositioned itself on the ground in front of her. She fired, piercing a black void where flesh should have been. Her bullet struck the building's brick, and as the silhouette retreated, she gave chase.

Lance didn't find Marcus outside, but the images of Donnell's blood-soaked bedsheets and Cedrick's brain-covered headboard would haunt him forever.

Regardless of what Ms. Lawson said and Gretchen feared, Lance believed his mother now: Peter was going around shooting up fools in the Gardens. Perhaps that was why Peter had gone missing beforehand: so he could ambush everyone. Why hadn't Peter also targeted him? Gretchen said she thought Marcus had a gun. Maybe that was why he'd gotten it: for protection from Peter.

Back in his room, Lance found the metal box peeking out from under Marcus's bed. It'd been missing the last time Lance searched for it. When had it returned? Had Marcus come home at some point while Lance had been outside looking for him?

Lance knelt, hoping all of his questions would be answered by the contents. Had Marcus really been meeting a future teammate? It was possible, but Marcus's head had been all over the place lately: preparing for college but buying a gun, giving a great graduation speech but blasting Peter in the chest with his fist.

He muffled the case with Marcus's pillow as he fit the paper clips into the lock and jiggled the box until it snapped open.

Inside rested Kendall's graduation photo. Lance's oldest brother held his rolled-up diploma, the gold watch peeking out from the fabric of his gown.

Kendall and Marcus appeared so much alike. It was uncanny. Marcus's graduation photo wasn't nearby, but if he put those images side by side, his older brothers would be the spitting image of each other. Would he resemble them when he was eighteen? Would he graduate like them or drop out like the other guys in their neighborhood? Or maybe he'd be dead before then.

He wanted to say *I miss you* to Kendall's picture, but it would have been weird to talk to a photo while sitting on his bedroom floor.

Marcus's black-and-white notebook was also in the box. Inside was a list of names of Hester Boys, including the ones Wiggly had rattled off in his text. Marcus had scrawled *justice* across the top. On the back, it said *Teachers and police are neither supported nor equipped to fix all the problems of bad social policy.*

"What the fuck?" he whispered. Lance flipped through the rest of the pages, searching for something to make it all make sense. No way Marcus had written this. Well, it was Marcus's handwriting—angular, with indentations in the paper—and it seemed to have been scrawled in haste, but why?

Lance remembered the V in Marcus's forehead, and how matter-of-fact Marcus had been when he'd said his writing was for Kendall, as if Kendall were still alive.

Lance tore out the list and ripped it up. He placed the picture of Kendall on Marcus's desk, where it should have been. He set the metal box next to it, open, with the paper clips still in the lock.

Lance took the scraps of paper to the bathroom and flushed them down the toilet.

Lance had never told anybody that when Kendall died, Marcus had started talking in his sleep. In the beginning, he'd mostly whisper, "Where are you, Kendall?" or "Why did you leave, Kendall?" but the closer Marcus got to his own graduation, the darker the nighttime chatter had gotten. One night, Lance had been startled awake when Marcus whispered, "They will pay."

Could Lance really still believe Peter had committed these slayings? Like a boulder resting on his chest, doubt forced him to have a seat, to stare out the window. That doubt even forced him to pray.

Forty

Nona's bedroom brought her no comfort. She couldn't sleep. The ringing in her ears stopped, but the silence was worse. She opened her closet, pulled down the bag with Kendall's shirt, opened a tiny corner, stuck her nose in, and inhaled.

The day had come when she could no longer smell her son's sandalwood mixed with cocoa butter. Now she smelled incense from Mable's conjuring between the fabric's threads. Tears stung her eyes. On days like this, when she was losing her grip on reality, when she might die of a broken heart, she really needed Kendall nearby.

In the hierarchy of grief, nothing touched the pain a mother carried. A wife could divorce. In the natural cycle of life, a child was supposed to bury their parents. A sibling never carried their contemporary inside their body, growing them for nine months and bringing them into the world. She'd once read that for the first few months, a baby believed it was still attached to its mother, that it was a part of her body. For the mother, that feeling continued for the remainder of her life. So her pain was not just a broken heart. She had lost her whole heart. Her entire everything.

That last week of his life, Kendall had been humming a song, one she didn't know. When she'd buried him and was able to form words again, she'd hummed the melody for Lance one night. Asked him what the tune was.

"Song by a white girl," Lance had said.

"Who?" Nona had asked.

"Avril Lavigne," Lance had answered, seeming confused about why she was asking.

When Nona had finally gotten to the business center at the church to look up Avril Lavigne, she discovered the track was called "Here's to Never Growing Up."

Had Kendall known? Not outwardly, but did everyone have some deeply ingrained sense when their clock had about run out?

She sealed the bag again and placed it on the pillow next to her head.

In the hallway, the bathroom door squeaked open. It wasn't Lance. Wasn't Marcus either. Across the hall, a shadow rose in the light-filled bathroom. The figure was watching her. It wanted to destroy her, Marcus, Lance, and what was left of their home. NaDarius. Only eighteen. Somebody's baby. An entire future ahead of him. He had every right to be angry. She and Vance had taken his future away. Nona deserved this haunting.

And she wasn't the only one who did. There were too many ghosts in Hester Gardens. What of all the young boys and girls, all the people in their twenties and thirties killed each year? How different her community would be if they were all allowed to live and be free.

And what of all the folks in prison too, like Vance? He was a ghost as well. His absence sat in his old chair, was the spot in the refrigerator where his beer used to rest, was the fingers snapping to a Jill Scott tune on the radio. There were too many ghosts in Nona's house, and she was starting to feel like one too.

She spread out her hair and let her tresses cascade down her face, her pillow, the crinkly bag that used to contain her son's scent.

She should have waited as Marcus left earlier that evening, waited until he entered the shadows on his walk to Prescott.

Marcus should have waited too. For the headlights and for the car door to open and take him away.

She closed her eyes and kissed the plastic. Red lights strobed through her windows. Raindrops pelted the glass, slowly at first and then rapidly, like frightened fingers tapping, desperate to be let in and kept safe.

Part Five

Forty-One

At eight a.m., before Nona walked onto the factory floor to begin her shift, she broke down and reported Marcus missing.

On the call, the officer's voice dropped. "You say the last name's McKinley?" he asked, as if already aware Marcus was in trouble. Something was wrong.

Pastor had called and texted her nonstop that morning, but she hadn't answered. *Nona, please call me. Are the boys okay? I'm worried sick about you all.* She couldn't hear Pastor's voice. She couldn't hear anyone's voice except Marcus's.

After phoning the police, she inspected the bottles on the machine in a daze. She thought back to his first day of school, when he was tiny, when he'd held onto her and asked, "How long I gotta be 'way from you?"

At ten a.m., Nona got the visit. She removed her wrist braces and motioned to Lena, who, along with all the other employees in the middle of boxing bottles, placing the cartons on dollies, and pushing the stacks to the loading docks, slowed her work and stared open-mouthed at the approaching officers.

Nona pulled up the stool she'd been given for rest, though the packages of iced-tea bottles came down her line so quickly she never had a chance to use it. She sat down hard on the elevated cloth chair, tipping the seat to the right on its uneven wheels. Her wrists throbbed. Her neck muscles tightened. This was going to be bad news.

Sgt. Prager stepped toward Nona with bloodshot eyes. "We found your boy." The woman's metallic badge caught the overhead fluorescent lights.

"Where?" It had been two years since Pastor had held her hand in front of Kendall's casket and told her the streets were cursed, that the devil himself walked the Gardens like in the Revelation, and the beast did all he could to "steal, kill, and destroy." There was no way God would see fit for her to lose two sons.

Her co-workers, whom she'd not told of her fears that morning, seemed to be bracing themselves for her news as well. They cut furtive glances at one another and voyeuristic ones at Nona. They wanted to watch her, to witness her life falling apart from a safe distance, since today they didn't have to worry about their children.

Sgt. Prager placed her hand gently on Nona's shoulder and moved Nona out of earshot of everyone else. As Nona stood from the stool, Ashford stepped out of his office and eyed her from the balcony above. He didn't seem angry, but he looked worried. Did he already know? He would have been the one to tell the receptionist where to find her.

Nona's feet were on the ground, but they could as easily have been on the ceiling. She floated. Everything was upside down. *Please, God, let Marcus be okay. I can't go through this again, Lord.*

"We found Marcus at Kitledge." Sgt. Prager squeezed Nona's shoulder like she had at the morgue when Nona identified Kendall. The affection from the officer acknowledged the women's shared history. "Marcus died from a self-inflicted gunshot wound."

Nona didn't fully understand Sgt. Prager's words. Marcus couldn't be dead. He was going to Brown in two weeks. He was going to walk across the manicured lawn in Rhode Island, surrounded by trees and books. So he wasn't dead. He'd been accepted. He'd enrolled. He'd been cleared to register for his classes. He'd met with his basketball teammate at some point during the previous night, and they were going to be roommates.

"You must be mistaken."

"He had his identification on him." Sgt. Prager's voice quivered.

"This must be a mistake." Nona searched Ashford's face as he made his way to the bottom of those steps, his hands clasped in front of his waist like a priest awaiting mass. She wanted her foreman to fix this misunderstanding like he fixed the jammed machines.

"Tell them, Ashford. They're confused. They must be talking about Kendall. My oldest. You remember, Sergeant Prager? He was killed two years ago. Somebody shot him. So you must be thinking of him. I've been dealing with that all this time since then. Marcus too. Marcus has been dealing with it too. So you must be talking about Kendall. We've already . . ."

With a pained expression, Ashford shook his head. The entire factory was on rollers now; the room wasn't exactly spinning, but everything was mobile: the walls, the machines, the floor, the ceiling, the foreman, and the co-workers. Lena had stopped the machine; the belt screamed as it came to a halt, and Ashford didn't seem to mind.

Nona returned to her stool, sat, and turned the machine back on. As it clunked and roared back to life, bottles came down the line. Nona lifted one, inspected it, and placed it back on the belt. In tears, Lena walked over, gently took Nona's wrist, and placed it in Nona's lap.

"We can do this," Lena said. And the other co-workers nodded.

"I got it!" Nona yelled. "Damn! You don't even know how to inspect these!"

Her co-workers stepped back with their hands folded at their waists too, like Ashford. Their heads were low, probably because she'd never yelled in front of them. Nor cursed.

She lifted another bottle of iced tea.

"Ma'am. I know this is hard." Sgt. Prager was whispering still.

"Oh, no. It's not hard. You're just confused."

"Ma'am, we're here to . . ."

Nona was up again. She reached for another bottle. Had Sgt. Prager said "self-inflicted"? They weren't talking about Kendall. Kendall had been shot by somebody else. She let the bottle slip from her hand and land on the ground, where it shattered at her feet. Cool liquid sprayed her pants and shoes, and she turned to Sgt. Prager.

"Did you say self-inflicted?"

Sgt. Prager nodded.

"You mean like . . . he killed himself?"

Again, Sgt. Prager nodded, and she seemed to struggle to not avert her eyes.

Not homicide? Nona had faced homicide. Homicide was familiar, maybe even inevitable, but Sgt. Prager hadn't said "homicide." She'd said "self-inflicted." Which meant suicide. Suicide was foreign and in no way a decision Marcus would make. Would he put her through this knowing what she'd already endured? Of course he wouldn't.

Unless.

The word "rifle" underlined thirty-four times.

The gun.

Unless.

The violent song lyrics.

The hand trembling at his side, ready to strike.

Unless.

He'd packed up all his clothes and given them to his brother.

The voice—*It's me.*

The curse, the stench, the shadow lurking in the hallways. The thing in Medford Lake.

"Marcus wouldn't do that."

Two suit-wearing men stood at the glass-enclosed entrance to the assembly floor. Detectives. Detectives wouldn't be here only for a suicide.

Marcus's face had pulled into itself with disappointment, shame, and sadness when their father was arrested in the middle of their living room. She'd argued with their dad on the phone because she would not allow her boys to visit him in prison, and when she hung up, Marcus had held her for several minutes. She hadn't known whether she was comforting him or he, her. She'd been so torn about the decision, but she didn't want them to ever know the inside of a prison. Their home was prison enough.

"Mrs. McKinley?" Sgt. Prager had been speaking.

"Yes?" The thing she'd feared came into Nona's head so assuredly it seemed God had spoken the words: *It was Marcus who killed the others.*

Sgt. Prager glanced over her shoulder at the suited men, then back at Nona. "The detectives believe—"

"Don't." Nona didn't need the officer to say it. Didn't want her to say it. She had the evidence already. The bizarre ending to his graduation speech. The angry bedsheet he'd hung in the middle of his room to wall off his brother. His scuffle with Peter at his graduation party. The fistfight. The gun. The detectives believe . . . Nona believed too. Only it hadn't been Marcus. It had been her curse. It had been NaDarius.

No "proper" way to respond to tragedy existed. The common way was to scream, to rip at the hairs at the front of the head, to yell *How? Why?*

When she'd learned Kendall had been killed, she'd responded in the common way. Back then, when she'd arrived home from identifying Kendall's body, she pounded her fists on Marcus's chest and screamed until he placed her on the couch.

Marcus had sat awake, holding her hand as she sobbed until morning. Him needing to comfort her was probably another bad parenting thing she'd done. She should have been comforting Marcus, not the other way around.

"I need to get Lance." That's all she could manage this time. No wailing. Not yet. Not now. She needed to get her one remaining son—her only reason to not take a knife to her arteries—before NaDarius got him too. "He's at summer school. I need a ride."

She put her earrings on again and removed her house keys from her pants pocket. Lena and her other co-workers stepped aside, pushed the chair out of Nona's way, and made sure the path was clear as she departed. The worker at the end powered down the machine again, stopping the bottles from rolling down to her section.

Another co-worker grabbed Nona's handbag for her from the cubby under the loading machine. Nona took the bag and nodded, and her arms seemed to be filled with so many things.

Her foreman was inches from her now. Why didn't he ask her to come to the lobby to meet with the officers instead of allowing them to come in and make a spectacle of her? Here she was on display for everyone: the woman with one son killed and another who was a killer, a killer who had also killed himself.

"I need to get Lance. He's at summer school. At school. Yes. I need to get him. Give me a ride? I need to get him. I need to get him right now."

"Ma'am, I can have a unit pick him up," Sgt. Prager said.

"No!" She hadn't meant to scream the word until she became hoarse nor drop the keys, which clattered against the floor, but she didn't want Lance around anyone with a gun. No gang members. No random police unit. "I'll get him. I need to get him. Just me. You take me, Victoria."

Ashford touched her shoulder and said, "Take all the time you need, Nona. Don't worry about a thing."

Lena nodded, as did the others. Did everyone already know? Why was she the last to find out? She was Marcus's mother. Why were mothers always the last to know?

Sgt. Prager drove her from the plant through Medford, past the Gardens, and to Lance's middle school. It was two blocks over from Kitledge High, where months ago, she'd listened to Marcus's valedictory speech. In a matter of months, she'd gone from the height of his graduation day to such an unbelievable low. She'd never predicted it. She never could have.

Something brushed against the side of her neck right where it met her shoulder, and she thought it was a finger from the cursed hand poking at her, but it was, in fact, her hair, which had flopped out of its bobby pins and hair ties. Her bun had spilled down her shoulders and back. She was undone. Every part of her.

The car ride seemed to take a full day, though it was less than thirty minutes. As they drove by Hester Gardens, she sat silent and motionless because even blinking hurt. The Gardens' front doors were propped open with grief, the bereaved moving sluggishly like dying fish in a bowl, and as the projects disappeared out her window, she wished those buildings would vanish forever.

Forty-Two

No one ever called Lance to the main office for anything, especially at summer school. Not for anything good he'd done nor for anything bad. He was always below the radar, answering questions when called on but never raising his hand. Doing just enough on the assignments so the teachers didn't phone his mother but also not doing well enough to be lumped in with the brainiacs and folks who thought they were hot shit.

So, when the administrative assistant entered his classroom and whispered to the teacher that he was needed in the main office and should bring all his things, it served as a sign that Marcus was gone. There would be no other explanation.

This was just life. This was just what should be expected. His time would come one day too, likely soon. Would his mother even cry for him when he was gone?

She stood near the receptionist's desk, her face dry until she saw him, when she broke down sobbing and shouting, "Lance, baby!" She ran over and wrapped her arms around him. Hugs from her were rare and never actually about him.

Her hair was loose and hung down her back. Some strands were stuck to her tear-soaked cheeks. He wasn't used to seeing his mother's hair uncombed and untied like this. He had the urge to back away, but he didn't like to see his mother cry either.

No, he wasn't her favorite, and even though that resentment ran deep, he still struggled when his mother came apart like this. Her scrunched-together eyes, mouth pulled into a wail, and shuddering shoulders as she sputtered to catch her breath. She seemed younger than he was.

He'd seen her weep like this when the pigs hauled off his father. When Kendall died, she'd wailed like this for months straight and he and Marcus had to keep the house running because his mom just woke up and sobbed every day. And now, her grief seemed to start in her feet and tremble up her entire body.

He held her. "What happened, Mom?" He asked as if she were the child and he was the parent trying to calm her with a *there, there, now.*

She pulled away, covered her mouth and nose with her hands, then looked around wildly to discover all the women who worked in the office had risen from their chairs and were staring at her. "Not here," she whispered.

She pulled his hand and took him outside to the front steps of the middle school, usually a crowded spot during the academic year, but since it was summer, they were the only people around. "I have to tell you something about Marcus." She was hyperventilating now. "You're going to hear it from so many people."

She gripped the banister, moaning and grabbing her chest. "Oh, God."

"Mom. Just say it."

"I can't. I'm trying."

He rubbed her back. A police car was parked in the lot with that same lady officer who'd picked him up and brought him home. The woman stood, wide-legged, arms folded, staring at them. What exactly had Marcus done? Was his mother about to tell him about Schoolboy Marcus, who, like Kendall, was a victim of something? Or was she about to tell him about Evil Marcus, who maybe had been the one to do the hurting to someone else this time? Because why else would the cop be there?

"Did Marcus kill them?"

His mother abruptly stopped crying and pushed his hand off her back. "What?"

He motioned his head toward the cop without looking over there. He didn't want the officer to know they were talking about her. "She's here, so I figure . . ."

Already, he was envisioning the coming storm in his life. He wouldn't allow his mother to keep him from Marcus in prison the way she'd kept him from his father. He couldn't imagine Schoolboy Marcus behind bars. He didn't like the thought at all, but wherever Marcus went, Lance would be there telling him he still loved him. That he still had his back.

"Oh, Lance." His mother was sobbing again, and she pulled him into her and whispered in his ear between huffs of jagged breath, "Marcus killed them all. Then he . . ."

Lance made eye contact with the officer then. "Then he what?" Lance was glad he'd gotten rid of the list. He would need to get rid of the game and the music too. He wanted to go through the rest of Marcus's writings, in his notebooks and folders and binders and the sheets of papers he kept tucked between the pages of his books, and he wanted to get rid of anything Marcus wouldn't want them to know. What proof did they have, he wondered? Were officers back at his home now, going through his and Marcus's stuff? Had his mother agreed to a search? Had they shown her a warrant?

"Then Marcus killed himself."

The world grew dim. Lance's breaths were shallow. Tears stung his eyes, and a lump developed in his throat. "What?" She was crying so hard that he must have heard her wrong. "Killed himself?"

She wailed, but her voice sounded a hundred yards away. He couldn't breathe, and a pain tore through his stomach. He could see Marcus killing Peter. He could even wrap his brain around Marcus offing the HBs, as wild as that was, but never in his most stretched-out thoughts did Lance think Marcus would kill himself. Would leave his mother. Would leave him. So he would never talk to Marcus again? Marcus would never steal his eggs? Give him books to read? Argue with him? Chastise him? He'd already lost Kendall. Solomon, Donnell, Cedrick. The list continued. His father was in another part of the state, and now Marcus? He was supposed to live without Marcus too? How was he supposed to do that? He didn't know if he *could* do that.

"Let's go home, Mom." He led her down the steps, numbness growing on his scalp and creeping down his body. It was too much to feel, so he would just stop doing that.

"Did you hear what I said, baby?"

He nodded and kept his hand on her back and brought her down to the bottom, where the officer walked over to him.

"I'm so sorry, Lance," the officer said.

Lance eyed her but didn't speak. The officer opened the back door to the car and motioned for them to get in. Lance said, "We'll walk."

And when his mother gazed at him, tears still spilling down her cheeks, her face incredulous, he just tugged her hand to lead her to the bus stop. "Did you really understand what I just said, Lance? What I said about Marcus?"

He nodded again. Pulled her to him. He felt himself growing older and stronger the closer they got to the covered station. When they'd boarded and he'd placed his sobbing mother in the seat next to him, he peered out the window at the cop, who held her car door open as she stared at them, likely planning to watch them until the bus was out of sight.

Lance blinked, and standing beside the cop was Kendall in his white shirt and shorts. Lance blinked again, and standing next to Kendall was Marcus, and Lance realized his brothers had died in almost the same clothes.

The bus turned the corner, and Lance could no longer see the parking lot, but he couldn't shake the image of his two brothers standing together, watching him.

As soon as she answered the door, Pastor rushed in, wild, panicked, his eyes red, the gray of a beard and mustache growing on his face. She fell into his arms and sobbed for hours as he held her and stroked her hair.

"You said he would be fine," she whimpered against his chest. "You said God wouldn't take another of my boys."

Pastor cried with her. "Let me get you out of here," he repeated in whispers between her sobs. "I need to get you and Lance out of here, Nona."

Forty-Three

Weeks passed, and Lance spent all that time drunk or high. Whiskey. Weed. Some prescription pills Wiggly gave him. He didn't sleep or eat. Just numbed everything and avoided his mother.

The envelope fell off the kitchen counter when he walked by as if intended for him. It was from Brown University. He tore it open, imagining Marcus still at home packing to move away. Marcus's departure date for Brown was three days away, and yet it was his burial day. Lance couldn't wrap his brain around that.

The university's housing department wanted to notify Marcus of his room assignment. He could pick up his keys at his residence hall's front desk. He only needed to present a photo ID.

Lance folded the letter, returned it to the envelope, and placed it in the pocket of his funeral suit, an outfit he'd found at the back of his closet. It had probably been Kendall's and then handed down to Marcus and now him. He was wearing the suit of his two dead brothers. Why was he still alive? Maybe he should be dead too.

A part of him was waiting for this all to be a misunderstanding and for Marcus to show up at the doorstep and say, *Mom. Lance. Don't worry. You know I'd never do anything to hurt you. Now I need to know how to get my dorm key.*

At the hall closet near the front door, Lance stepped into Marcus's dress shoes. From the corner of his eye, a shadow floated into view. He jerked his head in the direction of the shape, but it had moved farther right. He pivoted and followed it, the thing always just out of view, until he had made a full turn and was back in his original spot. He stared straight ahead into the closet filled with coats on hangers and duffel bags mixed with sneakers on the floor, but he focused on his peripheral vision, where the figure closed in on him.

Heat washed over him as he closed his eyes. Was it Kendall? Marcus? Neither of them? Had it been the footsteps in the hall that day when he played video games? Had it been the thing Gretchen spoke of when she said Marcus was possessed? The thing couldn't have him, he decided as he opened his eyes. He would fight it. With whatever anger and sadness and love he had inside of him, he would keep it from entering him and making him do things. He scanned the room again, but this time the shadow man was gone.

The shoes were wide but snug at the toe. Lance flexed his feet as much as he could. If Marcus were alive and packing for Brown, he would have been thinking about that housing letter. An exact copy of it was probably sitting in Marcus's email inbox. Marcus would have seen the assignment, ordered the small refrigerator he'd picked out online, and maybe purchased used coursebooks.

And the dude police said had waited on Prescott to meet up with Marcus. Where was he now? For him, this entire episode would be something strange he could tell his family as his parents drove him to the airport and gave him kisses goodbye with promises to get together for Thanksgiving.

Dude would arrive at school and attend his first team meeting with all the other basketball players and say, *Yeah. I was the one waiting for him out there the night he went berserk. You should have seen the place where he lived. A real dump. It even smelled like garbage. So glad he didn't come here, because what if he had shot us all up?*

It's sad about the boys he did kill, someone would say. And his future roommate would argue, *Not really. They were all in a gang.*

His mom trudged into the kitchen and stopped like she'd forgotten why she'd entered. He swayed as he watched her. He tried to stand straight.

She searched the counter. What was she looking for?

"Did you wish it was me instead?" His voice sounded especially loud in his ears. Was he yelling? He hadn't meant to speak loudly.

"What?" Her cheeks flushed red.

"Am I enough?"

"What are you talking—?"

"Been wanting to ask you that since Kendall was killed, but I knew you'd say you love me, I'm your baby, you love all your boys the same—and you and I both know that's a lie."

Her mouth fell open, and he waited for her to cry. For her to actually feel bad. She didn't. She just continued to stare at him.

"That's what I thought." He removed the envelope from his pocket, handed it to her, and left, letting the door bang against the frame. A mother who actually loved her son would go after him, but she didn't.

He glanced over his shoulder and saw her through the screen door as she tore open the envelope. She read the words, and slowly her face crumpled into a sob.

Forty-Four

Nona closed her front door, located her purse in the hall closet, and put the envelope inside. Lance didn't understand her. No one understood the pain of being a mother. Motherhood had been mostly suffering for her.

A knock at the door. She wouldn't answer.

Knock. Knock. Knock. Knock.

"Mrs. McKinley?" A white woman's voice. "We want to talk, ma'am."

Knock. Knock. Knock. Knock.

"Did you see it coming? Did you know your son was in the gang?"

She almost answered that time. She compressed her hands under her armpits, holding them there. She bit her lip. She wanted to throw open the door, shout, *Heifer, my son was headed to an Ivy League school. Get your ass away from my door.*

It wasn't like Hester Gardens hadn't always been infamous, but now it was horrific. Bloggers came to report on the "bizarre" slayings, which "wiped out half of the Hester Boys, who sold drugs and terrorized the residents of H.G." Every report referred to the crime as "gang-related."

The *Sebastian Hills Chronicle* sent a reporter who took pictures of the bullet holes in the doors and interviewed the police officers but never spoke to residents. He'd theorized that Marcus had had help from one or more other young men, because how could he have killed so many on his own?

Harlan had said, "Never answer the door. They'll use your sound bite as evidence their gang-related theory is correct."

Harlan had spoken plainly with Nona about what these killings were: a mass shooting, no different than the ones he'd been covering, but because the victims and killer were Black, the deep analysis the media typically brought to killing sprees at malls, movie theaters, and suburban schools would not come to bear on this crime.

As soon as she'd gotten home after learning of Marcus's death, she'd phoned Harlan, told him about the curse. He told her spirits weren't real. That everything that had happened had a rational explanation. He'd been acting strange since he'd been the one to identify Marcus's body. Nona had done it once with Kendall but couldn't bear to do it with Marcus.

She listened for Harlan's secret knock. It was specific to the two of them and was how she'd know to answer the door for him.

Knock. Knock. Knock. Knock.

Harlan still wasn't there.

Her phone rang. She didn't answer. Might be reporters or folks from her job. Or Pastor. She couldn't talk to him right now. She mostly wanted to be left alone.

Knock. Knock. Kn-knock. Knock. Boom. Boom.

Harlan.

She stood to the left of the door and opened it without allowing any part of her body to be in view of the cameras as she let him in.

He stormed in with the early-morning air. Smelling of un-showered funk, he didn't make eye contact, and when he did, the whites were bloodshot.

"You know. I can't sleep. I've been thinking about Marcus. What he did. And how I missed the signs, Auntie. How he— I should have seen the signs. Should have known them from my research."

"Harlan. You are shaking." She got him a glass of water. He was worse now than he'd been at Kendall's funeral.

"Hear me out." He took the glass of water from her and set it on her counter. "That essay. The one you told me he'd written about the shootings and gun violence. He'd made the connection. They are all the same. The shooters. No matter their background, ethnicity, class, or location, they are all exposed to the same things: They are victimized, they have access to guns, they consume a diet of violent media, they have dealt with trauma, they don't have mental health resources, they—"

"Stop, Harlan."

"My research doesn't lie. Eighty percent of youth homicides involve guns. Young, inner-city, Black and brown shooters, gang-affiliated or not. Young, white, suburban school shooters or mass shooters of color. They often come from dysfunctional homes, they become fascinated with violence and guns, they have access to weapons, and in every single case, they were victimized or suffered some recent trauma before turning to violence."

"Don't do this to yourself."

"And we were the first wave. Our deaths were ignored all those years. Shootings are acceptable as long as they happen in the bad neighborhoods to bad people or to innocent people who live next to the bad people, but it's not acceptable. And since they ignored our shootings and deaths, now the shootings and deaths are coming for everyone. White, Black, and other people of color. Urban, suburban, and rural. Poor and rich. At the malls, the movie theaters, the schools, and the nightclubs. I know all of this, and I still missed it. I was covering the fucking stories. The same fucking stories as Marcus's story, and I missed what you were telling me. I missed what Marcus was telling us."

"It wasn't Marcus. I mean, it was Marcus, but it wasn't Marcus. This place is haunted. Cursed. This place has a power, a force that uses our young men to destroy the community."

"Cursed?"

"Yes. Don't give me that look. I've seen it with my own eyes. I've felt it. I've been possessed by it myself. I—"

"You can't be serious." Harlan's eyes rolled up to the ceiling. Tears spilled down his cheeks. He looked at her again.

"The dead are here," Nona said. "They are not at peace. You can't take on this guilt over Marcus."

"But why Kendall? Why Marcus?"

"That's my fault. That's your uncle's fault. And we can't fix that right now. For now, we need to go out this door, get in that car, and make it through today."

She opened her door to find someone had replanted her zinnias. An index card sat atop the dirt, and it read, "Much Love. DBs." She stooped and placed the card in her purse, considering how the Dempsey Boys had remained true to who she'd known them to be—rough, but with heart and love for their community.

Pastor had sent a fleet of limousines to Prescott Road. As she and Harlan rushed across the courtyard, Harlan told her the first vehicle was for her and Lance.

She brushed by reporters shouting questions at her: "Mrs. McKinley, what do you say to the mothers of the boys your son killed?"

When she was alone in the vehicle, she sat stiffly because she'd never been in a limousine before and didn't want to ruin anything. Even the leather seats seemed delicate. She wished Lance were sitting beside her.

"Can you avoid Willowbrook Road?" The massive car swallowed up her voice.

"No problem." The chauffeur's eyes were kind. "It will take us longer if we don't go that way."

"That's fine. I just can't see that street today."

Many of Medford C.O.G.I.C.'s congregants were buried half a mile away from church at Proctor Cemetery. The burial ground bore the name of Medford's most popular mayor, and the folks at rest there had been of money or had access to city hall.

A husky-voiced woman sang "Precious Lord, Take My Hand," and Nona winced from her grief over losing Marcus and the painful memories of Kendall's funeral brought up by the song.

Deep green lawns sloped up and down around them, and someone had decorated the awning and chairs with purple lilacs—Marcus's favorite color. Harlan and Pastor must have been footing the bill for everything. Pastor must have done the planning.

Harlan didn't look good. His hands trembled, and he repeatedly muttered, "I can't believe this." "I can't believe he did this." "I can't believe he . . ." "I can't believe I lost another . . ." His on-again, off-again girlfriend had joined him. She rubbed his shoulder, took deep breaths with him, and seemed to be the only thing holding him together.

Nona hugged her nephew. His sobs drew stares and eventually pats on his shoulder. He was overcome and making dry-eyed people into choked-up people.

Pastor's eulogy focused on First Corinthians: "Oh, death, where is thy sting?" Afterward, he shook hands and gave hugs liberally but was unusually reserved in his speech.

For once, Pastor didn't seem to have much to say. He kept stroking Nona's hair, and he repeated "We'll get through this" enough to annoy her. His inability to say Marcus's name or mention any of the good things about him seemed to be Pastor judging Marcus for what he'd done. It was a marked difference from how he'd spoken after Kendall's death.

When the burial ceremony ended and several attendees headed to their cars to leave, she willed herself to rise from her seat in front of the coffin, but she couldn't move. Not only was she too tired, but the few people there were bending to kiss her. Her co-worker Lena planted a kiss on Nona's forehead. "You've always been there for me," Lena whispered. "And I'm going to continue to be here for you." Nona squeezed the woman's bony hands, encouraged that her co-worker, her friend, no longer smelled of cigarettes.

Vega and Esmé stood the entire time, though there were enough chairs for them to sit. Esmé had obviously done Vega's hair in a French twist to match her own. Vega made her way to Nona, patted Nona's shoulder, and said, "Don't beat yourself up. Nobody saw this coming. Not even me."

Nona loved Vega. With everyone's attempts at words of comfort, Vega was the only one who said the exact thing Nona had been turning over in her mind: whether once she'd pieced everything together, she could have stopped him.

Vega shifted to her other foot, motioned for Esmé to give them a moment alone, and sat, finally, in Lance's empty chair next to Nona.

Where was Lance? She wanted him to stay within sight. She scanned the area until she noticed him talking to Gretchen, the young woman patting his back as he cried.

The wind blew, and Nona welcomed the breeze.

"Never got around to telling you"—Vega leaned in and lowered her voice— "the real reason I was cursed."

The woman smelled of coffee even though she wasn't holding her stained coffee mug. "I got rid of Solomon and Esmé's father because he was a lot like Vance, and I wasn't going to put up with it."

"Got rid of him?" It was a relief to not be talking about her own troubles. Maybe that was Vega's point in sharing: to distract Nona from the pain.

"That's what I said. I used to hold things for him, including his pistols. Would polish them, keep them loaded and organized. I'd even wipe that holster with a leather cleaner, get it nice and shiny for him. But I needed him gone. I didn't mess around with the poison and didn't associate with anyone who did. When I caught him slanging, I confronted him, and he put his hands on me. That was the last time he put his hands on anybody."

Nona thought of the moment she confronted Vance. She wished with every ounce of her being she had left him that day.

"So he called me all frantic one night, saying he had to take care of some business and he needed his heat. I rounded up all the polished and pretty things I kept for him, and he came in angry as the devil, cussing and fussing, and was in such a rush when he dashed back out, he never even inspected the things. And I know those guns were a lot less heavy when they were empty, but he was in too much of a rage to notice. He was shot to death that evening with a gun in his hand, chamber empty, not one bullet left in his weapon because there were none there."

"Oh my God, Vega."

"Now you know."

"So he . . ." Nona looked around to check that no one was within earshot. She lowered her voice. "He came back to take your kids?"

"He took Solomon away from me because he knew Solomon was my favorite."

"I'm sorry, Veg—"

"You didn't do it. Don't be sorry. You find out why you're cursed?"

Nona shrugged. "How did you stop your curse, Vega?"

"Who said I stopped it?"

"Esmé is still alive."

"That's because I've trained her to survive, but I don't know how much longer that will work. The devil will come for you if you don't hunt him down first."

"How do I hunt him down? You saw what he did to me in the lake."

"What if your curse doesn't want revenge, Nona? What if he wants peace?"

"Peace?"

"Where is his home? Where is he buried?"

"I don't know."

"Well, maybe it's time you do." Vega rose, closed the gap between her and Esmé, and glanced back at Nona with a warm smile.

The crowd shifted as more people left and others lined up to offer Nona their condolences. Kiandra approached. When Nona asked Kiandra how Mother was doing, Kiandra whispered, "She was still worried about Peter maybe moving out because she was too strict, but then I finally broke down and told her that Peter was a gang member and everyone thought he'd killed Kendall."

"I can't even imagine her hearing those words."

"It was pretty bad."

"She must have been devastated."

"She had a stroke two days ago, and now I wish I'd never said anything."

Nona had thought she couldn't feel any more despair, but this news made her feel worse.

"I think she's going to be fine," Kiandra tried to reassure her. "It was a mild stroke."

Nona could only muster a nod. There was nothing but loss between her and Kiandra, really. It was like the grief had come in and filled up all the spaces where the love used to be.

"How are you holding up?" Kiandra's eyes filled with tears. She and her parents hadn't held a funeral for Cedrick, and maybe Marcus's service was her closure. "This is . . . too much for one person." Nona nodded. She had something she wanted to say, but Kiandra continued. "I guess with your faith."

"My faith?" Nona chuckled. "I see now my faith hasn't done anything for me but keep me stuck. Anyway, I'm surprised to see you here. Surprised but grateful."

"I came to honor Kendall. I know Kendall is up there, heartbroken." Kiandra tilted back her head to stare at the sky. She blinked away tears and made a move like she was going to stand again. Nona put her hand out to keep her from going so soon.

"You know I'm sorry, Kiki, for—"

"You can't apologize for him." Kiandra seemed angry, then surprised by her own anger. She stared at Nona and softened her eyes. "I mean, you don't need to do that."

The second statement was gentler, and Nona took it to mean Kiandra had forgiven Nona, but she wanted everyone to absolve Marcus as well. It was a feeling she couldn't describe, but she still didn't want his image sullied. She didn't want people to think ill of him. She didn't want people to forgive him so much as she wanted them to understand how he'd been possessed.

If he'd joined the gang—like Peter—and killed as many boys over the course of his life, she wouldn't have been shunned like this. No one shunned Mother or Vega or Mable for their boys' crimes and killings. Nona had no right to her feelings of resentment, but she was powerless to stop them.

Kiandra's hair was cut short to her scalp, and she had an engagement ring on her finger.

"I haven't seen you since . . ." Nona couldn't finish the sentence.

"I haven't been back since that night. I can't go back. Been staying with my friend." Kiandra glanced at her ring but seemed self-conscious about wearing it. "I mean, my fiancé."

When Kiandra was a young girl, Nona used to braid her hair. Nona kept magazine clippings in the drawer of her living room's side table of the wedding dress and tuxedo that she'd thought Kiandra and Kendall would one day walk down the aisle in. Those two had been so in love. If Nona had let Kendall move out and start a life with Kiandra at the end of their senior year the way they wanted to, maybe life would have been different. Nona raised her hand to pat Kiandra on the shoulder but stopped short.

Kiandra returned to her fiancé's side. Nona watched them until they got into his car and drove away.

When they lowered Marcus into the ground, Nona dropped her flowers on the coffin as well as a corsage someone had pinned to her blouse. She wanted to jump into the grave with Marcus and let them bury her too, but Pastor handed Lance a shovel, and Lance's downcast face as he took the wooden handle shifted something inside of her. She couldn't leave Lance.

After the pallbearers added dirt to the grave, Pastor opened the limousine door for Nona and Lance. She glared at Pastor, removed her shoes, and ambled away.

"Nona?" Pastor whisper-shouted. He glanced around nervously at the congregants in the crowd. "Nona. Where are you going?" He seemed to stop caring about the people staring. He closed the gap with her, grabbed her arm, and spun her around. "Put on your shoes. Where are you going?"

She removed his hand from her arm. "For a walk." She started down the path again. He got in front of her and blocked her way.

"For a . . . ? Get in the car, Nona," he whispered. Pastor was a much different man than Vance, but in both cases, even when they were being gentle and caring and attentive and helpful, there was always the underlying expectation of obedience from her—that she would listen to their counsel, accept their gifts, go along with their plans.

She wasn't sure what her facial expression had become, but fear entered Pastor's gaze.

"Step aside . . . Timothy."

And he obeyed. "Nona," he whispered. "I'm worried about you."

She sauntered off. She was worried about her too.

The few miles home destroyed the soles of her stockings as she carried her shoes in her hand. She wore the same blouse and pencil skirt she'd donned at Marcus's graduation, though the fabric was looser this time. She hadn't been eating.

She passed the cash advance store where she and Vance as newlyweds had gotten a loan with twenty percent interest because their lights were going to be shut off if they didn't have payment by the fifteenth of the month, and their next paychecks weren't set to arrive until the thirtieth.

She passed the plasma center where she'd regularly give blood, and once, even though they'd given her a banana and apple juice before sending her on her way, she'd still fainted in the lobby on the way out.

She passed Medford Church of God in Christ. All those days and nights she'd climbed the stairs to make it on time for service, a meeting she was running, a picnic she was volunteering at, and what good had it done her?

Pastor would always say *God is not going to stop the troubles, but he is a balm in Gilead. He will be a comfort during the storms.* Easy for Pastor to say when he lived in a mansion. What good was invisible comfort?

What a mess her life had become, and she couldn't say she was surprised. By the time she was nine, she was well-known at the library and read three books a week, many of them beyond her emotional age. She had been curious about the sky, the trees, the color of water, why music had a certain rhythm, why God had made her. Her mother had become her protector and the one she'd ask all her questions. Her mother instilled in her the need to be independent. To strike out on her own in the world and travel and have hobbies and cook and maybe learn another language, all dreams her mother had growing up in 1950s Michigan. When her mother died, Nona turned to her journal to do all her thinking and asking. Her diary was the place in which she realized all she wanted was to be free, but she wasn't free. She was cursed.

NaDarius had taken Vance away. NaDarius had taken Kendall. Now he had taken Marcus. And did she have four years with Lance still? Was NaDarius waiting until her baby was eighteen to snatch him away like the others? She and Mable had unleashed

NaDarius. And now that he roamed free in her home, in Hester Gardens, maybe NaDarius would take Lance now instead of in four years. He was stronger than Kendall. He was stronger than Nona.

Back at the Gardens, she passed the alley where she'd caught Vance with the pistol she'd told him to get rid of. NaDarius had been somebody's baby. Somebody's child. Vega's words flashed in her mind: *Where is his home? Where is he buried?*

And when the funeral procession made it back to the Gardens, they found Nona sitting in her business suit and stockinged feet in the rickety white chair Vega normally occupied. Nona sipped from a bottle of wine with the cork and opener resting in her lap. She stared into the alley and whispered the names of her dead boys.

Forty-Five

A week later, Nona was worse. She was down to a cup of chicken broth a day that Lance forced her to sip. She stayed up all night pacing, ignoring Pastor's phone calls and text messages, listening for the dark figure slithering down the hall.

Then one morning, the stench from the dumpsters seemed more powerful than ever and had permeated the strands of her hair and the fabric of her nightgown. At dawn, she snapped.

In her ankle-length red robe, she stomped to the kitchen, ripped open the bric-a-brac drawer, and pulled out ten boxes of matches she'd bought in bulk. She slammed open her front door and stormed out to the alley she always avoided. With electricity in each of her steps, she marched straight up to the dumpsters.

Hester Gardens was eerily quiet. A man who walked to the bus did not speak to a woman headed to the same spot. Nor did they wave to each other.

When Nona spotted that blue ball sitting at the head of the alley, she kicked it so hard toward the courtyard that it made a loud pop and squeak as it slammed into the brick façade of one of the units. It was loud enough to wake the residents inside, but she didn't care.

Nona struck a match and placed it on the pile of garbage. Another she chucked beside the heap. A final one she was about to wedge between two dumpsters when she saw a scuffed-up pair of red Air Jordans with the tongues sticking straight up like rabbit ears.

Autumn offered hints of its arrival in Medford, but that wasn't the reason goosebumps spread up her arm.

With flames burning around her, smoke filling her nostrils, and heat washing over her from both the rising sun and the fire, she bent toward the shoes and glimpsed a pair of outstretched legs lying beneath a mattress. A brown arm, frozen stiff, poked crookedly from the gap. Was it a large doll? Was it an apparition? Was this real? Could it be they had all gotten so used to the vile odor coming from the dumpster they hadn't noticed the stench of a body?

She backed up and accidentally bumped into Vega.

"What are you doing?" Vega stared down at the rectangle in Nona's hands and slapped the box to the ground. It hit the concrete and broke open. The long, slender matches rolled into crevices alongside persistent weeds. "If you gon' burn the trash, you need to do it in a drum, otherwise you'll catch everything here on fire."

Nona grabbed Vega's hand and yanked her toward the big dumpsters. "I . . . I was tired of the trash. I started burning it. Then I found . . . We don't have time. Help me move this." Nona pointed to the mattress.

"I'm not touching that."

Nona lifted a corner and showed Vega the shoulder she knew would be there.

Eyes wide, Vega reached down and pulled on the mattress with Nona until they'd cleared it away from the body. Heavy bags of trash and discarded furniture fell to the side as they stared down at the figure.

"Have y'all lost your ever-loving minds?" Mable Cleveland stood behind them.

Nona and Vega turned to Mable, and they both stepped aside so Mable could see. Nona had not spoken to Mable since they'd lost Marcus and Donnell, and Mable did not meet Nona's eyes. Nona wanted to make a connection, wanted Mable to let her know she didn't hold anything against her, she didn't blame her, but Mable did not give her that satisfaction.

The plump woman walked between Nona and Vega, her mouth falling open as she approached.

They all covered their noses with their robe sleeves and took in the white T-shirt, the eyes still open but only showing the upturned sclera, the hand curling into a fist. The flames died down as humid air soaked the fuel in the trash pile, which was already wet from the previous night's rain. How did everyone miss this body?

The three women backed away from the corpse, panting and fighting back tears. Nona had spent so much time hating Peter. Now, as she stared at his mangled, blood-crusted flesh, his wide eyes, the bullet hole in his head, just like the six young men Marcus had killed, just like Marcus himself, the enmity floated from her chest, both constricting and loosening her airways. He'd gotten what he deserved, but who deserved death? Did anyone? If so, then maybe so did everyone.

"Police combed this entire place and didn't see him. How did he get here?" Vega's voice was deadpan, as if a body in the trash was a normal occurrence. "I told you he was dead," Vega said to Mable.

"One of you call the police," Mable said. "I'll go tell Mother Lincoln." And just before Mable stepped away, Nona reached for the woman's hand. Mable stopped, took both of Nona's hands in hers. She stared into Nona's eyes and nodded. "We'll get through this won't we, Nona? We always do."

Something broke inside of Nona. She nodded and sobbed as Mable released her hands and headed toward Mother Lincoln's.

Nona didn't move. She let Vega phone the police. She wanted to know who had killed Peter. Who had placed his body here seemingly overnight? It couldn't have been Marcus. And the only other people left in the place who could have done it had already been killed. Except for Lance, but her Lance couldn't do this. Wouldn't do this. NaDarius was still slithering around her home, wasn't he? Was dragging his legs across the floor of her hallway at night as she lay awake, sweating, in a panic, praying that he didn't go into Lance's room. Into her room.

Vega's questions about NaDarius replayed in Nona's mind: *Where is his home? Where is he buried?*

As Mother Lincoln's wails emanated from the southernmost part of Hester Gardens, Nona decided she would no longer let NaDarius come for her. She would find him.

Part Six

Forty-Six

Nona arrived at the Medford police station and asked for Sgt. Prager. No, she didn't have an appointment, she told the uniformed officer with droopy eyes who sipped from his travel mug, but she added that she knew the sergeant would see her.

After phoning Sgt. Prager's line, the officer said, "Mmhmm," took a final swig of his drink, and left his post at the front desk to usher Nona to a conference room. The newly renovated space had windows for walls that let her see into the hallway.

Was his side-eye in recognition of her name or in reaction to her appearance? She glimpsed herself in that reflective wall: a black shoe on her left foot, a navy blue one on her right, still in her pajama bottoms, hair in a messy bun with wispy strands floating above her head. She saw she was off by one button on her blouse, but she didn't care to refasten them.

The carpet smelled new, and she sat at a table encircled by thirty chairs, rubbing her hand over the polished wood. The repetitive gesture soothed her.

Sgt. Prager cast her eyes low as she approached the door and met Nona's gaze upon entering. When Sgt. Prager took in Nona's unbrushed hair, poorly buttoned shirt, and mismatched shoes, she neither reacted nor commented. Nona was grateful for the woman's compassion.

"How you holding up?" Sgt. Prager carried folders, and Nona hoped one of them was related to Marcus.

"I'm not holding up."

"I'm sorry, Mrs. McKinley."

"I think we're long past you calling me 'missus.'"

Sgt. Prager nodded. "What can I do for you, Nona?"

"Harlan said you were the first one to make a connection between Marcus and the others."

"Yes." Sgt. Prager checked the hallway, where a group of burly, suited men sauntered by, grinning at one another as if they'd just shared a joke.

"How?"

"Because I found the gun. It was a Bushmaster XM15-E2S—"

"Do you know where he got it?"

"That's all I can say."

"Please, Victoria."

"I'm sorry, Nona, but that's all—"

"Have you ever lost someone?"

"Excuse me?"

"Maybe you've never lost anyone. Never felt this kind of pain. I want so badly to stop it. To turn it off."

"This isn't about me."

"But it is. Because if you know where I'm coming from, where I'm really coming from, you would tell me what you know."

Sgt. Prager leaned back in her chair and sighed. "Look. I'm from Medford. Grew up rough and at the bottom. My dad was an officer. Was killed in a high-speed chase. My first partner was killed trying to protect kids in a school shooting. We both entered the building. I came from the north entrance and he from the south, and it just so happened the shooter was headed out the south entrance. Had we decided on different doors, I'd be in the ground, and he'd be sitting with you right now. So don't tell me about what I don't know."

"Then you know how gut-wrenching this is. You must have experienced days where you didn't want to go on living. You wondered why you were forced to carry this burden."

"Nona, please—"

"I think . . . I think I've been cursed. And I need to know how to stop it, to save Lance, and I think to stop it, I have to know how the curse won. Where did Marcus get the gun? Did he make a plan or did he think it up that night? How can I protect Lance? Or did the curse die with Marcus? These are the questions that keep me up at night."

"But I—"

"I've lost two sons, Victoria. Two. I—"

"I believe you about the curse, Nona."

The room shrank. Her ears rang.

"You do?" Nona choked down a sob.

"Yeah. He wouldn't be able to get the jump on six young men in one night by himself. Either there was more than one shooter, which is unlikely based on the evidence, or he had some sort of supernatural help. It's several feet up and down from half those windows. He removed bars from some of them. All of the young men were asleep. Nobody was startled awake? He was silent the entire time? Nobody else in their homes heard him enter and leave?

"One person, Kiandra Harris, thought she heard someone in her brother's room, but when she got in there, the suspect had just left, only she didn't see him outside the window.

"Like I said, there's no evidence he worked with an accomplice. The only way he'd be able to do all this is if he slowed time or could move more quickly than a person is capable of. And then I . . ."

Sgt. Prager paused. Cleared her throat.

Nona leaned in. "You what?"

Sgt. Prager gave a sheepish grin then went back to her stern police-officer face.

"Say it, Victoria."

Sgt. Prager cleared her throat again. Checked the hallway. It was empty. "I'm a skeptic. I've never seen anything odd in my life. I don't believe in an afterlife."

"What happened, Victoria?"

"Something," Sgt. Prager whispered. She leaned in close enough for Nona to smell cigarettes on her breath. "A person high up on the building at the school, in a spot he couldn't really get to that fast and without a ladder, and then I chased him all the way back to Hester Gardens and didn't see him anymore."

Laughter filled the hallway as two officers palming coffee mugs strolled by and waved at Sgt. Prager. She nodded at them and sat up straight again.

"Like, the person disappeared?" Nona could feel the hairs on her arms standing on end. "Was this after Marcus was already . . . ?" She couldn't say the word.

"Yes. This was after I found his remains. Someone was there, and then they weren't. But I need you to pretend I never told you that."

Nona nodded. She wasn't breathing. Her mind was racing. Ever since the night at the lake with Mable and Vega, NaDarius's presence had been palpable. Now, with Victoria seeing a figure after Marcus was already gone, Nona had proof that NaDarius had possessed her boy. This was also proof he was still in her home.

Nona rose, steadying herself by leaning the bulk of her weight against the conference table.

"I have one more piece of information, Nona. It's about your pastor."

"My pastor?" Her pulse quickened. What could the woman possibly have to tell her about Pastor?

"Pastor Davis isn't innocent in all this."

Forty-Seven

Nona was well put together again—clothing, hair, shoes, handbag—and she approached Medford C.O.G.I.C.'s front door as if made of flames. It's not like the space in the parking lot labeled "Pastor" with a gold Mercedes in it was new to her. She'd ridden in that car, and only today did it dawn on her that Pastor could only afford these expensive things by collecting money from his poor congregants, like Nona.

Most church members rode the bus, and not only were they bankrolling the reverend's luxury vehicle, but the saints also bragged to folks at nearby Rodgers AME or Medford World Outreach Ministries about how *their* pastor drove a *Mercedes* because the Lord's favor was shining down on Medford C.O.G.I.C.

She'd been an idiot for handing over ten percent of her measly paychecks to this church, to this man, all in the name of "tithes and offerings." And she had even given her body over to him too.

When she entered, the church was subdued. Many congregants lived at Hester Gardens and were in mourning. Also, Pastor and First Lady were separated, and members of their flock—from the cook staff to the deacon board—had to choose sides.

Dim lights filled the empty vestibule. The cleaning crew packed away vacuums, dusters, and wipes.

"Nona?" Pastor appeared in a gray suit tailored to his muscular frame.

"I see you don't have your security with you today." She brushed past him, walked beyond the cloth pews red as blood. The altar's two theatre-sized screens—usually set to broadcast the sermon to folks in the balcony—were in screensaver mode and displayed a photo of Pastor and the first lady with their dazzling smiles.

"What?" Pastor had obviously been heading out, likely to an appointment, but she didn't care. His smile dissolved as he turned and fell in line behind her. He reached for Nona, but she raised her arm as she stormed past the altar and down the sunlit hall to his office.

"We need to talk . . . Timothy."

Pastor's office was outfitted with a better couch, bathroom, and refrigerator than her nephew's suburban home. She bet state politicians and businessmen had lesser office digs. How was she only noticing all this now? Losing Marcus had removed a veil from her eyes.

She took the chair where she and Pastor had first made physical contact. He sat in the one next to her but was not flirty, seemed to be bracing himself, perhaps mentally scrolling through his lies and misdeeds to determine which one she was about to call him out on.

"What did Marcus do with the money he earned from you this summer?"

It was a simple enough question, but Pastor's face twisted into confusion.

"Marcus never spoke to me about his finances, but I'm certain he was a prayerful financial steward. I assumed he gave his earnings to you."

"I'm going to ask you this question one time, and your answer will determine whether we ever speak again."

"Nona, you're scaring me."

"You get one answer."

"Have I done something wrong?"

"Do you know anyone named Jalani?"

Something stirred behind Pastor's eyes, the recognition evident on his face. Sgt. Prager had no reason to lie, and to date, the woman's facts had never been wrong. So of course Pastor knew Jalani. Nona just hoped he would level with her.

Pastor remained poker-faced and, after a long pause, said, "I do not."

And she was done.

Completely.

Unequivocally.

The moment her relationship ended with Vance was when she realized the man he'd claimed to be was different from the one he actually was. Vance didn't need to be perfect; he just needed to be honest with *her*. And the same was true of Pastor.

"So you don't know a Jalani?"

Pastor shook his head.

"Someone whose street name is Heat?"

"Nona, can you tell me what this is about?"

"There's a Jalani Holmes among the congregants here. Big donor. Five thousand a year for the past three years and Lord only knows how much more under the table. Never shows up to Sunday service yet is present at youth ministry events. On the streets, he sells guns. Got a seven-page rap sheet. I know because I combed through it. Ever see Marcus and Jalani hanging out at your events?"

"As I've said, I know not of whom you speak."

Nona reached into her purse. Pulled out her phone. Scrolled through her photos and showed the screen to Pastor. In the background of most of her photos from Marcus's graduation party stood the out-of-place young man.

"Took me a while to put two and two together. Your security guy? I remember seeing him at Marcus's graduation party. He wasn't one of the musicians. Saw him again when I came here to do research and your wife threatened my job. And he drove you to my home. Remember, I asked you why you needed security? I certainly thought it odd. And he's young, not much older than Marcus, sells semi-automatic weapons."

"Nona. There's a perfectly good explanation for—"

She rose, snatched her phone away, and, before turning to go, said, "Don't ever contact me again."

"You have to know I'd never do anything to hurt you or Marcus."

She walked to his office door.

"Okay. Nona, wait." He took her hand in his to stop her. "Yes. Jalani is a congregant. Yes. He's also a big donor. Remember how I told you the church was in financial trouble? Debt? All that? Well, the thing I've been keeping from you is that I've been turning a blind eye to our biggest donor being a weapons dealer because his gifts to the church were the only thing keeping us afloat. It's not like I've been letting him sell weapons here or at our events. He just . . . hangs around the young people and I . . . I mean . . . and I certainly would have put a stop to it if I knew Marcus had purchased a gun from him."

"But I asked you whether Marcus had gotten a gun."

"You did, but Marcus is the last person I'd ever think would buy a gun. He was headed to Brown!"

"But you must have suspected."

He paused, began to speak, but stopped himself.

"And you're still not leveling with me," Nona said. "If I had a gun, I would use it on you right now."

"Okay. After we found out what happened, when I learned what kind of gun Marcus had used, I suspected, but it was too late then. And you know I'm leaving the church. My ties to Jalani are severed."

"Right. Your ties are severed *after* I lost another of my babies. You are no better than Vance. You belong in prison. Man of God?

Stay the fuck away from me." She pushed him aside and opened the door.

"You have to know . . . Nona. You know how I feel about you."

She was out the door and down the hallway before he could continue, and when she stormed past the first lady's office, the woman, horrified, rose and stood behind her desk but didn't move when she saw Pastor chasing after Nona.

"Look, Nona. I don't blame you for leaving, but I have information about NaDarius."

She accidentally dropped her phone when he uttered NaDarius's name. She swung around to face him.

"Are you threatening me?"

"What? No. Absolutely not." Tears filled his eyes. He stepped toward Nona, and over his shoulder, Nona saw the first lady return to her seat and stare out at them. Nona didn't care what that woman thought. If she wanted him, she could have him. "I hoped the information would help you."

He reached in the pocket of his blazer, pulled out a pen and a grocery store receipt. He wrote on the back and spoke rapidly. "I discovered his mother is a congregant here."

He handed the sheet of paper to Nona. "This is her address. I was going to contact her myself, but if I can't talk to you again, I won't be able to share with you what I find. I was hoping . . . I mean, I . . ."

Nona snatched the paper from him, picked up her phone from the marble floor, and ran down the hall. She sprinted from the church all the way back to the bus stop. When she boarded and grabbed a window seat, she was numb the entire ride, until she passed the house on Willowbrook. Seeing that they'd purchased dainty white rocking chairs for the front porch, with a cute little wicker side table, Nona burst into tears.

Forty-Eight

The next day, Nona got off at the Plymouth Woods bus stop in the nicer part of Medford, where the city bordered Sebastian Hills and the homes were brick and square. Glancing at the back of the receipt in her hand where Pastor had scrawled the address, she trudged down Cantor Street, teetering between nervous and determined to get answers.

Midsized sedans filled the street and driveways, and it seemed everyone used their garages for tinkering or home gyms. The kids played hopscotch on the sidewalk, men mowed their lawns, and women added mulch to their tree beds. NaDarius's home had a front porch with bushes, a red door, and a brick walkway between two patches of lawn.

Trying to appear as if she belonged, Nona had chosen a plain black housedress fixed up with a belt and a necklace, but she still felt like an intruder.

She'd had Harlan search for the woman in the newspaper's database and found she lived alone. Husband passed away about five years after NaDarius went missing. No other kids.

When Nona saw her sitting outside, reminding her of Vega, she headed toward the woman's porch without a clue of what she'd say. Nona smiled at the woman, who was narrowing her eyes. Nona hoped to put the woman's suspicions at ease.

"May I help you?" The woman had a soft face with perfect skin she seemed to moisturize twice daily, at least. Flecks of gray dotted her sideburns. If Mable had seen the thin woman, she'd have referred to her as a "bag of bones." The skin sagged around her eyes, crowded with hair-thin lines. Apparently, the woman carried her grief there.

"I was walking down the street when I looked over," Nona said, her voice quivering. "I think we go to the same church."

"Oh, yeah?" The woman folded her arms across her chest, suspicious but curious. The gospel song "Mary Don't You Weep" flowed from her home.

"Medford C.O.G.I.C.? Timothy Davis is your pastor?" Saying his name sent a surge through Nona.

"He's my pastor," the woman said, still hesitant but perhaps curious enough to continue the conversation. "Honestly, so many folks go to that church, I can't keep track. I've been there since the beginning, but I stopped counting the saints after he hit five thousand."

The woman chuckled; her face grew younger and sweeter. Nona regretted she and Vance had ever caused her any pain. She imagined the woman cradling NaDarius as a baby, then, later, holding his tiny hands as he took his first steps.

"I'm Nona. I sometimes run the women's ministry."

"McKinley?"

"That's me."

"You're the one with the son heading to college back east, right? I heard Pastor talking about him."

Nona tried to keep smiling, but the tears came.

"Yes. That's me as well. Well, he *was* going." The tears fell.

"Oh, no, sweetheart. I'm sorry. What . . . ? Here. Have a seat."

The woman rose just long enough to pull a chair forward for Nona. The rocker was sturdy under Nona, and with her sore back, knees, and ankles, she was glad to be off her feet.

"I'm sorry for getting emotional. He was killed. I live at Hester Gardens."

"I'm so sorry. Was it over there with all that shooting recently? All them boys?"

"Yes. That's the one." Nona didn't like the way she was straddling reality and make-believe.

"The Lord will carry you. He carries us all. I'm Beth, by the way. Short for Elizabeth. I'm on the church roster as Bethanne. What brings you over this way, sweetheart?"

"Visiting a friend. I'll be heading back to the bus before too long. Don't let me keep you." Nona rose.

"Don't be silly. You're not keeping me. Maybe I'll see you at church sometime. I haven't been going recently. I lost a son too. I always get so down when it gets close to his birthday. Another year without my baby."

Nona's stomach dropped. It had been fourteen years since this woman lost her son, and not only was she still suffering, but she still referred to him as her baby.

Nona thought of all the holidays, birthdays, good days, and bad days she still had to get through without Kendall and Marcus, and she wished she could make her suffering stop, if even for a few moments.

"I'm sorry. Was he killed too?"

"I assume. Never came home, and the police never really looked for him from the beginning. I searched for him all around Medford and halfway in and out Michigan for years, but I never got a handle on what happened.

"He just went to work one morning and never returned. I kept his bedroom how he left it. I guess it's different for me, since you have a grave site, probably."

Nona nodded. Two boys buried at different cemeteries . . . The wave of grief made her gasp.

"Officer said my boy was selling drugs. That he might have been selling in an area with a lot of competition. And that was an injustice all to itself. My boy didn't sell drugs."

The words stung. Nona's mind raced. Back to that day when NaDarius was on the ground. To her argument with Vance in the living room. Had Vance lied about that part? Why would he have beaten NaDarius if there wasn't turf competition?

"I mean . . ." Beth looked sheepish. "He *used* drugs. He had . . . a habit, but he didn't sell them."

Nona had been slapped. Vance had killed an addict. Maybe NaDarius had stolen drugs from Vance and Vance had beaten him to prove a point, but this wasn't some gangster who was encroaching on his turf. Vance had killed a young man who was addicted to the product that he'd sold to him. If Vance weren't locked up, she'd go beat him herself.

Then she caught herself. Did it really matter whether NaDarius was a gangster or not? Was Nona any different than the journalist she'd slapped, who had painted Kendall out to be a gang member? That's what she'd allowed Vance to do to her, hadn't she? Absolve her of some of her guilt by saying that NaDarius had been no angel. Same way everyone absolved themselves of guilt, of their hand in the deaths of young "urban" men, some who were like Kendall, some who were not.

"For me, it's the not knowing that hurts." Beth's voice dropped to a whisper, and the sweetness in her face devolved into a vacant stare.

She thought about Vega's words. What if he didn't want revenge? What if he wanted peace?

"Would it help if you had him back? Could bury him?"

"I think so, but what do I know?" Beth gave a self-conscious chuckle. "I really wish I had gotten him out."

"I know what you mean. I was gearing up to get my boy out."

"You married?"

"Not really. He's in prison. When we'd finally saved the money to get out of the Gardens, officers showed up and carted him off. The part they don't tell you is, getting locked up is expensive. Court bond. And they seize your assets, anything you have in the bank."

"You have any more kids?" Beth seemed sympathetic, and Nona knew she didn't deserve any of the woman's compassion.

"My youngest is in middle school."

"Get him out."

Nona nodded her agreement.

"I don't care what it takes, get him as far away from Medford as you can. Out of Michigan even. If I could do my life over again, I would have had urgency about my boy's problems as soon as they surfaced. If I could go back, I would have gotten him out, sent him south, or got him into a boarding school or something. Just anywhere but here."

Nona agreed with Beth, but where could she go? Pastor was her only way out, and she would no longer hitch herself to that man. To any man, really.

"You hear me, Nona?"

"I hear you."

"Out. Far from here. As far away as you can. And when you get gone, just look ahead, ahead, ahead. Only ahead."

Nona: I talked to his mother. She has no idea what happened to him.

Vega: Was she at peace? Did she seem at peace?

Nona: No. She said not knowing where he was and what happened made her grief worse.

Vega: You know who knows where he's buried?
Nona: Yes. But I don't understand how any of this will help.
Vega: You can't keep running. Your past is here, staring you in your face. You know who you need to talk to. Who you've been needing to talk to.
Nona: I really don't want to.
Vega: I know. But you will.

Forty-Nine

The penitentiary was about two hours outside Medford, which was an-other reason she'd never taken her boys. By the time she rode the bus there, had the visit, and headed back home, the sun would be on its way down.

This was the first time she'd seen Vance since he was taken into custody. When he entered the room and sat in the chair behind the glass opposite her, he stared at her tenderly.

He lifted the phone receiver and tears filled his eyes. The lines in his face had deepened, and his close-cut hair had gotten gray about the sideburns. He'd always been a beautiful man, and even with gaunt cheeks and dark circles beneath his eyes, her insides stirred when she saw how attractive he still was.

"My forever." His voice, raspier than it used to be, traveled through the receiver in her hand, the sound filling her ear. Thick glass separated him from Nona, and she was grateful for that. Grateful he couldn't touch her. Couldn't hold her.

The sketch he'd mailed to her came to mind. His artwork hadn't been the sum of all he was doing in prison. He was surviving, and the drawings were likely holding him together.

"You are still so beautiful, Nona. I . . ."

He stopped abruptly. She was not smiling.

"I never expected you to visit me. Either you're divorcing me or someone's dead."

The only other soul in the room was a guard waiting by the door, and he wasn't looking at them.

"I'm not divorcing you."

Vance's eyes narrowed as he seemed to brace himself for the news. "Please tell me it's not my dad. He and I aren't on speaking terms still, and I . . . Please say it's not him. Not before I had a chance to fix things with him."

"It's Marcus."

A small grin emerged at the corners of his mouth. "What about Marcus? He already need more money for college? I can help, if—"

"He's dead."

Vance's eyes grew wide, and he searched her face. "Is this . . . some sort of cruel joke?"

His long pause gave her enough time to think about the words she'd spoken. She was on autopilot. She was dead inside too, right along with Marcus and Kendall.

"Nona. I . . . I . . . What do you . . . ?"

She let the news sink in. It was only fair this information should destroy someone in addition to her. Let Vance share some of her pain for once.

"But . . . he's at college, I thought," Vance said. "Harlan told me Marcus was headed to college." His voice came out in a shudder, and he grew crimson about the neck and cheeks.

"You're crying? You left me with these boys. You don't have a right to cry."

"Of course I have a right to cry over these boys." He was choked up and whispering. Fat tears settled in the crevices on either side of his nose. "Otherwise, you wouldn't have come here at all."

"That's not why I came here. I could have called to—"

"What happened to him, Nona?"

"I don't really know how to tell you, other than to tell you. He shot and killed everyone in the Hester Boys, and then he turned the gun on himself."

He stopped crying, and his face stretched in surprise. "What?"

She told him everything, from Marcus's graduation day to Solomon getting killed. Peter's confession about killing Kendall. The watch. She even mentioned the 911 call and finding Peter's body in the trash.

Air hissed as it escaped a vent. Vance let out a yelp as he sobbed. The guard glanced at the two of them and then looked away again.

"You're a damn lie, Nona." He spoke through wails. "I don't believe it. Not one word. Not Marcus. Marcus wouldn't do that."

"He did it, but deep down, I know it wasn't really him."

"But wh—"

"I need to know what you did with NaDarius."

Vega's words popped in her mind: *Where is his home? Where is he buried?*

"What?" Vance was panting, the way a person struggled to catch their breath after a sprint.

"You heard me. Where'd you put NaDarius?"

"I . . . I have no idea who you're talking about." He turned his tear-soaked face toward the guard, who was staring through the glass into the lobby. Vance eyed her again and leaned forward, whispering. "Need I remind you we're being watched?"

"I'm well aware."

"And need I remind you I'm likely to get out of here with good behavior before my—"

"And need I remind you that two of our sons are dead?"

"What does that have to do with what you're asking?"

"NaDarius is after our sons."

A long pause. His eyes grew suspicious. Snot flowed from his nose and over his top lip. "What?"

"He's terrorizing me in my own home and has used the shitty housing situation you left us in to take Kendall and Marcus, and I won't let him have Lance."

"Look. I know your grief is heavy, but you're talkin' crazy. Listen to yourself, Nona."

"I am listening to myself."

"What are you saying?"

"A curse."

"You're really serious right now?"

"He got inside of Peter and made Peter kill Kendall. Then Vega's curse, a different curse, got inside of Peter and made him kill Solomon. Then NaDarius got inside of Marcus and made Marcus . . . do what he did. Now Lance is skipping school, drinking, doing drugs, breaking into homes."

"This is all in your head!" His voice boomed through the earpiece. She got a flash of the bear he'd been in the alley and shortly thereafter in their home. She'd not seen this angry Vance in a long time and had forgotten how she'd flinched during their disagreement about NaDarius, when Vance had slapped his palm for emphasis. How she'd feared his wrath coming down on her that day, but not this time.

"A guilty conscience, Nona." He lowered his voice that time. "Nothing more. Making you think you're cursed. I didn't even think you believed in all that."

"I didn't think I believed in all that until the shit started showing up in my house."

His mouth opened into an O. He seemed shocked that she'd sworn. "There's no such thing as curses. I can't believe I even have to say this to you, of all people. Folks who think they're cursed have let their minds play tricks on them. It might have been that Marcus's anger at losing Kendall and maybe his fear of the Hester Boys took hold of him. No different than Peter. But . . . I mean . . . You want to talk about a curse? Yeah. We're cursed, all right. Generation after generation. Shitty housing, high crime, poor education, no jobs. Those are our curses. The curse of Hester Gardens. Not what revenge a certain dead person might be after."

Vance was convincing. He always had been. And for a moment, Nona's conviction waned. Had she made up everything herself?

Then she remembered she hadn't been the only one to see. If she were hallucinating, then Mable was too. And Vega. Kiki. Gretchen. Harlan. And Sgt. Prager.

"Like I said . . . you're talkin' crazy."

"I'm talking . . . ?" She raised her voice. "You pistol-whipped an eighteen-year-old named NaDarius Rucker to death in the alley near our home. You killed an addict, Vance, not a drug dealer, someone who was hooked on the product you sold him, you low-down, no-good—"

"Hey. Hey. Hey." Vance stood, dropped the receiver. Muscles rippled beneath his orange jumpsuit as he clenched his fists. The guard shot him a look, and Vance opened his palms, wiped his eyes, seeming sheepish. "Death in the family," he said to the guard, who nodded and glanced away again.

Vance was probably paying off this guard. She hadn't spent any time in prisons before, but it seemed unusual for her and Vance to have an entire visitation room to themselves and a warden looking the other way when she was screaming about a murder.

Vance slowly picked up the receiver again. He sat and leaned all the way in so his face was inches away from hers. She knew it killed him to be unable to touch her.

"Nona. Baby. Stop. I know you hate me, but what are you trying to do to me?"

"I don't hate you," she whispered. "Not anymore. And I'll probably never divorce you. I don't think I'm capable of loving anyone but Lance nor hating anyone but this curse."

"Then what—"

"You will give me the information, and, if you're smart, right this very moment." Her breathing sped up. His eyes grew wide as she worked hard to remain calm, to steady herself, to lower her voice. "If I have to, I will come through this bulletproof glass to get it. I will call the authorities. I will have it written up in the news. I will send someone in here after you while you sleep. Whatever it takes. For once, you're going to put your son before yourself. Tell me where to search." She slammed her fists on the glass. "Tell me. This instant. Or I will come for you. I will burn down this entire fucking prison around you. I. Will. Not. Lose. Another. Son!"

Her voice echoed off the empty chairs and cement walls.

All the tears that had welled in Vance's eyes spilled down his face. He nodded.

"Do you remember our first time?"

"Don't change the subject—"

"I'm not changing the subject, baby. Listen to me. Our first time. Do you remember it? You got in my car. Let me kiss your sweet lips. And I drove you somewhere for the first time. Made love to you. Made you my forever."

"What about it?"

"Do you remember where I drove you? Remember where we went? It's where I later popped the question. It's where we would picnic on the blanket with those delicious deviled eggs you used to make."

He was pointing her to the lake, where NaDarius's spirit had nearly drowned her. She couldn't believe that, of all the places Vance could have chosen to stash a body, he'd picked a place tied to the beginning of their relationship.

"I remember." She wanted to slap him. To gouge out his eyes, but also to cry in his arms. He had made a mess of their lives, and she had let him.

"That's where you should go, baby. That spot, way far out there. In the clearing, where even the trees can't provide shade. It's nothing but sunshine out there on that part of the lake. That's where forever is."

Nona: You won't fucking believe this.
Vega: He wouldn't tell you.
Nona: Oh, he told me.
Vega: Then what?
Nona: The lake.
Vega: I guess it makes sense since you and Mable damn near drowned in that lake.
Nona: And now I need to somehow get him back home.
Vega: You'll figure it out. You always do.

Fifty

Within a week of her prison visit with Vance, Nona had Sgt. Prager check the lake, NaDarius's bones were found, and Harlan wrote up a story about how the mother of NaDarius Rucker finally had him home, how police had no new leads and appreciated any help from the public. She was grateful that Sgt. Prager never asked how she knew to search the lake and that Harlan's article referred to "an anonymous source."

On her way to work one morning, Nona rode the bus to Beth's street, got off, and walked past the woman's house just so she could wave to her.

"They found my boy," Beth said as she waved Nona to the seat next to her on the porch. The woman's smile was brighter, happier than when she'd first met her.

"What a blessing," Nona said as she hugged the woman in an embrace reminiscent of ones from her own mother and Mother Lincoln. A wave of sadness passed through her, but she wouldn't let it stay. This was the moment she'd been waiting for. She could finally breathe again. Her curse was finally broken.

"I've been thinking about you," Beth continued as Nona sat and settled into the chair. "About your boy. Your middle schooler. When you said you wanted to get him out. Wait right here."

The woman rose, went inside, and returned with a thick white envelope. She handed it to Nona.

"What is this?" Nona didn't feel she deserved any kindness from the woman, and she sensed there was money between the paper.

"I was finally able to get a death certificate for him, and because of that, some insurance money. I want you to use it to get your boy out."

"What? I can't. I—"

"I want you to get him out the way you couldn't get your other boys out. The way I couldn't get my boy out."

"There is no way I can accept this, Beth." Nona could barely speak because she was choking down a sob.

Then it hit her. Beth had said "boys." Plural.

Nona let the tears fall. "My . . . boys?"

"Your boys, Nona. Both of your boys. I looked you up. I know who you are. I know who your husband is. I know the rumors."

Everything stopped. The car engine from down the street. The robins singing in the trees. The kids laughing as they played hopscotch.

"You have to forgive me, Beth," Nona whispered as she sobbed.

"You don't need forgiving. Your husband's sins are not your sins. You know that. I know that. And most importantly"—Beth pointed to the sky—"God knows that."

Nona broke down, and Beth did as well. The woman took Nona's hands in hers as they sniffled and tried to compose themselves. "I want you to take this money and get your remaining boy out," she whispered. "For my boy. For your boys. Remember what I said. Please. Look ahead, ahead, ahead. Only ahead."

Lance felt like a ghost. He knew he was still alive, but it was like he was haunting his home instead of living in it. After the funeral, he hadn't touched a drink or smoke. The shadow man in his peripheral vision hadn't returned, but Lance went about his days in silence, eating, bathing, sleeping, and with Marcus gone, he had no one to talk to. Whenever he and his mother were home at the same time, she just sat and stared into dark corners, at high shelves in closets, down their empty hallway, like she was still waiting for Kendall and Marcus to arrive.

Lance felt everyone in the Gardens was a ghost, too, because they weren't really living anyway, were they? The residents just hadn't passed out of time yet, but he knew the longer they stayed, the closer they would get to their transition.

When Lance and his mother had packed their belongings into the U-Haul, Lance waited in his empty room for his mother to sign the landlord's papers to break the lease. He wore the gold watch; the band snagged the tiny hairs on his wrist as he turned it around and around. Kendall and Marcus used to be in this very space with him, laughing and shoving, wrestling over a chocolate candy bar they'd pilfered from Lance's backpack.

Back when Kendall still slept in the room, Lance's oldest brother had his own twin bed, and Lance and Marcus had a bunk bed, with Lance up top. At first, Lance had been afraid to climb up there, and Marcus had told him he couldn't be weak, but Kendall had actually shown Lance how to do it and had practiced with him until he got the hang of it. Kendall never complained whenever Lance asked him to spot him by waiting at the bottom of the ladder until he made it up. Kendall would repeat the chore with an amused grin until Lance's fear disappeared and he didn't need the help anymore.

Once Lance was able to get up there on his own "like a big boy," Kendall gave him a popsicle before bed. Then Lance had woken with a bellyache and asked Kendall to help him back down so he could go to the bathroom. Lance had been so tired after the trip, he'd just climbed into Kendall's bed and fallen asleep in his oldest brother's embrace. Kendall didn't complain, and when

Lance woke up, Marcus had somehow managed to squeeze in the bed too, between Kendall and the wall. Lance used to feel safe in Kendall's arms. It was just like having a dad, but better because Kendall was cool too.

Medford's weather had switched to gray and breezy. He could have used a sweater like his mom had suggested, but he'd never give her the satisfaction of knowing her nagging was justified. The Gardens had grown quiet with the Hester Boys gone. Out of respect, the Dempsey Boys had come around to place flowers outside the doors of the mothers who had lost sons that night. No fights. No gunshot blasts. No loud music blaring from speakers. And the helicopters had taken a break from flying overhead. Lance finally had the peace he'd been longing for, but at the price he had to pay for the quiet, he couldn't say he much liked it.

Leaning his head against the wall where his bed used to be, Lance held *Monster,* the book Marcus had given him after they'd both been jumped by the Hester Boys. The book was about a Black sixteen-year-old on trial for the murder of a convenience store owner. Lance always assumed Marcus wanted him to think about the "prison industrial complex," but after losing Marcus, Lance wasn't so sure.

The front door banged open. Footsteps in the hall, and his mother was standing in the doorframe. "It's time."

She'd chopped off all her hair. Some mornings, he could hear her in the bathroom, using Kendall and Marcus's clippers to shave down her curls to her scalp. She'd also stopped getting on her knees each night for prayer. She didn't say grace before meals anymore. She didn't talk on the phone and never answered it when it rang. For the first couple weeks, she drank wine every night, and then one night, she poured out every ounce of alcohol in the house and never took another sip.

He rose, filled the empty space of the doorframe as his mom headed down the hall. He took one final look at the dingy-walled space he'd shared with his brothers his entire life. Out the window, a cardinal that had been resting on the jagged branch of an elm tree flew away. The branch bobbed in the pale sunlight as if the tree were waving to him. He was leaving this room, this home, and he'd be lying if he said it didn't feel like a betrayal. Didn't he owe it to them to stay?

Harlan was on the scene of a shooting in Seabury Falls. It was orientation day at the suburban high school, and a freshman, whom witnesses said had been laughed at for his bad acne, had brought a gun to school—police wouldn't yet say what kind—and shot four classmates and a teacher before killing himself. Six dead including the shooter.

Harlan's phone rang. He exited the school parking lot, where parents were hugging their kids and local news crews were stationed and interviewing people. He positioned himself across the street on the curb, where he could talk but also keep an eye on the school in case there were any developments.

An editor from *U.S. News Daily* was on the line, telling him they were interested in buying his pitch about youth violence in America.

Harlan stepped away from the police tape and walked past additional victims and bystanders who were outside their cars, the vehicle doors hanging open. He'd already interviewed many of the moms and dads, who were standing in place with that shocked countenance all parents got in this situation, because they hadn't known, when they'd woken in the morning and combed their hair and tugged on their shorts and slipped their feet into their sandals, that they'd be picking up their kids from a school massacre.

The editor told him he had three weeks to submit a draft. Harlan's stomach dropped as the editor discussed the length of the piece and another expert he wanted Harlan to add to his interview list. He couldn't believe that after multiple pitches, this was the first time they'd bought one of his stories—at the exact moment Harlan wasn't sure he had the strength to actually write it.

Feeling he'd gathered enough information at the scene to write his daily article, Harlan got back in his car. He was supposed to drive to his girlfriend's house for dinner, but he was on deadline now and really needed to get home to work on the story. Yet instead of starting his car, he just stared ahead of him at the row of police vehicles.

Kendall appeared in Harlan's passenger seat and Marcus in the back. Harlan could see Kendall from his peripheral vision and Marcus in the rearview mirror, and they were seated just as they had been the day he'd driven them to the university talk on economic oppression. They giggled, and the laughter echoed against the windows. Something stirred in his chest. His grief was psychosomatic; the pain radiated throughout his body. When he blinked, Marcus and Kendall vanished.

He pulled his laptop from his work bag, wedged it between the steering wheel and his middle, and opened a new document. He typed, jabbing at those keys like he was writing for the last time:

One late August night, so hot that even the most cautious Hester Gardens residents left their doors and windows open, high school graduate Marcus McKinley entered the home of six young men who lived within his public housing complex, and, as they slept, he executed each one with a semiautomatic rifle and then fatally shot himself.

Tears stung Harlan's eyes as he removed his hand from the keys. He reached into the pocket of his collared shirt and took out the picture he'd been carrying around since that morning, when he'd stopped by to help Aunt Nona and Lance pack up and load the U-Haul.

He'd found a scrapbook with a photo she'd taken when he was younger, an image he'd not known existed, of a day he had long forgotten. In it, Harlan is sixteen, and he is at Aunt Nona's sitting outside on the grass with large picnic blankets nearby. Kendall is ten years old, as are Donnell, Solomon, and Kiandra, and the four of them are sitting cross-legged on one of the blankets next to Harlan, eating ice cream sandwiches with their shorts and tank tops on but no shoes.

Gretchen and her twin sister Grace, Esmé, Peter, and Marcus, all eight years old, are on one of the other blankets, holding hands as if playing ring around the rosy and they've all just fallen down.

Cedrick is five and Lance is four, and the two of them are shirtless and eating red, white, and blue Superman popsicles, the dye dripping down their arms.

All the kids are smiling, their faces spread so far apart in laughter Harlan could almost hear them through the image in his hand.

They are not wearing sunscreen to protect them from the summer sun. They are not covered in repellant to keep the mosquitoes from biting their flesh. They are not in bulletproof vests nor listening to their families' fuzz buzz to let them know when the police are in the area. They are just kids, being free, and probably don't even know they have nothing and live in a country that mostly wishes them dead.

That morning, without asking his aunt, Harlan had taken the photo and tucked it in his breast pocket. He would scan it later and make it the wallpaper on his computer screen so he could study it as he drafted his feature story. He wanted to see all their smiles, their joy and freedom. The long-form article would include all the mass shootings, school shootings, and so-called gang shootings he'd been covering since Kendall died, as well as the photo, and it would begin with the opening paragraph he'd just written about Marcus's mass shooting. Harlan would title the feature "Living Ghosts."

Fifty-One

Nona packed boxes, suitcases, and books into the moving van, wishing she could have said goodbye to Mother Lincoln. The woman passed away from another stroke after learning Peter had been killed. Nona had not been invited to the funeral that First Lady Davis put together, but Nona had shown up to the cemetery and stood next to a tree.

Pastor spotted her and texted, I never had a chance to tell you, but I love you. I am in love with you. I am sorry for everything. You must know that. And I am here if ever you want to come back to me. Are you never going to speak to me again? She let her silence serve as the answer to his question.

It had been weeks since Beth gave Nona the money. The bullet in Peter's body matched the one from Marcus's gun, so Peter's case was closed as well. The dumpsters were back to being emptied weekly since every local newspaper ran the story of Midwestern Waste letting the garbage pile so high it had hidden the decomposing body of a murdered resident. Medford ended its contract with Midwestern Waste, created trash management jobs in the city, and hired local residents as municipal workers to remove their own refuse.

Vance wrote to say he'd helped the police solve some random cold case and was getting out. "Prison informant," Harlan had told her. And she figured Vance had probably lied through his teeth to be free. *I will look for you,* he'd written. *You are my forever.*

He'd, for once, put Lance before himself by telling her where NaDarius's body had been. She hoped this meant Vance had changed and could be a grounding force in Lance's life. She would probably not divorce Vance, but she was going to be on her own. She thought about Vega asking her why she always needed a man, and for once, she didn't.

Leaning his head against the refrigerator, where Kendall's taped photo had reappeared that morning, Lance held *Monster.* He'd begun asking why Marcus had given him the book.

Nona didn't know what to make of all the sharing Lance had been doing, but she assumed his pain was so acute he had no other choice but to let it out. Wiggly, and every other friend he'd thought he'd had, abandoned him when they discovered it was Marcus who had killed everyone.

"Listen to this passage," Lance had told her the night before, as she labeled the boxes from his bedroom. He read her a line in which the main character talked about how much he hated being in jail. And the protagonist repeated the declaration of hate over and over again.

"What do you think that meant to Marcus?" Her voice sounded foreign to her. It was kind and calm, while her insides were a heartbroken mess.

"Marcus hated living here just like in the book, how Steve hated being in jail. Maybe Marcus thought Hester Gardens was a kind of jail. I think Marcus wanted me to hate it as well. I think it's why Harlan gave us *Soledad Brother.* So we could see how much of what we face is by design. The bad housing, the not having, the schools that ain't really teaching . . . excuse me . . . the schools that *aren't* really teaching. It's exactly what this country intends for us."

"And do you hate this place?" She hoped he'd say yes. Hoped he could finally see the Gardens was a place of destruction.

"Not when they gave me the books, but I do now."

Nona taped the final box and moved it near the door. She thought of the envelope that had arrived from Brown with a check for one thousand dollars along with kind letters from the financial aid and admissions offices, as well as the staff from the athletics departments, many of them apologetic for the bureaucratic oversight that had prevented him from registering for his classes in the first place. They'd issued a refund and offered their condolences.

He would have done well at such a fine university. One of the nation's best. It had hurt to place the money into her account, but she'd felt it was Marcus's final gift to his younger brother. She had no choice but to put it to good use. Coupled with the money from Beth, she was getting Lance out. Her job at the plant was now vacant, and she'd gotten both Mable and Mable's niece Tah-leasy hired in her stead.

A breeze passed over her. Since she'd chopped off all her hair, she still wasn't used to the cold air on her scalp and neck.

"You're different, Mom," Lance had said the first week she'd skipped church. "But, like, good different."

She checked under the sink and in all the kitchen drawers, making sure she'd not left anything behind. There was only one bit of unfinished business. She looked at Lance.

"I didn't love them more than you."

He seemed stunned. She'd broken her silence, had answered the very question he'd asked her, and it seemed he longed to escape the conversation now that it was finally happening.

He stared out the window toward their moving van, which was parked on Prescott Road. Outside that window, cars zoomed by fast enough to shake the truck, and as he watched, she continued to stare at him.

"I don't even think it's possible for a mother to love one child more than the other. Did I have a favorite?" Her voice was not soft and sweet. "Kendall was my favorite. I'm not going to sugarcoat it for you. Not because I thought he was better than you or Marcus, but because he desired the same things I did. I thought I understood him. I thought I understood Marcus, but now I see I didn't understand either of them at all. If I treated them differently from you, made you feel a certain way about it—"

"I don't want to talk about this." He taped the box labeled *tools*.

"I'm sorry, Lance. You remind me of your father. Everything about you. Your face, your voice, the way your lip curls, the tight coils on your head. I've been shutting you out like I shut Vance out. And I'm sorry."

"It's whatever, mom." He removed his phone from his pocket.

She took the device from his hand and gently set it on the empty counter.

He rolled his eyes and peered out the window again. Vega was sitting in her lawn chair. Mable was outside her unit as well, placing bowls of pink water around her front door.

"We're moving because of you, Lance. I want to make that clear. I can't lose you." She was sobbing again, and he couldn't "whatever" her when she was crying.

He leaned over, hugged her, and patted her back until her wails ended. She wished he'd said, *You won't lose me, Mom*. It seemed he wasn't convinced yet that he had a future, but she was.

He'd taken to carrying around a packet of face tissues in his pocket for her tears, so he reached in and gave her one.

When she pulled herself together, she pointed to the final box. They each stepped into their shoes, and she grabbed her keys and phone. She would lock up, go to the housing authority to drop off those keys, and then they'd drive away from Hester Gardens for the final time.

With the box in his left hand, Lance reached for the iron with his right, but the lock snapped down before he even made contact. The front door slammed shut. The windows banged closed, one by one, each with a loud *thwack*. The locks fastened.

The stove ticked, and the flames on all the burners roared to life. Behind them, in the hallway, the dragging noise began.

Vega's story flashed in her mind. Of the mother trapped in the unit, the locks fastened, while her toddler headed for Prescott Road. What more could Nona do? She'd lifted her curse, hadn't she? NaDarius was at peace; his mother had him home. What more did this place want from her?

It hit her. Vega's story! About the mother and her toddler. It meant the curse had been here before Nona and Vance had ever moved in. What if Vance had been possessed in that alley when he brought that pistol down on NaDarius? What if Vega's husband had been possessed when he came back for his guns? What if the curse had taken Gretchen's twin sister Grace when they were playing with dolls on the lawn? What had Vega said? *Spirits walk the same grounds our feet are resting on . . . Ask me? It's because they stole this land from Black folks a long time ago. Drove us right off of it, and now are renting it back to us like it belongs to them.*

What if Nona's curse wasn't just Nona's curse? And Vega's wasn't just Vega's? What if the curse belonged to everyone in the Gardens? What if there was one spirit, an original spirit, that was beyond appeasing?

Lance set down the box. She and Lance tried the key in the iron and deadbolt. They tried to lift the kitchen window and kicked at the glass with their shoes. They did the same in the bathroom and both the bedrooms. They raced from room to room and then back to the front. They tried their phones but had no reception. The iron door remained locked.

"Vega!" She hoped her voice would travel across the courtyard, but it was drowned out by someone blasting "Alright" by Kendrick Lamar. "Mable!"

While she pounded on the doors and windows, Lance removed his shirt and tried to beat down the fire on the stove. The flames shot up, the bright red licking the ceiling, and the blaze spread down the walls. The room filled with smoke and heat, and the irons . . . the irons would not budge.

She faced the door. She was not giving up. A siren wailed in the distance, and she prayed it was coming for them.

"Kendall! Marcus!" she yelled.

All she needed was for someone to arrive with a tool that could remove the bars.

Wait!

She had a tool. In the box Lance had set down. She ripped off the tape, yanked open the cardboard flaps, and snatched up the screwdriver. As the heat rushed across the floors, eating the wood in its run, she turned the screw that held the iron in place. She got it to budge a quarter inch to the left.

Lance grabbed another screwdriver from the box. He worked on the bottom screw while she worked on the top. The siren was louder. In the distance, on Prescott, where their moving van was parked, she thought she saw Kendall and Marcus. They'd heard her.

"Please come to us," she prayed to that siren, to her dead sons.

In her mind, she and Lance drove away.

The farther down Prescott they got, the stranger she felt. She never thought they'd leave for good.

Lance would finish school and find a young lady he could marry.

Lance would have children of his own. Two sons. And he'd name them after Kendall and Marcus.

Flashes of the red brick of Hester Gardens would come to her in the rearview mirror, but she wouldn't look at the disappearing image. She would only focus on the road before them, which would seem wider and longer now that they were on it for the final time.

Flames rushed to her heels. Panicked, Lance dropped the tool and let out a scream.

In her mind, they were already in the truck. *She'd say, "Ready, Lance?" Never glancing away from the lane in front of her, phrasing it as a question when it was really a statement of hope.*

Lance would nod, and like her, he would look ahead, ahead, ahead. Only ahead.

"I. Will. Not. Lose. Another. Son!" She chanted the phrase again and again and again until she was larger, stronger. She was the bear now, with her back spreading, her veins protruding. With all the might from every trembling muscle in her body, she pulled at the now-loose iron door. The fury grew inside of her, spread from her bulging shoulders, tore down her arms, and electrified her fingers. The rage was overtaking her, but she fought back. "I will not lose another son. I will not lose another son." And when she screamed, she shouted down the anger and called up love. She drew in a breath and pulled one final time. The metal creaked, bent, and spread apart under the power of Nona's own hands.

Acknowledgments

First and foremost, I am giving honor to God, who is the head of my life and who guides all that I think, do, am, and will become. I keep five scriptures on the home screen of my computer—Proverbs 16:3, Isaiah 54:17, Proverbs 19:21, Psalm 91:1–2, Isaiah 60:3—and God has always kept His word. Even when things don't go the way I want them to, God reminds me that I am not in control, but He will ensure that all things work together for my good. And for anyone who needs to hear it, when God says, "No weapon," He means NO weapon.

Thank you to the grieving family members, survivors, experts, and elected officials who were generous with their time and stories. It has been an honor to hold and carry your words.

I must thank my rock star agent and all-around wonderful soul, Rebecca Podos, for championing this book and guiding me on this path. My deepest gratitude goes to my DREAM editor, Diana M. Pho, whose insight and wisdom allowed me to fully render Nona's story. I am grateful for the entire Erewhon and Kensington teams, especially Michelle Addo-Chajet for all things marketing and publicity. Special thanks to Crystal Patriarche, Grace Fell, and Leilani Fitzpatrick at BookSparks for keeping me calm when I would have otherwise been bouncing off the walls.

I must heap praise on my literary comrades Black Women in Horror, especially Sumiko Saulson, Kenya Moss-Dyme, and Linda Addison, as well as the San Francisco Bay chapter of the Horror Writers Association, especially Francesca Maria. I am indebted to early readers and close literary friends Charlene Adhiambo, Bernard Harris, Alexandria Lynch, MJ Pankey, and Joe Nassise for seeing the merit in these pages. I must thank my teachers Reyna Grande and Mark Sarvas for saying the right thing at the right time. Colleague and friend Regine Darius gets her own mention because she held my feet to the fire on this project, and if she hadn't gotten me together, this book would not exist in this form.

I have been blessed to have lifelong and close friendships with brilliant people who have become my family: Ha-Hoa Hamano, Adrienne Christian, Manju Dawkins, Shawneé Pickney-Forrest, Audrey Eatherly, Chetna Joshi, Megan Isser, Ian Wenger, Pallavi Dhawan, and Eraina Ferguson. You all hold me up and make me better.

Thank you to my parents, Corliss and (the late) Edgar Thomas, especially my Mother Extraordinaire, who always believed I would get her to the red carpet. Hopefully this book will do. A shout-out to my siblings Deondre Knight, Kevin Thomas, Kim Davis, and Gregory Pressley, to my brother-in-law, Elen Thompson, as well as to my cousin (who is really my sister) Sherry Cole. All my love to my mother- and father-in-law Pat and Len Thompson for always supporting my work, as well as to the aunt and uncle who helped raise me, Auntie Phyllis and Uncle Roosevelt Cole.

My fire comes from my late grandmothers, Jessie Ambers and Alma Thomas, both Southern women from Georgia and Alabama, respectively, who loved hard, worked harder, prayed, cooked like nobody's business, and knew their way around a gun. I am grateful for their blood, which flows through my veins, and for their spirits, which guide me each day.

I want to thank the aunts and uncles who either prayed over me or sent me cash when I was a broke college or grad school student (some did both)—Lore and (the late) LeRoi Ambers (aka "Uncle Cookie"), Anna Woodford, Lucille Gibson, Flora McGregory, Mary Gibson, Floyd Thomas, Ernestine Fountain, Annette Haston, and John Thomas.

To my husband, Lendell, whose ongoing support afforded me the time and space to create this project. You have held it down for this career to blossom, and I am eternally grateful.

And finally, to my kids, my miracles, my muses, Morgan and Ellis, who are the embodiment of joy, and who have shown me that unconditional love is possible. I feel immensely blessed and honored to be your mother, and I will love you forever, in and out of time.

Author's Note

The gun culture in this book is not happenstance. The continuum from abolition to the total proliferation of guns in our society includes deeply held opinions and values, and the outcomes differ depending on whether you are a member of a marginalized group or of the dominant culture. I believe this difference, this unevenness, has impacted Americans' views on guns.

This unevenness existed in my background and showed up in my research. I grew up in a high-crime neighborhood, where guns were kept in our home for protection and sport, yet I survived a carjacking attempt as a teen. Experts I spoke to discussed the need for gun control but also the need for social investment and a revamp on approach to mental health.

For Black people in particular, there are a multitude of nuanced perspectives on gun ownership.

As dangerous as their neighborhood is, and as perilous as their lives are in relation to the criminal justice system, Nona McKinley and Mable Cleveland do not agree on whether guns should be in the home and accessible to their sons.

The "bad negroes" Mable Cleveland mentions, as well as Donnell Cleveland's ownership of Grave Digger, grew out of my family's (legal and illegal) ownership of guns, as well as my research on the use of guns among African American people for defense and survival in a country where the right of the people to keep and bear arms is codified in its constitution, where gun ownership is pervasive, and where every citizen is a soldier.

For further reading on gun culture, gang culture, and youth violence that informed this book:

- *Code of the Street: Decency, Violence, and the Moral Life of the Inner City* (W. W. Norton), Elijah Anderson;
- *This Nonviolent Stuff'll Get You Killed: How Guns Made the Civil Rights Movement Possible* (Duke University Press), Charles E. Cobb Jr.;
- *There Is a River: The Black Struggle for Freedom in America* (Harvest), Vincent Harding;
- *The Deacons for Defense: Armed Resistance and the Civil Rights Movement* (The University of North Carolina Press), Lance Hill;
- *We Refuse: A Forceful History of Black Resistance* (Seal Press), Kellie Carter Jackson;
- *Let Nobody Turn Us Around: Voices of Resistance, Reform, and Renewal* (Rowman & Littlefield), edited by Manning Marable and Leith Mullings;
- *The Almighty Black P Stone Nation: The Rise, Fall, and Resurgence of an American Gang* (Lawrence Hill Books), Natalie Y. Moore and Lance Williams;
- *Murder Is No Accident: Understanding and Preventing Youth Violence in America* (Jossey-Bass); Deborah Prothrow-Stith and Howard R. Spivak;
- *Deadly Consequences: How Violence Is Destroying Our Teenage Population and a Plan to Begin Solving the Problem* (HarperPerennial), Deborah Prothrow-Stith and Michaele Weissman;

- *We Will Shoot Back: Armed Resistance in the Mississippi Freedom Movement* (New York University Press), Akinyele Omowale Umoja;

And to read the books that Vance, Harlan, and Marcus passed on to their loved ones:

- *Soledad Brother: The Prison Letters of George Jackson* (Lawrence Hill Books), George Jackson; and
- *Monster* (Amistad and Harper Teen), Walter Dean Myers.

Discussion Questions

These suggested questions are to spark conversation and enhance your reading of *The Curse of Hester Gardens.*

1. The McKinley family and other Hester Gardens residents interact with a number of institutions: the housing authority that oversees Medford public housing, Medford "Deadford" Hospital, Kitledge High School, Medford Church of God in Christ, Up North Tea Company, and the state penitentiary. How do these establishments impact their options, choices, and quality of life?

2. Before reading this book, what was your understanding of inner-city gang culture? How do the Hester Boys, particularly Peter, Solomon, and Donnell, inform your thinking on the matter? Considering Nona's mention of the Dempsey Boys replanting her zinnias and her frequent protests that the DBs "aren't that kind of gang," what differences are you able to notice between the Hester Boys and the Dempsey Boys?

3. Later in the novel, Nona's husband Vance tells her that he doesn't believe in curses. Considering his disagreement with Nona, what do you make of the title of the book?

4. Individual guns play a prominent role in this book, from Sgt. Prager's "service weapon" to Mable's holstered pistol, from Peter's

AR-15 style rifle to Donnell's prized possession, Grave Digger. How does each character's relationship to their gun reflect modern U.S. gun culture?

5. In Chapter 13, Nona and Mable have a disagreement about gun ownership within their households. How do Nona and Mable's differing views on gun ownership reflect attitudes held by Black Americans and all Americans more broadly? How has losing Kendall perhaps colored Nona's view, if at all?

6. Faith, or lack thereof, is an important element within the story, from Nona's membership in a Christian church to Vega's atheism—"You know I think religion is no different than magic"—as well as to Mable's multiple faith traditions, including Yoruba orishas and honoring the faith practices of her Muscogee ancestors. What effect do these characters' faith traditions have on their identities? Does that change throughout the book? If so, how?

7. Medford Church of God in Christ, led by Pastor and First Lady Davis, is a well-regarded and powerful megachurch at the start of the story. What is your impression of the church at the beginning of the book? Does that impression change by the end? Considering the financial means of most of Medford C.O.G.I.C.'s congregants, what do you make of the church's wealth?

8. When taking out the trash, Nona considers the city of Medford's contract with Midwestern Waste Systems, which doesn't empty the garbage at Hester Gardens with any frequency: "Detroit had abandoned homes, Flint had poisonous water, and Medford's projects had sky-high trash." Considering that Nona is thinking of all three issues, what is your takeaway about trash collection in Hester Gardens?

9. Nona repeatedly implores Lance and Marcus to use American English. She specifically takes umbrage at use of the word "ain't." Considering the differences in speech among the characters (e.g., Nona, Pastor, Vance, Lance, Marcus, Vega, Mable, and Donnell), how does language reflect the characters' pasts and life outlooks? What do you make of Donnell's use of "nigga"? How about other

characters' use of African American Vernacular English (AAVE)? Why do you think this is important to Nona? How do you think AAVE is perceived relative to other dialects like American Southern English and Caribbean English creoles?

10. Birds, elm trees, and zinnias play significant symbolic roles in the text. What do you think these natural elements symbolize, and how does the motif change throughout the story?

11. Considering Mable's Southern roots, Harlan's sprawling suburban home, and Nona's dream home on Willowbrook Street, how do each of these characters relate to the idea of land and home ownership in the United States? How do each of their visions of home reflect the American Dream?

12. Throughout the text, a blue ball repeatedly appears around Hester Gardens. What do you think the blue ball symbolizes? How does it relate to Grace's baby doll in the pink gingham dress?

13. In a discussion with Nona, Harlan shares his views on how white and Black shooters are treated differently in the mainstream media: "When the shooters are white, the write-ups are all about how they came from a wonderful family . . . But let that same shooter be Black. He's just a criminal." What do you think of his assessment? What life experiences may have colored his perspective?

14. What do you make of Sgt. Victoria Prager and her interactions with Nona? Does being a Black woman seem to change Sgt. Prager's policing style? If so, how?

15. Considering Pastor's final text message to Nona, how might her relationship with Pastor unfold in a sequel? How about her relationship with Vance, considering his final letter to her?

Playlist

Music is central to the setting of Hester Gardens. The characters' ancestors sang to communicate routes of escape. They sang while working in the fields or tethered to a chain gang. They sang while doing domestic work or during praise and worship service. So, music, whether at church or flowing from car speakers, contributes to the soundtrack of these characters' lives. Below is a complete list of the songs that appear in *The Curse of Hester Gardens*:

"Real Love," Mary J. Blige;

"Speak to My Heart," Donnie McClurkin;

"Angels," Chance the Rapper;

"Bling Bling," B.G. ft. Big Tymers and Hot Boyz;

"Lift Every Voice and Sing," various artists;

"Four Women," Nina Simone;

"Hail Mary," 2Pac;

"He's Working It Out for You," Shirley Caesar;

"The Question Is," The Winans;

"It Was a Good Day," Ice Cube;

"Low Life," Future;
"Standing in the Need of a Blessing," Rev. James Cleveland;
"I'll Always Love My Mama," The Intruders;
"Nobody Knows the Trouble I've Seen," Louis Armstrong;
"Psychosocial," Slipknot;
"Sorry," Beyoncé;
"Lord Knows," Meek Mill ft. Tory Lanez;
"Victory," Yolanda Adams;
"Bitch Better Have My Money," Rihanna;
"What Good Can Drinkin' Do," Janis Joplin;
"Is My Living in Vain," The Clark Sisters;
"Don't Trip," The Game;
"My House," Flo Rida;
"Don't Worry, Be Happy," Bobby McFerrin;
"Storm Coming," Gnarls Barkley;
"See You Again," Wiz Khalifa ft. Charlie Puth;
"Here's to Never Growing Up," Avril Lavigne;
"Take My Hand, Precious Lord," Mahalia Jackson;
"Fool's Gold," Jill Scott;
"Mary Don't You Weep," Shirley Caesar;
"Good Morning Heartache," Billie Holiday;
"Soldier," Erykah Badu;
"Alright," Kendrick Lamar.

Content Note

The Curse of Hester Gardens contains depictions of gun violence, horror-level violence, swearing, drug and alcohol use, and references to racism, self-harm, suicide, and suicidal ideation.